W9-CNL-769

Marcia Willett was born in Somerset and lives in deepest Devon with her husband and their large dog. A former ballet dancer and teacher, she is the author of thirteen previous books, including *The Children's Hour*, available from McArthur & Company.

THE BIRDCAGE

THE BIRDCAGE

Marcia Willett

McArthur & Company

Toronto

First published in 2004 by
McArthur & Company
322 King St. West., Suite 402
Toronto, Ontario
M5V 1J2
www.mcarthur-co.com

This paperback edition published in 2005 by
McArthur & Company

Library and Archives Canada Cataloguing in Publication

Willett, Marcia
The birdcage / Marcia Willett.

ISBN 1-55278-491-6

I. Title.

PR6073.I277B57 2005   823'.914   C2005-903261-8

Cover Photo Credit by Masterfile
Printed in Canada by Webcom

10 9 8 7 6 5 4 3 2 1

To Pam Goddard

My thanks to Mr Anthony Brunt for allowing me
to place Felix's flat on the first floor of the
Yarn Market Hotel, Dunster.

PROLOGUE

The child, waking suddenly and finding herself alone, sat up anxiously amongst the makeshift bed of cushions and rugs. She could hear her mother's voice, echoing oddly – now loud, now quiet – a murmuring duet with a deeper voice, flaring and dying so queerly that she scrambled to her feet and went out into the passage. Small, tousled, without her shoes, she hurried along until she emerged into a Looking-Glass world where painted gardens ascended into cavernous shadowy places, a flight of stairs revolved gently away, and walls drifted silently apart. A cluster of lights, perched aloft, lit up an interior as neat and bright as a dolls'-house room, with cardboard books on painted shelves and shiny plaster food set upon the small table; almost she expected Hunca Munca to appear.

Standing quite still, just beyond the circle of light, a draught shivering round her legs, she watched her mother, who talked and smiled and stretched her hands to someone whose arm and shoulder, clad in severe dark cloth, could just be glimpsed; but, before she was able run to her, a sudden surging roar pinned her in the dark corner. As it beat up, swelling then receding dizzily about her head, she squared her mouth to cry out in fear, and then there were people all about her, lifting her, soothing her, carrying the small struggling figure away from the woman who remained on stage as the curtain rose and fell, again and again. She yelled aloud in panic as she was borne off – 'Angel!' she shouted – but her voice was lost in the backstage bustle and she cried out again.

No sound came and she wakened – properly now – to the present, her head at an uncomfortable angle against the arm of the chair, her mouth dry. The fear was still with her, a sense of terrible loss clinging with the fragments of the dream, so that she passed her hands over her face as if to wipe away both the dream and the panic together.

'Sleeping in the afternoon,' she told herself disparagingly. 'What do you expect?' and glanced hopefully at her watch. Twenty-eight minutes past five. Once, not so long ago, this would have been a time of preparation, of nervous tension; swallowing black coffee, forcing down some bread and butter, before going to the theatre. There, the world beyond the stage door brought its own particular brand of comfort. Snuffing up the familiar theatre smell – dust, greasepaint, sweat – hearing the chatter in the dressing-rooms, a kind of comradeship and relief that sprang from the security of being where you belonged, concentrated the mind on the work ahead. Still nervous, oh, yes! But excited now and part of the family: listening to the gossip as you sat at the mirror and applied the colour to your face.

Lizzie Blake straightened in her chair, shrugging her shoulders to ease the crick in her neck, stretching her long, still-glamorous legs. She rose from the armchair, humming. She'd discovered that humming held thought – and fear – at bay and she knew plenty of tunes. Today it was *South Pacific*: 'This Nearly was Mine'. She waltzed into the kitchen, exaggerating the beat, hamming it up, humming and singing alternately, slipping back nearly twenty-five years. Lizzie filled the kettle and switched it on; not that she wanted a cup of tea but that dread, empty, early evening desert between five and seven had to be filled somehow – especially now that Sam was gone.

She hurried herself away from this thought at once, humming again – 'A Cockeyed Optimist' this time – and began to make the tea, tapping out the rhythm on the caddy with a teaspoon, wondering whether she might allow herself a ginger biscuit: just one. After all, her weight never increased. She remained as tall and slender as she'd been at twenty – her work and self-discipline had kept her fit and supple – and the masses of dark reddish-gold hair were barely touched with grey. It was pinned, as usual, into a mysterious bundle from which screwy tendrils escaped and tortoiseshell hairpins occasionally slipped; her ivory skin was dusted with freckles and her amber-brown eyes were rather shy beneath the feathery brows. As she'd grown older – too old for the roles of Nellie or Ado Annie or Bianca – she'd been cast in small comedy parts and had also had a great success in a television sitcom that had run for several years. Meanwhile, her singing voice had carried her into voice-over jingles for television commercials and now, if she'd wanted to, she could have listened to herself at least three or four times each evening, extolling a particular brand of face-cream, or watched herself at the wheel of a popular family car complete with two small children and a delightful mutt-like dog. This last was a very amusing and popular commercial and she'd become a household face – something she'd never quite achieved through those long years on the stage nor, even, with the sitcom – and she was getting used to passers-by doing double-takes and crying, 'Oh, you're that lady in the advert . . .' She longed to be blasé about it, to shrug and smile distantly, but, truth to tell, she rather liked the recognition and was quite ready for a little chat, a bit of a chuckle with these friendly admirers. Deep down she felt rather ashamed at the pleasure this gave her but there was no harm and it cheered her up, boosting her ego and warming the heart: reactions not to be sniffed at, especially since Sam . . .

Lizzie seized the biscuit tin: *two* biscuits and a good look at the latest holiday brochure would be an excellent distraction from the long empty hours ahead. Perhaps her friends and her agent had been right when they'd advised that she shouldn't leave London to return to the house in Bristol where she'd grown up with Pidge and Angel. It was simply that London had been so awful without Sam; so lonely and . . . just wrong. She lifted the mug and tasted the hot tea, glancing at the highly coloured brochure advertising the beauty of the West Country.

'Will you be travelling with a party?' the young woman in the travel agent's office had asked earlier that morning.

'No, no. Quite alone.' She tried to make it sound adventurous and gay but the words had a rather pathetic ring and the woman glanced curiously at her.

'I lost my husband three months ago.' The words leaped from her mouth and seemed to lie on the counter where they could both look at them: Lizzie with dismayed surprise and the woman with shocked pity.

'I am *so* sorry.'

The hushed tone and special sympathetic expression had an odd effect on Lizzie; she could feel wild laughter creeping below her diaphragm. Instinctively she breathed in, tightening her stomach muscles, beaming so madly that the woman almost flinched away from her.

'So am I,' she answered brightly, speaking clearly. 'Terribly, terribly sorry.'

The woman's expression grew anxious; she seized some brochures, and pushed them across the counter, muttering unintelligibly, her eyes averted.

Remembering, Lizzie burst into a fit of laughter, nearly choking on her tea; tears streamed from her eyes and she dabbed at them. Could it be that she was crying? Resolutely she took her mug and the booklets and went to sit at the dining-table.

In this big first-floor room, the kitchen had been divided from the living area by the simple means of placing an upright piano in the middle of the floor. Its back, which had a square deal table placed against it, was turned to the sink and cupboards and shelves, hiding the smaller working area very cleverly. On its other side, a long refectory table was set about with assorted battered wooden chairs, one wall was lined with bookshelves, another hung with paintings, and a long sofa, which fitted comfortably into the wide bay window, kept company with three unmatched armchairs and a low carved chest used as a table.

Sitting in the wide-armed carver, pushing an old silk cushion into the small of her back, Lizzie set down her tea, took the brochures from under her arm and opened the biscuit tin. She began to turn the pages. Beyond the window, the plane tree trembled in the light, soft breeze; the June evening was warm and the voices of the children, playing in the square, echoed through the open casement. The room faced west and the pattern of the leaves shifted and changed in the sunlight, flickering over faded linen chair covers. A crimson petal fell soundlessly from one of the roses in a vase on the piano, their scent drifting in the high, airy spaces. Lizzie turned another page.

'Dunster Castle towers above the little village huddled at its gates . . .'

She stared at the picture, frowning, her mind balancing on the edge of a memory: the sandstone castle, glowing rich and warm at sunset, the mosaic of red and grey slate roofs silvered by gentle rain, a peaceful, sheltered garden; the sea breaking on grey stones and shingle, the ache of weary legs on the long walk home from the beach . . . And Angel, restless, brittle, never still.

Lizzie put the brochure aside. She saw a tiny cameo, a sliver of the past: a meeting, charged with tension and excitement, and Angel staring at a woman of her own age whilst she, Lizzie, gazed at the small boy who held the woman's hand.

The telephone bell shivered the memory to pieces and made her jump.

'Hello, dear heart.'

Lizzie smiled with relief to hear her agent's voice and sank into a deep-lapped armchair.

'Hello, Jim. How are things?'

'Things are good. Very good. That holiday you were talking about. You're not going too far away?'

'No, no.' Her eyes strayed to the table, the open brochure, the glossy photographs. 'I thought, maybe, the West Country. On the coast somewhere. Why?'

'Just as long as you're in Manchester on Monday week.'

They talked for a few moments longer, Lizzie replaced the receiver and returned to the table. She stood for a long while, staring down at the picture.

Dunster Castle towers above the little village huddled at its gates.

She slept late the next morning. Half a sleeping tablet had finally released her from an exhausting mental circling, resurrecting memories and sharpening grief, which dogged her into the early hours. Her dreams were curiously vivid.

Pidge and Angel are sitting together at the table, a bottle of wine between them whilst she sits on the floor beneath the long board with her toys. Angel's feet are bare and fidget constantly, rubbing one upon the other or tucking themselves into the long, cotton wrapper that ripples round her legs. Pidge's feet are placed upon the long bar and her shoes, with pointed toes and little heels, are soft dark blue leather.

'I loved him so much, d'you see?' she is saying. Her voice is full of pain and, more than that, there is a kind of desperate need to be understood, forgiven even. Her narrow feet remain quite still, planted firmly there on the wooden rail, whilst Angel's white, rounded toes, with their brightly painted nails, push at each other restlessly. She murmurs at intervals, in soothing counterpoint to Pidge's recital, comforting her.

'After all, sweetie, he didn't belong to me either. I mean, did he?' Her chair creaks a little as she leans forward. There is a tiny chink of glass, a liquid gurgle. 'To be honest, it's *quite* extraordinary. Rather fun, *I* think . . .'

Pidge's feet come down from the rail, her shoes are eased off and she hitches her chair forward an inch or two: Angel's toes cease to rub together, she crosses her legs, drawing the wrapper about her knees, and sits back comfortably. With the voices murmuring above her head, listening to bursts of smothered laughter and the occasional exclamation, the child continues her game; setting the scene that her toys enact on the soft silky rug, with the refectory table like a roof, the broad end-leg as a wall, sheltering and enclosing them.

Lizzie pushed back the quilt and sat on the edge of the bed. The dream, like yesterday's, left her feeling edgy. Had she sat so, beneath the table, whilst Angel and Pidge talked? Had she wakened in the dressing-room one evening, alone and frightened, and run to find her mother? She was not a stranger to dreams but these had been touched by an almost hallucinatory quality. Her behaviour of late might have given rise to a slight anxiety if she could only bring herself to care. She'd posted a nice little cut of steak in the letter-box outside the butcher's shop, gone off with someone else's trolley in the supermarket, forgotten the car and, leaving it behind in the car-park, walked home from the library. Small things of no great moment, taken separately, yet the dreams seemed part of the same pattern.

'Perhaps I'm having a nervous breakdown.'

Lizzie spoke the words aloud, tilted her head as if waiting for a response, and pattered away to the bathroom for a shower. Talking to herself made her feel less alone and, more importantly, kept anxieties in proportion. It was much more difficult to take herself seriously when she spoke out – rather loudly and very clearly – as if to an audience. She grinned brightly at herself in the glass above the basin as she cleaned her face, slapped on moisturizer and plunged the horseshoe-shaped pins into her hair.

She began to hum: 'I'm Gonna Wash That Man Right Outa My Hair.'

Still with *South Pacific*, then. Well, that was fine, lots of good numbers to carry her through the day. She remembered the little tap routine that had accompanied that particular song and tried it out, her leather-soled slippers clapping softly on the lino, thinking back to her first lessons in the basement room with the painted concrete floor at the dance studio.

Shuffle *hop* step tap ball change. Shuffle *hop* step tap ball change. Shuffle *hop* step, shu*ffle* step, shuffle *step*, shuffle ball *change*.

She could hear, inside her head, the dancing mistress shouting the steps above the clatter of tap shoes, accentuating the beat; her body could remember the rhythm, arms swinging loosely, head up. She couldn't have been more than seven or eight. How she'd loved the music, the movement, the disciplining of the body; the *barre* that had been fixed to the wall in the attic room forty years ago was still there where Lizzie had once performed her daily exercises, her little routine: *pliés*, *battements*, *port de bras*, watching herself in the glass on the opposite wall. She still did a regular work-out.

'But not this morning,' she muttered as she dressed quickly, pulling on jeans and a black T-shirt.

An appointment with the hairdresser hurried her down the stairs for coffee and some toast. The brochure was lying where she'd left it but she glanced away from it, humming to herself again, concentrating on what Jim had told her about the possibility of work with a touring company in the autumn. Could she cope with the arduous routine, the travelling, the same performance night after night?

'Just what you need, heart,' he'd said reassuringly. He was very kind, very professional and insisted that his extravagant speech and flamboyant behaviour were simply by-products of a lifetime working with actors. Lizzie adored him.

'I feel a bit wobbly,' she'd told him before she'd left London. 'I need a break. I'm going to Bristol.'

'Back to the Birdcage?' That's what the tall, narrow house had been dubbed back in the early sixties once the agency had learned that three women lived in it, one of them called Pidgeon.

Standing in the kitchen, drinking black coffee, waiting for the toaster to fling its contents on to the floor, Lizzie thinks of Angel's delight at the joke and how she pleads for them to change the address officially.

'It's all very well for you,' retorts Pidge, 'but how would you like your letters to be addressed to "Miss Pidgeon, The Birdcage"? Have a heart.'

Instead, Angel finds a pretty, gilt birdcage – from some prop room? – complete with two brightly painted, little wooden birds perched on a trapeze. Shortly afterwards an even smaller chick, made of soft yellow material, is added.

'That's you,' says Angel to Lizzie. 'See? You're a swinging chick. How do you like that?'

The birdcage hangs above the piano in the sitting-room for years. It becomes a symbol, an in-joke.

'That's us,' Angel tells visitors. 'Three little birds in a gilded cage. Well, one chick and two old boilers . . .' she adds – and waits for the inevitable denial, the compliments.

The birdcage is such a part of their lives together that it is impossible to imagine either Pidge or Angel getting rid of it. When Angel dies of complications following the onset of pneumonia, Pidge lives on alone until she, too, dies after a series of strokes. She leaves the house with all its contents to Lizzie.

'I can't sell it,' Lizzie tells Sam. 'I just can't. Not yet, anyway.'

'No need,' he answers easily. 'It will be useful as a little bolt-hole.'

'That's about right,' she agrees. 'I always bolted back to it. Between productions, after your disastrous love affairs. I always finished up in the Birdcage with Angel and Pidge.'

'That's not quite what I had in mind,' he says, putting an arm round her, knowing how hard she is taking Pidge's death. He makes a face, rolling his eyes, guying a saucy leer, hoping to make her smile, holding her closer. 'More of a love nest, perhaps, than a birdcage?' and she laughs at his feeble joke, winding her arms about him.

Ten years ago since Pidge died, thought Lizzie, swallowing her toast with difficulty. And less than two years ago Sam and I were here together. And now?

She began to clear her breakfast things, the action distracting her from such thoughts, concentrating instead on the missing birdcage. It would be good to see it again; to hang it up as a gesture to the past. She decided that as soon as she was home again she would have a thorough search for it.

All the while, as she collected her keys, hunted for her bag, the photograph seemed to cry continually for her attention. Reluctantly, almost fearfully, she paused to look at it again. 'The Yarn Market is octagonal and dates from the fifteenth century . . .'

Lizzie bent closer to look at the smaller, inset picture. Another fragment, just like the scene in the shop, slid clearly into her mind.

The Yarn Market. She remembers running in through the doorless entrance, calling to Angel, who stands on the cobbles outside in the sunshine, and leaning through the big window spaces.

'Look at me? Can you see me?'

'I can see you, sweetie, I can see you.' But Angel is looking up the High Street, her eyes darting from shop doorways to peer at the occupants of a car; distracted, preoccupied, always on the watch.

Lizzie feels the slubby crispness of her yellow and white gingham frock, bare feet in sandshoes, and her long plait, thick as Angel's wrist, knocking against her back as she jumps along beside her mother down the sunken, narrow, cobbled pavement. They pause beside the hotel, with its big medieval porch, before crossing the road to the Yarn Market. It is cool and dark beneath the slated roof and she dances, singing breathlessly to herself, a small, bright flame of colour amongst the shadows, whilst Angel waits, watching and watching. But for whom?

This question occupied Lizzie as she walked into the town: as she chatted to the friendly girl who blow-dried her hair; as she did her shopping; all the while she was trying to pin the memory down, to capture it. If she could remember which year it had been, then other things might fall into place; but why should Angel, of all people, decide to take a holiday in a tiny town on Exmoor? Angel liked bustle, unexpected outings to restaurants or pubs, friends dropping by for impromptu drinks: she became restive and bored after ten minutes up on Brandon Hill. Nor did she consider it necessary for Lizzie to be taken on holiday except during the summer of that one year. That Dunster year.

Back at home, Lizzie kicked off her shoes, put away the shopping and collected the ingredients for her lunch. Mostly she couldn't be bothered to eat formally – it seemed such an effort for just one person – but today she felt a need to prepare something almost as a rite to the shades of Pidge and Angel rather than for herself. Just now, here in the Birdcage, she felt that they were very close to her: Angel, eyes closed, stretched along the sofa in the window, with Pidge sewing nearby, arguing across the table or perhaps pottering in the kitchen. Pidge was responsible for most of the cooking, although Angel liked to experiment – either disastrously or brilliantly. 'I am never commonplace,' she'd say grandly, shovelling her mistakes into a newspaper whilst Pidge, resigned, began to make an omelette. 'I don't do things by halves.' Because of going down to the theatre each evening, mealtimes were movable feasts and Pidge remained flexible at all times.

Now, as Lizzie set the table, she felt as if she were making them an offering, a simple little puja: smoked salmon with chunks of lemon, rings of tomato in a vinaigrette with herbs, thin slices of cucumber in mayonnaise, and new brown bread. She chose the dishes with care: round, white bone-china for the salmon; oval, blue earthenware for the tomatoes; a yellow bowl for the cucumber. Oddly, the palette of colour and texture worked. Lizzie felt that Pidge and Angel would have approved. Unable to afford the best, each of them had made a point of buying and using things that caught her attention and appealed to her own particular taste.

Pleased with her puja, Lizzie poured herself a glass of chilled Sancerre and sat down.

'I know I shouldn't be eating this because it's for you,' she said aloud so as to placate the shades of Pidge and Angel. 'It's not a real puja but it's the best I can do.'

The little meal was delicious. Afterwards, she cut herself some cheese and made coffee, strong and black. Sitting quietly, she stared out across the room, through the branches of the plane tree outside the window, to the rooftops and the sky beyond, listening to other things beside the city's sounds.

Later, she climbed the steep stairs to the attic room. Once her own special eyrie, now it was full of those things that had been put aside for later use – 'It might come in,' Pidge had been fond of saying – as well as the items which, out of sentimental attachment, they'd simply been unable to throw away. It was years since Lizzie had used this room and it was here she hoped to find the birdcage. Which one of them would have decided that the joke was too stale to want to keep it hanging above the piano? Perhaps, after Angel died, Pidge had found it too painful a reminder.

Lizzie moved slowly between cardboard boxes, bulging bin-liners and small pieces of furniture. Old books, with broken spines and ragged leaves, were stacked on the small bookcase she'd used as a child, whilst a chair with a broken leg held a faded tapestry stool in its lap. There was no sign of the birdcage. It was too big to be stored in the boxes which were marked clearly with felt-tip pen; too bulky for the bin-liners, weighty with their burden of old curtains and blankets, which she moved carefully aside in case they'd been piled on top of it. She peered into a tea-chest, which was packed with sheet music and theatre programmes, and stared for a moment at the cardboard box bearing the legend 'LIZZIE'S TOYS'. To distract herself from the mixed emotions that this evoked, she turned aside and glanced along the shelf at the books. Amongst these battered copies were several Reprint Society editions. Elizabeth Bowen's *The Heat of the Day*, two Rumer Goddens, Maugham's *Theatre* and an Iris Murdoch.

Lizzie leafed through the Bowen and then picked up *Theatre*. She remembered that Angel had given it to Pidge as a birthday present and, still feeling their shades close at hand, she decided to take the book down to read later. She looked about her, frowning: the birdcage was nowhere to be seen and she was acutely disappointed. It was foolish and irrational but she'd cherished the hope that she would discover it here amongst these artefacts of the past, but suspected now that it must have been thrown away. Angel's rooms, which Lizzie now used, had no cupboard large enough to conceal it and Pidge's quarters, cleared out and redecorated, were let to a young woman taking a post-graduate course at the university.

Lizzie went into the sitting-room and lay full-length on the sofa. She felt deeply hurt that the birdcage had been disposed of without her consent.

'After all,' she said aloud, crossly, as if to admonish the accompanying shades, 'I was part of it too.'

She can imagine it quite clearly. The two little wooden birds have been so delicately painted that it seems that the feathers, blue and green and yellow, must stir; that at any moment the wings might be stretched for flight. Angel, professional as always in the setting of a scene, places a tiny bowl of seed on the floor of the cage and hangs a round mirror beside the trapeze. Pidge refuses to let her put a second bowl of water beside the seed.

'It'll get stale and smell,' she says firmly, 'or get knocked over when people peer in.'

Angel grumbles, her artistic sensibilities affronted, but Pidge won't budge. There is only just room on the swing for the yellow chick, probably an Easter toy from a cardboard egg. She leans rakishly, her bright orange feet wound about with wire so as to attach her to the wooden bar, her fluffy wings poised as if she fears that she might tumble from her precarious perch.

How Lizzie loves them: to begin with, tall though she is, she has to stand on the piano stool so as to see them properly. Angel is the bird whose head is thrown back, beak parted in joyous song: Pidge has her head on one side, as if listening. Lizzie is thrilled to be a part of this little tableau: the chick, safe within the confines of the cage, not quite ready for flight.

Lizzie stirred. Now that she was back in Bristol, her earlier instinct – to block the past, to hum and dance away from those dreams and memories – was beginning to change very gradually into an acceptance; even into curiosity. The mad conception that, somehow, Pidge and Angel were here in the Birdcage with her was beginning to be a comfort rather than a threat.

'Crazy!' she announced to anyone who might be listening. 'Potty. Nuts. Doolally.'

She hitched herself a little higher on the sofa, found that she was still clutching *Theatre*, and, holding it by its spine, shook the book gently so as to dislodge the dust. The pages clapped lightly together and a card slipped from between its sheets and fell to the floor. Lizzie picked it up and looked at it. Even in black and white the Yarn Market was instantly recognizable. The castle's towers and battlements rose from behind the trees on Castle Hill and across the street from the Yarn Market stood the Luttrell Arms with its high medieval porch.

Shocked and disbelieving, Lizzie stared at the postcard. Its appearance at this moment, hedged about with mystery and coincidence as if it were some sign or portent, knocked her off balance and it was some time before she could bring herself to turn it over, so hopeful was she that it should contain some kind of message for her. The ink was faded but Angel's writing was clear enough.

Darling Pidge,
　　So here we are and the cottage is sweet.
　　Lovely weather but it's rather a trek to the beach for poor little Lizzie's legs. Dunster is the most gorgeous village but – you'll be relieved to know! – not a sign of F. I haven't given up hope, though!
　　Love from us both. Angel xx

There was no date, only the word 'Tuesday' scrawled across the top of the card and the postmark was blurred. Lizzie reread the message anxiously, as though by further study the words might give up some secret; the answer to her question: why the holiday in Dunster? The first lines were innocent enough; it was only the words 'not a sign of F' that held the clue to the mystery.

21

Lizzie lay down again, holding the card, closing her eyes, remembering. Gently, as in that Looking-Glass world of backstage, with its silently collapsing walls and revolving staircases, her memory began to open, layer upon layer, before her inward eye. It was a long while before she stirred, rousing slowly to the sounds of evening outside the window, aware of the coolness of the shadowy room. She shivered a little, reaching a long arm for Angel's yellow silk shawl, her eyes still dreamy and unfocused.

It was strange that a part of her life once so vital could be so completely written over, hidden beneath the palimpsest of subsequent experiences. F was for Felix: oh, how could she have forgotten someone she loved so much? The smell of him was in her nostrils, the feel of him beneath her fingertips, which clutched the postcard. For years he was a part of their lives here in the Birdcage; joking with Pidge, bringing presents for the small Lizzie, going down to the theatre with Angel. He'd arrive at the Birdcage on Sunday evenings; Pidge would be thinking about supper whilst listening to the Palm Court Hotel orchestra on the radio. Nothing could have persuaded Lizzie to go to bed until after she'd seen him and very often she was allowed to stay up late as a special treat.

'Hello, my birds,' he'd say, holding out a bottle to Pidge, fielding Lizzie with his other arm, looking across at Angel with that tiny heart-stopping wink. 'How's life in the cage?'

Perhaps, after all, it was Felix and not Angel's agent who had named it so? For years – or so it seemed – that one Sunday in the month was the high spot of her small existence. Lizzie frowned, drawing the shawl about her, still holding the postcard. There could be no doubt that F stood for Felix – but what had Felix Hamilton, her mother's lover, to do with Dunster? She sat up, feeling about with her toes for her shoes. Placing the card on the table beside the brochure, she went into the kitchen to pour herself a drink and, sitting down with it at the table, she stared at the postcard as if by sheer willpower she could wrench an answer from its picture of Dunster and the faded inky message.

Closing her eyes, Lizzie groped towards the words that defined Felix: the smell of his tweed coat; the feel of his long brown fingers holding her hand; the queer sensation of an emotional stability. Crazy! For years she hadn't given him a thought whilst now, for some reason, the memories had come crowding back, green and fresh, and filling her with an unsettled longing; a need to see him again. It wasn't so odd that, back in Bristol, she should feel the presence of Pidge and Angel – even her sudden passion to find the birdcage was not unreasonable – but this desire to seek Felix out, talk to him and tie up loose ends, was extraordinary. But why Dunster?

Lizzie opened her eyes; the question continued to puzzle her. The postcard lay face upwards and, as she looked at it, suddenly the tiny cameo, that sliver of the past, slid back into her mind: Angel staring at the woman in the grocer's shop whilst she and the little boy gazed at one another. She recalled the atmosphere of tension, communicated by the sudden tightening of Angel's hand on hers and the expression of resentment on the woman's face. Her memory made another connection: Felix explaining why he couldn't be her daddy, telling her about his son with the odd name who lived in the country.

Gasping with a kind of triumphant relief Lizzie leaned back in her chair, the pieces of the puzzle clicking neatly into place. It seemed clear, now, that Angel had gone to Dunster hoping to see Felix and almost certainly against Pidge's advice: . . . *You'll be relieved to know! – not a sign of F. I haven't given up hope, though!* It was the kind of mad plan that would have appealed to Angel. Perhaps Felix had been on holiday from the office for a while with no excuse to visit Bristol: perhaps his passion had been cooling off a little. Had Angel hoped that, by appearing on his home ground, she might force his hand? Lizzie longed to know what had happened between Felix and Angel; why had he stopped coming to the Birdcage? Frustration seized her. Why, when it was too late, did she feel this passion to unearth the past? She picked up the postcard with its faded message. Were they still there, in Dunster somewhere, Felix and his son – and that woman with the bitter, resentful face?

It suddenly occurred to her that Felix, like Angel and Pidge, might be dead. In remembering the young Felix she'd forgotten that he would have grown old too. Only then did she realize how much she'd been counting on finding him again; of talking to him once more. An unexpected and inexplicable sense of despair galvanized her into action. She reached for her mobile and, peering at the page in the brochure, dialled a number.

'Hello,' she said, swallowing in a suddenly dry throat. 'I expect it's hopeless but I suppose you don't have any rooms empty at the moment? I'd like to come down to Dunster for a few days next week . . . Oh, really? Four nights? . . . No, no, not too soon at all. Monday night to Thursday night. Fine . . .'

She gave the details required by the receptionist, replaced the receiver and sat quite still; the room was full of early evening sunshine, dappled with the pattern of plane leaves, peaceful and full of memories. She half expected to see Angel come yawning from her afternoon sleep, waving to Lizzie with her crayons at the table, calling to Pidge clattering about in the kitchen.

'I need you, sweetie. Could you just hear me in that bit in Act Three? It's the scene with Orlando . . .' And Pidge, quickly drying her hands, taking the script, read the part in a quiet, colourless voice, whilst Angel lay full-length on the sofa with her eyes closed, responding to the cues.

'I'm sure you realize,' Lizzie said aloud to them, 'that this is a wild-goose chase. Utterly crazy . . .' but her voice trembled with anticipation and she was filled with a new sense of purpose. She must decide what clothes she'd need, find the map, telephone Jim to let him know where she'd be; if she managed an early start on Monday morning she could be in Dunster in plenty of time for lunch.

In Dunster: at these words a thrill passed through her frame. With her head full of plans and hopes Lizzie rose from the table and, pausing only to pick up the postcard, hurried away to her bedroom.

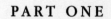

PART ONE

CHAPTER ONE

Dunster 1956

The village is quiet this afternoon and Marina Hamilton hurries through her shopping, Piers skipping and jumping at her side. She says, 'Walk properly, Piers,' but he takes no notice, knowing that today she is happy and he does not have to be so careful. He looks with pleasure at the castle on its wooded hill, its battlements and towers framed by the dense trees, whose leaves are the colour of the new pennies he has in the pocket of his corduroy shorts.

Remembering, he thrusts his hand deep down into the pocket and feels the smooth, roundness of the pennies, warm from his body, and the little sharp-edged threepenny piece that his father has given him earlier.

'Buy a stick of chocolate, old fellow,' he says while Piers looks with awe at so much money. 'Go on, put it away.'

Anxiously Piers tucks the coins into his pocket for there is that tiny edge of urgency in his father's voice which he has come to recognize, although he doesn't understand it, just as he recognizes that state between his parents which he calls to

29

himself 'uncomfortableness'. It is present in the atmosphere like cold or heat – not visible, but there – and he tries to dispel it by talking loudly, showing something – a book, a toy – or demonstrating some new skill: standing on his head, turning a cartwheel. In the cottage, on the toll road just out of Porlock, such antics have sometimes caused trouble, the breaking of an ornament, the knocking over of a table, but not any longer; today, when they drive back home from Dunster, they will be going not to the cottage but to Michaelgarth.

Piers gives another big bounce of happiness, swinging on his mother's hand, beaming up at her, remembering how she told him the wonderful news.

'Grandfather can't manage on his own any longer,' she explains, 'so we are going to move to Michaelgarth to look after him.'

Piers hears the lilt in her voice; he knows how she loves the place where she was born and grew up with her beloved brother, Peter: the big grey-stone house standing up on the hill looking out to sea, with the sunny, sheltered garth behind it, held within the two wings of the house. He loves it too. There is space to run, to make secret dens; his tricycle judders and jolts over the cobbles in the garth but, once out on the drive, he can go like the wind whilst Grandfather's springer spaniel, Monty, bounds along beside him, barking madly. If only he had a brother they could play such splendid games at Michaelgarth.

This afternoon, he stands patiently beside his mother as they wait in Parhams to be served with cheese and tea. Perhaps now is the time, now that she is happy, to ask for a brother – or even a sister. Outside the shop he changes his mind; something deep inside warns him not to spoil today's happiness. Already at seven years old he knows how fragile it is.

'There's Daddy,' he cries with delight. 'Look, he's talking to Mrs Cartwright.'

He feels his mother's grip tighten on his hand and looks up

at her. The smoothed-out look her face has been wearing all day has gone: she frowns and her mouth turns down. It is as if the sun has disappeared behind a cloud; anxiety is heavy in his stomach – as if he has eaten rice pudding too quickly – and in a sudden panic he shouts aloud.

'Daddy,' he calls across the street. 'Hello, Daddy. Hello, Mrs Cartwright.'

They both turn and Mrs Cartwright smiles, waves her hand. 'Hello, Piers. How are you, Marina?'

His father raises his hat to Mrs Cartwright, as if bidding her goodbye, but she accompanies him, crossing with him to where they stand outside the post office.

'Hello, darling,' says his father easily. Piers sees him move, as if to kiss her mother's cheek, but a stiffening, a tilting of her chin, makes him hesitate.

'Hello, Marina,' says Mrs Cartwright. She looks amused, her eyes sparkle, and Piers decides that she is very pretty, with her little feathered hat and tall-heeled shoes. 'I hear that you've moved back home.'

'Yes, that's right. How are you, Helen? How's James?'

Piers tugs at his father's sleeve. 'Are you coming home to tea with us, Daddy?' he asks eagerly.

His father glances at his watch and Piers sees him look at his mother's face as if he might find an answer written there.

'I expect your father has to get back to the office,' she says. 'He'll be home later.'

'I've been with old Mrs Baker at Myrtle Cottage.' He says it to Piers but rather as if he is telling the others as well. 'The roof is leaking like a basket. Well, I'd better be off. See you later.'

He raises his hat again and turns away. Helen Cartwright smiles down at Piers.

'This boy is just like his father, Marina,' she says. 'So you're back at Michaelgarth. That's such good news although I'm sorry to hear that your father isn't too well. Your mother's death must have been a great shock to you all.'

'It was very sad but I hope he'll pick up a little now.' Her voice is cool but polite. 'You must come for tea soon, once we've settled in properly.'

'That would be very nice.' Mrs Cartwright still looks as if something is amusing her. 'Felix was saying that James and I should come in for drinks one evening but I'd love to come to tea.'

'Goodbye, then.' His mother turns away, pulling Piers with her into the post office, but he twists back to smile at Mrs Cartwright.

'She's pretty, isn't she?' he says later, hurrying along at his mother's side. 'I like her.'

'Perhaps that's why she says that you're like your father.'

Her voice is sharp, the happiness is gone, and as he trudges back to the car his spirits flutter down and make a tiny cold pain inside him. He fingers the two sticks of chocolate in his pocket: one for him and one for Grandfather, and he still has two pennies left. He climbs into the car, kneeling up on the front seat so that he can see out properly, and as they drive down The Steep he remembers that they are going home to Michaelgarth and he is happy again.

As she drives along the familiar narrow lanes, between high-banked hedges, Marina is unaware of autumn's magic. The haws gleam crimson against fading leaves of yellow, hiding the luscious purple blackberries which cluster on rich-red brambles, and the sun is slipping below the blue-black rim of Dunkery Hill. Marina sees none of it: inside her head is a muddle of images and she is torn between guilt and suspicion. She sees Felix – hands in his pockets, laughing with Helen Cartwright – and remembers the instant twisting fear that stifles every other normal reaction. She knows that there is no reason why he shouldn't talk to an old friend yet she is incapable of responding naturally; of calling across the street to him, as Piers did, or crossing to join them.

32

'Hello, Helen,' she could have said, 'hello, darling,' and let him kiss her as he had wanted to, just a little affectionate kiss on the cheek. Instead, fear and rage held her aloof, recoiling from his gesture, hating him for standing with pretty Helen Cartwright in her silly hat and, no doubt, paying her compliments. If only she could have slipped her arm within his own, smiled back at Helen from a position of strength by his side, instead of remaining apart, mistrusting Helen's look of amusement, sheltering behind disdain.

Marina's hands tighten on the wheel: misery and anger war within her. Each time she vows that she will be different, that she will change, but each time that reaction is so sharp, so quick, that she has no time to fight it down and to remember that she means to trust him. She loves him – and hates him – because he is good-looking and attractive, because he likes to laugh and draws other people to him. She suspects every woman who comes near him and feels some kind of need to punish him for that quality, that warmth and generosity, which is like a magnet to men and women alike. He tries to understand and works hard to show that her suspicions are unfounded. That remark to Piers, 'I've been with old Mrs Baker at Myrtle Cottage,' was meant for her and, decoded, meant: 'No, I have not been having lunch with Helen Cartwright.'

She bites her lips with agitation, feeling remorse. As they climb away from the coast she sees Michaelgarth, standing strong and invulnerable on the hill, and she feels balanced again, more calm. She will pour Felix a drink when he comes home, cook something special for dinner, and later they will make love. She relaxes a little, changing gear to turn up the drive, and smiles at Piers, kneeling beside her on the passenger seat, looking eagerly up at the house.

'We're home,' she says to him and sees his answering beam of relief. For the moment all is well.

CHAPTER TWO

The old Morris bumps through the stone archway that leads into the garth and comes to rest in the open-fronted barn. Piers has to use both hands to open the door but then he is out, running across the ancient cobbles and in through the scullery.

'Grandfather,' he shouts. 'Where are you?'

He glances round the kitchen and passes into the hall. Even though he is in a tremendous hurry he hesitates here, tilting back his head to stare up at the soaring stone walls, dazzled by the light that pours through the high arched windows which face both north, towards the sea, and across the garth to the south. Michaelgarth is built on the ruins of an old priory and this room used to be the chapel. To Piers it has a special quality that imposes itself on the day-to-day: despite his need to be quick he finds that he must pause for a moment, to acknowledge whatever it is that lives here in the heart of the house.

His mother is coming into the scullery; he hears her drop her basket with a dull thud on the kitchen table, and he crosses the hall, flinging open the door of the drawing-room.

His grandfather, the newspaper fallen across his knees, jerks upright.

'What is it? What's up? Where's the fire?'

Piers laughs to himself for he always finds this question very funny. The fire is where it always is: in the big marble fireplace. Monty is stretched out on the rug but his tail beats a welcome on the floor and Piers pauses to stroke him before he feels in his pocket and takes out the sticks of chocolate.

'I bought one each,' he says confidentially, placing one of the sticks on his grandfather's knee. 'Only don't tell Mummy. I'm not allowed chocolate except on Saturdays. You can have yours later.'

His grandfather looks at the two small sticks in their shiny blue and silver wrapping, debating whether he should reprimand his small grandson for being deceitful. The grey eyes with their black lashes – just like his father's – look up at him with trustful glee and David Frayn takes his stick of chocolate with a wink and puts it in his trouser pocket.

'Very decent of you, old fellow. It'll go down a treat a bit later.'

'That's what I thought.' Piers frowns. 'Do you think Mummy might like the other one? We could say that you bought it. She was a bit down in the mouth just now.'

He likes the phrase 'down in the mouth', which is another of his grandfather's expressions. It is exactly right for his mother's face when she's not happy and the corners of her mouth turn down.

'Was she?' His grandfather sounds thoughtful; his eyes scan his grandson's face as he rubs his fingers over his clean-shaven jaw. 'And why would that be, I wonder?'

Piers shrugs – or rather his face shrugs: his lips purse and his eyebrows rise up towards his hairline. He rolls his eyes. 'Don't know.' He thinks of something else. 'We saw Daddy talking to Mrs Cartwright while we were shopping but he couldn't come back for tea.' He hooks his elbows over the arm of his grandfather's chair and slowly levers himself up so that his feet swing and bump against the chair. 'She said I was just like Daddy.'

'Helen Cartwright? Pretty girl.'

'She had a hat made of feathers. I think she's pretty too, but Mummy says that's why Mrs Cartwright thinks I'm like Daddy.'

David Frayn folds up his newspaper; although his suspicions have been proved correct he wishes it were otherwise. He is well aware of his daughter's jealous tendencies and his uneasiness is growing. Her mother had been of the same disposition and he knows what it is like to live with suspicion and mistrust; she'd poured all her energy into their son. Peter's passion for Michaelgarth and Exmoor, his wicked love of practical jokes and his unquenchable kindness had held at bay those spectres of jealousy and fear, and when he'd been killed in the war it was as if his mother's life had ended with his. David doesn't want history to repeat itself with Marina and Piers. He's very fond of his son-in-law, who is a chartered surveyor and land agent, and very proud of him. When Felix returned to his flat in Dunster, after the war, he'd taken over the management of several small estates in Somerset, one of which is Michaelgarth. It is soon clear to her parents that nobody but Felix will do for Marina; she loves him much more than she ever shows, even when they are alone together, but David Frayn knows his daughter very well and wonders if it would be better if she were to love Felix a little less. Once they are married, and after Piers is born, he sees a possessiveness growing, a desire to control, which he recognizes and fears. He hopes that his presence might exercise some restraint although he fears that he is an interfering old fool.

'Don't kick the chair, Piers, I've told you before.' Marina comes into the drawing-room. 'Are you ready for tea, Father?'

'*I* am.' Piers gives one last big swing and drops back to the floor. 'Mrs P said she'd make a chocolate cake.'

'And don't call her Mrs P. Her name is Mrs Penn.'

Piers wonders whether to say 'That's what Grandfather calls her' but doesn't want to get him into trouble. Mrs Penn has been coming up from Luccombe to clean the house and help with the cooking for years but she's getting too old for the long walk across the fields, and now that they've moved to Michaelgarth, Mummy is going to collect her in Grandfather's Morris. Piers likes Mrs Penn, who is very small and bundly and whose hair is so thin that he can see the pink top of her head shining through the strands of grey.

'How old are you, Mrs P?' he asks, knowing that the answer is always the same.

'As old as my tongue and a little older than my teeth.'

He likes this familiar exchange in the same way that he likes Grandfather asking where the fire is, although he doesn't quite understand what either of them means, and, anyway, when he looks carefully it seems that Mrs P doesn't have very many teeth. Sometimes, when she's known that he is coming to tea, she makes him gingerbread men. Now that he lives at Michaelgarth he wonders if she might make them every day.

'Although, to be honest,' says Marina later, as they sit beside the fire and she pours the tea, 'she's getting too old to do anything thoroughly. I wonder if we should get someone younger, though I shall be able to do so much more myself now.'

Sitting on the leather pouffe, managing his plate with difficulty, Piers licks the crumbs anxiously from his fingers. He is distracted from the pleasurable feel of Monty's heavy head on his feet and the way he raises it occasionally to lick Piers' knee. Mrs P would be very hurt if she knew that she was too old to do her work properly.

'Can't get rid of Mrs P,' says Grandfather, drinking his tea. 'She's been coming up to Michaelgarth since I can't remember when. Hurt her feelings, poor old duck.'

'She might be relieved,' suggests Marina. 'Perhaps she'd like the chance to take it easy.'

'No-one likes to be told that they're too old. Mind you, she must be getting on a bit.'

'She's as old as her tongue and a little older than her teeth,' offers Piers.

Marina looks at him with exasperation; his face is smeared with icing but he smiles at her contentedly: the chocolate cake is excellent. She melts with love for him but doesn't let him see it; he mustn't be spoiled.

'Do you have a handkerchief?' she asks, hardening her heart as she watches his smile fade into anxiety as he rootles in the pocket of his shorts.

'Here it is,' he cries, pulling it out triumphantly, but even as he flourishes it the chocolate stick falls to the carpet and he gives a little gasp, his teeth sinking into his lower lip, his cheeks bright as poppies.

'What is it?' She stretches across to pick up the chocolate, frowning. 'Who gave you this?'

'Nobody. I bought it,' says Piers, his heart bumping in his side.

'Nonsense,' replies Marina. Her face is cold, disdainful at what she perceives to be a lie. She remembers that he dawdled behind her at the post office whilst she was talking to a friend outside on the pavement. Can he have taken it? 'Tell me the truth at once, Piers,' she insists.

'Good gracious!' exclaims her father, who has seen the chocolate just too late. 'What's all the fuss about? *I* gave it to him.'

All three of them know that this is a lie and there is an uncomfortable silence: the happy tea-time atmosphere is dissipating and David Frayn heaves himself forward on to the edge of his chair.

'That was very good cake,' he says cheerfully, as if nothing has happened. 'And now, young man, it's time you got your revenge on the snakes and ladders board. Since you've got that nice handkerchief, why don't you use it? Come on, let me help you . . .'

They go away together, followed closely by Monty, into David's study next to the drawing-room, and Marina is left alone on the long sofa before the fire. The windows face north and west and the room is washed with a golden light, which glances off the silver teapot and shows the crumbs scattered on Piers' plate. She feels frustrated by her father's action and disapproves of the way he sprang to Piers' defence. It is the sort of thing that sets a bad example, but she can guess the truth of it. Felix has been irresponsible: giving Piers money without her knowing. She sits in the firelight as the sunset glow fades, thinking of Felix, waiting for him to come home.

CHAPTER THREE

He is slightly later than usual, suspecting that there is to be a scene about Helen Cartwright, taking his time on the journey from Minehead. It feels odd, turning off at Headon Cross rather than driving on towards Porlock to the cottage on the old toll road where he and Marina have lived since they were first married. It is Marina's idea, backed strongly by her mother, that they should start their married life in the cottage, which is part of the Michaelgarth estate. Even when they are engaged, Marina will never go to his small flat in Dunster.

'Mummy would have a fit,' she tells him. 'After all, it's so public, isn't it?'

'Does it matter?' he asks. 'We're getting married in a few months' time. Who cares if people talk? I'm only suggesting that we have a cup of tea together.'

She is so set against it that he wonders if she thinks she will find evidence of former entanglements: she wants no part in anything that has had a role in his bachelor state. He is sometimes hurt – and occasionally irritated – by her refusal to share his former life but he tells himself that she is unconfident and that she needs time.

She is such a pretty girl, with delicate features and fine dark hair, rather self-effacing and painfully shy. Despite this shyness, however, there is no question of her wanting him: from the beginning, when her father introduces them, she quietly but determinedly annexes him away from other girls. He finds it flattering, rather amusing, and is intrigued by her silent intensity. Having discovered that she is in love with him he begins to love her, encouraging her confidence in him to grow, gently drawing her out. As the months pass, he feels certain that, once they are married, she'll relax into an easiness with him and later, taken by surprise – and gratified – by her physical passion, he waits for other expressions of her affection. He longs for loving warmth, an unexpected hug from her, or to hear her say 'I love you' but, seven years on, accusations and jealous silences have been the only evidence of how much she needs him: cold comfort for a warm-hearted man.

He parks his car beside his father-in-law's Morris and stands for a moment on the cobbles wishing that he was climbing the stairs to his little flat in Dunster: no stress in that first-floor room overlooking the High Street; no anxiety that an unconsidered word might shiver the atmosphere to ice. As he looks up at the tall windows of the hall, light shines out from the landing of the east wing, casting long shadows across the garth. Piers will be going to bed, hoping for a story, and David will be waiting to offer him a drink. His spirits rise and, pausing to pluck a late-flowering rose from its stem against the wall, he goes inside.

Leaving his briefcase and the rosebud on the kitchen table, he goes into the hall and climbs the staircase at the eastern end. He can hear voices from the bathroom and there, through the open door, is Piers in his pyjamas, his toes curling away from the cold lino, his damp hair standing on end. All he can see of Marina is her hands, now buttoning his jacket, now brushing his hair whilst Piers winces away, his face puckered.

'That's too hard,' he complains. 'I won't have any hair left if you go on, Mummy. I'll look just like Mrs P.'

'I won't tell you again, Piers.' Marina's voice is edgy. 'It's very disrespectful for a little boy of your age—'

Felix pushes the door wider, cutting her short, and Piers cries out, 'It's Daddy.'

'Hello, darling.' He leans to touch Marina's forehead with his lips before lifting Piers high up, swinging him round, whilst he screams with delight. 'Come on, old son. It's time for our story. Bet you can't remember where we'd got to.'

He bears him off along the landing whilst Piers protests that he *can* remember, of *course* he can, and Marina gets to her feet and folds the bath-towel, retrieves the celluloid duck and the clockwork steamer, and lets the water run away. By the time she arrives in the bedroom Piers is half in bed, half cuddled up to Felix, listening to Chapter Three of *The Wind in the Willows*. Felix's ability to be naturally affectionate embarrasses her and she shows by a little frowning glance that she disapproves of this abandonment. Piers should be sitting properly in bed, with Felix beside him on the chair, and she pulls at the blankets in an attempt to dislodge Piers, to tidy him into the bed and Felix on to the chair. Piers frowns at her and clings tighter to Felix, who hugs him, gives him a kiss, and she shrugs, says 'Goodnight' to Piers and goes downstairs.

Piers is glad to see her go. He still feels uncomfortable about the chocolate and Grandfather telling a lie but doesn't know how to begin to explain. He becomes engrossed in the story and presently forgets all about the chocolate; soon he drifts into sleep and Felix lays him gently down, covering him warmly.

Felix goes quietly downstairs, hesitates in the hall but decides that he mustn't take refuge with his father-in-law: not just yet. He can hear noises in the kitchen and goes to find Marina.

'He's asleep,' he says. 'Dear old chap. Ready for a drink?'

'That means that you are,' she answers, putting potatoes into a dish and slipping them into the oven. 'You're so late that I assumed that you'd stopped off to have one on the way home.'

'Am I late?' He makes his voice casually surprised. 'I don't think so. Look, isn't that pretty?'

He offers her the rose and she takes it, rather nonplussed but jolted for a moment out of her grievance with him. She'd planned it differently: she was going to be welcoming and make some light remark about Helen Cartwright, but in that half an hour of waiting she'd already imagined him in a pub somewhere, joking with friends, flirting with the barmaid. She thinks of him standing with Helen Cartwright, laughing in the sunshine. Now, as she looks at the tightly furled bud, smoothing it with her finger, he watches her anxiously, willing her away from suspicion towards trust.

'I've been thinking,' he says, 'that you might come to Bristol with me this weekend.'

She hates his monthly visits to the Bristol office and, during those early years before Piers was born, he persuaded her to accompany him to Bristol, staying with him in the flat owned by the company above the office in Clifton. He hoped that, by introducing her to his colleagues and their wives, by showing her that these two days are not passed in riotous living and parties, she would be reassured. Once Piers was born, however, these visits tailed off and a new resentment – that motherhood is a ploy that she has been tricked into – began to develop.

'I suppose you have to go?' She raises the bud to her lips, inhaling its faint scent. 'After all, we've only just moved in here and there's so much to do.'

'You know I have to go to the partners' meetings,' he says gently. 'Come with me, Marina. You used to enjoy it, didn't you? Piers will be perfectly safe with your father for two nights and he's at school for most of the day. Perhaps Mrs Penn would stay over. We could go to the Old Vic or to the Hippodrome. I wish you would.'

He watches her smooth the velvet petals, wanting to accept yet unable to give in, and sees the exact moment when she rejects the gentler powers of loving reason for the destructive need to punish and destroy.

'I can't possibly go,' she says impatiently, as if he has demanded some enormous sacrifice, fiddling with the bud. 'There's still a huge amount of unpacking to be done here, even if I could just go off leaving Piers with his grandfather.' She gives a little disdainful smile as if to imply that only he would make such a selfish suggestion. 'If you want company perhaps you should ask Helen Cartwright. I'm sure she'd be only too pleased to go with you and from the way you were all over her earlier, I'm sure you'd like it too.'

He stares at her for a moment, swallowing down furious words, and then goes away to find David in his study. Marina stands quite still, biting her lips, shredding and rolling the rosebud to and fro between her thumb and fingers until finally she throws it away in disgust and turns on the tap to wash her hands.

It is David who makes peace possible between them and helps Felix to persuade Marina to go to Bristol. As soon as he comes into the study, David Frayn sees the angry set of Felix's mouth, the distraction in his eyes, and guesses that there is trouble. Knowing Marina, remembering his conversation with Piers, he suspects that it will be to do with Helen Cartwright. Pouring Felix a whisky he feels a bond of sympathy: he knows what it is like to live on a knife-edge, to crave for normal loving companionship.

These poor women, he thinks, trapped into bitterness and misery, unable to seize a lifeline. But I mustn't interfere . . .

He talks to Felix about his day, about his own morning in

court – he is a JP and sits on the local magistrates' bench each week – they discuss the local farmers, land that is for sale, property that is being developed, and all the while his kindly eyes note the signs of relaxation: the unforced smile, the easing of his shoulders as Felix stretches his legs towards the fire. It's a comfortably untidy room, the oak shelves holding not only leather-backed books but also the clutter of the old man's shooting paraphernalia; on a sagging sofa, covered by a faded rug, Monty curls, dry and warm, his eyes glinting in the firelight.

David sighs contentedly as he fills his pipe; if Marina's mother were still alive he'd now be hauled off to remove his disreputable old tweed and told to tidy himself up. It's been years since he's changed into black tie for dinner at Michaelgarth – the war put a stop to all that sort of thing – but Eleanor insisted on maintaining standards. He wonders if Marina shares her mother's liking for formality but a glance at his son-in-law's firm chin and the set of his lips makes him suspect that Felix can only be pushed so far. He wonders if Marina has mentioned the matter of the chocolate. Perhaps that is what the trouble is all about.

'Good little fellow, that chap of yours,' he begins carefully. 'Thoughtful. Brought me home some chocolate this afternoon. His mother couldn't think where he got it.'

Felix seems unmoved; he even smiles. 'I should have thought he'd have had the sense not to have shown her,' he says. 'He's only allowed sweets at the weekend but I found a few pennies in my pocket and gave them to him as a half-term treat. Perhaps it was wrong of me. Marina will think I'm undermining her authority.'

His smile fades, as if he is remembering other occasions of his failure to live up to her high standards, and David shifts about in his high-backed leather chair.

'If you can't bend the rules from time to time,' he mutters, 'it's a poor sort of show.'

A silence: neither is prepared to discuss Marina more explicitly but they sense a rapport and gain comfort from it.

'I suggested that she should come to Bristol with me this Sunday,' says Felix, anxious that his father-in-law shouldn't read too much into the silence. 'I think she feels it's rather cheeky to leave Piers with you, especially as we haven't finished unpacking yet.'

'But that's an excellent plan,' cries David, sitting up, reaching for the decanter. 'I'm sure the boy and I can shift for ourselves for a couple of days.'

'That's what I told her.' Felix holds out his glass gratefully. 'I wondered if Mrs Penn might be persuaded to stay for a couple of nights. I know she's getting on a bit . . .'

'As old as her tongue and a little older than her teeth.' David grins, thinking of Piers at tea-time. 'He's a tonic, that boy. No need to worry about him.'

'I don't,' answers Felix grimly. 'Piers is the least of my worries.'

They both jump as the door opens and Marina comes into the study. Both men notice that she has changed from the slacks and jersey she was wearing earlier into a long-sleeved frock with a full skirt. David looks at her uneasily, wondering if this is to be the thin end of the wedge, waiting for some remark regarding the shabbiness of his tweed jacket and rubbed cords. Felix, however, guesses that Marina has had time to regret her outburst and has been making herself look pretty so as to boost her own confidence before she attempts some kind of bridge-building.

He is on familiar territory here and, relaxed and peaceful after this short time with David, he throws out the first line.

'How nice you look,' he says, smiling at her. 'Are you ready for some of this excellent whisky? Of course, I only agreed to move up to Michaelgarth because of your father's cellar. You know that, don't you, David?'

His father-in-law, delighted by this promising beginning,

gives a snort of approval whilst Marina perches on the fender, arranging her spreading skirts carefully. Her dark hair is twisted up into a smooth French pleat and she manages to look both sophisticated and vulnerable. The leaping glow of the flames warms her pale skin and she finds it difficult to look directly at Felix.

'Sherry for me,' she says. 'You know I hate the smell of whisky,' but, for once, this is not criticism, the usual reminder that she doesn't like the smell of it on his breath. 'Dinner's nearly ready so I mustn't be too long.'

'I was just telling David that you won't come to Bristol with me.' Felix decides to take full opportunity of having a third person present. 'He agrees with me that Piers would be perfectly safe for just two nights. Won't you change your mind, darling?'

Marina, who has been cursing herself for ruining this chance to be with him, cross that once again she has failed to control her demon, is taken aback by such a direct approach. So is David, who looks with admiration at Felix before coming in on his side.

'We'd be perfectly fine,' he says impatiently. 'He's not a baby, Marina, and neither am I. We'll survive, I promise you.'

'I think that Piers will see it as some kind of adventure.' Felix leans forward, as though to touch her arm, but she instinctively draws back. Even at moments like these, when she'd like to make amends, she can't endure any show of physical affection. 'And, after all,' he adds rather wearily, 'we shan't be that far away. You could drive back if you needed to.'

He sits back in his chair, hurt by her continual rejection, suddenly uncaring whether she joins him or not.

Seven years of marriage, he thinks bitterly, and I'm still only allowed to touch her when we're having sex. She thinks that those frenzied acts make up for this continuing lack of affection.

Marina sees that he is upset and, remembering how Helen Cartwright looked at him and how other women look at him, she feels the pang of fear.

'Oh, very well,' she says. 'If you insist, but I must have a word with Mrs Penn to see if she can cope with bath-time.'

'Piers won't die if he doesn't have a bath for two nights,' says David cheerfully. 'Stop fussing, woman. Won't that dinner be ready yet?'

She hurries away, taking her sherry with her, relieved now that the matter is resolved. She will make it up to Felix later on tonight – and in Bristol.

'I'll go and wash my hands.' Felix rises reluctantly to his feet: the peace and harmony is shattered and he feels irritable. 'Thanks for the whisky, David.'

The old man lays an arm along his son-in-law's shoulders and gives it a little squeeze; their eyes meet and Felix realizes that the old man knows exactly how he feels. Warmth steals round his heart and he smiles at him. He begins to speak – to justify himself? To explain that he is not an adulterous bastard? – but David shakes his head. No words are needed here. Marina calls to them that dinner is being taken into the dining-room and they go out together, Monty following along behind.

CHAPTER FOUR

So it is that Marina is with him that evening when he first sees Angelica Blake as Rosalind in *As You Like It*. One of his colleagues and his wife are 'Friends of the Theatre' and have bought the tickets.

'I was hoping that we were going to have an evening on our own,' says Marina sulkily, sitting at the small dressing-table, screwing in her earrings. 'I thought that was the whole point of me being here.'

'They thought it would be a treat.' Felix transfers his loose cash to his trouser pocket, stows away his cigarette case and lighter. 'Molly and Tom are very kind to me when I'm up on my own. We can hardly refuse.'

'But they had no idea I was coming,' she persists. 'How did they know to get two tickets?'

Her suspicions are out in the open and Felix wonders how he should answer so that the evening is not ruined. Sometimes he makes up a foursome with Molly's sister, whose husband was killed in the war, but how is he to explain this to Marina without opening a floodgate? He knows that there is simply no time to work through the wearying but familiar pattern of accusation, explanations, arctic silence, gradual propitiation on his part and remorse on hers, which finally spends itself in an exhausting bout of love-making. After seven years he is beginning to find it humiliating and distasteful, and Tom and Molly will be here in fifteen minutes to collect them.

'I expect someone has let them down,' he answers casually, praying that Tom doesn't make an ill-timed joke about the occasional foursome. 'Perhaps Molly dashed out to buy the tickets this morning. Does it matter? Can't we just enjoy it? It's one of your favourites, isn't it? Didn't you tell me that you once played Rosalind in the school play?'

Staring at him as he bends to look into the mirror, his head beside hers as he swiftly brushes his hair, Marina remembers that she has vowed not to spoil this time with him. She's had a very pleasant day, exploring old Clifton before walking down to Whiteladies Road for lunch in Brights, followed by a stroll on Brandon Hill, and Felix is making every effort to spend as much time with her as possible.

'I played Celia, actually,' she says, trying for a lighter note, 'and hated every moment of it. I wasn't cut out for the stage but it was a poor year for artistic talent and I was the best of a bad bunch. I'm sure it will be great fun.'

Grateful for this attempt, Felix bends to kiss her. 'At least you would have looked beautiful, if nothing else,' he murmurs.

As usual she is embarrassed by his extravagance and turns her head aside, making a show of fastening her pretty garnet necklace, checking her hair. Felix straightens up, too relieved that the awkward moment has passed to feel the usual resignation, putting on his jacket. When the doorbell rings he hurries out to greet Molly and Tom, who arrive in good humour and over drinks explain that, after the show, a visit backstage has been arranged: Molly knows Angelica Blake, the actress who is playing the part of Rosalind. Felix sees at once that Marina is not too keen on this suggestion but she is too well-mannered to object in front of their hosts and there is no time to voice her feelings to Felix. He hopes that, when the time comes, she'll simply allow herself to be carried along with the general fun.

The atmosphere of the theatre works its magic: the air of expectation amongst the audience, who talk and laugh and peer about to see if they recognize friends, the shabby gilt of the tiers and ornate pillars, the soft, dusty plush of the seats and – at last – the sudden hush as the lights dim and the curtain rises.

Marina is relaxed, her shoulder rests against his arm and, briefly, she is transported to this other world, to the Forest of Arden, her own fears and tension forgotten. Afterwards, as they pass through the swing door, she holds his arm and he squeezes it with his elbow against his side so as to reassure her.

The small dressing-room seems full of people and noise so that Marina hesitates, pushing Felix ahead of her. Molly and Tom are already greeting one of the actors and Felix has time to take in the scene: the long dressing-bar with sticks of greasepaint and a bowl of flowers beside the mirror; a huge tin of grease with a mound of cotton wool; a screen with clothes flung over it; the sound of the departing audience relayed through the Tannoy.

The girl who played the part of Celia is sitting before the glass, cleaning her face with cotton wool, but Angelica Blake stands beside the screen, tying the belt of a dark blue cotton wrapper round her slender waist, her ash-fair hair pulled back casually from a face that, already wiped bare of its make-up, is as fresh and clean as a child's. She is listening intently to the tall, dark-haired man in jeans and green jersey who gesticulates, explaining something, until suddenly he gives a shout of laughter and leans forward to kiss her.

'You were terrific, darling,' he says, 'but just don't forget to take that line slowly. The timing is absolutely vital,' and she smiles gratefully at him and they turn together as the stage-manager calls: 'You've got visitors, Angel.'

As her glance touches his, Felix feels a tiny galvanic shock, a thrill of something that could be described as a kind of recognition. It is so strong, so compelling, that he instinctively turns away from her to Marina, who is still just behind him in the doorway, as if the sight of his wife – cool, smart, emotions well under control – might restore him to his senses. She doesn't respond as he smiles at her, standing to one side so that she can edge past and precede him into the dressing-room, but he keeps his eyes carefully away from the girl who is now making her way towards them. The tall, dark-haired man is the first to be introduced; he already knows Molly and Tom, and now he holds out his arm so as to draw Angel into the circle.

Felix briefly grasps her warm hand, barely glancing at her again, talking instead to the tall man and one or two other people who have now squeezed into the overcrowded dressing-room. Presently, they go in a group to the Llandoger Trow for supper but, before very long, Angel and the girl who's played Celia gather up their coats, preparing to leave, joking about beauty sleep. There is much kissing and noisy farewells, but when she comes face to face with Felix, Angel simply holds out her hand.

'We haven't talked properly.' She speaks so quietly that he has to bend his head to hear her. 'I wish we had.'

'So do I,' he mumbles inadequately, foolishly – and looks at her again.

Her hand tightens around his and then she turns away; only a few seconds have passed, nobody has heard or noticed them. A moment later he's finishing his pint, laughing at some amusing remark, and even Marina hasn't noticed how forced his laughter sounds or how his hand shakes when he replaces the empty glass upon the bar.

It is ironic, he thinks, that when, for the first time, Marina has reason to be jealous she suspects nothing. He knows why: it is as if, after the exchange of that very first glance, he's been in shock, his usual friendliness and charm temporarily suspended.

'You seemed a bit off,' Marina tells him later, once they're back at the flat alone. Her voice is a strange mix of brittle sarcasm and curiosity. 'Not your usual self at all.'

'I've had the most fearful headache,' he answers. 'I was hoping nobody noticed. I didn't want to be a wet blanket.'

He tries to take her in his arms but she wriggles away from him, saying that she is going to make some coffee, and for once he makes no effort to detain her. The next time he goes to Bristol he goes alone.

CHAPTER FIVE

'I've asked someone for a drink tomorrow evening,' says Angel to Pidge one Sunday evening in January. She looks slightly self-conscious. 'Before I go down to the theatre. Could you be around? I'd like you to meet him.'

She speaks quite low, so as not to arouse Lizzie's attention, and Pidge looks up from her book, quirking her eyebrows so that Angel becomes even more embarrassed. This is so unlike her that Pidge feels a qualm of anxiety.

'Married, is he?' she asks lightly, laying the book face down on the broad arm of the chair.

Angel pulls a face and draws her cotton wrapper round her more tightly. She always sleeps in the afternoon and doesn't dress again properly until it's time to go down to the theatre.

'Isn't it typical, sweetie?' she asks ruefully. 'Why is it I only fall in love with married men?'

'Oh dear.' Pidge reaches for a cigarette and pushes the packet towards Angel. 'Very married?'

Angel purses her lips, pretending to consider, gives Pidge a sideways glance. 'Well, perhaps not *that* married.'

'Another Mike?'

They both glance instinctively towards the table where Lizzie, humming to herself, is filling in a picture in her colouring book. She works busily, unaware of their conversation, and Angel kicks off her flat leather slippers and tucks her feet up on the seat.

'He's a bit like Mike to look at – dark hair and that very direct look – but he's not as tough and forceful as Mike. He's nice, Pidge.'

There's a wistful note in her voice and Pidge watches her sympathetically, tapping ash from her cigarette, remembering Mike: General Sir Hilary Carmichael whom the troops nicknamed 'Mike' just as he nicknamed her 'Pidge'.

'Then I'll certainly be here.' She grins. 'Let's hope we don't repeat our performance.'

'At least this time I shall get in first.' Angel wriggles along the sofa so that she is leaning a little closer to Pidge. 'His name's Felix Hamilton . . .'

Kneeling on the chair, working carefully with her crayons, Lizzie is aware of their voices murmuring together but she is too busy telling herself a story that goes with the picture to take any of it in. The woman holding the baby is Angel and she is the baby: 'There, there, sweetie,' she mutters, 'don't cry. Look, here's Daddy coming home; he's bringing a rabbit skin to wrap poor Baby Bunting in.' She sings the nursery rhyme just under her breath whilst she colours the tall sunflowers that frame the cottage door a satisfyingly brilliant orange. She sits back on her heels to study her efforts, flexing her fingers, which ache a little from clutching the crayon, listening to the voices. There is a quality in the conversation between Angel and Pidge that hints at something private – some secret knowledge that they share – which is how it has been from the beginning: from that first moment when she and Angel arrived on the doorstep. Lizzie remembers Angel's excitement when she returned from that first meeting with Pidge after an evening performance; excitement and something else.

As soon as Pidge opened the door and welcomed them in, Lizzie was aware of an undercurrent running beneath the polite introductions. The house had been carefully arranged and divided to accommodate lodgers: the ground floor kept as Pidge's private quarters, the first floor and the attic room for the tenant. This little room beneath the eaves was to be Lizzie's and, as they climbed the short steep flight of stairs, her heart thumped with hope. Angel and Pidge stood aside and allowed her to enter.

As Lizzie looked about her in the high attic room, her first impression was that she was standing inside a tent. Rafters criss-crossed high above her head and the ceiling sloped sharply, nearly to the floor. There was a bed with a patchwork quilt, a white painted chest for her clothes and a wickerwork chair with a cushion that matched the quilt. She ran to the dormer window, kneeling so as to look down into the leafy square.

'Will she be able to cope with the stairs?' Pidge asked anxiously, still standing at the door. 'They're a bit steep.'

'Oh, *yes*,' Lizzie cried at once, lest Angel should take fright and deny her this magic place. 'I can be very careful. Please, Angel. Anyway, it's too small for *you*.'

Angel chuckled; that warm, easy laugh that makes her so many friends.

'It's simply perfect,' she answered – and Lizzie, washed through with relief and joy, perched on the edge of the bed, looking about her with delight, longing to bring her small suitcase containing all the treasures that would make the room truly hers. Later she went very carefully down the short steep flight of stairs to find Angel, who was being shown her own bedroom across the landing from the big room which was divided into a sitting-room and kitchen. A lavatory with a separate bathroom complete the first-floor accommodation.

'It's just right for us, isn't it, Angel?' Lizzie, always alert to mood and atmosphere, was anxious to make up for her mother's unusual silence, sensing Pidge's nervousness, puzzled by those undercurrents she could not understand.

'It's simply perfect,' Angel repeated slowly. 'But the rent seems very . . . modest for all this space . . .'

It was almost as if she were testing Pidge – or even teasing her slightly – and Lizzie instinctively tensed as if for some kind of physical action.

'It's more important that I have the right people in my home, you see.' Pidge broke in quickly. 'It's not just the money . . .'

Her distress communicated itself to Angel who, apparently regretting her former feigned reluctance, slipped an arm about Pidge's slim shoulders in a spontaneous gesture of comfort. 'My dear, don't think I'm complaining! I couldn't be more thrilled. I'm just knocked sideways at our luck.'

'That's good, then. So it's "yes"?'

Angel looked from Pidge's anxious face into Lizzie's plead-ing one. 'Oh, I think so,' she said, chuckling again. 'I'd say it's definitely "yes".'

Whilst Angel and Pidge disappeared into the sitting-room to deal with the business side of the arrangement, Lizzie climbed back up to her eyrie, looking about her with joyful amaze-ment, wondering how soon they could move in so that she might arrange her few belongings to her own satisfaction. After a few weeks it seemed as if they had lived here with Pidge for ever.

Now, slipping from the chair, carrying the book, she goes across to the two women, who stop talking to look at her.

'See what I've done,' she says, and Angel takes the book, holding it at an angle so that Pidge can see it too.

'That's pretty good, Lizzie,' says Pidge, blinking a little at the brightness of the sunflowers. 'Very imaginative use of colour.'

Lizzie too peers at the picture. 'That's Mummy and me,' she explains, 'when I was a baby. And that's my daddy coming in at the gate. See? I wish Daddy could come home.'

She imagines him at the front door with Angel standing at the top of the stairs looking down at him holding her, Lizzie's, hand. She knows exactly how it would be: he would drop his case on the floor and hold out his arms to them and they would run down the stairs together. His coat would be rough to touch but he would swing her up in his arms and say: 'I can't believe that this is little Lizzie. How she's grown . . .'

'Oh, sweetie.' Angel puts an arm about her. 'I wish it too. But so many people were killed in the war.'

Lizzie knows this, her very best friend at her new school is also fatherless, and she leans against Angel's leg, pulling her heavy red-gold plait over her shoulder to rub it against her cheek for comfort.

'He was very brave,' says Pidge, attempting to console. 'He was a King's Messenger.'

In the odd little silence that follows Angel glances warningly at Pidge but Lizzie is never surprised by those unexpected remarks that indicate that Pidge knew her father almost as intimately as Angel did. Instead, she frowns, remembering *Through the Looking-Glass* and the picture of the King's Messenger in the chapter headed 'The Lion and the Unicorn'. In her mind's eye she sees an odd-looking rabbit with huge ears, one foot pointed, delving in a bag for a letter for the White King. The creased photograph of her father that Angel has shown her is rather blurred but it is at least that of a man in uniform. Nevertheless, she is confused.

('Wouldn't it be heaven,' Angel says in the early days to Pidge, 'if we could have a proper photograph of Mike framed for her? We could stand it on the piano.'

'Completely crazy,' answers Pidge forcefully. 'We might as well put up a photo of Winston or Monty or Mountbatten. Everyone would recognize him at once. That photo of your brother will simply have to do. Thank God he was called Michael. We both promised . . .')

'Tell me about him,' demands Lizzie, hitching herself into Angel's lap. 'Tell me again.'

Angel settles them both comfortably. 'His name was Michael Blake,' she begins.

She is describing her brother, who was killed in Korea, and Pidge knows that she is feeling, as she always does, guilty at this deception: ashamed that Lizzie can never know who her real father is, distressed at using the brother whom she loved as a kind of replacement.

'Michael wouldn't have cared,' Angel often says defensively, after these uncomfortable times. 'He was always kicking up a lark, he'd have understood, but it just feels . . . well, you know . . .'

And Pidge can imagine how difficult it is and tries to do what she can. As she listens to Angel she thinks of Mike, whose driver she was in the last year of the war and the first months of peace.

'I'll want the car at three o'clock' – a tiny pause – 'but it'll be a late one, Pidge,' he'd say; this is their signal.

She'll never know how the rumours started but once Mike hears of them he is ruthless.

'Nothing I can do, darling Pidge,' he tells her on that last meeting. 'I've told you how it is with my wife. She's quite helpless physically and I could never leave her. We agreed, didn't we?'

But she still clings to him, unwilling to believe that she will never lie with him like this again, warm in his arms.

Pidge looks about her and then back at the two curled together on the sofa: this is Mike's house. He owns a great deal of property and when he found that she was taking up a job at the University Library in Bristol, he offered her the house on a very reasonable rent.

'No strings,' he said. 'That's all over, Pidge, but it might help out while you get settled.'

It was nearly nine years before she heard from him again: a

letter outlining another plan, this time an attempt to assist the mother of his child.

'See what you can do, Pidge,' he wrote. 'No names, no pack-drill. You'll like Angel and I'd like to think of you all together, looking after each other since I can't – not directly, anyway.'

It could so easily have been a disaster – they might have been jealous of each other – but it was a brilliant plan.

Mike always was a great judge of character, thinks Pidge, listening to Angel describing Michael's schooldays to Lizzie – and now there is a new man: Felix Hamilton, who will be coming for a drink tomorrow.

In his nervousness he rings the wrong doorbell.

'Hello,' says Pidge, appearing as suddenly as a jack-in-the-box, and he looks at her almost in dismay. She raises an eyebrow, registering his confusion, liking the look of him. 'Can I help?'

'I'm so sorry, I must have muddled the address.' Disconcerted, he bundles the bunch of flowers – yellow roses – into his left arm and feels anxiously in his pocket. 'I could have sworn it was this number.' He steps back to check the number on the door whilst Pidge watches with amused interest.

'Right number, wrong door,' she says kindly when she feels that he's suffered enough. 'I expect it's Angel you're looking for.'

'Yes it is,' he agrees gratefully. 'I thought . . . she said that . . .'

At this point the door at the top of the stairs opens and Angel stares down at them.

'Darling,' she cries warmly, addressing both of them. 'Whatever are you doing down there? I hope you're not giving Pidge my flowers, Felix.'

'No, no,' he says hastily and, instantly embarrassed at this ungallant denial, adds, 'not that I wouldn't have bought some more if I'd realized . . .'

'So I should hope,' says Pidge indignantly. 'I'm not some old concierge, you know, sitting about here waiting for the doorbell to ring.'

He begins to laugh and Pidge sees exactly why Angel has been behaving like a woman who is head over heels in love. 'I give in,' he said. 'Would half each settle the point?'

'Certainly not,' cries Angel. 'They're all for me. Come on up and we'll have a drink. And you, Pidge! Don't go all tactful on me. I want you to meet this man properly. He's coming down to the theatre with me later.'

They climb the stairs and, once inside the big first-floor room, Felix and Pidge shake hands solemnly.

Pidge's level brown-eyed gaze continues to unnerve him a little. 'And will this be the first time that you've seen the play?' she asks.

He reddens slightly, suspecting that she already knows the answer, guessing that he is being teased, and Angel, pouring drinks, chuckles triumphantly.

'This'll be the third time, sweetie. How's that for devotion?'

'Very commendable.' Pidge continues to watch him, assessing him, and Felix has the uncomfortable suspicion that these two women have no secrets from each other.

'It's a good play,' he answers lightly.

When Lizzie comes downstairs from her high attic room he shakes hands with her just as if she is grown up.

'Did you bring me a present too?' she asks when she is shown the roses and Pidge chuckles at the expression on Felix's face.

'He forgot me too,' she says to Lizzie. 'Shocking, isn't it?'

'I had no idea,' he pleads, addressing Lizzie, 'that there were *three* ladies living here. May I come again and make up for it?'

'I like chocolate,' says Lizzie warningly, lest he should bring the wrong kind of presents. She likes flowers too, but chocolate is best. 'And Pidge says diamonds are a girl's best friend.'

'Does she indeed?' Felix laughs as Pidge covers her face with her hands and shakes her head in despair. 'Well, the truth will out. I'll have to see what I can do.'

'I like him,' says Pidge much later to Angel. 'I like him a lot. So does Lizzie. I'm just warning you that you've got competition.'

'Oh, Pidge,' Angel's eyes are huge with joy and love, 'he is rather nice, isn't he?'

'Mind you,' Pidge tells her, touched by the evidence of Angel's feelings, 'I'm not committing myself just yet. It's all hanging on those diamonds.'

CHAPTER SIX

'Have you thought of going to Bristol with Felix next week-end?' asks David Frayn. 'It's about time you had another break.'

He stands at the drawing-room window looking out into the dusk. Earlier a blizzard has swept in over the Channel and the branches of the fir trees are weighed down with smooth, rounded snowy domes, which fall from time to time in soft powdery explosions. Below, on the rocky, ice-glazed slopes of the hill, a fox moves cautiously in the shelter of the furze, a note of warm russet in the freezing landscape, whilst the silver disc of a moon, thin and insubstantial, is already setting behind Dunkery.

Piers, cross-legged on the hearth rug, is collecting up his toy soldiers and putting them away in the big wooden box. Grandfather has been advising him – 'Now, you put your artillery *here*, d'you see? And the infantry *here*' – and they've had a very good game, but he senses a tension in the old man as he stands at the window; there is a note in his voice that Piers can't quite place. Although he doesn't know why, he feels anxious. He leans back against Monty, who stirs in his sleep, whining a little, his paws twitching as if he were running. Piers leans over him tenderly, smoothing the soft coat, murmuring reassurances.

David Frayn turns away from the window and Marina glances up from her book.

'To be honest with you, it doesn't really appeal in weather like this,' she answers. 'It was quite fun, last autumn, but the days are rather long all alone in a poky flat and you can't spend all day walking about. I don't see much of Felix, you know, Father. He has to fit quite a lot in during those two days each month. Perhaps in the spring I'll go.'

'Is it snowing again?' asks Piers eagerly. The village school has closed early because of the weather and he has built a splendid snowman in the garth: his grandfather has lent a shabby old felt hat and a long woollen scarf, and Piers can hardly wait to show his father.

'I hope not,' answers Marina. She glances at her watch. 'I hoped Felix would be home early, before it begins to freeze again.'

Even as she speaks they hear a door slam and suddenly here is Felix, ruddy-cheeked, rubbing his hands together, smiling at his family all happily together in this warm, comfortable room.

'There's a strange person in the garth,' he says solemnly. 'A very cold person. I introduced myself and tried to shake hands with him but he refused.'

Piers flings himself at his father's legs, roaring with laughter. 'That's my snowman,' he cries, his face bunched up with mirth. 'He hasn't *got* any hands.'

Felix bends to touch his lips to Marina's brow, smiles at his father-in-law and sits down by the fire with Piers in his lap.

'He has a very smart hat,' he says to Piers. 'What's his name?'

Marina watches them with her familiar half-frowning, half-smiling expression, as if she cannot understand how Felix can be so undignified, so natural with the child. He lies back in the chair with Piers kneeling astride him, almost shouting into his face with excitement, as relaxed and interested as if he too were six years old. What can it matter whether a snowman has a name? She gives a little disdainful shake of the head and, out of the corner of her eye, catches her father's look. He watches Felix almost narrowly, as if trying to detect something, and she feels an odd pang of fear.

'I was just saying to Marina,' he says to Felix, 'that she should have another trip to Bristol with you when you go on Sunday.'

Accidentally, or otherwise, Piers moves suddenly, so it is impossible to see Felix's expression and when he speaks his voice is muffled by the child's embracing arms.

'Why not?' he says, emerging from the tussle. 'Good idea.' He looks at Marina questioningly. 'Would you like to?'

David Frayn notices that he makes no attempt to discourage her – he even sounds quite keen – and wonders if he is misjudging Felix. Lately his son-in-law seems calmer, more able to deal with the silences, the unspoken criticism, those accusations that occasionally he cannot help but overhear. There is something detached about Felix, some external power is giving him the ability to be patient, cheerful: more, there is an ill-concealed happiness, a smile that lingers on his lips when he is caught unawares. If he were asked to define it he'd say that here is a man who's fallen wildly in love with someone who loves him just as much in return. Unfortunately there is no such change in Marina – which is why he feels anxious.

'I was explaining that I find it rather bleak,' Marina is saying. 'The flat has that unused feel, doesn't it? It's not so bad in the summer when you can be outside for most of the time but it's not much fun in this kind of weather.'

David watches Felix thoughtfully. He makes the facial shrug that Piers sometimes copies: the mouth turns downward at the corners whilst the eyebrows lift and the eyes roll a little. It's not a dismissive expression but more one of consideration.

'Oh, I don't know,' he says, after a moment. 'It's not a bad place. Of course, you can't have an open fire, and it's not what you might call cosy, but it's quite a nice little flat. And it must be rather a pleasant change to see some decent shops. We could go to the cinema . . .'

'It's all right for you,' says Marina rather defensively, feeling that both men are now ganging up on her. 'You're working most of the time. I can't spend all day shopping.'

'Absolutely not,' agrees Felix at once. 'I see that. Perhaps when it's warmer . . . ?'

David cannot decide whether Felix is being very clever or if his fears are simply unfounded; and, after all, if Felix is able to manage his marriage more happily, does it matter why? He has no right to interfere, he tells himself, but still he watches him; seeing that fleeting smile, the far-away look in his eyes, as if his son-in-law is hearing other voices and looking upon other scenes. Surely the ever-vigilant Marina would have guessed if there were something? David Frayn shivers involuntarily and moves back into the room, nearer to the fire.

It is extraordinary, Felix is thinking, how quickly he has become a part of the little family in the narrow house near the university. His monthly visits are settling into a natural routine and he is welcomed as readily by Pidge and Lizzie as he is by Angel. They are a tight-knit little group; the bond between Pidge and Angel is strong and he is confirmed in his belief that they have no secrets from each other.

'You're quite right,' Angel agrees when he suggests this to her, 'we don't. We've shared a lover, you see, and as soon as we discovered that, well, it changed everything for us. It broke down any barriers and brought us very close.'

'I can believe that,' he says sincerely; by this time he's been often enough to the Birdcage to realize that there is nothing ordinary about either Pidge or Angel. There is an atmosphere of warmth and ease that has a healing quality; he is able to laugh and tease the two women without the fear of those misunderstandings which, with Marina, result in long, arctic silences.

'We were both mad about him,' Angel tells him. She is curled on the sofa, curtains drawn against a cold, wet Sunday evening in March; Pidge has disappeared downstairs and Lizzie is tucked up in bed. Angel wears one of her favourite long wrappers, belted tightly, bare legs tucked beneath her, a cigarette in her fingers. She looks unusually serious, the lighted lamp lending a glowing lustre to her pale hair and skin as she reflects upon the past, and Felix feels a sudden, piercing sense of exclusion.

'He must have been pretty special,' he says lightly.

'Oh, yes.' She glances at him, tapping the cigarette ash into a small enamelled bowl. 'He was. His wife had had a riding accident not long after they married and was not only crippled but suffered some kind of brain damage. It was terrible. Mike loved her so much and there was absolutely nothing he could do but keep her comfortable and well cared for. Pidge met him towards the end of the war – she was his driver – and then someone found out about them and Pidge was transferred. He owns quite a bit of property and when the war was over he got in touch with her to say that the flat downstairs had been vacated and she could have it for a very reasonable rent. Pidge got a job at the library and moved in. No,' she shakes her head at his expression, 'there was no ulterior motive. He just wanted to help her.'

'And where did you come in?'

'I met him at a party. He's quite a bit older than I am and I was rather bowled over by his sophistication, to tell you the truth. He never pretended that there could be a future but, like Pidge, I didn't much care. He's that sort of man.' She glances at him, drawing on her cigarette. 'Are you sure you want to know all this?'

'Quite sure.' His sense of isolation has vanished and he is curiously bound up in this little history, feeling a sympathy for the man who has lost so much but accepts love when it is offered.

'Well, unlike Pidge, I was the foolish virgin who got caught out. Lizzie is his child.'

'Poor Angel.' He gets up and goes to sit beside her, and she moves so as to make room for him. 'How did you manage with a child and your career?'

'Rather badly to begin with.' She chuckles, leaning against him. 'My mother, after the initial shock, was surprisingly good. I had to tell her who the baby's father was and that helped. Mike's a war hero and he's a very popular public figure. My mother instantly decided that it wasn't really his fault and, since he was ready to help to support Lizzie financially, she was actually a tremendous comfort. We agreed that Lizzie shouldn't know the truth – he has a son of his own, you see – and afterwards he simply continued to contact us through his lawyers.'

'So how did you end up here with Pidge?'

'Oh, that was just so typical of him.' Angel stubs out her cigarette and settles comfortably in his arms. 'When he found out that I was coming to Bristol he sent a little note to Pidge suggesting that she should come to see me at the theatre. On the opening night he sent flowers, something he never did, saying that he hoped I'd found comfortable digs. It was just so odd. And then darling Pidge was shown into the dressing-room, looking all nervous and twitchy and saying that she'd heard I was looking for somewhere to live which could take a small child. I smelled a rat at once.'

'But you weren't upset that he brought you both together?'

Angel frowns. 'Pidge asked that. She was so anxious about it, she felt so guilty. But after all, she'd had him first, and, let's face it, he didn't belong to me.' She makes a little face. 'Actually, I thought it was rather fun. It connected us together, made a little family of us, and he's been so good to both of us in an odd kind of way. That's what's so special about him, I suppose. We've never felt resentful or hard done by. Perhaps it's because he's so much older?' She shrugged. 'Anyway, that's how it happened.'

'And Lizzie?'

'Oh, Lizzie's happy here. We've stuck as close to the truth as we can and told her that her father was a soldier who was killed in the Korean war, which, let's face it, is hardly an unusual situation these days. Of course, it's wonderful having Pidge around. She looks after Lizzie when I go down to the theatre and takes her to school on the way to the library each morning. Between us we manage to look after her very well. Yes, Lizzie's fine.'

'She wasn't too impressed with Pidge's diamonds,' he says ruefully.

Angel chuckles. 'It was very clever of you, sweetie,' she says, 'but poor Lizzie couldn't grasp it all.'

Discovering that Pidge has a passion for playing patience he bought a charming double pack of tiny cards for her.

'Twenty-six diamonds,' he said, holding out the little box, grinning at her expression. 'Unfortunately there're also twenty-six clubs, twenty-six hearts and twenty-six spades.'

'It's a joke,' Pidge had to explain to the disappointed Lizzie who was, nevertheless, very pleased with her own present: one Punch bar, one Five Boys and a Fry's sandwich bar with plain and milk chocolate. 'Rather a good joke, actually.'

'Lizzie's not impressed,' said Felix, 'and I don't blame her' – but she smiled at him and said, 'Thank you for my chocolate,' and carried it away, stumping up the steep narrow staircase to her attic room.

'I think,' said Pidge, suddenly overcome with a fit of tactfulness, 'I'll go and have my bath and then we'll cook supper.'

Now, together on the sofa, aware of Lizzie in her little attic room, Felix slips an arm about Angel and she holds him tightly.

'Oh, Felix,' she says, 'I've missed you. I'm terribly in need of some soothing.'

'When you say "soothing",' he murmurs cautiously, 'is this an occupation which might frighten Lizzie if she came upon it suddenly or am I letting my imagination run away with me?'

She begins to laugh, still holding him. 'The answers to those questions are "Yes" and "No", in that order, sweetie,' she says. 'I suppose you couldn't possibly slip away tomorrow afternoon just after lunch, could you? Lizzie is home from school by half-past three.'

'Oh, I think I could,' he says, his lips against her throat.

So it begins.

CHAPTER SEVEN

All through that summer Marina too is aware of a change in Felix. Her naturally suspicious temperament suggests the obvious reason for it but she is unable to find any proof. He is rarely late home, he makes no excuses so as to stay away, there is no evidence that she can find – and she looks, hating herself but unable to resist; searching in his pockets, smelling his clothes and examining them for traces of lipstick – and even when they go out together she cannot really fault his behaviour except in the usual way: that he is too friendly with other women. It is as if he has, in some indefinable way, moved beyond her reach and yet he still makes every effort to show that he cares for her. He is not indifferent to her moods but now it's as if he feels compassion for her, as if – she flinches away from the idea – as if he pities her.

It is no longer in her power to flick him on the raw with stinging comments regarding his flirtatious friendliness; he no longer jumps to defend himself or turns angrily away. It is impossible to wound or shame him into acts of penitence; he seems unmoved by the icy silences. Once he would have cajoled her back to warmth with little offerings: a cup of tea, the removal of Piers so as to give her some peace, a little posy of flowers beside her plate. She's never considered the ready hugs or kisses to be a sign of love: these are merely evidence of his weak, licentious nature. Yet, because *he* no longer reacts to her jealousy, *she* is no longer able to reach those heights of remorse that once drove her into his arms in acts of almost violent reparation. Now, love-making must either be the result of those very hugs and kisses that she despises as weakness – or she must initiate the act herself without the necessary overture of guilt that has hitherto smothered the embarrassment and humiliation of showing that she wants him.

She stands at her bedroom window staring into soft dense cloud through which thick fingers of gold stab and probe the land below. The sea-borne mist parts for a moment to reveal a patch of sky, the colour of blue cotton, and the curve of a rainbow which trembles and flashes above Bossington Hill. On the drive, which winds up from the lane, two figures are climbing towards the house hand in hand: her father uses his walking stick to help him onwards and even Piers looks weary, not hopping and skipping as he usually does. Only Monty races ahead, fresh and excited as when they all set out, darting away from the path, dashing back, his tail wagging madly with anticipation. They pause: her father's arm shoots out to indicate something in the furze. It might be a stone-chat or a rabbit – Marina shrugs, amused – whatever it is Piers will be full of it later, passionate about this corner of Exmoor just as her brother, Peter, was in those idyllic years before the war. How Piers loves these explorations with his grandfather: walks over the heathery slopes of Dunkery or down in Horner Wood; the sighting of a tiny dappled fawn curled in a nest of rusty bracken or a dipper bobbing on a smooth grey boulder down on Horner Water. Her father has taught him to keep a nature book and he carefully labours at making a record of the year's passing, starting with the early snowdrops in the woods near Cutcombe and finishing with a sprig of bell-heather still blooming on Porlock Common in December.

The figures resume their climb, looking forward no doubt to some tea, and Marina turns away from the window, picks up a cardigan and goes downstairs. It is too damp to have tea in the garth and, even though it is July, the sitting-room feels cold and chill. Marina is persuaded to have tea in the kitchen, which is always warm because of the solid-fuel range, and as she pours Piers' milk she listens to their duet describing the walk. Monty stretches himself comfortably on his old rug beneath the window, which looks south into the garth, one eye fixed hopefully on the floor beneath Piers' chair. Sometimes there are accidents – once, half of a scone dropped face downwards on the flags – and he holds himself ready for a quick dash.

Presently, when Piers has asked to get down and has gone away to bring his nature book up to date – although the sea mist has prevented any unusual sightings – Marina pours more tea for her father, her face thoughtful.

'I was wondering,' she begins, 'whether I might go to Bristol with Felix next weekend. He's on holiday next month so it will be my only chance for a while. I feel rather restless. Do you think you could manage if I get Mrs Penn to help?'

'Of course we can manage. Haven't I been suggesting it for the last few months? I think it's a very good idea.'

He wonders if he sounds rather too enthusiastic and takes a sip of his tea. David Frayn is on the horns of a dilemma: he is unhappy at the idea of Felix being unfaithful to Marina yet there is an even tenor these days in their relationship – not quite contented tranquillity, nor yet detached indifference – that creates a better atmosphere than Marina's icy silences and ill-concealed criticism countered by repressed irritation and long-suffering on Felix's side. Part of David is unwilling to upset the status quo; part fears what might happen if Marina discovers an affair. He is convinced that, if his son-in-law *is* having an affair, then it is happening in Bristol and he believes that Marina's regular presence on those monthly visits would quite naturally put an end to it. At least the idea is hers, this time; he has not persuaded her into it. Why then does he feel so full of fear?

Felix is shocked at how much he minds losing his few precious hours at the Birdcage with Angel and the others. To his surprise Marina has never questioned his departure after tea on Sunday afternoons, never asked why he can't leave later in the evening or even – in the summer months – very early on Monday morning. She accepts his casual murmurings of arriving in time for a chat over a drink with Tom in order to catch up with things and to discuss the partners' meeting on the following Monday morning. Marina thinks – he allows her to think – that these chats take place at Tom and Molly's house in Caledonia Place, not far from the offices in Portland Street, and her antennae, usually so keen, have completely let her down in this respect. The chats *do* take place – but are kept fairly short and are generally conducted at the end of a telephone.

'The only thing is,' he tells her, hoping that it might put her off, 'it's Molly's birthday this Sunday and they're having a cocktail party in the evening. I don't see how we'll be able to get out of it.'

He's been planning to drop in for a short while, drink Molly's health and then quietly disappear; now he hopes that Marina will be dissuaded from her trip. She is ill at ease socially and has never been able to achieve the easy comradeship with her own sex that might have brought comfort and relief, but Molly's natural sweetness of character and down-to-earth warmth have made her one of the few women with whom Marina has any kind of rapport.

'Well, I expect we'll manage,' she says now, to his surprise and frustration. 'It might be quite fun although their friends are all very Bohemian, aren't they? They've always read the newest books and seen the latest films, and I always feel like a country mouse, but I suppose we needn't stay too long.'

'No,' says Felix, swallowing down disappointment. 'No, of course not, and we can find somewhere for dinner afterwards. I know Molly will be delighted to see you.'

Only David, coming out of his study, sees his expression as he pauses for a moment in the hall, realizing that he won't see Angel now until the end of September. He stands with his hands in his pockets, head lowered, biting his lip, before he crosses the hall and runs lightly up the stairs. David moves out of the shadows and stares after him, his sense of anxiety increasing.

CHAPTER EIGHT

'We won't see him this weekend,' says Angel, her voice tragic. 'Marina's coming up with him and he won't be able to get away.'

Pidge hides her own disappointment in the face of Angel's and attempts to console her. 'It's bound to happen occasionally,' she says. 'And, after all, she is his wife.'

'Oh, I know all that,' Angel says miserably. 'But a few hours a month, Pidge! That's all we get. It's not much to live on, is it?'

She smooths out the letter and Pidge sees her expression change: Angel's eyes narrow thoughtfully and she purses her lips consideringly.

'He tells me that they'll be going to the Curzons' cocktail party tomorrow,' she says – and smiles brightly at Pidge across the table. 'The usual Friends of the Theatre mob, of course, and I know that quite a few of the cast are going. I've been invited, actually.'

'But you get fed up to the back teeth with the dear old Friends,' says Pidge lightly, her heart sinking. 'Not your kind of thing at all.'

'Oh, Molly's OK,' answers Angel casually. 'She's rather a sweetie. I might just pop along for an hour.'

'Please,' says Pidge, abandoning caution, 'please don't, Angel. Imagine how difficult it will be for Felix if you show up.'

'Oh, I shall behave myself.' It is clear that Angel is enchanted by her plan: her eyes sparkle at the prospect. She can feel the *frisson* of meeting Felix in public with such a delicious secret between them. It is irresistible. 'Don't fuss, Pidge. I'm not quite an idiot, you know.'

'It's not just you,' says Pidge almost crossly. 'Felix is our friend too; mine and Lizzie's. He's terribly important to Lizzie and she adores him. She's old enough to know what she's missing when she see her little friends with their fathers. Being a father himself, Felix understands her; he fills a huge need. You simply mustn't risk it, Angel.'

Angel looks sombre. 'I simply must see him,' she says, 'even if we don't speak. He won't be coming up next month because he's on holiday. I won't see him until the end of September. I promise I'll behave but I must just see him.'

Pidge sighs heavily; she shakes her head. 'It's all wrong,' she says.

'Of course it's all wrong, sweetie,' agrees Angel, but she smiles winningly at Pidge. 'You and me and Mike were all wrong; Felix coming here is all wrong. But I love him. So do you. So does Lizzie. We need him.'

'Then don't risk it,' begs Pidge. 'From the few things that Felix has let drop we know his wife is a jealous type. Can't you see how dangerous it is?'

'Your name should have been Hen, not Pidgeon,' grins Angel. 'His wife won't suspect a thing. After all, you're forgetting that I *am* an actress.'

'"Love and a cough cannot be hid",' quotes Pidge warningly.

* * *

The moment that she sees Felix in Molly's high-walled garden, talking to Tom, she knows that Pidge is right. She feels the hot colour wash into her cheeks, her body feels languid with longing, her eyes grow large. From the shelter of the dining-room she stares avidly at the woman at his side; taking in every detail. Her dark hair is pulled back into a French pleat, which in Angel's view doesn't flatter her: she is too thin, her features are too sharp. Her frock is unremarkable, the ubiquitous little black dress, and the low heels of her plain court shoes sink into Molly's smooth turf. At regular instances she casts quick glances round at the guests, almost as if she is looking for someone; there is an intensity in that swift, searching, radar-like probe and Angel feels a spasm of terror grip her heart.

Suddenly she realizes how very dear Felix is to the three of them, how terrible it would be to lose him, and she knows that she is in danger. Her gaze is drawn back to him, at ease and attractive in his dark suit, listening to Tom, and she acknowledges that in coming to this party she is being both selfish and foolish. The excitement of it, the danger, is no longer appealing and she doesn't want to see his expression of shock or, even worse, disappointment. For a moment she is angry that she cannot stand at his side as Marina does: his wife, acknowledged, in her rightful place. As it is she must skulk here in the shadows and the secret is no longer exciting, it is grubby and shaming.

'I can't leave Marina,' Felix says, as Mike has said of his wife before him. 'I have a son, you know, and I could never abandon Piers. I have very little to offer you so, in the light of what I've just said, you'll find it difficult to believe it when I say that I love you.'

But she does believe it – and watching him now she knows she loves him too. Even as she turns back into the dining-room, so as to make her escape, a fellow actor with some friends swoop in through the opposite door and, despite her very real protests, carry her with them down the steps and into the garden. It needs all her skill to present a calm exterior, a polite, almost indifferent smile when Tom introduces her to Felix and Marina.

'But haven't you met before?' Tom asks in his breezy, cheerful way. 'We took you both backstage to meet Miss Blake if I remember rightly.'

'Of course we did. I remember now,' she says smoothly as she shakes Marina's hand.

She is aware of Felix's brief shocked stare, almost instantly replaced by a guarded friendliness, and she turns away from them as soon as it is possible to do so naturally, taking Tom by the arm on the pretext of discussing when she should give Molly her present. She pays them no further attention, flirting instead with another of Tom's friends, although there is an unworthy satisfaction in the prospect that Felix will see her flirting and feel as miserable as she does; a hope that is swiftly followed by a sense of shame, as if she has degraded herself in his presence.

'You were right,' she says to Pidge later, high-heeled shoes kicked off, hair dishevelled round her shoulders.

'Of course I was,' answers Pidge calmly.

'But it's not *fair*,' Angel bursts out.

'Who said anything about "fair"?' asks Pidge. 'Shut up and have a drink.'

CHAPTER NINE

David Frayn sees their return with relief. Nothing, it seems, has altered between them and Marina is looking forward to having Felix under her eye for most of August. David feels guilty, rather as if he has accused Felix unfairly, yet deep in his bones he continues to feel that something is wrong. As the summer progresses he notices that whatever source has been supplying Felix with the strength to cope with Marina's whims and fancies is failing him. He becomes less able to deal with her accusations and sometimes David overhears a desperate note in his voice.

'I promise you, darling, that it was nothing more than dinner-party fun. I wasn't flirting with her. Oh, I know it might have looked like it but we were simply laughing about something – no, I've no idea what it was. It was completely unimportant. Please, Marina, it is *not* a sin for a married man to laugh with another woman . . .'

Marina has begun to suspect that Felix is entailed with the rather disreputable wife of one of his colleagues and gradually the icy silences, the tension, reappear. As autumn draws on and half-term approaches, Piers begins to suffer from his mother's uncertain temper.

'We saw a cormorant on the beach,' he tells her, noting the event laboriously in his nature book. He sits at his grand-father's desk, a cushion on the chair to lift him high enough, his legs twisting together in his efforts. 'He'd eaten so much fish he could hardly fly and we were able to get a really good look at him.'

'It would be much more useful,' answers his mother sharply, 'if instead of wandering about watching birds all day you were practising your tables. You know how weak you are at your sums.'

He stares at her, stricken, his happy mood shattered, his pleasure in the cormorant with his grey eye and snake-like neck completely spoiled.

'I *do* practise them sometimes,' he protests. 'When I'm out with Grandfather I say them as we go along. Daddy says he was bad at sums too, when he was my age.'

'Then he should encourage you to practise more,' says Marina angrily. She resents the way Piers shows such affection to his father when he, Felix, is so indifferent to her own happiness: it is hurtful and shows insensitivity on Piers' part. 'The trouble is that Daddy doesn't care. If he really cared about you he'd make you work instead of reading you silly stories. You'll find as you grow older, Piers, that the people who are easy-going are not the ones who have your true welfare at heart.'

She goes away, taking the Hoover and her dusters, and Piers is left sitting at the desk, his heart cold with terror. *The trouble is that Daddy doesn't care. If he really cared about you . . .*

His innocence is tarnished; his confidence shaken. Nothing will ever be quite the same again.

After a great deal of anxious thought he decides to take his own soundings: Grandfather first. He waits until his parents have gone off to a dinner party and then climbs out of bed, pulls on his plaid dressing-gown and slips downstairs. In the hall he hesitates: here, as usual, he is aware of a presence, an invisible comfort that soothes his troubled heart. Sometimes he lies on the flagged floor, watching the light that streams through the tall, high windows, or he might climb into one of the pair of heavily carved chairs that stand against the staircases, one at each end of the hall. Occasionally he takes a toy into the hall, running a small car or a fire engine over the slates, muttering to himself, but before too long the stillness here in the heart of the house takes hold of him so that he finds that he is lying quite still, listening to the silence.

This evening he waits only for a moment – the prospect of this first test interferes with his ability to hear that all-embracing sound of silence – and presently he crosses the hall and moves quietly down the passage towards the study. Outside the door he stops, his ear pressed against the panel. Several voices are speaking in loud, urgent tones and suddenly there is a burst of music; Grandfather is listening to the wireless. Piers recognizes that music, which sounds like a great train pulling out of the station, gathering speed, thundering rhythmically along the track with sparks flying and smoke pouring from its chimney: it's the theme tune from the weekly serial *Paul Temple*.

Piers turns the handle and goes into the warm, firelit study. Monty's tail beats a welcome from the rug and David Frayn, seated at his desk, screws round in his chair to peer at the small figure standing just inside the door.

'Hello there,' he says. 'What's up? Where's the fire? Had a bad dream?'

He gets up, switching off the wireless, and Piers closes the door behind him and goes to sit on the fender beside his grandfather's armchair.

'I haven't been to sleep yet,' he admits. He stretches out his slippered foot so that Monty can lick his bare ankle: he finds the warm, wet caress oddly comforting. 'I've been thinking, Grandfather.' He's thought very carefully about what he should say, basing it on what his mother has said to him, and now he tries it out. 'If I don't get better at my tables I might not pass my entrance exam in the spring and I've been wondering if I should give up the nature book, Grandfather? It takes up quite a lot of time, these days, when I could be practising my tables.'

David Frayn looks down upon the boy's dark head, watching him stroking Monty with the fringed edge of his dressing-gown's corded belt. He doesn't question the fact that the boy has to go away to preparatory school but he guesses that Marina has been putting pressure on him to work harder and he knows that his daughter, like her mother before her, always uses a hammer to crack a walnut. He feels his way towards a compromise between discipline and kindness.

'I think you've come on very well,' he says, so as to make an encouraging start. 'You rattle them off like a good 'un when we're out on our sorties.'

'It's not just saying them that I mind,' says Piers earnestly, turning to look up at him. 'It's dotting about. Like nine sixes or seven eights. I get muddled then, you see. Mummy nearly always catches me out.'

Hunched on the fender, dressing-gown trailing over his drawn-up knees, he wears an anxious expression that makes him look almost careworn and David thinks of Piers' uncle Peter, killed at Arnhem before he was able to have a child of his own. How often he looks back, regretting hasty words, wrong decisions: now, with Piers, he attempts to put his experience to good use.

'Tell you what,' he says thoughtfully. 'How would it be if I took over the nature book for a bit? You could advise, of course, on what we decide to put in; read it over, keep me up to scratch and so on. But it would save you some time, wouldn't it, without breaking the flow?'

Piers' face is alight with joy and his grandfather smiles back at him, touched that the nature book is so important to his grandson, unaware that he has passed a crucial test. The book *is* important but not so important as discovering that his grandfather, by putting work before pleasure, has shown that he really cares about him. The sensation of relief cannot be suppressed, it must be allowed a physical expression, and Piers crawls along his grandfather's outstretched legs and cuddles into his arms just as he does with his own father.

Holding the child, watching the firelight leap on the dark-panelled walls, David reflects sadly on how rarely he held Peter in his arms once he'd grown out of babyhood. It simply wasn't done – even if Eleanor had allowed it – and he'd been afraid of showing his emotional side to the boy. This might have been more acceptable with his daughter but Marina had never encouraged physical displays of affection. Peter had been a true male Frayn, cheerful, good-humoured, warm – and he'd been loved by everyone who knew him – but it had taken Felix, who had come amongst them and broken the taboos of the past, to show that the comfort of a cuddle, the warmth of a hug, releases tension and dissipates anger or fear.

'How about a bite of supper?' suggests David, feeling that the boy deserves a little reward.

'What is it?' asks Piers, sitting upright, distracted by the thought of food. 'Has Mummy left you something nice?'

'Baked potato.' David edges himself off the chair. 'Bit of chicken. Might be some of that trifle left.'

Piers is filled with pleasurable anticipation as the three of them leave the study and cross the hall to the kitchen.

'I like lots of butter on the potato,' he mentions hopefully. 'But I don't like the outside skin.' He chuckles aloud, thinking of another of Grandfather's odd sayings: 'Only potatoes wear jackets; gentlemen wear coats', and his grandfather winks at him.

'That's Monty's treat,' he says. 'Plenty for all. Foraging party to the fore. Quick march.'

CHAPTER TEN

Watching Felix across the polished surface of the dining-table, Marina is aware that she is changed: different from the girl who fell in love nearly ten years before. She does not analyse this difference, she merely acknowledges it; almost relieved that the uncontrollable flutterings and wild desperations are rarely felt nowadays. In truth those tenderer, gentler powers have hardened into a sense of possession, a need to control, and the passion between them, once given an edge by her need to assuage her guilt, has become dulled. Without this edge physical love is an unnecessary embarrassment, building to a loss of that necessary control so that, afterwards, she feels humiliated.

She looks with faint resentment at Felix who is talking to Helen Cartwright, smiling at some story she is telling him. Marina notices the intimate way Helen sits half turned, so that she leans a little against him, whilst Felix, head bent on one side, turns and turns his glass, his other hand jammed into the pocket of his black jacket. He looks relaxed, comfortable with himself, and yet not totally absorbed. Marina dislikes Helen Cartwright, still fearing that she has the power to make Felix behave foolishly, wishing that she could annihilate whatever it is within him that attracts women. Her physical need for him might be growing less but she still has all the rights of ownership. Anyway, there is something degrading in this silly flirtation between people of their ages.

Marina glances at the other women around the table. Her sixth sense insists that Felix is playing a double game yet she still can't quite decide with whom he might be involved. Her suspicion alights first on one acquaintance and, when no proof is forthcoming, on another; yet, despite his apparent innocence, some instinct warns her that he is betraying her. She looks at him again and, at that same moment, he raises his eyes and stares at her. His eyes narrow into a smile, tentative, almost questioning, and she realizes with a tiny shock that she almost dislikes him; that she wants to punish him for being attractive, generous, warm-hearted. She turns her head away without responding, addressing some random remark to her neighbour, James Cartwright, who hastens to make himself agreeable.

Felix, wondering if sharp-eyed Helen has seen the exchange, straightens in his seat and counts the days that must pass before he can be in the Birdcage again. Those few days each month are so precious that he wonders how he ever managed without them. It is another world, there in the narrow house in Bristol; a world in which he can be himself. He arrives as early as he can on Sunday evening, feeling the tension drop away from him as he enters that big room where the three of them are waiting for him: Angel stretched out along the sofa; Pidge pottering in the kitchen area behind the piano; Lizzie kneeling at the table, colouring a picture.

'Hello, my birds,' he says. 'How's life in the cage?' and it is as if this is how they always are and always will be: waiting for him. In summer the warm breeze trembles through the branches of the plane tree beyond the window; in winter the curtains are drawn and the lamps lit. On the following

Monday he very occasionally manages to get away so as to take Angel out to lunch but, even if he can't, those few hours in the afternoon are kept sacrosanct. 'Soothing time,' Angel calls it – and he needs soothing just as much as she does. Oh, the comfort of Angel! – releasing the pent-up tensions and humiliations, restoring him to confidence. He hurries away before Lizzie comes in from school, back to the office, but much later he returns to the Birdcage so as to spend the evening with Pidge and Lizzie before going down to King Street to meet Angel from the theatre so that they can have supper together.

As he looks at Marina across the table, he is continually amazed that she hasn't suspected that there is someone in Bristol; especially after Angel's appearance at Molly's cocktail party.

'I'm sorry, sweetie,' she said at once, when she saw him again. 'It was just such a long time not to see you that I simply couldn't bear it. I know it was crazy. Pidge is furious with me.'

It *had* been a shock to see her there, with Marina standing so watchfully beside him, but even in his horror he'd been aware of undercurrents of shame. Angel had every right to be at the party and he'd felt hypocritical as he'd stood with his wife whilst his mistress pretended that they hardly knew each other.

'I hoped that Marina wouldn't want to come to the party,' he began to explain but Angel simply shook her head.

'Forget it, sweetie. All over now.'

Watching Marina across the table Felix realizes that Angel never demands excuses, she simply requires his love. He takes a deep breath of gratitude and smiles at Helen Cartwright.

'A penny for your thoughts?' she asks archly – but he shakes his head.

'They're far too expensive,' he answers lightly, 'even for you.'

*   *   *

'She never gives up, does she?' asks Marina on the way home in the car.

A light mizzle of rain mists the windscreen and the narrow road, winding ahead between coppery beech hedges, gleams black and shiny in the headlights' beam. Felix tenses himself.

'She?' He answers her question with a question, although he knows the answer.

'Helen Cartwright.' Marina's voice is contemptuous. 'Still flirting and wriggling about as if she were sixteen instead of nearly forty. It's so undignified.'

Felix knows that if he is to have a comfortable journey back to Michaelgarth and a peaceful night then he must agree with her: he must condemn Helen. But Felix dislikes belittling his friends; he refuses to heap contumely upon people simply because they are fun-loving, friendly or kind. He doesn't care to compromise his own standards for the doubtful benefits of a quiet life.

'Old Helen's all right,' he says lightly. 'No harm in her really, you know. I didn't get chance of a word with James. How is he?'

'I hardly spoke to him,' she answers coolly. 'He was too busy talking to Mary Yates. His manners are nearly as bad as Helen's.'

Suppressing a sigh Felix drives on towards Michaelgarth, wishing that he were able to get to Bristol more often, and, as if she guesses his thoughts, Marina speaks the words he has grown to dread.

'I'm thinking of coming to Bristol with you next weekend. I want to get some Christmas presents. It's rather early but the weather at the end of November is usually so miserable.'

He changes gear noisily, apologizes and brakes suddenly as a dark shape streaks across the lane. He instinctively thrusts out his arm to prevent Marina from being thrown forward and feels the soft warm fur of her coat.

'Sorry,' he says again. 'Fox, I think. Too quick for a badger,' but the little shock has cleared his brain. 'Yes, Bristol. Well, why not? Piers could come too. It's his half-term that week, isn't it? I can't get out of it, I'm afraid, but at least I shall be back for Bonfire Night.'

This is a very special occasion. The village school traditionally celebrates Guy Fawkes on the hill behind Michaelgarth and Piers feels a special responsibility as host.

'Damn,' says Marina irritably. 'I'd forgotten that. It's rather too much to ask Father to look after him for two days and he'll be rather under my feet in that tiny flat. There isn't even a second bedroom. Well, that's that, then.'

She sounds ill-used and Felix refrains from making encouraging suggestions, although he feels very guilty. There is a long silence, which lasts until they drive through the arch into the garth. Felix puts the car away and follows Marina across the wet, slippery cobbles and into the house. The kitchen is unusually tidy and Marina looks about her with narrowed, calculating eyes: Monty's tail beats a cautious welcome as he watches them from his bed beneath the window.

'Well,' says Felix, rather puzzled both by the spotlessness of the kitchen and his wife's expression. 'Old David's done his bit by the look of it.'

'He never washes up after himself,' replies Marina tartly, 'unless Piers has been down and there are extra plates and so on which have been used. He washes it all up, so as to cover himself, and he imagines that I don't notice.'

'Does it matter?' asks Felix wearily. 'Perhaps the poor little chap had a nightmare. I think it's rather nice of David to share his supper with him. Fun for both of them.'

She turns to look at him. 'You have no idea about discipline, do you, Felix?' she asks icily. 'Either self-discipline or any other kind?'

He stares at her. 'No,' he says at last. 'No, I'm a profligate bastard with a set of unprincipled friends. Look, I'm not particularly tired so I'll spend the night in my dressing-room. I wouldn't want to keep you awake by having the light on. Goodnight, Marina.'

Upstairs, in the room next to Piers' bedroom, he stands for a moment staring at nothing, his fists bunched in the pockets of his dinner jacket. He hears Marina pass his door, on her way to the big bedroom on the north-west corner, and waits without moving until he hears the lavatory flush and the bathroom door close, followed by the click of her bedroom door. With a sigh of frustration he begins to drag off his jacket and he's already untying his tie and kicking off his shoes when he hears the movement next door. As he lets himself out silently onto the landing he sees a light flash up under Piers' door.

Felix turns the handle and goes in, switching on the lamp.

'Hello, old chap,' he says. 'Can't sleep?'

'Oh, Daddy,' cries Piers with relief, 'I wondered if it was a burglar.'

He switches off his torch – he's not allowed a bedside lamp in case it encourages him to read when he should be asleep – and beams at his father.

'We're just home,' Felix tells him, 'and I couldn't sleep either. So I'm staying in my dressing-room so as not to disturb Mummy. I might read for a bit and she can't get off if the light's on.'

'I wish I could read when I can't sleep,' says Piers enviously. 'I just have to tell myself stories instead.'

'Well, what about a story now?' asks Felix, picking up the newest book, an abridged version of *Treasure Island* with exciting colour plates. 'It might make us both sleepy.'

If he really cared about you he'd make you work instead of reading you silly stories.

Even as his father picks up the book, Piers sees his way to his next sounding; coming so soon after his success with his grandfather he feels hopeful that he might be lucky a second time.

'I've been thinking, Daddy,' he says, hauling himself higher on the pillow, his heart beginning to thump in anticipation. 'I was thinking that perhaps we ought to practise my tables each evening instead of reading stories.'

His look is so anxious, so intense, that Felix is startled. He sits on the edge of the bed, putting an arm about his son, but Piers wriggles free. He is frightened now, terrified that his father will prove his mother right. *If he really cared about you* . . . He kneels upright so as to make his point.

'I'm very weak at maths,' he says urgently, 'and we mustn't forget that I have to take the entrance exam in the spring.'

These are his mother's words and Felix, still angry at Marina, feels a terrible compassion as he stares down at his son's white, frightened face, misreading the reason behind that fearful, oddly expectant expression.

He is too young to be threatened and bullied, thinks Felix, and he will learn quicker if he is happy and more confident.

'You're doing very well,' he says gently. 'A bedtime story won't make any difference, I'm sure. All work and no play makes Jack a dull boy.'

He opens the book but Piers stares at his father almost with a kind of dread.

'I don't think I will, if you don't mind,' he says politely. 'I think I can sleep now.'

He gets down quickly under the blankets, pulling the sheet over his head so that Felix can only bend to kiss him and go quietly out. Back in his dressing-room he wonders if *Treasure Island* with blind Pew delivering the black spot is rather frightening – if fascinating – for a small boy: perhaps he is too young for it. Suddenly tired, Felix flings off his clothes and climbs into bed.

Next door, his face buried in his pillow, Piers sobs himself to sleep.

CHAPTER ELEVEN

Early on Sunday evening, up in her attic room, Lizzie arranges the various items that she intends to show Felix when he arrives later. She sets them out on the patchwork quilt, singing to herself, imagining his pleasure when he sees these good things. There are several pictures, some crayoned in a picture book, but there is also a rather ambitious painting executed with a certain amount of dash. She is especially pleased with this because it is Felix who has given her the blue enamelled paintbox with its dear little square cakes of paint and a separate channel for the brushes. She can hardly bear to use it to begin with, it is so pretty and the brushes are so soft against her cheek – just like the end of her thick, silky plait – but soon she longs to dip the brush into water and swirl it over the reds and blues and yellows. She makes several attempts, none quite to her satisfaction, but at last she achieves a very creditable creation and Pidge has helped her to back it onto some stiff card so that it looks most professional.

As well as the painting she has a page of writing, adorned with a highly cherished gold star, which she has been allowed to bring home from school. 'Very good, Lizzie' is written in the margin and she peers with pride at this accolade. She places it carefully on the quilt so that the white ruled paper shows to advantage against a square of ruby velvet and stands back to view the effect. A sharp nod of approval and away she goes to the white chest to transport a plasticine family over to the bed: first there is Angel, yellow hair pressed down onto a pink head, then Pidge wearing a rather exotic hat – no black plasticine for Pidge's hair – and then, on a smaller scale, Lizzie herself modelled with a bright red plait. Lastly there is Felix, long-legged, with a lump of hair that looks like a doormat. Try as she might she cannot improve it and she hopes that he will understand how difficult it is for small fingers to mould the stiff clay-like material.

She carries them carefully, lest a leg or an arm might separate from its parent body, and sets them in a little group. They don't look quite so impressive against the multicoloured background and briefly she considers leaving them on the white chest; but no, she shakes her head, rejecting the idea, her display will be diminished without the central group and she rearranges them, standing back to survey her efforts.

A pair of new plaid slippers finish the display, the red and blue felt showing up splendidly on a square of pale, sprigged cotton, and she drags forward the basket chair so that Felix will be able to sit at ease while he inspects the painstaking efforts produced during the four long weeks of his absence.

She hears the doorbell and in the time it takes for one long, last critical look at her display, and the careful climb down the short, steep flight of stairs, Felix is already here. He holds out a bottle of wine to Pidge, kisses Angel and braces himself as Lizzie hurtles through the door.

'Hello, my bird,' he says, swinging her up, and she wraps her legs about his waist and hugs him tightly, snuffing up the Felix-smell of his tweed jacket: tobacco, dog, rain, coffee.

He sits down next to Angel on the sofa with Lizzie in his lap and she cuddles into the crook of his arm, content to wait, to share this moment with Pidge and Angel, before she shows him the delightful surprises upstairs. She draws his arm around her, holding his hand in both of hers, revelling in the sense of safety, rubbing her cheek against the soft material of his shirt. He slips his other arm about Angel's shoulders, drawing her close, so that the three of them are grouped together just like a proper family. Lizzie feels excitement rise inside her as she contemplates the treat in store for him – and there is something else.

She tenses, hardly able to contain herself, and Felix, aware of the sudden contraction, smiles down at her.

'And how are you, little Lizzie?' he asks.

The loving welcome, the warmth, are doing their work. He lets himself relax: sinking down into the comfort of the sofa, liking the weight of Lizzie across his thighs, breathing up Angel's familiar scent. Pidge brings him a drink, grinning at the sight of him almost submerged by Lizzie and Angel, and he winks back at her, wishing that he could do more for them. He feels that he must only spend on them the money that formerly he would have spent on himself and so he goes without small luxuries so that he can bring presents to the Birdcage.

'I've got a surprise for you,' Lizzie announces a little later.

Felix looks interested. 'For me?' he asks – and she hugs herself with secret pleasure.

'It's upstairs,' she tells him. 'Come and see.'

The two women smile at him as he puts down his glass and allows Lizzie to haul him from the chair and away to the attic.

'Close your eyes,' she instructs him as he enters the room and he obeys at once, letting her lead him to the wicker chair. He feels for its arms and lowers himself carefully.

'Now,' she cries, almost bursting with excited anticipation. 'Open your eyes, Felix.'

He does so at once, staring at the delights spread before him, and she stands at his knee, ready to begin the inspection. First are the plaid slippers which, though delightful, are not of her creation and therefore the least important in her eyes. She shows them carefully and they agree upon the cosiness of the lining and the brightness of the plaid. Then, at his request, she puts them on and dances a few steps for him and, keeping them on, she next selects the page of writing. Felix is suitably impressed.

'Did you do this yourself?' he asks. 'With no help? And what does it say here? "Very good, Lizzie." Well, that's absolutely first class . . .'

She allows herself several minutes of his heart-warming praise before turning to the plasticine family.

'Only you must be very careful with them,' she warns as he reaches to pick up one of the figures. 'It's very difficult to make them stick together, you know.'

'I'm sure it is,' he murmurs, looking at the little family intently.

'It's us,' she says, lest he hasn't realized. 'This is Angel. See, she has yellow hair but Pidge is wearing a hat. And this one's you . . .'

He turns the little figures carefully and she sees that his face is serious: perhaps he doesn't like them.

'Your hair isn't quite right,' she says anxiously, not wishing him to be hurt.

'It's very good,' he says quickly. 'It's jolly hard to make plasticine soft enough to work it properly.'

'Yes,' she agrees with relief. 'It is, isn't it? But I wanted to do the four of us together.'

'That's nice,' he says, after a moment. 'The four of us together.'

The colouring book comes next and then, last of all, the painting. As she lifts it up, Lizzie is grateful to Pidge for pasting it on to the card so that it isn't limp any more. She holds it so that he can see it properly and he smiles as he recognizes that this is her first effort with the paintbox.

'It's wonderful,' he says sincerely. 'What a dear little house.'

'It's our cottage in the country,' she tells him. She doesn't quite know what that is except that Angel sometimes says, 'Oh, sweetie, just wait till we get our cottage in the country,' and Pidge always answers, 'You'd die of boredom in a week.' Lizzie has seen pictures of cottages in her nursery rhyme books so she knows that it should have a thatched roof and roses round the door. 'And this is Angel outside the door and this is me. Pidge is inside cooking lunch so we can't see her but this is my daddy coming in at the gate.'

She leans over his arm, pointing, her plait hanging over his shoulder, and so she cannot see the expression on his face. Presently she looks up at him, to see how he is liking it, and prepares to explain her most precious offering.

'My daddy's dead, actually.' A deep breath. 'You can be my daddy, if you like.'

Young though she is, Lizzie instinctively knows that the long silence that follows her suggestion is not one of gratified delight. She looks back at the picture so Felix doesn't see the disappointment on her face. Perhaps her work isn't good enough yet for him to be able to consider the idea.

'I expect I shall get better if I practise hard,' she offers hopefully.

'Oh, darling,' he says, and his voice is so full of love – and something else she can't quite place – that she looks at him again, wondering if he is going to agree after all. 'It's nothing to do with the painting. It's beautiful and you're a very clever girl. The thing is,' he pauses, biting his lip, frowning, and then looks at her, holding her between his knees. 'The thing is, Lizzie, that I'm a daddy already. I have a little boy.'

She is so surprised that her disappointment is temporarily displaced by curiosity.

'A little boy?' she repeats wonderingly. 'How little? Is he as big as me?'

'Bigger,' answers Felix. 'He's a year older than you are. He lives a long way away, in the country near the sea, which is why I can't get to see you very often. I need to be with him just like Angel needs to be with you.'

To his relief she doesn't ask the obvious question; she is too busy imagining this little boy.

'What's his name?' she asks, trying to picture him.

'His name is Piers,' he says – and she laughs.

'That's a funny name. Peers.' She has a mental vision of a little boy peering over walls and round corners.

'It's a different form of the name Peter,' Felix explains. 'He was named after his uncle Peter who was killed in the war.'

Lizzie looks sombre, feeling a sense of kinship with this little boy who has also lost someone dear to him in the war.

'Do you love him very much?' she asks wistfully.

'I love you both very much,' he tells her firmly, 'almost as if you were brother and sister. I know it's difficult to understand, Lizzie, but you are very special to me.'

Pidge calls up the stairs to tell them that supper is ready and they go down together, hand in hand. Lizzie tells Angel that Felix has a little boy called Piers and Angel says, 'Yes, I know, sweetie, isn't that nice?' and is so calm that Lizzie accepts it too. She is beginning to adapt to the idea, to pretend that this boy with the odd name is a kind of brother and that Felix is father to them both. She absorbs the information and sees that there is no threat to her; no need for her to be anxious. Nothing has changed, after all.

CHAPTER TWELVE

'I thought he looked the least bit muted,' mentions Pidge later. 'What did Lizzie say to him?'

'She asked if he'd like to be her daddy.' Angel grimaces. 'He told her the truth but he was afraid that she might be upset about it.'

'Knowing Felix, I expect that he was the one who was upset,' says Pidge. 'I suppose it was bound to happen sooner or later.' She hesitates. 'I suppose there's no chance that he might leave her?'

Angel shakes her head. 'He's devoted to his little boy. He's always been quite open about it – that he'd never leave her, I mean – but I have to admit that I never quite give up hope. Oh, Pidge, it's such a bloody mess, isn't it? He never talks about her but you can see that he's not happy. The really infuriating thing is that I'm quite convinced that it's his visits to us that keep him going. Crazy, isn't it? Two days a month; not much of a ration, is it?'

'Not much,' agrees Pidge.

*   *   *

Driving back to Michaelgarth on Tuesday afternoon, Felix is still suffering from the shock of having his two worlds collide. It happened once before, when he saw Angel at Molly's party, and now, as then, he feels ashamed and frustrated.

Lizzie's face superimposes itself on the road beyond the windscreen, and he sees again that expression of hope and expectation, the longing for something that he cannot provide. It reminds him of Piers asking if they should practise his tables instead of having a story and, although that was quite different, Felix has a sinking feeling that he has in some way failed both of them. So far, it has been possible to hold the two worlds apart; to imagine that neither world need impose on the other. Now he sees how much damage might be done.

Caught in the wake of a Royal Blue coach, chugging on its stately way towards Torquay, Felix changes down a gear and lights a cigarette. Well-worn arguments begin to rehearse themselves inside his head: might Marina actually be happier without him? Can he actually see himself living in the Birdcage with all three women? If not, would it be fair to break up their happy little group? The whole question hinges on Piers and he knows that Marina will never let Piers go; he probably would not even be allowed to see his father if Felix were to abandon his family to live with an actress and her illegitimate child.

Felix smokes steadily, pulling out from time to time, watching for an opportunity to overtake. He feels a huge dissatisfaction with himself; a wearying disgust. He sees himself as a pathetic figure, living in his father-in-law's house, only able to preserve his marriage by monthly visits to his mistress in Bristol. In a fit of frustration he flings the cigarette butt out of the window, puts his hand on the horn and, changing gear noisily, roars past the coach.

As he drives along the familiar road it is now Piers' face he sees, wearing an expression that Felix has noticed lately: a kind of puzzled, searching look, as if he is examining his father; waiting – longing – for something to show itself. But what? He has become more remote, resigning himself to a hug rather than sharing it, holding back rather than running to greet Felix, accepting his offerings – whether it is a stick of chocolate or the suggestion of a game of draughts – with reserve or even, oddly, with disappointment, as if he suspects some hidden meaning. His gut churns as he imagines Piers discovering the truth about Angel, explained brutally to him by Marina.

For a bleak moment, Felix imagines his life without the comfort of the Birdcage; without that distant promise of warmth and laughter. He shakes his head in despair. Soon Angel's contract will be up and she will go to one of the other classical reps for a year or two. That is when the moment of truth will come, he tells himself: he need not face it yet.

It is late spring before Marina makes another trip to Bristol. This time, Felix determines to take no chances but reckons without Molly and Tom, who have extra tickets for *Much Ado About Nothing* and have invited them for cocktails before the performance. Marina is quite pleased at the prospect and Felix is comforted by the thought that at least he will see Angel, if only at a distance, but he makes his own plans. He books a table for dinner at a little restaurant in Clifton, arranging to be collected by taxi as soon as the curtain falls, so that there can be no time to go backstage afterwards or join the cast for drinks at the Llandoger Trow or the Duke.

Perhaps it is because he feels that he has taken every precaution that he allows himself to relax as the curtain rises. Angel is an enchanting Beatrice and he watches her with delight tinged with pride and mixed with a frustrated sadness that they cannot be together. When she says '. . . there was a star danced, and under that was I born . . .' he murmurs assentingly beneath his breath, smiling with such tenderness, his hands gripping so tightly together, that Marina glances at him curiously. He is too rapt, too intent on Angel's exit, to notice and Marina looks back at the stage, curiosity hardening into wariness.

During the intervals she exchanges pleasantries with Tom but spends much of the time examining her programme and especially Angel's photograph and short biography. She is quiet during dinner, asking a few questions about how often he gets to the theatre, which make him cautious. He racks his brains on how he might distract her – the invitation for her to replace her father who wishes to retire from his position as JP on the local magistrates' bench is a good subject – and they walk back through the quiet streets in a fairly amicable silence.

When they let themselves into the flat the telephone is ringing and Felix seizes the receiver whilst Marina stares fearfully, still clutching her wrap. He speaks quickly, keeps it short.

'It was Mrs Penn,' he says at last, going to her, taking her hands. 'She's been trying to get hold of us all evening. Your father is ill. We must get back at once.'

Their last afternoon together is one that Piers will never forget. They take Grandfather's old Morris and drive to Stoke Pero to see the little church set deep in its encircling hollow. Grandfather tells him how, in Edward the Confessor's time, the church was held by the beautiful Queen Editha, passing to William de Mohun after the Conquest and later owned by Sir Gilbert Piro, from whom it took the second part of its name. Piers listens carefully, feeling this new responsibility to learn as much as he can, but distracted by the glory of the hot May afternoon. As they chug along the East Water Valley below Dunkery he can hear a cuckoo calling in the woods. Here the coombe falls so steeply away from the narrow road that he is staring into the topmost branches of trees sixty feet tall. The dense green leaves form a shaking, shadowy canopy above the valley floor and, when the car stops and he scrambles out to stare dizzily down, Piers can hear the music of the East Water, tumbling and rushing along its invisible bed. In the rocky wall that rears up behind him, cushiony mosses and tiny, frondy ferns grow, brilliant emerald green, and miniature waterfalls cascade over the uneven stone-face, pouring down from Robin How high up on Dunkery. The air is full of birdsong, echoing with the sound of water, and Monty runs along the road, uttering wild, excited barks that send a jay swooping skyward with a flash of blue feathers. He splashes through the ford and up onto the old bridge with Piers close behind him whilst his grandfather waits beside the car, leaning against the bonnet, lighting his pipe.

Later, inside the church it is hot and silent. Piers gazes up at the arched wooden ceiling whilst Grandfather reads aloud how Zulu the donkey carried the timber all the way from Porlock – two loads a day – and he examines the harmonium, wishing that he had the courage to strike a chord. Presently he joins the old man in his pew as he sits resting, his eyes closed, and he too says a silent prayer, asking God to make his father really care about him. Grandfather is a solid, comfortable bulk beside him and he slips his hand into the crook of the tweedy arm.

'What's up? Where's the fire?' It seems that Grandfather has nodded off to sleep and Piers beams at him, showing that he doesn't mind, that it's quite all right to have forty winks in this peaceful place.

'Home for tea,' says Grandfather, swaying slightly as he stands up, grabbing at the pew for support. 'Come along, young feller-me-lad.'

Out they go together, hand in hand, past the yew tree and the leaning gravestones, back to the car where Monty waits impatiently, his head sticking out of the half-open window; home along the familiar lanes that wind through Luccombe and Huntscott, their cottage gardens awash with red and white blossom, and on to Michaelgarth. Piers feels the usual upthrust of joy as they pass into the garth beneath the arch, and he and Monty play on the cobbles, running and jumping, as Grandfather fumbles for the key and unlocks the scullery door. He leans heavily on his stick, staggering a little, and Piers looks up at him anxiously as he opens the door.

'Are you tired, Grandfather?' he asks. 'Shall I make you a cup of tea? We don't need to wait for Mrs Penn. I make tea for Mummy sometimes when she's tired.'

The old man shakes his head, murmurs that he'll sit down for a moment and stumbles through the kitchen into the hall. Piers, feeling rather grown-up, though concerned, begins to make the tea just as his mother has shown him, dragging a chair across to the dresser so as to reach the tea caddy, only just managing the heavy kettle on the range. He carries the cup and saucer carefully, walking slowly lest it should slop over, and is surprised to see that Grandfather has made it no further than the hall where he is slumped in one of the big carved chairs. Piers sees now that he must have been very tired for he has fallen asleep, his head on one side, his hands lying loosely on his knees. Piers stands the tea on the flagged floor and kneels down beside him, taking one of the hands in his own. There is no answering pressure, no reassuring squeeze, so he knows that his grandfather is truly asleep. Puzzled, Monty lies down too, nose on paws, and Piers settles himself more comfortably, resting his head against the old man's knee. He stares up at the high, arched windows where a butterfly with sulphur-yellow wings beats against the glass. He knows that it is a brimstone and he reminds himself that it must be recorded in the nature book along with the jay and the cuckoo. He glances up to see if Grandfather is stirring yet but his head seems to have sunk even lower on his shoulder and Piers turns back again to watch the butterfly. It has left the window now and soars higher and higher, up into the airy sunny spaces of the hall, and he watches it in delight, washed through with peace, whilst the tea grows cold and his grandfather's hand stiffens within his own small, warm one.

It is here that Mrs Penn finds them when she arrives nearly an hour later.

CHAPTER THIRTEEN

'He is too young to attend the funeral,' says Marina coldly –
and Felix is silent, unable to express his feeling that Piers
should be able to make his own farewell. So far he has been
very quiet about it all, though clearly he is missing his
grandfather.

'There won't be anyone to do the nature book,' he says,
'not now I have to do my tables.'

Felix glares warningly at Marina, who is about to observe
that the nature book is the least of her problems, and suggests,
diffidently, that he might take it on if Piers will help him.

'I expect I shan't see so many things now, without . . .' Piers
swallows, and his mouth turns down at the corners, but
quite suddenly he remembers the butterfly and it is as if
his grandfather has reached out to lay his hand upon his
shoulder.

'We could still see things,' says Felix carefully. 'You could
show me where you went, couldn't you? It might be rather
fun.'

Piers stares at him and Marina shrugs impatiently, dreading
any kind of emotional outburst.

'He'll be going away to school in the autumn,' she says bracingly, 'won't you, Piers? Lots of new things to do and see.'

Piers looks from one to the other, weighing the two suggestions, remembering something: . . . *the people who are easy-going are not the ones who have your true welfare at heart*. Then he nods.

'Come along, then,' she says. 'Time for your bath.'

He looks back at his father as he goes out with her and Felix sighs, hands in pockets, feeling a familiar sense of frustration.

On the evening after the funeral, when everyone has left, he finds Piers sitting in the carved chair in the hall.

'Has he gone now?' he asks his father.

'Yes,' Felix answers gently. 'He's gone now, the grandfather we used to have with us, but there will be a part of him that's always here.' He stops, aware of his inadequacy, afraid of a misunderstanding.

'Which part?' asks Piers rather anxiously.

'It's difficult to explain,' says Felix quickly. 'Not actually a piece of him as such. When people die there's a kind of metamorphosing.' He pauses, praying for help, and has an inspiration. 'You know how a dragonfly leaves its cocoon behind, don't you? Well, it's rather like that. There's a prayer, it's from the Bible actually, which is read at funerals. It goes like this. "Behold, I shew you a mystery. We shall not all sleep, but we shall be changed. In a moment, in the twinkling of an eye".'

He has closed his eyes in an effort to remember and opens them again, already regretting his impulse, for how can a child be expected to understand? But Piers is actually smiling; he stares up into the shadowy hall as if looking for something.

'Yes,' he says with relief. 'Yes, I like that. "We shall be changed".' He repeats the phrase thoughtfully. 'I suppose it could be into anything?'

'Yes,' agrees Felix cautiously, wondering what is in his son's mind but glad to see that he looks happy and at peace. 'Something rather nice, I think, don't you?'

'Oh, yes,' answers Piers confidently. He looks again for the butterfly but the shadows are gathering and he guesses that it is already asleep, wings folded for the night. He hopes that Monty understands that Grandfather has changed: poor Monty is grieving for his master and refuses to be comforted.

'I wish we could tell Monty,' he says. 'About being changed, I mean. Oh, if only dogs could talk.'

'I'm sure you are a great comfort to him,' says Felix. 'He looks upon you as his master now, don't you think?'

Piers is amazed at such promotion: amazed and pleased.

'But what about when I'm at school?' he asks. 'I know that Mummy will feed him and let him out but she won't . . .'

He hesitates, trying to think of a phrase which doesn't sound disloyal, and Felix knows that he means that Marina will do her duty but nothing more. She's already suggested that Monty's bed be moved into the scullery: a move that Felix has fiercely vetoed.

'I've got an idea,' he begins, 'and you must tell me what you think of it. How would it be if I took Monty with me to the office each day during term? I go out quite a lot, round farms and woodland, seeing lots of people who like dogs. He could sleep under my desk when I'm working. Would he like it, d'you think?'

'Oh, yes,' cries Piers. 'I'm sure he would. And we can take him for long walks at the weekend.'

'That's good, then,' says Felix. 'But you're his master, remember. He'll look to you for lots of love and you must learn to groom him and feed him. When you go away to school in the autumn I'll take that over during term-time but you'll still have long holidays together, remember.'

'I could brush him now,' says Piers eagerly, edging himself off the chair. 'He'd like it, wouldn't he?'

'No doubt about it,' says Felix. 'Grooming's like having a cuddle. Do you both good.'

Piers dashes away across the hall and pauses at the door to look back at this man who says and does such kind things; at this father of his who doesn't really care about him. He is puzzled and confused – but the idea of being Monty's master takes hold of him again, comforting him, giving him a purpose, and he disappears towards the scullery.

Felix stands alone in the hall, head bent, remembering the funeral service, seeing again the quiet grave in the small country churchyard. *Thou knowest, Lord, the secrets of our hearts.*

His eyes burn with tears and he would give much to feel David Frayn's arm laid along his shoulder, to hear his voice. He passes across the hall towards the old man's study, knowing how very bleak life will be without him.

CHAPTER FOURTEEN

'We're going on holiday,' Lizzie tells Pidge with great excitement as soon as she comes upstairs, one July evening. 'We're going to the seaside and Angel is going to buy me a bucket and spade.'

Pidge stares at Angel, stretched along the sofa, her eyebrows high with disbelief.

'To the *seaside*?'

'Isn't it exciting, sweetie?' Angel doesn't move and she keeps her eyes closed. 'I do think it's time Lizzie had a little holiday. A proper holiday near the sea.'

'We're going on a train.' Lizzie clasps her hands together, hardly able to believe her good fortune. 'And there's a castle.'

'Hold on,' begs Pidge. 'This is very exciting but why the unexpected need for ozone, Angel?' A thought occurs to her and she looks suddenly grave. 'And does this place, which has a castle and is near the sea, happen to be on Exmoor?'

Angel sits up suddenly, dragging her wrapper around her.

'Sweetie,' she says to Lizzie, 'just go into my bedroom and see if you can find my cigarettes, would you?'

'What are you up to?' asks Pidge in a low voice as soon as Lizzie disappears. 'This is madness, Angel. Much worse than Molly's party. Remember how you felt then?'

'I can't help it.' She stares up at Pidge miserably. 'He can't come up this month because he's taking his holiday and next month the office here is closed for some repairs or something and they're postponing the partners' meeting until September. It'll be three months until I see him again, Pidge. Three months. How can I bear it?'

'It'll be three months anyway, Angel,' answers Pidge urgently. 'Or . . .' she frowns, 'do you mean that Felix has set this holiday up?'

Angel shakes her head, pressing her lips together, looking away.

'No, of course he hasn't,' says Pidge impatiently. 'Stupid of me to think that he'd be so foolish. Please don't do this, Angel.'

'You don't understand.' Angel stands up, taking Pidge's arm. 'You see, it's simply that I can't just go on waiting. There's something so . . . oh, I don't know, degrading about it. It's not his fault, I know that, but I've got to make a move of my own. Do you see what I mean?'

'Yes,' says Pidge gently. 'Yes, of course I do, love, but it's the wrong move. You won't see him or if you do it'll be like the party all over again and you'll just feel horrid about the whole thing. Can you imagine how Felix will react if he comes across you and Lizzie in Dunster High Street? Especially if he has his wife and son with him? You'll blow it wide open and then what will you be left with?'

'I don't know.' Angel looks distressed. 'But sometimes I think it's better than doing nothing at all. One day he's going to leave me anyway, Pidge.'

Pidge looks at her compassionately, seeing that this is not the moment to talk about Lizzie's part – or her own – in the relationship, or about Felix himself.

'Think it over,' she pleads.

'I've booked the cottage,' says Angel defiantly. 'I saw it advertised in the Sunday paper weeks ago and kept it just in case. Anyway, Lizzie will love it.'

Before Pidge can reply Lizzie is back.

'I can't find them anywhere,' she tells Angel. 'I've searched and searched.'

'Oh, here they are,' cries Angel, retrieving the case from the side of the chair where she has hidden it earlier. 'I *am* an idiot. Sorry, sweetie.'

'I wish you could come with us,' says Lizzie to Pidge, her eyes bright with excitement, 'but Angel only has a few weeks between her contracts and she says you can't get away from the library in August.'

'No,' agrees Pidge after a moment. 'No, I can't get away from the library.'

'We'll send you a postcard, sweetie,' says Angel.

She looks at Pidge with a wheedling grin, rather as a naughty but penitent child might seek forgiveness, and Pidge cannot help but smile back at her.

'Yes,' she says. 'You do that.'

Lizzie hurries away to her attic room and wonders what she will take with her on holiday. She drags out her little suitcase, puts it on her bed and opens it: how small it looks. The battered teddy, which belonged to Michael Blake, must certainly go to Dunster and the small felt penguin – a present from Felix after a memorable birthday visit to the zoo – must also be of the party. She holds him in her hand, admiring his smart black-and-white coat and cheerful yellow beak and feet. Eyes closed, she remembers walking between Angel and Felix, just like a real family, and how they sat in the sunshine outside the small café and she ate an ice whilst the others drank coffee.

The penguin arrived by post later: 'I came across this Penguin Person from Porlock on his way to Bristol Zoo,' Felix wrote in the card, and she named him Porlock because it has rather a good ring to it. She still has the card.

Singing to herself, Lizzie begins to pack her case.

Sitting in the shade of some furze, up on the hill behind the garth, Piers dries his eyes on his handkerchief and puts his arm about Monty's neck. Nobody has told him how unexpectedly grief strikes, catching you between a moment and a moment, crippling you with pain, making it impossible to swallow. Just now, as he watched the little bird, swinging and hopping in the topmost branches of the wind-shaped thorn, he turned instinctively to point it out to his grandfather: to confirm that it was the male stonechat, with his chestnut breast and black head. It was a terrific shock to find himself alone; no old man, leaning on his stick, watching the tiny bird with that dear, familiar expression that combined wonder, joy and gratitude, even though he'd seen the sight a hundred times before. Piers felt bereft then, as shocked and lonely as when his mother had explained that Grandfather had gone away and couldn't ever come back.

Each week he rides down to the churchyard on his new bicycle, Monty racing alongside, and goes to see the old man's grave. Although Monty is always put on his lead, his mother is not happy about dogs going into churchyards but the old sexton agrees with Piers that David Frayn would like to know that his dog visits him from time to time.

'Although that's just his chrysalis,' explains Piers. 'He's changed now, you know.'

The sexton nods wisely and leaves them to it, sitting together on the grassy mound in the sunshine, the little boy talking and talking to the dog – and to his grandfather – whilst he watches them from beneath the shadow of the yews lest the young fellow should get upset.

But it's at the most unexpected moments that Piers gets

upset; moments that take him by surprise and which he can't control.

'Big boys don't cry,' warns his mother, so that Piers knows that he must never show the tears and he wipes his face again now as he hears her calling from the garth below. They are going shopping in Dunster and he hurries down the hill, slipping on the dry, loose scree, still rubbing his face with his handkerchief.

'Goodness, you do look hot,' she says, pushing back his hair from his eyes, straightening his Aertex shirt. 'What a ragamuffin! Come in and be tidied up. No, we can't take Monty, it'll be far too hot for him in the car.'

Sometimes, as they drive through the lanes in the Morris, Piers remembers that last journey to Stoke Pero but today he stares the tears away, looking for the first blossoming of bell heather on Dunkery, seeing the white scut of a rabbit running in the ditch.

The village drowses in the afternoon sunshine, the rose-red castle standing guardian on the hill, and he follows his mother from the post office to the chemist and finally to Parhams. There are several people in the shop but his attention is immediately taken by a little girl, rather younger than he is, who stares about her, singing just beneath her breath. She wears a yellow frock and her thick plait is reddish gold and tied with a yellow ribbon. She turns suddenly, seeing him for the first time, and he sees that her eyes are amber-brown and rather shy although she looks friendly, as though she would like to smile at him.

He straightens up, stealthily trying to let go of his mother's hand in order to show that he is not a baby but a big boy who is going away to school next term, yet his face cannot help but respond to that cheerful little look. Alerted by the wriggling of his fingers, his mother glances down at him and then immediately at the object of his interest. At this moment the woman with the little girl turns too, and the four of them seem fixed for a brief moment in time, gazing at each other, until Piers feels his hand gripped even tighter and he is pulled away.

'I can't be bothered to wait,' says his mother.

Her cheeks are red and hot-looking, her mouth pinched, and he looks up at her anxiously as they hurry back to the car.

'Are you ill?' he asks, remembering his grandfather. 'Are you all right, Mummy?'

'Quite all right,' she answers briefly but, as they drive back to Michaelgarth, he knows that there is something wrong, as if her thoughts are rushing ahead of the car, and he feels frightened.

All the time that she is putting away the shopping, making his tea, it seems that she is waiting for something; as if, deep inside, her feelings are twisting tighter and tighter, like a spring. When his father comes home he passes through the hall and into the study to pour himself a drink and, from his position up on the landing, Piers watches his mother follow him. He slips quietly down the stairs and into the hall, creeping along the passage until he can see them both through the half-open door.

'. . . What a fool I've been,' his mother is saying, 'haven't I? I should have guessed long ago. Oh, don't pretend any more, Felix. I saw that woman today in Dunster. That actress. She's your mistress, isn't she? She had a child with her. I suppose she isn't yours, by any chance?'

Piers knows at once that she is talking about the people they saw earlier in Parhams: the fair, pretty woman with the little girl. But what does it mean? He thinks confusedly of his kindly old schoolmistress but, even as he moves a little closer, he sees his father put down his glass with an angry exclamation and come striding towards the door and guesses that he has been seen.

He turns at once, running across the hall and out through the scullery, into the garth where Monty is sleeping on the cool cobbles, and all the while the words beat in his brain in time with his running feet. *She had a child with her. . . she isn't yours, by any chance?*

By the time Felix arrives at the scullery door, both boy and dog have vanished.

PART TWO

CHAPTER FIFTEEN

Dunster 1998

The birdcage hung in the first-floor window where anyone looking up from the High Street might see it. The morning sun glinted on the gilt bars, and on the little birds, but the chick's once-fluffy egg-yolk yellow feathers were dulled to pale lemon and her orange feet were faded now, although they clung just as tenaciously to the wooden bar of the trapeze.

Piers, rising from his chair, ducked as usual to prevent his head from touching it and his father smiled at him; there was humility and compassion in his smile. He suspected that Piers saw the birdcage as some symbol of his father's past but, if he'd ever wondered about its provenance, he'd never mentioned it.

Piers, bending to kiss his father lightly on his brow, experienced the old frustration of his boyhood: an instinctive deep affection for his father that battled constantly with his sense of loyalty to his mother. Her face, with its bitter mouth and wary eyes, seemed to get in the way of the kiss and Piers straightened up, fighting back an increasing need to kneel beside his father and question him.

'Why,' he longed to ask, 'did you need them when you had *us*? Why did you make her suffer?' Instead he turned away and went out, shutting the door gently behind him.

Felix took a deep breath, allowing his hands to unclench. With each visit he expected the storm to break and prepared himself accordingly. Ever since Piers' wife left him and, less than a year later, his soldier son, David, was killed in a road traffic accident, Felix had been waiting for his own son's self-control to crack beneath the strain of his grief. He intuitively felt that these two events were breaking down that barrier of amicable reserve from behind which Piers had conducted his adult relationship with his father.

He leaned forward in his chair, watching for Piers to appear in the street below. A tall fair girl, her baby in a carrying-chair, was passing along the pavement opposite. Her thick yellow hair was wound into a knot and her face was head-turningly arresting in its true, bone-deep beauty. She looked about her, elegant and graceful even in faded jeans and an old white shirt, and suddenly she smiled at someone Felix could not see. He waited. Piers emerged suddenly from a door beneath the window, glanced up at his father with his usual salute, and crossed the road to meet her. She took his arm with a warm affection and they stood for a moment in conversation before turning away up the High Street. She raised her hand in brief greeting to Felix, still watching from his window, and he waved back, his heart filled with gratitude, although she'd already turned back to Piers.

Sitting in the wing-backed chair, revelling in the warmth of the morning sunshine, Felix wondered why it should be impossible to break down Piers' reserve. Why had he not long since simply battered down that wall, built out of old loyalties and resentment and fear, which stood between them? Yet the thought of attempting it appalled him: what harm might it do?

Was his love for Piers strong enough to sustain them both through the breaking-down process? How often it had been the same with Marina: she, shut up in her silence, pinched with reproach; he, trying to penetrate the barrier with words? Felix was gripped with helplessness, thinking of past failure.

Marina's pride in her son becomes the mainspring of her life: she is determined that he shall be best, first, a genius. Slowly, as he grows, all her passion is finally directed to this end; Piers shall not fail her as Felix has failed her. As for Piers – torn between his love for both of them, made increasingly aware of his mother's unhappiness – he tries to sow harmony, to repair the damage as best he can. Marina's claim on their son is the stronger; she sees more of him, deals with his small day-to-day needs – and she is upheld by her self-righteous sense of injustice. Felix continues to be cast into the role of sinner and the knowledge of his weakness undermines his confidence in his dealings with his son. It is only after Piers' marriage that some touch of grace – a softening that allows Felix to draw closer to her – gradually releases Marina from the iron grip of resentment. Their last years together are overshadowed by the cancer which, to him, seems like some final physical manifestation of that banked-down, lifelong jealousy that has so destroyed her peace: yet during her illness he is able to minister to her, touched by her bravery, able to demonstrate his love which, at last, moved by his affection and grateful for his care, she is able to accept.

Once Marina dies, and he moves back to his flat in Dunster, Sunday afternoon tea and supper at Michaelgarth become a weekly ritual. He suspects that this is his son's way of trying to repay him for abdicating so cheerfully and he goes along readily with it, knowing that it eases Piers' sense of guilt. Piers finds it difficult to believe that his father no longer wishes to stay at Michaelgarth and suspects that Felix simply feels selfish at occupying so much space whilst Piers and his family manage in their much smaller cottage just outside Porlock, where his parents began their married life.

Standing together by the fire in the study at Michaelgarth, where Felix spends most of his time now that he is alone, he tries to explain his reasons for deciding to move back to Dunster.

'After all, Michaelgarth's not even mine,' he says – and seeing Piers' expression change to wariness, even hurt, he hurries on, 'Michaelgarth belongs to you now, which is how it should be. You know that the estate belonged to your mother's family, not mine, which is why she left it to you and not to me. She grew up here, just as you did, and I think that it's right that David should grow up here in his turn. Anyway,' he tries for a lighter touch, 'it's too big for one old boy on his own.'

'Nonsense, you're barely sixty,' Piers dismisses his father's age with a shake of his head, 'not that we wouldn't love it, of course.' He sounds a touch stiff in his effort to suppress an upsurge of excitement, wanting to be certain that Felix has really made up his mind. 'But do you really think you'd be happy in that flat? After this?'

Looking at Piers' unbelieving expression, Felix almost chuckles aloud. Impossible for Piers to imagine that anyone could prefer the small flat to this rambling, inconvenient old house – but then Piers, like Marina and the whole Frayn clan before him, adores Michaelgarth.

'Of course,' he adds, 'the house is big enough for all of us . . .'

He looks around the room and Felix knows that he is thinking of how they'd lived at Michaelgarth with his grandfather. He racks his brain to think of ways to explain the difference: to say that David Frayn had owned the house, Marina was his daughter, and in those days it was fairly normal for the old to be cared for by the young. Piers' wife, Sue, runs her own business in Taunton, as well as looking after young David and Piers, and she makes certain that their lives are organized along efficient lines on a tight schedule. Felix feels exhausted simply thinking about her.

He picks up the heavy, square decanter and the splintered light gleams and flashes as he pours whisky into two tumblers. How often he and David have performed this ritual: how much he missed him in those early, empty years.

'I'd get under Sue's feet in no time,' he says cheerfully. 'Anyway,' he attempts a little joke, 'I'm rather looking forward to being back in my bachelor pad after all this time.'

He bites his lip, regretting the quip; knowing how Marina would have reacted to such a statement.

Piers looks uncomfortable. 'Well, there's always the cottage,' he says, 'if you should feel a bit cramped in the flat. I shan't let it for a bit. It needs a bit of work done on it.'

'But the flat is *mine*, you see,' Felix wants to say to him. 'It's where I started as a young fellow back from the war and it's where I want to finish.'

The sunny flat, above the High Street, welcomes him home as though nothing has changed through the intervening years. When he brings the birdcage back from Bristol, he hangs it in the window as a reminder of the warmth and humour of those happy times with Angel and Lizzie and Pidge.

'Angel wanted you to have it', Pidge writes. 'She was very positive about it and I feel I must respect how she felt. Come and see me, Felix . . .'

And so he goes for the last time to the narrow house near the university. Pidge's gaze is uncompromising as ever, though the once-sleek, dark cap of hair is now grey. They talk of many things and, at last, she gives him the birdcage.

'Take care of it,' she says. 'Angel had this presentiment that you should have it and I promised her, though it's taken me long enough to get round to it. I miss her so much and though Lizzie dashes down whenever she can, she spends most of her time in London or touring abroad.'

'I'd love to have it,' he answers, touched and rather shaken to be back in that place where there are so many memories. 'I can't tell you what it means to know that she forgave me in the end. I still think it belongs here with you, though. Or with Lizzie.'

'You know Angel!' She smiles at him, her eyes shadowy with remembrances. 'She had these strange presentiments and I shouldn't like to go against her wishes.' They embrace, each holding the other tightly. 'Remember the way we were,' she calls suddenly from the doorway as he goes down the little path, carrying the birdcage.

Now, staring up at the birdcage, at the little chick with her fluffy wings outstretched, Felix could visualize the small Lizzie showing him her work in her little attic room: the painting and the plasticine family.

You can be my daddy, if you like.

Felix grimaced, recalling his helpless distress at this show of pathetic longing and his clumsy attempt to salvage her pride and restore her confidence in his love for her: nothing less than absolute truthfulness had answered.

The sun had edged beyond the window and his chair was in shadow. Deliberately pushing the memory aside, climbing to his feet, Felix went into his small kitchen to put away the shopping that Piers had collected for him and to prepare his solitary lunch.

CHAPTER SIXTEEN

Backing the car out of its parking space, weaving carefully through the queue of Saturday morning traffic, Tilda was more than usually aware of Piers sitting silently beside her. He was an a excellent passenger: his foot never reached for an imaginary brake nor did he flinch as she tucked the car tight into the hedge to avoid a motorist who needed more than his share of narrow lane. She swore beneath her breath once or twice – as dilatory tourists braked suddenly to consult a map or, panic-stricken, refused to back their shiny new cars into generously wide passing places – but Piers simply looked amused. He remained relaxed in his seat, his thoughts elsewhere. Only his hands showed a different message: they rested lightly on his thighs, curled loosely into fists, except that each thumb was tucked within each fist and held tightly between the knuckles of his fingers. Tilda now knew that this was a sign of inward stress. Trying to gauge his mood, wondering what might have passed between him and Felix, she'd driven out of Dunster, through Alcombe, and was turning left at Headon Cross before she could think of something to say that was neither banal nor intrusive.

'I went round to Cobbles bookshop while you were with Felix,' she said at last. 'Adrian thinks he's tracked down the book you told him about but he wants to double-check with you. I completely forgot to tell you.'

Piers glanced about him, as if suddenly aware that he was travelling through the countryside with Tilda and not locked in some private world of his own.

'That's good,' he answered rather vaguely.

'I said you'd probably pop in.' Tilda shook her head. 'I'm hopeless. Utterly brain dead. He'll be wondering where you are.'

Piers turned to study his daughter-in-law: her white shirt-sleeves were rolled up over bare brown arms, her startlingly blue eyes were fixed on the winding lane ahead: she looked so young and strong but he knew very well how vulnerable she was. As usual he was filled with a brew of conflicting emotions: joy and grief; happiness and pain.

'I'll phone Adrian when we get home,' he said. 'It's not a problem.'

'That's OK, then. And don't forget that I shall be going down to the cottage later on to see if Gemma and Guy have settled in. I've asked them over to Michaelgarth tomorrow evening for supper. Remember?'

Piers, who had completely forgotten that these friends had taken their cottage just outside Porlock for a week, wondered how much Tilda suffered when she was in the company of young couples. Surely it must remind her of all that she'd lost: or perhaps their company and the links they'd had with David comforted her?

Words filled his mouth, meaningless placebos that seemed to coat his tongue and paralyse it. He sighed with frustration and she glanced sideways at him, smiling as if she recognized his dilemma.

'How was Felix?'

Piers shifted slightly, shrugging a little. 'He's looking pretty good. A bit frail, of course. I said that one of us would pick him up tomorrow at about half-past two. Of course, he wanted to drive himself out to Michaelgarth but I put my foot down. A hip replacement is no small thing at his age.'

'He shouldn't be driving yet,' agreed Tilda, 'but it must be awful to have to be so dependent. Especially for someone like Felix.'

'He certainly enjoys being driven around by you – but then . . .'

'But then?' Tilda prodded. 'Then what?'

He gave a little self-mocking snort. 'I was going to say that my father has always enjoyed the company of a pretty woman but I can't really blame him on that score, can I?'

'It's hardly an uncommon tendency, given your average bloke,' conceded Tilda. She grinned at him, liking him even more when his sense of fairness conquered his occasional flashes of bitterness. 'You're dead spoiled, of course. What with me *and* Alison dancing attendance on you . . .'

Piers looked embarrassed but was saved from answering by a sudden wail from the back seat; a pause and then another longer, stronger howling began.

'Shit!' said Tilda, putting her foot down a little on the accelerator. 'I was hoping he'd stay asleep until we got home.' She raised her voice above the now rhythmic shrieking. 'It's OK, Jake, we can all hear you.'

The drive wound away from the lane, across a wild open heath on which gorse bushes and bracken grew, and finally led through an archway into the old garth. High walls connected the house to the stables and barns opposite, so that the ancient cobbles were enclosed. Tilda drove her small hatchback into the open-fronted barn and parked neatly beside the rather battered four-track which belonged to Piers. As she hastily pulled the Tesco carrier bags from the back of the car, Piers lifted his screaming grandson from his bucket seat and rocked him comfortably. Jake's fists thrashed the air, his face was puce, and Tilda chuckled as she slammed the hatch and they set off over the cobbles towards the scullery that led into the house.

'You look just like your father when he needed a drink,' she told Jake.

Piers held the child closer, smiling, touched as he always was by Tilda's courage. He knew how much she missed David, how hard she was finding it to accept the bleak fact of his death, yet she kept his presence alive with these little references to him. It wrung his heart when he heard her speaking to Jake of his father as though David were still watching over them, caring about them, but from some remote place. Helplessly watching her struggle, he'd been both glad and grateful when Tilda had accepted his offer of a home whilst she came to terms with her terrible loss.

Several of his friends – and Alison was the foremost amongst these – had not hesitated to tell him that it was a mistake.

'A young woman and a child,' she'd said, almost disbelievingly. 'Can you imagine how they will disrupt your life?'

'We're talking about Tilda and Jake,' he'd pointed out. 'David's wife and child. They can't continue to live in their married quarter now. Where would they go? Her mother is about to move north to join her husband, and their house in Taunton is up for sale, and Tilda and her sister have never seen eye to eye. Not that there would be room there for Tilda and Jake. There's plenty of space here for them and, after all, Michaelgarth will be Jake's one day.'

'I think it's a most unselfish gesture.' A pause. 'If foolhardy. After all, Tilda has to come to terms with this somehow. She's only . . . twenty-six, is it? Twenty-seven? She can't spend the rest of her life at Michaelgarth.'

Looking at Alison, Piers had recognized signs of that jealousy which had destroyed his mother's life.

'I'm sure she won't want to do that,' he'd answered gently.

'Nevertheless, it is her home for as long as she and Jake need it.'

Now, as he passed Jake to Tilda, Piers wondered what she thought about Alison and, as if on cue, a step was heard crossing the flagstones of the scullery and Alison's voice could be heard calling, 'Anyone about?' She must have almost followed them home.

Bending over her baby, Tilda made a rude face. She knew exactly how Alison felt about her arrival with Jake at Michaelgarth – tiny hints about Piers' privacy or small indigestible gobbets of advice were handed out at discreet intervals – but, even if this had not been the case, Tilda would have still been concerned about Alison's growing relationship with Piers. Alison was a very possessive woman and Tilda longed to see Piers free, for once, and in control of his own life.

Tilda, who had grown up a few miles away across the moor, remembered his mother, Marina, as a distant, unemotional woman, rarely showing her feelings to either her son or grandson, and distinctly offhand with her daughter-in-law. Piers' wife, Sue, was a strong, capable, managing woman; great fun but with a very low tolerance of boredom. She'd organized Piers and David for more than twenty years with the same good-humoured efficiency with which she'd run her thriving business, selling reproduction country furniture in Taunton. Having seen her son safely through university and into the army, she'd waited until he was happily married before announcing that she was leaving. By this time her company had several outlets on the Continent and now she intended to expand it into the United States whilst her business partner continued to run the British end of the operation. She'd flown back for David's funeral, received the news of her expected grandchild with a quite remarkable lack of interest, and had hurried away again.

'It's over, you see,' she'd explained privately to the numbed

Tilda. 'You mustn't be hurt. We'll stay in touch, of course, but my life here has come to an end. Can you understand that? Not especially now, because of David, but long before that. Once he was settled I was able to look to pastures new. I was never a maternal woman, Tilda, but I did my best. The business has been just as much a part of my life as Piers and David, you know, and I'd given them all I had to give. During all those years I never put them second for a moment; my family was always my first priority, but time moves on.'

Tilda had frowned, swallowing down her grief, trying not to feel hurt. 'All those years,' she'd repeated, groping towards some kind of perception of Sue's feelings. 'But you seemed so happy. You and Piers and David. And Michaelgarth . . .'

'Well, we were, my dear. Of *course* we were. But things come to a natural ending, if you see what I mean. Life goes in phases and this phase has finished.'

'Does Piers feel that too?' Tilda, her hands clasped across her unborn child, wondered if she could really be having this conversation with David's mother less than half an hour after he had been committed to the earth.

Sue had glanced across the room at her husband, deep in conversation with the vicar and one of David's fellow officers. She'd smiled, eyes narrowing in a kind of amused assessment of Piers' needs. 'Don't underestimate your father-in-law, Tilda. He'll be fine, my dear, simply fine. He's used to tough women, first Marina and then me, but it's time he had a break. You'll find that he's a very self-sufficient character.'

Now, as she listened to Alison talking to Piers, Tilda felt she agreed utterly with Sue. Once she'd moved to Michaelgarth she'd had the opportunity to observe Piers at close quarters. Allowing for his grief – and he missed David a great deal – nevertheless it seemed that he managed extraordinarily well without Sue. Once or twice it was as if she could feel him stretching, breathing deeply, so as to fill this space that he was experiencing for the first time in his life. On these occasions she'd feel guilty that she and Jake had arrived to cramp his new-found style. Yet Piers remained very much himself; it was as if she and Jake did not impinge on his freedom.

'But then I would say that, wouldn't I?' she muttered to herself – and smiled at Piers and Alison, who were struggling to make themselves heard above Jake's roars. She could see Alison's disapproval – the little frowns directed at Jake, and a kind of proprietorial anxiety for Piers – all very slightly exaggerated for Tilda's benefit.

'Well, there's nothing wrong with his lungs!' she cried with a rather forced jollity above the row.

'Nothing at all,' shouted Tilda cheerfully. 'Chip off the old block is Jake. He likes to make his presence felt, especially when he's hungry. Why don't you give Alison a drink, Piers, while I sort him out and get some lunch on the go?'

Piers took the hint at once. 'Good idea. Come on through to the drawing-room, Alison.'

They disappeared whilst Tilda, heaving a sigh of relief, sat down beside the kitchen table and began to unbutton her shirt. She put Jake to her breast and instantly his shouts were stopped and a glorious silence filled the room: Tilda settled him tenderly, closed her eyes and began to think about lunch in an effort to distract her mind from the persistent, painful longing for David.

CHAPTER SEVENTEEN

The stone cottage, built into a fold of the hill on the toll road out of Porlock, faced out across the small chequered plain of neat, tidy little fields towards Hurlstone Point. Guy Webster, standing at the window and watching the dazzling golden light on the calm waters of the Channel, was filled with a familiar longing to be out there on the water: to feel a boat's keel lifting under the tide, a cat's-paw of wind dimpling the surface skin of the sea and filling the sail . . .

'Did you put the kettle on?'

His wife's voice brought him back to the needs of the moment but he did not turn quickly or offer any kind of apology, for that was not his way. He would make her some tea but in his own time and not because she'd made him feel guilty.

'I wish we could afford a place like this,' he said, still staring out. 'To see the sea when you wake up each morning . . .'

Gemma heard the yearning in his voice and rolled her eyes but she did not hurry him, nor did she make some veiled complaint about having to deal with the unpacking while he stood about doing nothing, for that was not her way either.

'I should think that you spent enough time on the wretched stuff without wanting to live by it.' She went to stand beside him, slipping an arm round his waist. 'It must be really grim here in the winter when it's pouring with rain.'

He shrugged. 'No worse than Dartmouth.'

'Darling, there's nothing *here* – or haven't you noticed? Oh, I know Porlock's just down the road . . .'

He turned from the window almost as if he hadn't heard her, examining his surroundings, crossing the room into the kitchen, whilst Gemma watched his tall lean shape, bending to peer into the fridge, reaching for mugs from a shelf.

'If you feel like that about the place,' he said, filling the kettle with water from the tap, 'why were you so keen for us to come? You know what it's like here; after all, you were at school just up the coast.'

'You know why.' She leaned on the wide pine counter, which separated the kitchen from the rest of the room. 'We came because you found yourself with a free week, Ma said she'd take the twins and the Hamiltons had had a cancellation. Of course Matt offering you some sailing hadn't anything to do with it.'

He grinned then, his thin dark face lighting with amusement, and she laughed too.

'I'm looking forward to sailing on this coast,' he admitted. 'I suppose you and Sophie have plans?'

'Oh, you needn't worry about me,' she said lightly, lighting a cigarette. 'I always have plans.'

Their golden retriever, Bertie, wandered in from the garden, where he'd been carrying out an inspection of his new territory, and Gemma bent to stroke his smooth head. Guy glanced at her, perched on a high stool, elegant and pretty, her short fair hair sliced through with tawny, amber colours and cut with a casual cunning. The raspberry pink, scoop-necked cotton vest and her stone-coloured shorts had a stylish flair and there was an air of relaxed expectation about her that had nothing motherly about it. Guy suspected that he should feel excited by the fact that they were alone for a week without the interruptions and distractions of two fifteen-month-old boys: instead he had an odd stabbing longing for his children. It was selfish to feel that he wished that the twins could have come with them, knowing, as he did, that the break would do Gemma good. He was the first to admit that he didn't find parenthood easy – his short fuse was easily ignited – yet he loved his boys and would have liked to have seen them in this big, light room, set down upon the floor with their toys or hauling themselves up and staggering from chair to chair. At the same time, he knew that he would enjoy sailing with Matt, and wandering down to the pub with Gemma in the evening, and that it would have been unfair to expect her to have all the worry of them.

Drinking her tea, looking about the room and approving its decoration, Gemma knew exactly what was in his mind. She knew just how hard Guy had to struggle with his character and to remember that times had changed: he could no longer take a can of beer from the fridge and sit down to watch the rugby on the television or get fish and chips from the village if he felt too lazy to cook. The twins demanded his time and energy whilst Gemma – easy-going though she was – had no intention of allowing him to shirk his responsibility. She knew that he loved his two small boys, just as he loved her, but she also knew that when he set off to deliver or collect a boat for one of his clients he was able to shrug away the cares of his family and give himself utterly to the peace and silence of his voyages. She recognized that he needed those moments of solitude and, since she had her own ways of making certain that she was never lonely, had decided that it would be unfair – even dishonest – to attempt to make him feel guilty about it.

'Tilda will be down later,' she said idly. 'I suggested that she might have supper with us.'

He was instantly irritated: he had no great talent for socializing and had already planned that they might stroll down to the pub for supper. In an effort to control his annoyance he put down his mug and went across to the bookshelf. Recognizing the signs, Gemma eyed him thoughtfully as he picked up a book from the shelf and flipped through the pages: she liked the look of his wide shoulders beneath the crisp cotton of his shirt, his long legs in faded jeans, the way his fingers turned the thin paper. She stretched suddenly, deliciously, smiling secretly to herself.

'We might all go to the pub,' she said casually. 'But, on second thoughts, she probably won't want to leave Jake with Piers. Oh, how wonderful not to have to rush back for baby-sitters or get up early in the morning.' She finished her tea. 'I thought I might have a shower.'

He heard the invitation in her voice and felt an answering flicker of desire, although he did not look up from his book.

'Good idea,' he said casually. 'I shall take Bertie for a stroll. I think he deserves it after a couple of hours in the car. I'll have a shower afterwards.'

'Could you sort the wine before you go?' She slid off her stool. 'Put the white in the fridge and open the claret. You might bring a couple of glasses up with you when you get back. I'm sure the sun's over the yard-arm, as my dear old pa would say.'

He heard her go away up the stairs and, closing the book and putting it back in the bookcase, he went outside to the car with Bertie at his heels. The late afternoon sun lingered in the leafy tops of the trees that grew up the steep sides of the high coombe behind the cottage. The small sheltered garden was warm, the paving stones hot beneath his bare feet. Butterflies hovered over the clumps of pink valerian that flourished in the cracks of the rocky wall, and honey-scented thrift blossomed in cushiony clumps along the path. Guy paused to stare out to sea again, watching a small sail shaped like a curved white wing skimming over the sparkling water. The sight of it filled him with a wild unreasoning pleasure: tomorrow he might be out there with the light touch of the wind on his cheek, the feel of warm, smooth wood beneath his hand, listening to the sound of the water as it chuckled under the keel.

He lifted the case of wine from the boot of the car and carried it into the cottage, wondering if there would be a corkscrew and cursing himself for not packing one.

'Darling?' Gemma's voice echoed down the stairs and he went into the tiny hall to look up at her. She wore nothing at all, although she carried a towel, and he shook his head at her casual indifference.

'Lucky for you it was me,' he observed pleasantly, 'and not Tilda or Piers.'

'Lucky for *you*, darling,' she corrected him saucily – and struck a pose to make him smile. 'Just to say that there's a corkscrew in the big bag. Don't be too long.'

Bertie waited at the door, watching hopefully, ears cocked. He wasn't too certain of these new surroundings, though exciting scents beckoned from the grassy slopes beyond the gate, and his tail began to wave expectantly as Guy finished sorting out the wine, pushed his feet into his leather dekkies, and came back outside.

'Ten minutes,' he said, opening the gate. 'We'll have a proper walk later.'

Bertie hurried eagerly out, lest he should change his mind, and ran up on to the open moorland amongst furze and bracken whilst Guy climbed behind him, turning from time to time to survey the scene: the steep cliffs, patched with tiny fields and scored by deep wooded coombes, leading on to Foreland Point and, beyond them, the sea whose purple horizon was piled with untidy bundles of soft white clouds. He walked quickly, listening to the mournful croak of an unseen raven, hearing the chinking call of a stonechat in the furze, glad of Bertie's presence. The old boy had been his companion before he'd married Gemma, before the arrival of the twins, yet, despite Bertie's devotion to his small family, Guy knew that he enjoyed these moments when they were alone together. He walked on, his irritation forgotten, until he glanced at his watch and reluctantly decided they must turn for home.

Back at the cottage Bertie settled at once at the back of the courtyard, stretching out on the cool paving beneath the rocky wall, and, having filled his drinking bowl with fresh cold water, Guy went inside, found some glasses and poured the wine. In the hall he hesitated, trying to invest himself with some of his wife's insouciance, but his cautious nature proved too strong and he locked the door before climbing the stairs to the bedroom above.

As Piers drove Felix home from Michaelgarth on Sunday evening he was conscious of an oddness in his father's behaviour; a kind of listening quality that lent a slightly detached air to his demeanour. At some point during supper he'd begun to imagine that his father could hear something that he and the others could not. Even Tilda had seemed to be infected by his abstraction, pausing in the middle of cutting herself some cheese to ask, 'Is that Jake crying?'

'Are you feeling OK, Father?' Piers asked, as they drove back to Dunster together through the winding lanes. The hedges were enlaced with trailing honeysuckle whose scent drifted in the soft, warm air, and the blossoms of the dog-rose were moony pale in the deepening twilight. Felix turned his gaze from a star, which hung high above the dark shoulder of Dunkery Beacon, and smiled with great affection at his son.

'Of course I am. I can't tell you how much I look forward to my Sundays at Michaelgarth. What a dear girl Tilda is; she must be a great companion for you.'

'I have to admit that it's very nice to have her around, although I wish that the circumstances had been otherwise.'

'Well, of course.' Felix looked distressed. 'How could we feel anything else? But given those ghastly circumstances I think it's such a blessing for us to have her near. But then Tilda's been part of the family for such a long time, hasn't she? Since she and David were small children at playschool together. Michaelgarth seems her natural home.'

Piers, struggling with an overwhelming sadness as he thought of his son, felt that his own reply had sounded stiff. He tried to be more open. 'I hope she feels that too. I still can't quite believe it even now . . .'

He spoke with difficulty, unused to exposing his private feelings, and Felix touched his arm lightly as if to indicate that he mustn't worry, that he understood.

'It was good to meet those two young people and their delightful dog,' he said. 'Bertie, wasn't it? Splendid fellow. Very nice manners. He reminded me of Joker. Have you had any more thoughts about getting a puppy?'

Piers smiled, grateful for the change of subject. 'I'm terribly tempted,' he answered. 'I was certainly going to after Joker died. With Sue gone the place seemed rather empty. Then David . . .' He hesitated. 'Then Tilda and Jake arrived and it got put on the back burner.'

'Everything happened at once,' agreed Felix gently. 'And I understand that Alison doesn't feel that a puppy is necessary now . . .'

His voice tailed away but Piers heard the question behind the words. Normally he would have found it impossible to discuss his feelings for Alison with his father but there was some peaceful quality in the midsummer evening, an affectionate ease flowing between them, that made it possible to communicate at a more personal level.

'She's not terribly keen,' he agreed. 'Alison's not an animal person, which complicates life a bit, but I wouldn't let that stop me if I wanted another dog.' He was conscious of a wave of approval, of relief, even, and his eyes narrowed in amusement. 'Don't worry, Father. Even if I were inclined to let Alison make decisions for me, Tilda wouldn't stand for it.'

Felix laughed. 'I rather gathered that it might be the case,' he admitted. 'Poor fellow! Nothing more uncomfortable than being caught between two women.'

There was a sudden awkward silence that shattered the fragile ease between them. Felix bit his lip, cursing himself, whilst Piers could think of no answer that didn't add up to 'Well, you should know', and so remained silent until he'd parked beneath Felix's window and climbed out so as to help his father from the car. Felix allowed himself to be hauled into an upright position, took his stick and felt in his pocket for his key.

'Shall I come up with you?' Piers spoke cheerfully in an effort to show that all was well.

'No, no. I'll put the light on when I get upstairs as usual.' He hesitated, head bent, then put his hand on Piers' shoulder, gripping it for a moment. 'I'm so sorry, my dear boy.'

He turned away, opened his front door and disappeared inside. Presently the light flashed on in the first-floor sitting-room and, after a moment, Felix appeared at the window and waved. Piers waved back. The birdcage glinted in the light from the lamp, as it swung there in the window, and Piers stared at it for a moment before he climbed into the car and set off back to Michaelgarth.

Felix sat down in his chair and closed his eyes. He was very weary yet as he sat, his hands clasped upon his knee, there was an alertness about his posture, as if he might be listening or waiting for something.

CHAPTER EIGHTEEN

Knowing that her father-in-law was a man who liked a quiet start to his day, Tilda made sure that she did not interfere with his routine. As usual, when Jake woke just after six o'clock, she changed and fed him and then went down to the kitchen to make herself a cup of tea, which she took back to her big bedroom on the north-west corner of the west wing. She loved this room with its views over Porlock Bay and delighted in the fact that it was hardly changed since it had belonged to David. From a small boy he'd loved the idea of sleeping alone in this wing, of having this floor of the house to himself: these were his own quarters and the bedroom his private sanctuary. Sue had redecorated it once he'd gone to Sandhurst, covering the scarred, Blu-Tacked walls with a warm cream paint and buying new thick rugs in shades of terracotta to hide the worn, stained carpet. She'd sanded down and re-polished the old mahogany desk, which had belonged to David's great-grandfather – and after whom he was named – and consigned the war-weary crew of Action Men and their weapons to a wicker basket at the back of the big cupboard, which doubled as a wardrobe. This was as much as she was allowed to do

('For God's sake, Mother, don't go all girlie on me!') and Tilda was comforted to see his battered old tuck-box stuck about with labels, and the bookcase holding the familiar titles sharing the shelves with the dog-eared comics that he'd loved so much. Even the double bed had been David's, for he'd fought against it being changed for a single one when he'd inherited the room at eight years old.

'I like having lots of space,' he'd pleaded earnestly with his father. 'I can play really good games in that bed and you never know who I might want to share it with. Mummy doesn't seem to understand that.'

Piers had glanced briefly at Sue and then back at the anxious face of his son.

'To be honest, old son, I think that she understands only too well,' he'd said – but David had kept his bed.

Now, Tilda carried her tea – and Jake – back to David's bed. She talked to him and cuddled him, comforted by his small, wriggling body, and presently they both fell asleep, waking again at about eight o'clock. Knowing that Piers would be finishing his breakfast by now, she showered and dressed and carried Jake downstairs.

Piers, who had already finished eating, smiled at both of them and continued to read the newspaper whilst Tilda put bread in the toaster and fastened Jake into his bouncy chair. A murmur here and a comment there, interspersed with periods of silence, slowly lengthened into a more regular exchange until conversation was flowing along its usual lines.

'Gemma was in good form last evening.' Piers folded the newspaper. 'I gather Guy's got some sailing planned. Is Gemma coming over later?'

'We talked about lunch. She wanted to meet at a pub or in Minehead but it's not quite that easy with Jake. I expect she'll phone later on but I shan't hold my breath. Gemma's very laid back and likes to play things by ear.'

'Well, that's fair enough when you're on holiday. I expect she's enjoying a break from the twins.'

He hesitated, about to observe that Guy seemed very proud of his children, realizing that this might be a painful topic of conversation for Tilda. He liked Guy, found his keen wit very amusing, but he sensed a well-controlled personality firmly banked down beneath the quiet, polite exterior. It would be difficult to get close to him. Gemma, with her open, friendly, flirtatious ways, was so startlingly different that Piers wondered how they'd ever found any common ground on which to begin a relationship. He understood that, rather like Tilda and David, they'd grown up together so this must mean that they knew each other pretty well, but he'd been aware of some undercurrent that made him feel uneasy.

'Busy day?' enquired Tilda, standing up to pour herself a glass of milk.

Piers forgot about Guy and Gemma, swallowed the last of his coffee and glanced at his watch. 'Pretty standard. I shall be in the office this morning but I've got a survey to do on a house in Lynton after lunch. It shouldn't take long, and then I'm going on to an equestrian property over near Exford. Quite an interesting problem with a right-of-way, I gather.'

Jake began to chunter, waving his fists, and Tilda sat down again, murmuring to him, spinning one of the little toys that were strung across his chair. Watching her, Piers had a recollection of Sue, sitting at this same table, feeding David. A wrenching misery twisted his heart and, sensing some change in the atmosphere, Tilda looked across at him questioningly. They did not speak but a wave of awareness passed between them, as though each acknowledged the other's sadness and was comforted. Tilda gave the toy another twirl and picked up her glass.

'Did you notice anything odd about Felix last night?'

As a change of direction it was effective. Piers hesitated in the act of piling his breakfast things together and frowned.

'How do you mean?'

'Well, he was kind of *distrait*, wasn't he? Like he was listening to something we couldn't hear. It was so real that I found myself wondering if I could hear Jake crying. He had an abstracted look about him.'

Piers put his porridge bowl on the draining board, his cup and saucer beside it.

'I thought he was a little . . . distracted.' He gave a kind of mental shrug: raising his eyebrows, turning down the corners of his mouth. It was a familiar expression that Tilda knew was not dismissive.

'I felt it was more than that,' she insisted. 'There was something almost . . . well, fey about him.'

He turned to look at her. 'What's that supposed to mean?'

She ignored the irritation in his voice; just as she recognized the facial shrug for what it concealed, she knew that his irritation covered a similar sense of anxiety. 'I just feel worried about him, that's all. It was rather like you hear about people who have this premonition that some disaster's going to happen. Do you know what I mean?'

'No, I don't.' He sounded cross. 'Are you telling me that you think something might have happened to him?'

'I don't know.' She stared up at him, the dark blue eyes wide with anxiety. 'I don't know what I mean. It was just a feeling that *he* knew that something was going to happen.'

Piers' irritability increased. 'You realize that I'm going to have to phone him now? Although I don't know what on earth I shall say to him at this time of the morning. We never speak much before half-past nine and I don't want him to think we're fussing about him. He'd hate that.'

'I'm sorry.' Tilda bit her lip. 'I'm sure it's nothing. Honestly, it's probably just me being peculiar.'

'Very likely it is; but he has just had major surgery and you've put a doubt in my mind.' Piers hesitated, remembering the drive back to Dunster and his father's last words to him. Panic edged in, quickening his pulse. 'He *was* a bit . . . quiet.'

'*I'll* phone him,' said Tilda quickly. 'I'll say that I've got to come into Dunster and can I take him out for coffee. How about that?'

'And given that we were there on Saturday morning,' Piers still sounded irritable, 'what would you be going for?'

'I'll think of something. You can give me details about that book and I'll go and see Adrian. Anyway, Felix won't ask. He's not like that.'

She grinned at him and his irritation dissolved: he couldn't resist Tilda's smile.

'Well, telephone me at the office as soon as you've spoken to him.' He bent to kiss the top of her head, waggled his fingers at Jake and went out.

'He gets rattled,' Tilda told Jake, 'but he doesn't like anyone to know.'

She sat with both elbows resting on the table, the glass held between her hands, and fought down her desolation. Sitting in this familiar kitchen, looking upon a scene that she had known all her life, sometimes made things worse. The Welsh dresser held china that had belonged to four different generations of women: an oval willow-pattern Wedgwood dish, more than a hundred years old, sat elegantly beside a stylish piece by Clarice Cliff whilst an art deco dinner plate, octagonal in red and orange, nudged a primly pretty Royal Doulton cereal bowl. On a lower shelf Peter Rabbit jostled the mice of Brambly Hedge and Tilda's blue and white Spode mugs hung in a row above the large breakfast cup that Piers used for his coffee. At one end of the large square table newspapers and magazines, letters and bills were divided roughly into two piles. The notice-board on the door of the big, walk-in larder had notes and photographs pinned to it, various garments hung on the airer over the Aga, and Joker's bean bag still lay beside it, beneath the window.

The kitchen looked west towards Dunkery and east into the garth. From her chair at the table, Tilda could see the windows of Piers' study and the well into which David had always threatened to throw her when she got stroppy. They'd ridden their bicycles over the cobbles, shouting and squabbling, and later, much later, she'd sat here talking to Sue while David fiddled with the engine of his latest car in the open-fronted barn. It seemed impossible that he wouldn't stroll in now, as he'd done then, throwing himself down on a chair, tilting it on to its back legs – 'Don't *do* that!' Sue would cry – telling them jokes, teasing his father. He would listen intently to small anecdotes, helping the teller to embellish the story – 'What, *really* ugly? Seriously ugly? Bulldog-eating-a-wasp ugly?' – whilst eating a biscuit, cutting a piece of cake, never quite motionless. He'd given the impression of always being tensed for action and Tilda missed his vitality, his insouciance, though she still felt the backwash of that love of life with which he'd imbued their relationship.

It got her up on to her feet, now, blinking the tears from her eyes as she cleared the table. Talking to Jake whilst she stacked the dishwasher, which Sue had installed, going through to the scullery to set the washing machine in action, Tilda wondered how she might earn a living.

'I don't want to leave Michaelgarth,' she'd explained to Piers at the weekend, 'and I certainly don't want to let anyone else look after Jake yet, but I need to know where I'm going.'

Piers thought about and rejected several suggestions. 'You know that it was my grandparents who turned Michaelgarth into one property,' he'd said at last. 'The hall naturally divides the house into the two wings and there's no reason why we shouldn't convert it back again.'

'But I like it the way it is,' she'd said. 'Unless you'd rather . . . ?'

'No, no,' he'd said quickly. 'I'm very happy. But there might come a time when you need more privacy.'

She'd shaken her head quickly. 'It's not that. It's just I need something to concentrate on. I want something to *work* for.'

'I can understand that,' he'd said at once – and she'd known that he was thinking about Sue leaving him; the emptiness echoing in the old house without her life-force to fill it to the brim with energy. Like her son, Sue was always busy, never still: always with a new idea, never without an opinion. They could be exhausting people but, with them around, life was never dull and Tilda was learning that it took time to adapt to a different pace.

Tilda could see that Piers had not only adjusted to being alone but had created his own rhythm. Despite his natural grief for the loss of his son, there was nothing sad about Piers – yet Tilda knew that there was something unresolved between him and Felix; something that preyed on his peace of mind and destroyed his tranquillity. David had dismissed it as a simple lack of communication.

'It's a generation thing,' he'd said. 'They're all so buttoned-up. It's not done to show emotion or discuss things. Fathers and sons and that stuff.'

'But Felix isn't like that,' she'd said. 'Not really. Nor is your father.'

'Not with you,' he'd said. 'But you're not their son, are you?'

'But you are,' she'd said.

'Oh, I just won't let them get away with it, that's all,' he'd answered with the confidence of youth. 'Life's too short.'

It had been one of his favourite sayings: with that phrase he'd refused to let resentment or anger or disappointment cloud his optimism or corrode his goodwill. How prophetically he'd spoken!

Swallowing hard, Tilda glanced at the clock and went to the telephone. Felix answered almost immediately and she gave a quick gasp of relief. She explained her mission, arranged to meet him at half-past ten, hung up and immediately telephoned Piers to tell him that all was well. Collecting Jake she went upstairs to get them both ready for their date with Felix.

CHAPTER NINETEEN

Earlier, down at the cottage, the sun was already shining into the small paved area as Guy carried his coffee outside and sat at the green-painted, cast-iron table, his eyes turned seawards, Bertie curled at his feet. Thick soft mist drifted gently above the silvery water, fingering the fringes of the little fields, dissolving and shredding as the sun drew it upwards. The luscious dew-soaked meadows spread fan-wise round the bay edged all about by woody hills and tiny villages to the east: Bossington, Allerford and Selworthy, still folded in the shadow of Bossington Hill. He heard the stutter of a black-bird's warning call in the coombe behind him, followed by the quarrelling of harsh-voiced jays, and breathed a great sigh of quiet delight.

This week, dropping suddenly as an unexpected gift from nowhere after an arrangement to collect a boat from Falmouth had fallen through, was a real bonus. It was Gemma who had suggested Exmoor, telephoning around her friends until she found that the Hamiltons had a last-minute can-cellation, and he was looking forward to a few days at sea on this coast. He'd sold the boat, a Hurley 26, to Matt some months earlier and an offer to sail in her had been made along with the deal: Guy suspected that Matt would be a pleasant, quiet companion, not one of those endless chatterers who drove him mad. He'd never been able to explain his deep-down need for solitude: for periods of silence away even from those he loved best. He'd managed it at school with difficulty and only then with the connivance of his own twin brother, Giles. Later he'd started his small business – a yacht brokerage – and when the opportunity had arisen to collect a boat from down in the Med, he'd seized it without a second thought. Perhaps, once he was married, he should have explored other aspects of the business but Gemma seemed content with their rather unorthodox life and rarely complained. As a member of a naval family she was accustomed to the idea of separation; nevertheless he'd expected a change of attitude with the arrival of the twins.

Stretching his legs in the sunshine, smoothing Bertie's head which rested against his knee, Guy felt a warmth of gratitude towards his pretty, good-tempered wife: presently he would take up a mug of coffee for her. He looked again towards the sea, frowning a little, watching for any evidence of a breeze as the sun climbed higher, burning the glistening drops of moisture from the green leaves of the fuchsia bushes, and warming the damp rocky outcrops. After a while he stood up and went back into the cottage to make some more coffee.

Upstairs, beneath the thin cotton sheet, Gemma turned and dozed, half-consciously listening for the early-morning sounds of the twins. Reaching sleepily across the empty spaces of the bed she realized that Guy had already risen, remembered where she was and sighed pleasurably to herself. Soon he would bring her coffee but meanwhile she could relax and plan her day. There were several old friends she could look up, places to visit; she began to plot carefully so that the truth might be told – but not necessarily all of it. She'd learned the art of throwing a little dust in everyone's eyes so that nobody could be absolutely certain where she might have been at any one time.

'I was having lunch with Sophie, darling – or was it tea? D'you know, I simply can't remember which but, anyway, she sent you her love . . .'

Oh, she knew it was dangerous – Gemma shivered instinctively, pulling the sheet a little closer – but then that was the whole point of this delightful game. Just as Guy needed those periods of solitude, sitting on a boat somewhere at sea alone, so she needed the forbidden excitement of the chase: those electrifying moments of awareness, the eye-meets and apparently casual introductions. These made her feel twice as alive and, afterwards, she was filled with a glorious sense of well-being. Of course, Guy had never suspected a thing – again that tiny shiver of fear prickled her warm skin – but there was no reason why he should. It made no difference at all to their marriage apart from lending it an extra dimension which, she told herself, was a plus factor. These tiny excursions kept her happy and lent a glow to her relationship with Guy.

She loved him, of *course* she loved him, there was no question of that: those others were simply a rather delicious taste of icing on a very good cake and it was nonsense to suggest otherwise; and, anyway, she'd never been able to understand what all the fuss was about when it came to seizing a few moments of fun. It would be different, of course, if she were to start a long-term, serious affair, but that was never in question although there was always the chance that one of these brief meetings might lead on to something more serious. Her mother had begun to talk about it once, beginning to relate something that had happened to her when she was young, but Gemma had stopped her.

'Too much information, Ma,' she'd said, embarrassed – and, truth to tell, very slightly frightened. Had she suspected something? Gemma shrugged. Even if she had, Ma would never speak about it to anyone else.

The door opened and Guy came in carrying a mug of coffee. She pretended to stretch sleepily and felt his light touch on her shoulder: hidden beneath the sheet Gemma's mouth curled into a smile.

'Coffee,' he said. 'It's a fantastic morning though we could do with a bit more wind. There's hardly a breath at the moment.'

Still hidden from sight, Gemma's eyes opened warily.

'Does that mean you won't be able to sail?' Her voice was lazily concerned, merely faintly anxious that he should miss a day at sea, nothing more.

'Oh, we'll go.' He sounded confident. 'We've got an engine, of course, but no-one wants to use an engine if they can sail. We'll probably pick up a bit of breeze once we're out in the Channel.'

'I expect so.' She sat up, the sheet sliding away from her, reaching for the mug. 'Anyway, you'll be able to keep in touch. I shan't worry about you if you just let me know you're OK and when you're getting in so that I can meet you. Or will Matt drop you off?'

'Probably. I don't know yet. We might go into the Ship for a pint and some supper. You could come down and join us. Just remember to keep your mobile switched on, that's all.'

'I do generally.' He didn't see her swift, private grin. 'I think it's more likely that I'm out of signal or something when you can't get hold of me. Pass me my cigarettes, darling, would you? Thanks.'

She inhaled luxuriously, smiling at him, eyes narrowed against the smoke, her unclothed body posed comfortably but slightly suggestively against the pillows. Guy turned away wishing, as he sometimes did, that she was less obvious: more modest. Just occasionally he would have preferred her to be interestingly unavailable – not quite so predictably up for it – yet even as he thought it he cursed at himself for being an ungrateful fool.

'Matt should be here soon if we're to catch the tide,' he said casually. 'I'd better get my stuff together and have some breakfast. Will you be down or do you want to have a lazy morning in bed?'

'Oh, I'll be down,' she told him. 'Perhaps I'll come and see you off.'

She knew before he spoke what his answer would be.

'No, don't bother,' he said. 'It's simply not worth it. By the way, don't forget that Bertie will need a walk. I've given him a little run down the road but it'll do him good to stretch his legs.'

He smiled at her before he went downstairs, reminding himself how lucky he was – that it was very touching that she liked to know where he was and that he was OK.

Gemma watched him go, smoking her cigarette reflectively. She knew that he hated any kind of public demonstrations of affectionate farewells but she'd made the offer: now she could think about the rest of the day ahead. As she pushed back the sheet she chuckled to herself: thank goodness for the mobile telephone. Matt arrived as she was pulling a T-shirt over her head and she quickly fastened her shorts and went down-stairs.

They were laughing together, easy and relaxed, Guy tower-ing over the shorter, stockier and much older man who turned as Gemma came into the room.

Guy saw that Matt was clearly rather pleased if surprised by her kiss and felt the usual mix of irritation and resignation. He'd hated that easy familiarity with which she greeted virtual strangers – kissing them as though they were old friends, touching them lightly – and it had taken several years and a great measure of self-control to learn to accept it as part of her character. Although he knew that it meant no more – probably less – than the caress with which she now greeted Bertie, he could not quite control that twinge of fastidiousness that reacted against such gratuitous displays of affection. Matt was watching her with admiration and Guy frowned slightly as he picked up his sail-bag.

'We'll give you a buzz when we're heading in,' he told her, trying to keep his irritation out of his voice. 'Have a good day.'

She kissed him, conscious of Matt's envious eyes, and went with them to the gate. Matt's car was parked behind their own in the parking space and she watched as he turned the car, waving as they sped away down the toll road towards Porlock. She listened until the sound of the engine died away and bent to pat Bertie who waited patiently by her side, rather dejected by Guy's departure.

'We shall have a lovely time,' she promised him. 'Honestly. You shall go for a really good walk in a minute when I've made a few calls.'

She went inside and, taking her mobile from her bag, pressed some buttons.

'Tilda,' she said warmly into the mouthpiece. 'It was really great to see you and Piers yesterday. And Jake too. He's terrific. And did I say thanks for leaving all the stuff in the fridge? Listen, any chance of coffee somewhere? . . . Oh, gosh, poor old Felix. Isn't he a sweetie? Of course I quite understand . . . Well, no, I can't do lunch after all. Sophie's invited me for the day but I hoped we could meet up before I dash off . . . Look, don't worry about it, we've got all week. Shall I give you a call tomorrow? Great – and listen, I hope Felix is OK.'

Gemma put the telephone down and went to the fridge. Pouring milk onto her cereal she picked up the mobile and pressed more digits.

'Hi.' Her mouth curled into a smile. 'Guess where I am!' She chuckled. 'Of course I managed it, what did you expect? So where shall I meet you? . . . Sounds good. I *have* got a dog with me . . . I know, I know, but imagine if I'd had the twins as well . . . Oh, it'll be an hour at least, I haven't had my breakfast yet . . . Sounds perfect. Just give me some directions . . .'

Presently, ready at last, she let Bertie into the back of the car and, throwing her bag onto the passenger's seat, she climbed in and drove away from Porlock over the toll road towards Lynton.

CHAPTER TWENTY

It was after twelve o'clock by the time Lizzie arrived in Dunster. Roadworks on the A38 and a congested bottleneck of traffic around Bridgwater had added nearly an hour to her journey. She'd grown increasingly jumpy as the morning wore on, and this combination of excitement and nervousness had given rise to an outward show of high spirits. She'd played some tapes, sung to herself, talked aloud from time to time: 'Now what do I do here? Where's the map? Oh, I see, straight on.' It was very hot and she'd opened both front windows and the sunroof, drinking now and then from a bottle of mineral water.

As the sun rose higher, she took her khaki-coloured cotton hat from the glove compartment and dropped it onto the thick curling mass of bronze-coloured hair, tilting it forward a little. She realized that she was humming 'I Whistle a Happy Tune' from *The King and I* and grimaced to herself. Why should she feel afraid?

When she saw the castle, high on the wooded hill, she caught her breath in a tiny shocked gasp: with its towers and battlements, its red sandstone walls all rosy in the sunshine, it was like a vision from a fairytale. Did it look familiar because she'd studied its photograph so often in the past few days – or was it because once, over forty years before, wild with excitement, she'd crowded to the train window with Angel: 'Look, sweetie, see the castle? Isn't it wonderful?'

Apprehensively, Lizzie turned on to the road that led into the village of Dunster, remembering the receptionist's instructions: 'The hotel doesn't have its own parking facilities so if you can't find a space in the street you'll have to put it in the big car-park next door to the Visitors' Centre.' She saw the car-park, hesitated and, seeing how much traffic was about, decided to park the car and find the hotel on foot. People were climbing down from coaches, taking cameras from cars, wandering up the road towards the village. Negotiating the busy area carefully, she backed into a shady space, switched off the engine and sat for a few moments watching the tourists who thronged about so cheerfully. Quite suddenly, the remains of her courage deserted her and she succumbed to a full-scale panic-attack. What on earth was she doing all alone in this strange town so many miles from the Birdcage? What utter madness had brought her on this journey? Deliberately she drew several very deep breaths, squared her shoulders and practised smiling a little – not that mad grin that seemed to afflict her of late – but a serene expression, which, she hoped, gave an impression of self-confidence.

'After all,' she reminded herself, 'you *are* an actress.'

Presently, feeling more in control, she bought a car-park ticket, dashed into the ladies' lavatory and went back to the car. After debating whether or not she should take her case she decided against it, locked up the car and looked around her. At the top of a short flight of steps a broad paved area was flanked by the Exmoor National Park Visitors' Centre and a large, modern store calling itself the Dunster Wearhouse. Deciding to explore these later, she resettled her hat, slung her long-strapped leather satchel over her shoulder

and followed the trickle of visitors up The Steep. There was
no pavement here, so keeping close to the side of the road
because of the traffic, her pace dictated by the elderly couple
plodding along in front of her, she found herself quite
suddenly rounding the corner into the High Street.

Lizzie stopped abruptly, staring at the Yarn Market. With its
eight small-paned dormer windows set above the encircling
slate roof that overhung the heavy wood-framed apertures,
through which one might enter from the street, this strange
octagonal building dominated the scene. Here she had
danced in the shadows whilst Angel stood on the cobbles in
the bright sunshine, watching for Felix. Had he been there?
Had he emerged from a shop doorway? Climbed out of a car?
Surely she would have remembered meeting Felix: she would
have run to meet him, calling his name, and he would have
held out his arms to her, smiling at Angel as he always did.
Or would he? Perhaps, here, with a wife and child close by,
he'd have avoided them, fearing that he might be observed.
Instinctively Lizzie looked down the High Street and up
into the first-floor windows of the flats above the shops.
Somebody bumped into her, apologizing as he hurried past,
and Lizzie, putting out a hand to steady herself, realized that
she was standing beneath the high walls of the Luttrell Arms
Hotel.

She could not bring herself to go in; not quite yet. Instead
she stared about, noting the sunken cobbled pavement with
its railing at road level; the stone and timber-framed cottages;
the backdrop of dense green trees – and high above this busy,
lively scene, the castle.

*Dunster Castle towers above the little village huddled at its
gates.*

An upsurge of excitement expunged her fear and, as she
crossed the road for a closer inspection of the Yarn Market,
Lizzie realized that she was smiling with genuine pleasure
and anticipation; at the same moment she discovered that she

was very hungry. This, at least, should present no problem. Pausing to look into the shadowy spaces of the Yarn Market, glancing about her with delight, Lizzie set off along the High Street in search of lunch.

Her room, which bore the name 'HOOD' on its door, was on the second floor at the back of the hotel looking over the garden. Now, at nearly half-past four, she lay on the bed nearest the window just waking from a deep, refreshing sleep. After lunch, she'd collected her bag from the car, signed herself into the hotel and, having unpacked a few necessities, had soaked in a long, relaxing bath. It was still very hot and a sudden weariness had overtaken her as she'd pottered about, examining the room and finishing her unpacking. She'd lain down – 'Just for a moment,' she'd told herself – stretching comfortably on the cool red and white cotton gingham cover and fallen into instant slumber.

She is back in her little attic bedroom in the Birdcage on a hot summer evening. The room, high in the roof, is airless and she wakes suddenly, short of breath, with her head aching. Frightened by the strange thumping of her heart, she pushes back the sheet, goes out of the room and down the short flight of stairs. The lights are on but there is no sign of Pidge or Angel and she begins to grizzle as she crosses to Angel's bedroom.

The sight of Angel and Felix together in the bed startles her, although Angel leans out at once to her, stretching a hand – 'What is it, sweetie? Couldn't you sleep?' – whilst Felix slips hastily but silently away in the semi-darkness. She feels confused, sensing that something is wrong.

'I was hot,' she says, still in a rather whiny voice lest Angel should scold, 'and my head aches and I can't breathe . . . What was Felix doing?'

'I felt *just* the same, honey.' Angel's arms are soft and

comforting, and she smells delicious. 'I was *so* hot and I ached too, and Felix was soothing me.'

'And do you feel better?' She snuggles closer, feeling Angel's chuckle rather than hearing it.

'I was certainly beginning to.'

Angel is laughing and her laughter is infectious so that Lizzie laughs with her, happy together with her mother in the big bed, her woes forgotten. She falls asleep and wakens when the sun is already high, with Angel still curled beside her . . .

Lizzie stirred, still smiling as she opened her eyes. The hotel room was cooler now, and she longed for a cup of tea. Rolling off the bed, she looked down into the garden where wooden slatted chairs and tables were shaded by umbrellas. Several people were already having tea and Lizzie began to dress quickly, pulling on a white linen shirt, tucking it into a long twill skirt. Slipping the key into her bag, she went down the stairs, ordered a pot of tea at the reception desk and went out at the back of the hotel and up the steps into the walled garden.

Choosing a table slightly apart from the other guests, she sat down, kicked off her sandals and stretched out her legs, resting her bare feet on another chair. The garden was at first-floor level and she could see across the jumble of cottage roofs, a mosaic of red tiles and grey slate, to the castle on the hill. The whistle of the old steam train seemed perfectly in keeping with this tranquil scene and Lizzie sighed contentedly. Just at present, the outside world with its griefs and terrors was held at bay. Her tea arrived and, as she poured the pale Darjeeling, she thought of Felix and Angel and began to chuckle: how discreet they'd been, how clever. She guessed now that further 'soothings' had taken place in the afternoons when she was safe at school and Pidge was busy at the library. No doubt Felix had slipped away from the office to join Angel in her after-lunch rest; at any rate, there had been no more chances taken during the evening at the Birdcage.

Leaning back, watching a robin pecking up crumbs on the grass beneath the spreading branches of a beech tree, Lizzie grew slowly aware of the interest she was creating from the middle-aged couple at the table set by the steps that led down into another sheltered garden area. She picked up her cup, wondering if they'd seen her laughing all by herself – 'Quite potty, poor thing' – and at that moment the church clock struck five. She glanced at her watch and then frowned. It seemed that the clock was continuing to chime, though not on the same note – and she suddenly realized that it was a carillon, which was playing 'Drink to Me Only with Thine Eyes'. It sounded as extraordinary yet as utterly appropriate as the steam whistle and Lizzie was enchanted: this is how it might have been forty years ago. Maybe, back then, she and Angel had listened to the carillon; they had certainly travelled on the old steam train.

The couple, who were now standing up and collecting their belongings, seized the opportunity to share the moment as they passed her table.

'Isn't it fun?' The woman beamed at her. 'It plays a different tune each day.'

'Does it really?' Lizzie did not want her peace disturbed yet was incapable of cold-shouldering her. 'Amazing.'

'I knew it.' She was nodding at her companion with a kind of delighted satisfaction. 'You're the lady in the advert, aren't you? The one with the car and that dog? We were sure it was you.'

For once Lizzie was reluctant to be drawn in, resenting the shattering of her mood, but she nodded and smiled all the same, and joked about working with children and animals. After they'd gone, she poured another cup of tea and tried to regain that sense of relaxation, willing herself back in time. It simply wouldn't work. She fidgeted, aware now of other sounds: the hum of traffic on the A39, a child crying. It was the insistent, demanding cry of a very young baby and other memories began to rise to the surface of her mind: grief and loss nudged at her consciousness.

She stood up at once, denying them, picking up her bag. It would be rather fun to visit the church, she told herself, and to see if she could find the cottage in which she and Angel had stayed all those years ago: it hadn't been in the High Street, she was quite sure about that. A walk would be very pleasant, now that it was cooler, and, after that, she'd have a drink in the bar before dinner . . .

These plans carried her through the awkward moment and out into the High Street but that feeling of light-heartedness, of holiday, had deserted her. Whilst she wandered about the narrow paths behind the village, pausing to gaze in awe at the ancient tithe barn and medieval dovecote, anxiety was her companion. Why should she find anything here to ease her grief or answer her questions? It was madness to think that Dunster should hold any answers.

She felt a little better with a vodka and tonic before her, sitting at a table in the bar. Heavily beamed, with a window looking into a small walled court, this was clearly a room that truly came into its own in the winter when a fire burned cheerfully in the inglenook fireplace, but Lizzie began to relax as she chatted to the barman and an elderly local man with a small, friendly dog. When the middle-aged couple came in she hid herself behind the menu, taking care to be absorbed in her book whilst she ate her dinner in the long dining-room, only smiling at them when she got up to leave.

It was still early, barely ten o'clock, and Lizzie hesitated in the hall, feeling an oddly pressing need to go outside once more before she went up to bed. The High Street was deserted but the soft midsummer air was warm and the flowers in their hanging baskets gave off a delicate scent. It was not yet dark, and the turrets and battlements of the castle stood clearly defined against the deep blue of the evening sky. As she watched, lights began to spring up; someone drew curtains, a window high in an attic was opened. Just across from the hotel, where she stood in the shadow of the porch, a lamp was switched on in an upstairs room. It lit a painting on a wall, the wing of a chair, but her whole attention was riveted on the object that hung almost in the centre of the illuminated square. The light shimmered on the gilt-wire frame, outlined the shape of the birds clinging to the trapeze: there could be no doubt in her mind. It was the birdcage.

CHAPTER TWENTY-ONE

The telephone bell disturbed Piers, bringing him back into the present. The garth was in semi-darkness now; an oblong of light from the kitchen window slanted across the cobbles and here, within the sun-warmed walls, the air was laden with the scent of roses. He stirred, straightening his back, but remained where he was, sitting on the bench under the covered way which, supported by stone pillars, stretched, cloister-like, across the back of the hall. The swallows were settled for the night, roosting in the barn, but bats swooped and dived silently in the dusk and he could hear the screech of an owl down in Tivington woods.

He could also hear Tilda, who was in the kitchen. Her voice sounded concerned and he abandoned his private meditations and tried to concentrate on what she was saying.

'It's not a problem, Felix. Honestly, it isn't. I can fetch them in the morning and drop them into Minehead.'

Frowning, Piers stood up and went into the house through the scullery. Tilda, standing by the table, telephone to her ear, looked up as he came in and mouthed 'Felix' at him.

'Is he OK?'

She nodded, said, 'Hang on a minute, Felix, Piers has just come in and I think he'd like a word,' and passed the telephone to him, murmuring, 'He's fine. It's just a problem with his specs.'

'Father? What's happened?'

'I was telling Tilda what an old fool I am.' Felix's voice sounded rueful. 'I'd been dozing in my chair and when I woke up it was quite dark. I sat up to switch on the lamp and my spectacles fell on the floor. The shank has fallen off and I seem to have lost the little screw that holds it in place. D'you know what I mean? I've been crawling all over the floor but I'm damned if I can find it. I wouldn't bother you but, just at the moment, I do rely rather heavily on them for so many things.' His voice faded a little as if he were turned away from the mouthpiece, concentrating on something else. 'The shank looks a bit bent. I think my book fell on top of it.'

'Do you think you could manage without them this evening?' Piers tried not to sound too unwilling to drive into Dunster to search for the little screw but his heart sank at the prospect. 'I can pick them up in the morning on my way to the office and drop them into the optician. I could have them back to you by the afternoon.'

'That would be fine. I'm so sorry to bother you so late . . .'

'Don't worry.' Piers cut short his father's apologies. 'It's really not a problem. I'll dash in at about twenty past eight. Is that OK? Not too early?'

'Of course not. I'll be ready for you. Perhaps some coffee . . . ?'

Piers bit back the urge to say that he'd have already had his breakfast and tried to sound pleased at the prospect.

'Great. See you then. No other problems? . . . Quite sure? Good. Sleep well then, Father.'

Sensitive to his abstracted mood, wanting to help, Tilda said, 'I would have been quite happy to do it. I'm meeting

Gemma somewhere for coffee or going to the cottage, anyway, so it wouldn't be a problem to go into Dunster.'

'You went this morning,' he answered briefly. His hands were in the pockets of his chinos, his head bent, and she watched him curiously.

'It must be horrid,' she said thoughtfully.

'What must be?'

'To be getting old and having to ask people to do favours all the time.'

'I do *try* not to make him feel that he's a burden,' Piers said, after a moment.

'Oh, I know that,' she said quickly. 'It wasn't a criticism. I could just feel his . . . humiliation coming down the line, if you see what I mean.'

'Well at least the boot's on the other foot for a change.' He spoke without thinking and then saw Tilda's face, her surprise at the bitterness in his voice. 'Sorry. Take no notice . . . Goodness, sitting out there in the garth I hadn't realized it was this late.'

She took the hint at once, kissing him lightly, picking up her book.

'See you in the morning.'

'Yes, of course. And thanks for offering, Tilda, but it's much simpler for me to deal with it.'

She disappeared and, with a bitten-off curse, he sat down at the table, resting his head in his hands. Her remark had been badly timed, coming so quickly after his period of reflection in the garth, touching a raw nerve. The memory had surfaced unexpectedly, prompted by an earlier remark made by Tilda.

'Young widows are rather bad news, aren't they?' she'd observed. 'Nobody wants to be reminded of their mortality. After all, if David had been killed out in Bos., driving his Land Rover to and fro on that logging trail between Travnik and GV, it might have made a bit more sense. Crashing his car after a mess dinner half a mile from home doesn't have the same ring about it, does it? Nobody really wants me going back for Families Day – and I can see why. But what about Jake? The army was David's life and part of me thinks that Jake is entitled to a bit of that, but I can't quite see how it can be achieved. I can't live on the edge of it, taking him to school and parties and that stuff, and having to say the same thing over and over, explaining about David . . .'

Perhaps it was the usual frustration of being unable to ease her grief that had triggered off the memory. How often he'd felt that same inability to help his mother out of her bitter silences, his sense of failure shadowing his small world and dulling his natural abilities. It was ironic that it was precisely her own character that inhibited him in his attempts to fulfil her expectations of him: her demands and hopes – and clearly shown disappointment if he was not first, top, best – began to paralyse him. Fearful of her displeasure, aware that he was failing her, he grew cautious, learning not to expose himself to the possibility of ridicule and shame.

As he'd sat in the garth, thinking of Tilda, reflecting on his mother's character, he'd recalled a little scene played out at his prep school one Sunday afternoon.

There has been a cricket match followed by tea. Piers is Captain of the Second XI and his team has scored a great victory over the visitors.

'Well done, Piers,' someone's mother says. She smiles at Marina. 'You must be very proud of him. Isn't Felix here to see it? What a shame. Oh, yes, of course, I've just remembered, he goes up to Bristol regularly, doesn't he? Susan Banks said she saw him at the cinema with a rather pretty girl. A friend of yours, I expect? Do give him my love. You must come over . . .'

Looking between the two of them, his cheerful grin fades, his sense of triumph is corroded by anxiety. His mother's lifted chin, her bright, hard smile do not disguise the sudden wash of colour in her cheeks nor the way her lips tighten with mortification. At eleven he is already beginning to understand certain aspects of his parents' relationship and his mother is becoming less discreet; letting slip little hints about his father's behaviour. Piers is furious with him for exposing her to such remarks, for spoiling a rare and happy moment. And underneath, lurking, ready to pounce, that other memory: his mother speaking in a contemptuous, disgusted voice which continues to have the power to make him feel sick and frightened.

We saw that woman today . . . She's your mistress, isn't she? She had a child with her. I suppose she isn't yours, by any chance?

It would have been so much easier if only he could have ceased to love his father but there is something about Felix – he cannot define it – an unusual combination of generosity of spirit, humility, compassion, that draws Piers and demands some kind of instinctive reaction that looks beyond weakness and human failing.

It was a demand to which, even now, he had never yet fully responded. Marina's shade continued to stand between them, still requiring his loyalty.

Piers stood up, went to the dresser and poured himself a night-cap: a small slug of brandy and a squirt of soda. He began to prepare for bed, thinking ahead: he must set his alarm a little earlier than usual, so as to be in Dunster in time to have some coffee, otherwise he would be late at the office . . . And he'd promised to have lunch with Alison. As he crossed the hall, he hesitated for a few seconds, thinking of his grandfather, and then went to sit on the old carved chair set against the wall. This part of the house – the old priory chapel – seemed to resist any kind of domestication. Attempts by preceding generations to use it as a sitting-room or study or playroom had been thwarted by its atmosphere. There was

167

a deep-down peace, a sense of astringent single-mindedness, that defied the day-to-day hurly-burly. Only on very formal occasions was the front door used, and the hall was simply a passage between the two wings. The simplicity of the stone walls and its lofty height was emphasized by the long oak table, placed centrally on a faded but still beautiful silky Persian rug, and the two heavily scrolled chairs placed at either end.

Piers sat in silence, allowing the peace to enfold him, remembering how, as a small child, running a toy car over the flagstones or bouncing a ball, he'd pause to look up, way up, to the soaring rafters high above his head, or he'd lie quite still, listening to the silence. Even when he'd tried to pray, voicing his childish fears and hopes in cautious whispers, his prayers had been lifted from his heart almost as he'd begun to utter them and he'd been rapt in an intense wordless joy. Later, he'd lost the knack of it but sometimes, even now, he was touched by that same piercing sweetness. He'd read somewhere that intercession meant simply standing in the presence of God on behalf of another: not talking, not asking, just being. Piers closed his eyes, allowing his awareness to centre on Tilda and her child, so that His love might flow between them all.

For a greater part of the night Lizzie sat at the window in one of the armchairs, staring out into the warm darkness. Seeing the birdcage had shocked her even more than finding the card from Angel in Pidge's book. Although she'd come to Dunster with some wild hope of finding Felix, it hadn't occurred to her that he might have the birdcage. Had Angel given it to him? Or Pidge, after Angel had died? Puzzled, Lizzie shook her head. She'd been with Sam by then, of course; busy with her own career, preoccupied with her own problems. How easy it was to be so self-absorbed that, by the time you realized that there were questions to ask, it was too late; there was no-one left to answer them. Grief and loss had been the catalysts that set her off on this trail that led here, to Dunster, and – unexpectedly – to the birdcage. She was certain, now, that she had found Felix.

She'd spent the latter half of the long night watches planning how she might approach him. There were several courses of action open to her: she could look him up in the local directory and, should his name be listed, try a cautious telephone call; or she might ask around to see if anyone knew him and so discover whether he lived alone; or she might hover about, hoping to see him emerge. However, by the time the short June night was beginning to warm into daylight, with the silvery monochrome shapes in the garden gently greening into flowery bushes and the eastern sky glowing into a pale radiance, Lizzie was battling with a simple longing to cross the street and ring the doorbell.

Rising from the chair, stiff with fatigue, she set the kettle to boil and went to have a shower. She stood for some minutes at the bathroom window, staring out over the picturesque huddle of roof-lines and chimneys to the castle, insubstantial and unearthly in this early, luminous wash of light. Trembling a little – 'Exhaustion,' she told herself firmly, 'you're too old to stay awake half the night!' – she showered, wrapped herself in the thick bath-robe, and padded back into the bedroom.

The hot, strong coffee was wonderfully reviving. Carrying it over to the bed, she propped herself about with pillows and sipped luxuriously, thinking of Angel. At what stage had the pre-theatre mug of black coffee been replaced by a shot of whisky – 'Just a tiny one, sweetie!' – which she referred to as her Dutch courage? How old was she when she became unreliable? Life with Angel had been charted by her roles: 'Wasn't that the year we did the Northern tour? Sheridan, wasn't it? I was playing Lydia Languish and Maria alternate weeks . . .' or 'No, I remember that autumn quite clearly, we were rehearsing *Private Lives* in some God-awful church hall in Manchester.' Then there were the Old Vic years at the Theatre Royal in Bristol: the long, settled time at the Birdcage.

By the time the cup was empty, Lizzie felt calmer – and braver. She settled herself – just five minutes with her eyes closed – and woke to find the sun well up and the birds shouting cheerfully outside the window. It was ten past eight. As she brushed her hair, twisting it into a loose knot and plunging in the pins, she decided that she'd just have one quick look at the birdcage before breakfast. She was beginning to wonder whether she'd imagined it; perhaps her pottiness was beginning to take the form of hallucinations. Joking herself along, swallowing down her nerves, she went down the two flights of stairs, hesitated by the restaurant door and then passed by into the porch.

The man was just coming out of the door directly beneath the window where the birdcage hung: he was frowning a little, feeling for his car-keys in the pocket of his trousers. The set of his head, that quick glance, was so suddenly familiar to her that she nearly cried his name. Sanity drove her back into the shelter of the porch as he got into his car, reversed out of the space and drove quickly away. Lizzie watched him go, fingers pressed against her lips, trying to control her confused emotions: the rush of joy quickly giving way to crushing disappointment. Not Felix, of course: this must be his son – that boy with the strange name – who lived in the flat.

Lizzie stared up at the birdcage, glinting brightly, clearly visible in the sunshine. How could she possibly present herself now? 'Hello, I'm Lizzie Blake. You don't know me, of course, but my mother was your father's mistress.'

Felix had probably been dead for years, along with Angel and Pidge. And now Sam was gone too, and she was alone. A tremendous sense of loss possessed her, paralysing her ability to plot or plan, and, presently, she went back inside to have her breakfast.

CHAPTER TWENTY-TWO

Bertie sat beside the small bouncy chair, ears cocked, staring at its occupant who gurgled and waved its starfish hands. The small bare feet kicked energetically and Bertie took an experimental lick at the tiny curling toes, retreating swiftly as the feet thrashed even more wildly. Tilda smiled at his reaction.

'I miss having dogs around,' she said to Gemma, as they sat in the sunshine together outside the cottage door. 'David and I had decided that we were going to get one as soon as Jake was born. We were hoping to buy a little house in Marlborough . . .'

She paused, biting her lip, and Gemma, her quick sympathy aroused, put her hand briefly on Tilda's.

'It's just so wretched for you,' she said. 'Everything blown apart, having to leave all your chums.'

Tilda glanced at her, surprised. 'Not many people understand that. They can't see that it's just not the same to hang around on the edge of your old life, pretending that you're still a part of it, especially when that life was the army. You simply don't belong any more. Oh, people are kind, they make an effort to begin with, but it's quite frightening how quickly you begin to feel like some ghastly dependant who's being invited to parties and dinners on sufferance. And being a widow – especially a young one – has a kind of dampening effect on things. I was telling Piers last night that nobody likes to be reminded of their mortality and I began to dread that change of expression, that wariness, that friends would adopt as soon as they saw me. They'd nudge one another so that nobody would say anything tactless but then conversation would become terribly forced and it was clear that most of our friends were frightened to talk about David.'

'I can understand it,' said Gemma thoughtfully. 'It's not easy to find the line between an apparent indifference and that kind of awful sympathy. You know? When people put on special hushed voices and their faces lengthen and go all dejected but underneath there's a horrid prurient nosiness.'

She made the sort of face she'd described and, despite her misery, Tilda burst out laughing.

'That's exactly it. You've got it perfectly . . . but why can't people simply be natural about it?'

Gemma took her cigarettes from the table and shook one from the packet, frowning consideringly. 'I think it's because they have this superstitious fear about death,' she said at last. 'You know how people like to brag about knowing someone rich or famous, as if simply knowing them – or even something remote like seeing them in a shop – bestows some magic on their own lives? Well, I think death has the opposite effect. There might be something unlucky about the person whose life has been touched by it. That kind of thing.'

She lit her cigarette, elbow cocked on the table, turning her head sideways to blow the smoke away from Tilda and Jake.

'But you don't feel like that?' asked Tilda.

Gemma shook her head. 'Not at all. Someone like David would be impossible to forget. He was so much larger than life, wasn't he? You'd still feel he was around and he's still a part of your life. Yours and Jake's. Jake is going to want to know about his father and, anyway, Tilda, you couldn't just pretend that your marriage was a brief interlude, something that happened between growing up and the rest of your life. You and David go back to babyhood, like me and Guy. It must be impossible for you to take it in, especially now that you're back at Michaelgarth. I expect you think he's simply going to stroll in with one of those devastating remarks of his. God, he used to make me laugh.'

'I do feel like that about him,' agreed Tilda, struck by Gemma's ability to understand. 'I miss him so terribly but here at Michaelgarth I feel that he's close to us. Oh, I can see that you can't live in a time warp and make your life some kind of shrine to the past but I hate this "Now you must put it all behind you and make a new start" stuff.'

'I can't imagine Piers being like that,' Gemma tapped the ash from her cigarette, 'nor your mother, come to that.'

'Piers isn't,' agreed Tilda. 'Piers is simply brilliant and I think he feels just like I do about David. I can't tell you how lucky we are, Jake and me, to be here. Mum's a bit more like it.' She glanced almost slyly at Gemma. 'I think she'd like to see me getting together with Saul.'

At the mention of her brother, Gemma's eyebrows arched disbelievingly: she stared at Tilda with an amused, speculative gaze.

'Seriously? With dear Saul?' She took a deep breath, pursing her lips. 'Well, I'm probably not a good judge, being his little sister and all that, but I can't quite see Saul in David's league.'

'I'm very fond of him,' Tilda felt a need to defend David's closest friend, 'and he's been terrific—'

'Oh, I can believe that,' interrupted Gemma impatiently. 'Saul's a kind person . . .' She hesitated. 'But that's the trouble really, isn't it? David was all sorts of things but "kind" isn't the adjective which leaps at once to mind.'

Tilda was taken aback. 'Well, he's . . . he wasn't kind in the way Saul is, I suppose.'

'Come off it.' Gemma grinned at her. 'Who needs kind? The unknown quality, that's what we want and that's what David had.' She drew on her cigarette reflectively. 'I've always liked your mum,' she said. 'She's fun. I expect she just wants to see you and Jake looked after, that's all. Didn't you say that she was coming for lunch?'

'I did.' Tilda glanced at her watch. 'I must get back. Are you sure you won't come and join us. She'd love to see you again.'

'I simply can't.' Gemma stubbed out her cigarette. 'Sophie's coming over. We've got so much catching up to do since her wedding . . . but give your mum my love.'

Tilda looked about for her bag whilst Gemma went to crouch by the little chair, studying the sleeping Jake.

'He's going to be just like David,' she said. 'He's beautiful, Tilda. David would have been very proud of you both.'

She stood up and put her arms about the older girl and Tilda felt a moment of enormous comfort in the warm embrace.

'Thanks,' she said. 'For the coffee and everything. You know where we are if you need us but you'll come for supper on Friday when Saul's at Michaelgarth, won't you?'

'Of course we will. I'm only sorry that we shall miss Piers' birthday.'

'So am I,' said Tilda sadly, picking up Jake's chair. 'It would have been such fun to have you both with us but the next lot of people will be coming into the cottage on Saturday afternoon and, what with Saul and Felix and Mum all staying overnight, we've got a full house at Michaelgarth.'

'It doesn't matter a bit. This week's been such a bonus that I'm certainly not complaining. We'll look forward to Friday but I expect I'll pop in before then.'

Gemma went with her to the car, helped her to settle Jake and blew her a kiss as she drove away.

Bertie wagged his tail, looking eagerly down the road, hoping for a walk, but Gemma shook her head.

'Later,' she told him. 'Honestly. We'll have a lovely walk over the moor just like yesterday – but not quite yet.'

She went into the cottage, grimacing a little to herself, wondering if she'd gone too far with Tilda: speaking as she had about David and Saul. She'd always rather admired Tilda, and until recently been rather in awe of her. At school she'd been two years ahead: head of house, with a very direct way of dealing with her peers and the younger girls. Her extreme good looks, combined with a willingness to listen, had saved her from being either resented or despised and she'd been popular amongst the older girls and admired by the little ones. It was later, once Saul and David became good friends, that Gemma had come to know Tilda better.

'But not as well as I knew David,' she murmured to the attendant Bertie. 'That was a bit of a close one, my boy.'

She took her mobile from her bag whilst Bertie watched, tail drooping. He wondered if this meant another day sitting patiently in the back of the car, in some shady and deserted spot, waiting for that moment of freedom.

Gemma bent to fondle his ears. 'Good job you can't talk,' she murmured as she punched in some digits. 'Hello? Did it go OK? Was Marianne back before you? . . . What a relief. No, no problems here. So where shall we meet today?'

Bertie lay down, resigned, nose on paws, and closed his eyes.

CHAPTER TWENTY-THREE

Alison was waiting for Piers, neat as a pin, smiling with pleasure. There was the usual little flurry of greeting, which lay somewhere between the easy embrace of lovers and the more formal brief touching of cheeks: a kind of prolonged hug with a kiss that always left Piers feeling faintly guilty. He suspected that she was waiting for some gesture on his part that would move the relationship forward but he was incapable of supplying it. Fond though he was of her, he could not make a deeper commitment: not yet. Although he'd worked with Philip for years, it wasn't until after he'd died that Piers had become friendly with Alison. She'd decided to sell the house in Minehead and he'd assisted as far as he was able with the process of buying the small, modern bungalow at Timberscombe and moving her into it.

They'd been struck by the coincidences within their private lives: Alison had lost her husband just as her daughter started at university and her son took up a job in Edinburgh and it was as if, in a few short weeks, her whole world had diminished; her family gone. Philip's heart attack had been so shockingly unexpected in a man who ate sensibly and sparingly, drank very little and kept himself fit. 'He's the last person . . .' Alison would repeat at intervals; dazed and uncomprehending at her loss. During the six months after David's death she and Piers had spent a great deal of time together sorting out the bungalow, organizing the move. The similarity in their situations, being able to share mutual grief and loneliness, pushed the relationship rather quickly into an intimacy that Piers had quite soon begun to question although Tilda's arrival had put a natural brake on things.

Now, as he glanced about him, made slightly uncomfortable as usual by the almost antiseptic orderliness, she smiled as though she guessed his thoughts.

'I hope you agree now that I was quite right to move,' she said. 'I know you told me I should wait but this place is so wonderfully convenient after that big house in Minehead. Of course, Philip loved it, and it was very nice to have all the space while the children were growing up, but I simply shouldn't have known what to do with myself, rattling about on my own.'

Piers followed her into the small, shining kitchen. 'As long as you feel the same when Sara and Mark want to bring the grandchildren to see you,' he said cheerfully. 'You'll be a bit cramped.'

Alison shrugged. 'I shan't hold my breath,' she said shortly. 'Mark never seems to find the time to telephone, let alone come home, since he moved to Edinburgh and Sara only makes it during the holidays for a few days here and there. She's changed so much since she went to university.'

Tilda would have recognized Piers' expression – the mental shrug that hid so much more than it implied. He knew that Alison felt bitter about her children's defection so soon after the death of their father and he hesitated to trot out the usual platitudes. He was very aware of how much she missed them and how empty the days were, despite her efforts to fill the hours with charity work.

'I think it's fairly standard behaviour,' he said with a cautious attempt at the positive approach. 'They're making new friends and they have their own commitments but they still like to know we're there.'

'Go through and sit down,' she said. 'Everything's on the table, I'm just bringing the soup.'

Piers went into the long, bright room where the dining table and chairs were set formally at one end, with a sofa and armchairs grouped round the television at the other. In this room he always felt larger than life, fearful that he might knock against one of the small, spindly tables that held ornaments or spoil the immaculate effect by putting his briefcase or newspaper in the wrong place. The large plate-glass sliding window was open into the pretty, tidy little garden and he stood in the sunshine, hands in pockets, staring out. She came behind him and he turned, smiling at her as she set the crock on the table and began to ladle the home-made soup into his bowl.

'This is very sweet of you,' he said. 'Jolly nice for me not to have to think about lunch on a busy day like this.'

'It's very nice for me too.' She sounded abstracted, a polite response to his compliment, and he could see that she was still thinking of his earlier remark. 'It's lovely to have some company – but to go back to what we were saying, Piers; yes, I know that they like to know we're here but don't you find that the young's particular brand of dependency gets a bit wearing?'

Piers shook out his napkin, accepted a bread roll and crumbled it thoughtfully. This type of conversation generally led into the same groove, which finally resulted in her giving advice on how he should deal with Tilda and Jake.

'I think it's a wearing time of life.' He tried to make it sound a bit of a joke. 'Between elderly parents and grown-up children it can be . . . interesting.'

Alison snorted derisively. 'That's one way of describing it.

As far as I can see it, my children want the privilege of worrying me to death with their problems whilst denying me any right to intervene in their lives – apart from sending them money, of course.'

Piers smiled rather wistfully. 'That sums it up perfectly,' he agreed. 'This soup is absolutely delicious. I have to say that I quite enjoy cooking for myself but I haven't got round to attempting soup yet. You must give me the recipe.'

She glanced at him, quick to pick up the deliberate change of subject, guessing that he was thinking about David. Sometimes, in her anxiety to put him straight about his dealings with Tilda, she quite forgot that David was dead. She took his cue, feeling that she'd been insensitive.

'I'm glad you like it, I was rather worried that it might be too hot for soup. I hope this weather lasts for your holiday. Have you made any plans yet?'

'Not too many.' He tried not to let a certain wariness creep into his voice. 'Two weeks of freedom! I intend to lie about in the sun and catch up on some reading.'

She removed the soup bowls, putting them through the hatch into the kitchen. 'If Jake lets you.'

'Oh, he's too young to be a problem,' replied Piers cheerfully. 'The garden's looking delightful, isn't it? Wonderful colours.'

'I've been working very hard.' Distracted yet again, Alison looked with satisfaction on her handiwork. 'Although I'm having to water it every evening . . .'

Piers watched her as she talked on about bedding plants and her new rockery; her brown hair, bobbed with a fringe, was neat and shining, and her face, animated now, and free from discontent, was small and pretty. She was stockily built though well-shaped, not very tall, but, all things considered, an attractive woman . . .

She turned suddenly, saw his intent, assessing look and blushed suddenly. Piers, feeling extraordinarily uncomfortable, cut some cheese so as to give himself something to do.

'I was wondering,' she sat down again and leaned forward, encouraged by that unguarded look, 'well, hoping, actually, that we might have an outing or two while you're on holiday. We talked of it before, didn't we? I was saying that I'd like to go to Knightshayes. I've never been there.'

'Absolutely,' he said, some kind of guilt lending enthusiasm to his voice. It was as if that calculating look had betrayed him into an intimacy he'd not intended – yet he couldn't refuse her.

And why should I want to? he asked himself, confused. Dammit, I'm very fond of her.

'I thought we might have coffee in the garden,' she was saying, 'if you've got the time?'

He glanced at his watch. 'Plenty of time,' he said, still with that same feeling that he must make some kind of amends – and followed her outside.

After he'd gone, Alison cleared the table and began to wash up. Her movements were neat and methodical, no action was wasted and, as she worked, she thought about Piers. In those early days, after Philip's death and with the children gone, she'd been shocked at how quickly Piers had become important to her. He'd been more than someone willing to help with the unexpected small problems; more than a friend with whom she could talk through the pros and cons of moving. She'd found herself excited by the prospect of seeing him, taking care that she was looking her best, and, after he'd gone, she'd remember things he'd said and the electrifying sensation of the brief clasp of his hand.

She'd been confused, almost horrified by her disloyalty to Philip, wondering if it might be some strange manifestation of shock, but during the long dark emptiness that stretched between bed-time and breakfast she'd brought her common sense to bear upon these reactions. Lying awake, eyes dry and aching from lack of sleep, she'd examined her feelings. There was no question that, though she'd loved Philip and been very loyal to him, the early magic had faded once the children had come along. He'd always been a man who put his work first: pragmatic, sensible – nothing of the romantic about him – but he'd been a good father and husband. The simple explanation was that she'd loved him but hadn't been *in love* with him.

To begin with, this realization in itself had been a problem for her: to love someone as she'd loved Philip – and as, no doubt, he had loved her – suggested all the good, solid, admirable aspects of the word. To be *in love* had always, in her book, implied a rather different state: a febrile instability that majored with feckless irresponsibility on the physical aspect. It was a condition that had more to do with the Latin temperament and with film stars than with your sensible, reliable, durable relationships. Now, though, as she thought about Piers in those endless night watches, Alison had strange fantasies that seemed incongruous in company with the non-iron striped polycotton sheets and her cosy winceyette nightdress.

For the first time in her life, the woman who'd been buried deeply, willingly, inside the roles of wife and mother began to cast off these constricting images. Emerging with new, fresh eyes, Alison realized something else very important: Piers was sexy – and Philip never had been. This startling knowledge required further rearranging of her ideas. Philip had been a good-looking man: very tall, clean-cut features, slim. Everything about him suggested that he should be attractive, in the real sense of the word; drawing people to him, especially women. Yet this had never been the case. He'd been rather a dull stick – she caught her breath rather sharply when she acknowledged this to herself – just a touch boring, though kind; very kind.

But now, the new Alison, lying all restless and yearning in her sensible sheets, wondered whether 'kind' was as valuable a quality as her mother had first led her to believe.

'He's a kind man, Alison,' she'd said, after the second or third meeting, 'he'll never let you down' – and this was true: bills paid on time (not too early, no sense in losing the interest) – the house re-decorated every two years (must protect one's investment) – impulse buying not encouraged – ('but do you really *need* another handbag, dear?'). She'd learned to expect that the rubbish – sensibly wrapped – would always be put out, the grass mown within an inch of its life, the car MOT'd on the right day, and, during the whole of their twenty-five years together, she'd never suffered a moment's disquiet about his behaviour (unless she counted that little twinge when she'd feared he might be boring his fellow guest at a dinner party) nor a second's jealousy when he was in the company of a charming woman.

Yet Piers was kind too: he'd helped her through those miserable winter months, advised on the selling of the house in Minehead, surveyed the bungalow and helped her with the move. Why then this ceaseless agony of wondering whom he was meeting, what he was doing? Her latent jealousy, banked well down and undisturbed by Philip, now flared into a bonfire of anguished possessiveness. Her newly opened eyes saw that Piers was not only kind but he had that indefinable attraction that drew people – especially women – to him: it was something about his eyes, the way he was so at ease with his body, his deep chuckle. She'd been so upset when he'd told her – so happily, clearly expecting her full approval – that Tilda and Jake were coming back to Michaelgarth that she'd had a migraine for three days. Not that she was jealous, not in that way, of his relationship with Tilda – it was quite clear that Piers looked upon her as a deeply beloved daughter – no, it was the thought of the time they would spend together that made her so furious: time in which she would not be included: time that would be deducted from her share of him.

She'd tried to hint gently to Tilda that she was being rather thoughtless in assuming that she could simply walk in, as though she owned the place, as though Piers had no life of his own which might suffer by this invasion, but Tilda simply looked back at her with those remarkable cornflower eyes as if she saw right down to what lay beneath Alison's nice drip-dry shirt, which had been such an absolute bargain from the charity shop in Minehead.

Alison swiped the cloth around the twin stainless-steel bowls, wrung it out and went outside to peg it on the line. She remembered the way Piers had looked at her earlier – nothing casual about *that* look – and her gut churned. She was pretty certain that he'd felt about Sue the same way she'd been with Philip: he'd loved her but he hadn't been *in love* with her. The phrase, which she'd once dismissed so disdainfully, now obsessed her: she was certain that she was in love with Piers. And he?

Alison bit her lip in frustration, fetched the secateurs and went to dead-head the roses.

CHAPTER TWENTY-FOUR

After breakfast, her plans dashed to pieces, Lizzie decided to walk down to the beach. All keyed up and ready for action, she found the ground had been sliced from before her feet and she was left feeling disorientated and rather shaky. Some kind of physical exercise was essential and she set out for Dunster beach, hoping that the walk would refresh her memory, even, perhaps, summon Angel's shade. Instead she found that she was utterly at a loss. She recognized nothing: not the underpass beneath the A39, nor the sign 'To the beach', which led her along Sea Lane, nor the small, neat bungalows of Haven Close and Bridges Mead: none of these struck a chord. Once she'd finally reached the beach she thought that she did remember the wooden chalets with their corrugated asbestos roofs, but if she'd once played on those flat stretches of sandy beach with its grey rocky outcrops, or paddled in that far distant sea, then she had no recollection of it. Tired, disillusioned and very hot, she made her way back to the hotel, ready for a long cold drink. No wonder Angel had written all those years ago, 'but it's rather a trek to the beach for poor little Lizzie's legs'. She rather suspected, given that long weary walk, that Angel hadn't spent too much time on the beach; she'd hung about the village hoping to see Felix.

Lizzie sighed as she sat in the cool garden, sipping an icy St Clement's: it seemed that she was to be defeated in her hopes just as Angel had been forty years before. After all, what could she possibly say to Felix's son? She could think of no way to introduce herself or explain the reason for her visit to Dunster; yet neither could she bear to go away again, leaving the birdcage behind, without knowing how it came to be hanging in that room across the street. As she ate a sandwich beneath the shady umbrella listening to the carillon – today the tune was 'Home Sweet Home' – she tried to plan a path ahead, inventing scenarios that might answer these questions.

He'd looked nice, Felix's son – *what* was his name? – with that easy gait and the swift turn of the head. His glance – though he could have hardly seen her in the shadow of the porch – had that intent quality that reminded her of his father: just so had Felix looked as he came in on a Sunday evening, with a smile for Pidge, the wink for Angel, yet in that brief moment assessing the general atmosphere or any new addition to the room.

'Hello, my birds . . .' He'd managed to be inclusive whilst making each of them feel special and, more importantly, showing his admiration for their unity. There was never any inclination to vie for his attention; no attempts for one to outdo the other, despite the fact that they'd all loved him so much.

Lizzie kicked off her shoes and rested her heels on the second chair, wondering why the relationship had finished, cudgelling her memory. How long had the Felix years lasted? At eleven she'd been sent away to school – oh, the excitement of it! The preparations and expectation! – but, by the time she'd returned home for the Christmas holidays, Felix had disappeared from the scene.

'When is Felix coming to see us?' she asks, planning to tell him her news, show him the small trophies of the term's successes.

'He could never get away at Christmas,' answers Angel rather sharply. 'You know that.'

Lizzie slowly realizes that beneath the warm welcome of her homecoming there are other, darker, layers of emotion: Angel is absent-minded, and occasionally impatient, whilst Pidge is watchful.

'I've made a card for him,' she says – they've always exchanged presents with Felix after Christmas during their own little ceremony. 'When shall I give it to him?' but Angel is offhand, as if the question irritates her.

'I'd simply forget all about it, sweetie, if I were you.'

She stonewalls any further questions, and Pidge is unforth-coming too, but kinder.

'He's finding it impossible to get away just now. He'd have been thrilled, of course, but we'll have to wait and see. Now what have you got there?'

The holiday passes quickly and once she's back at school, with new experiences and objectives opening out before her, she is side-tracked; her vision already turning to expanding horizons so that she is easily persuaded from pursuing the subject.

Now, remembering Angel's stonewalling, she was fairly certain that it had been Felix who'd called a halt but, if that were true, why should he have the birdcage? If there had been a reconciliation she would certainly have heard about it; despite her own career, her life in London, she'd kept in close contact with Pidge and Angel, and even when she was married they'd gone back to Bristol as often as they could to see them. They'd adored Sam.

The pain was so sharp that she crossed her arms beneath her breast, holding herself upright as the memory assailed her.

Tall, tough as a tank, unruly black hair, he watches her from a distance, meeting – always, it seems, by chance – at first nights, after-the-show suppers, at parties. Naïvely, she feels that it is odd that their paths should cross so regularly. Increasingly aware of him she tries not to show her interest but it has become almost impossible not to look for his unmistakable figure, always dressed in black – jeans, roll-neck jersey, a jacket flung over his shoulders – nor to prevent that tell-tale colour that stains her skin the moment their eyes met. He is company manager when she joins the production of *French Without Tears* and later he becomes the artistic director of his own company, Centre Stage. How proud he is of that highly acclaimed little company, which specializes in theatre-in-the-round and has its headquarters in an old factory in Islington. After *French Without Tears* they never work together again but, by the end of her six-month contract, they are married.

'Sweetie,' Angel says at the reception, full of goodwill and champagne, 'this is one production which is just going to run and run.'

Lizzie mopped her eyes discreetly with her handkerchief and reached for her drink. Swallowing it back with her tears she cursed to herself, suspecting that if she once gave way to her grief she might fall into pieces that might never be put together again. It had come from nowhere, that subversive little memory: recalling how Pidge and Angel had loved him. No use to think about it now. Think about Felix, the birdcage, anything but Sam . . .

And here, oh welcome diversion, was the friendly couple, just come in for lunch and wanting to tell her about the church with its extraordinary rood screen – dates and dimensions were supplied at this point – and the delightful memorial garden. *So* peaceful and quiet. Had she seen it? Oh, then she must go and have a look. She was looking a little tired – an inquisitive note here – was she feeling quite well? Oh, a walk to the beach! Goodness, yes, *such* a long way on this hot morning . . .

'But I've been sitting here, resting in the shade with a deliciously cold drink and my lunch,' Lizzie told them, gathering her belongings, 'and that little garden sounds exactly the right place to explore. Just behind the church . . . ?'

They explained, solo and chorus, and she went away with a happy smile and a cheerful wave – 'After all,' she told herself, 'I *am* an actress' – through the hotel and out into the High Street. She paused to stare up at the birdcage, in shadow now but still visible, and noticed that the sash-window was open. Trying to remember whether it had been open earlier, she glanced along the line of parked cars looking for the rather battered four-track whilst feeling pretty sure that she probably wouldn't recognize it again. She'd been too busy looking at – whatever *was* his name, Felix's son? – too shocked to notice his car. She wandered along The Ball and into Priory Green, peeping into secret gardens, marvelling at the rich, rough texture of the old stone walls and the vivid patchwork colours of the flowers, until she found herself once more beside the Tithe barn and saw the entrance to the memorial garden. The wooden gate stood open and, bending her head beneath the wooden portal, she passed inside.

She stood quite still, just for a moment, entranced by the scene before her. Gravelled paths led between beds of tall flowering shrubs and sweetly scented flowers, wooden benches were placed beneath leafy bowers, and here, beside the high stone wall, stood the well on a big round cobbled step. Lizzie walked softly, lest she should disturb the silence; pausing to watch a blackbird in the branches of some ivy, leaning to inhale the heady perfume from a spray of roses, she moved quietly along the paths, feeling a deep-down peacefulness creeping around her heart.

He was sitting on a seat in the shadow of the wall, his

hands clasped on the stick held upright between his knees, contemplating the small sundial. Coming upon him suddenly, imagining herself quite alone, she gave a tiny gasping cry of surprise. He smiled at her and the shock, even as she acknowledged it, was almost immediately absorbed into that sense of peace, which continued to hold her steady. Everything – the return to Bristol, the memories, the postcard – had been leading towards this moment.

Lizzie breathed in, a deep, deep sigh, and exhaled gently. She went closer, searching for confirmation in his face, and he moved a little so that there might be room for her on the seat.

'I was looking for you,' she said simply, sitting down beside him. 'Hello, Felix.'

He turned to examine her, with that familiar, assessing look, and then, smiling with relief and murmuring 'Lizzie,' he sighed too, as if something momentous had been accomplished. They stared at each other with wondering faces, until Felix began to chuckle.

'This is utterly extraordinary,' he said, 'and yet I've been expecting it. Well, expecting something. I wasn't sure what it might be. When you get old, Lizzie, you have strange fancies.'

'You don't have to be old,' she answered feelingly. 'I've been like a madwoman just lately. Crazy. My God, Felix. It really is you, isn't it? I'm not hallucinating.'

'My dear Lizzie, if you were hallucinating I should imagine that you could do better than this.'

His chuckle moved her so deeply and so strangely that she reached out her hand. He took it in his and held it tightly, his lips compressed to hide his emotion.

'Felix, I can still hardly believe that we're here,' she glanced about her, 'in this garden, sitting on a bench dedicated to' – she screwed her head round to read the inscription – 'Peter Horatio Shepherd. How did you know it was me?'

He frowned a little, as if trying to understand it himself. 'You've been in my thoughts so much lately,' he said at last. 'You and Angel and Pidge. So many memories. And I've just had this premonition that something was about to happen.' He shook his head impatiently. 'Sounds foolish, put like that, but it's the truth. What else can I say? You have a look of your mother about you? Second sight? Haven't a clue. I could ask you the same question. And please don't tell me that I looked like this when I was thirty-five or I might hit you with this stick.'

She began to laugh, the sound escaping in muffled bursts, and he grinned sympathetically.

'It's the relief,' she gasped. 'Felix, I thought you might be dead and there's so much I need to know.'

He was silent, still holding her hand, staring out across the sunny garden, and, looking at him closely now, she saw how frail he was. Her hold tightened as anxiety clutched at her heart and he turned his head, his eyes narrowing with amusement as if to dismiss her fear.

'That sounds a rather tall order,' he said lightly. 'I warn you that I shall draw the line if you become too inquisitive.'

She relaxed a little. 'I don't know where to begin,' she admitted. 'OK, yes, I do. How did you come to have the birdcage? I saw it, you know, last night after dinner. It was . . . so strange. I'd been looking for it in Bristol and wondering what Pidge had done with it. Did she give it to you?'

Felix nodded. 'After Angel died, she wrote to me, telling me that Angel wanted me to have it . . .'

'As a keepsake?' prompted Lizzie, as the pause lengthened. 'But why? After all that time and since she was dead . . . sorry, I just can't see why.'

'The parting was a painful one,' said Felix. He looked distressed. 'It was my fault. There were reasons . . . but I think the birdcage was her way of letting me know that she'd forgiven me at the end.'

Some people came out of the door from the church and began to move about the garden, talking in lowered voices and gesturing at the flowers. Felix watched them for a moment and then turned to Lizzie.

'Would you come back and have tea with me?' he asked. 'I'm taking it for granted that you're staying somewhere round here? On holiday?'

'I came to find you,' she answered. 'I'm staying at the Luttrell Arms. I'd love to have tea with you, Felix, it's just . . . well, I saw your son this morning, leaving the flat. Does he know about me? Is it OK if he comes in and finds me with you?'

Felix had risen to his feet and now stood regarding her across the sundial with a kind of shocked surprise.

'You saw Piers this morning?'

'Piers!' exclaimed Lizzie. '*That* was his name!'

'But how could you possibly know it was him?'

'Oh, Felix,' she shook her head at him, 'I came to Dunster to find you. And first I saw the birdcage hanging in the window and then I saw Piers coming out of the flat. Apart from the fact that he looks pretty much like how I remembered you, there wasn't too much detective work required. Mind you, I put two and two together and made a rather staggering total. I assumed that he lived in the flat. That's why I said I thought you were dead. I couldn't see why Piers would have the birdcage otherwise.'

Felix, his heart sinking, imagined Piers coming back with the mended spectacles, being introduced to Lizzie. Lizzie watched him, guessing his thoughts.

'He doesn't know, does he?' she asked soberly.

'He knows that Angel and I were lovers. He has never been able to . . .' Felix cast about for the right phrase, 'come to terms with the fact that I was unfaithful to his mother. It might not be a very easy meeting.' He looked at his wrist-watch and straightened his shoulders, as if coming to a decision. 'It's barely three o'clock and Piers won't be here until after six. Plenty of time for some tea. Come along.'

He held out his arm to her, sketching a little bow, and they set off together along the gravelled path.

CHAPTER TWENTY-FIVE

Tilda poured tea into two blue and white mugs, feeling a mix of emotions as she watched her mother cradling Jake in her arms, talking to him.

'He's smiling at me,' she said delightedly. 'See, Tilda? You know, he's really got a look of David about him.'

'Yes,' agreed Tilda after a tiny pause. 'Yes, he's a real little Hamilton.'

Teresa Burton cast a quick questioning look at her daughter. 'Oh, darling,' she said remorsefully. 'I'm sorry. I just wasn't thinking . . .'

'Oh, don't!' cried Tilda, almost crossly. 'Don't, Ma. It's fine. Honestly. Jake *does* look like David. I want him to.'

'Of course you do,' murmured Teresa, touching her grandson's fist, feeling the powerful clutch of the tiny fingers. 'But it doesn't help you to get over it, does it? Not with this reminder so constantly with you.'

'I don't want to get over David,' said Tilda fiercely. 'I love him. He was everything to me and I don't want him to be air-brushed out of my life as if he never existed.'

Teresa settled Jake, fiddling with his little T-shirt,

uncomfortable as she often was in the face of Tilda's passion. She'd never been as much at ease with her older daughter as she'd been with Julia: but then, Teresa reminded herself, Tilda was her father's child. Where Julia – so like herself – was biddable, open to advice, Tilda had always been stubborn. Justin had backed her up, undermining her mother's influence, encouraging Tilda to be headstrong.

'I shall marry David,' she'd said when she was six – and so she had, despite her mother's warnings of the problems of being a soldier's wife. Teresa pursed her lips as she bent over Jake, murmuring to him. It wasn't that she hadn't liked David, quite the contrary; in fact, when she'd been a young woman she'd had quite a serious crush on Piers: all the Hamilton men had something special about them. The fact remained, however, that from his birth upward it was clear that David was going to be a handful: if there were anything difficult or dangerous going, then David was up for it. Remembering, Teresa couldn't help smiling to herself. He'd been irresistible in that indefinable, attractive, sexy Hamilton way – but a worrying prospect as a son-in-law. She'd pointed all this out to Justin but he'd refused to attempt to persuade Tilda to wait a few years; to enjoy her job in London as a PA to the director of an advertising agency; to meet other men. He'd been so proud of David, sure that he had a brilliant career ahead of him in the army. What a tragedy then that, after the tour in Bosnia, he should have been killed in a car accident half a mile from home; what a pointless waste of his life.

'I'm not suggesting that you should forget him.' Teresa took her mug of tea. 'Of course not, but—'

'But what?' Tilda sat down opposite and looked at her challengingly, though she smiled at her mother, remembering her conversation with Gemma earlier.

Teresa looked back at her daughter's lovely face, seeking for words that were neither banal nor instructive.

'I just care about you,' she said at last, defensively.

'Oh, Ma, I know you do.' Tilda sighed with frustration. 'Now I've got Jake I'm beginning to understand, at last, how you've felt about me and Jules all these years. It must be hell watching your children deliberately taking risks or putting themselves into danger. I'd kill anyone who hurt Jake and I can see just how easy it would be to wrap him up in loving, caring, smothering bubble-wrap and never let him out of my sight. Don't think I don't know what you want for me.'

'I just want you to be . . . sensible,' muttered Teresa.

'I know.' Tilda grinned at her. 'How d'you spell it?'

Teresa smiled unwillingly. 'Hopeless,' she said. 'Just like your father . . . Have you heard from him?'

'I had a postcard of the Yorkshire Moors a couple of days ago. You'll be glad to get the house sold up so that you can join him, won't you, although I shall miss you. He said that he's booked out a few days' holiday for Jake's baptism in September so you must let me know if you want to stay here with us. We'll probably be having one or two people overnight. Saul will be staying, of course.'

'Saul.' Teresa put down her mug and stared at Tilda. She repeated the name brightly, as if this was a whole new idea to her. 'Now that's nice. I'm very fond of Saul.'

'So am I,' agreed Tilda calmly. 'And of course he was David's greatest chum, which is why he's going to be Jake's godfather. Did I tell you he's coming down next weekend for the party?'

'Yes, you did say something about it.' Teresa hesitated, longing to ask a few questions, took one look at Tilda's warning expression and beamed at her instead. 'That'll be fun for you, darling. Piers is a sweetie but it's good to have people of your own age around and Saul is just the person to . . . well,' she hesitated beneath the steady gaze, 'to take you out of yourself. I mean,' she went on hurriedly, 'that it's good to have a change.'

'You're hopeless, Ma,' said Tilda good-naturedly. 'I know

just what you mean – in fact Gemma and I were discussing it this morning. It's a pity she couldn't come to lunch. I told you that she sent her love, didn't I?'

'You did,' said Teresa. 'I should like to see her again. Such a pretty girl.' She shook her head. 'I must admit that I had my doubts about that marriage.'

'She and Guy had known each other for ever,' protested Tilda. 'Just like me and David.'

'I don't think that it was quite the same. Gemma was always such a naughty girl and, though I don't know Guy very well, he seems a rather forbidding young man. He makes me feel nervous, quite unlike Saul. You'd never imagine that Saul and Gemma were brother and sister, would you? She's so blonde and he's so dark.'

Tilda remembered Gemma's remark. 'Do you think he's too kind?'

Teresa looked at her, puzzled. 'Too kind? Can anyone be too kind?'

'Gemma thinks so. She says that the unknown quality is what women like in men.'

'The unknown quality: how typical of Gemma,' Teresa snorted scornfully. 'Oh, we might *think* we want the challenge of a man with a reputation, we flatter ourselves that we're the one who will reform him, but when we're two months into our first pregnancy what we long for is the kind of man who will boost our morale and make us feel good.' She hesitated. 'The truth of the matter is that women don't know what they want and I have to admit,' said Teresa with the air of one who is trying to be fair, 'that I've always felt that it's rather unreasonable for women to expect men to know that today it's the time of the month when we'd like to be dragged upstairs and made passionate love to but tomorrow we'll want to sit in a corner feeling tearful and needing someone to make us cups of tea.'

'Well,' said Tilda lightly, rather taken aback by her mother's unexpected burst of outspokenness, 'I have to agree with you and, though I can't say that David was a great hand at making cups of tea when I had PMT, he *did* have a certain unknown quality.'

Teresa smiled down at the sleeping baby. 'He certainly did. So Saul will be staying here and Felix will need a bed for the night, won't he? Are you sure that it will be OK for me to stay overnight?'

'Of course it will. And what do you think of my plan to get Piers a puppy for his birthday? Don't you think it's a great idea? Alison totally disapproves.'

This last remark was quite enough to distract Teresa from any thoughts of Saul; Alison, as an in-comer, was poaching on old preserves and Teresa disliked her on principle.

'I think it's a splendid idea,' she said warmly. 'Piers has always had a dog about although Joker was very special, wasn't he?'

'Joker connected him with Sue and David,' said Tilda rather sadly. 'He was a kind of continuum when everything was falling apart and he helped Piers to get through some very dark times. When Joker died it was rather as if a whole era had come to an end. Poor old Piers was absolutely gutted. He wept buckets when he thought no-one was looking and I think that it enabled him to grieve for everything at once. Queer, isn't it, that you feel you can weep and despair over an animal's death when you can't if it's a person? Joker's death released some of the pain for him. His bed's still there.'

'I always look for him when I drive in.' Teresa blotted a tear or two of her own. 'He used to lie out in the sunshine in the garth when he got old and couldn't go about with Piers any longer. Poor old Piers really has had a rough ride one way and another. Sue was terrific fun but she was utterly exhausting, about half an hour of her company was quite enough, and, of course, his mother was such a difficult woman. Very possessive and tough as old boots.'

'Did you get on with her?' asked Tilda, her curiosity roused. 'I can remember her a bit. She was here, in those days, of course, and Piers and Sue were in the cottage in Porlock. I came out with David a few times when he was small, to visit her and Felix, and I remember her as being fearfully distant and terribly critical. Felix was quite different.'

'Oh, everyone adored Felix but Marina was a real cold fish,' said Teresa. 'Piers always gave the impression that he stood between them as a kind of mediator – awful for a child – and then Sue came along and simply took him out of it. She was like some Act of God, sweeping everything before her. There was a crusading spirit about her which was difficult to resist. Of course, Marina was awful to her. She was terribly jealous of all Piers' girl-friends but Sue simply took no notice of her. I'm not certain that Piers ever knew quite what hit him.'

'But wasn't it extraordinary that she should just pack it all in and go off to the States like that?' Tilda shook her head. 'It was so . . . unexpected.'

'It was typical of Sue. She was completely committed to whatever it was she was doing at the time. She started her little business when David went away to school, you know, and it was then that she realized that she had a real flair for business. It was typical that she managed to run her shop and still be such a dedicated wife and mother, but once David went into the army those wifely, maternal instincts simply seemed to have burned out. That scene came to its natural end and she turned her whole attention to building up her business and expanding it abroad. It was a very amicable separation.'

'She was so good at being a mum, that's what made it so odd,' said Tilda. 'She was so competent and kind and they were all so happy here at Michaelgarth. And then, finish!'

'Does Piers miss her?' asked Teresa curiously.

Tilda wrinkled her nose thoughtfully. 'I don't think he does, not really. Or, at least, only as you miss something you've got used to and rather liked. He's certainly not heart-broken.'

'That's what I thought,' agreed Teresa. 'I think that Sue was a kind of bridge for him, away from Marina's clutches, and that in an odd kind of way the break was right for him too. I agree, he's never seemed heart-broken or angry, just happy to move on. Although I understand that Alison is trying to worm her way in.'

'Oh, don't,' said Tilda involuntarily. 'She's a nice person, actually, but she's just not right for Piers.'

'What does he *see* in her?'

'Well, she lost her husband at about the time that David died and I think he feels sorry for her and now he's got himself a bit stuck.'

'That's just so like Piers,' sighed Teresa. 'Marina got him into the mind-set of feeling guilty if he doesn't please women at all costs and he's still in the habit of it. He'll simply have to unstick himself. I think a puppy is an excellent start.'

'I know Piers is thinking about getting one but it's as if he can't quite bring himself to do it yet. You don't think it's too soon after Joker?'

'No, I don't, but I think it might be difficult for Piers to actually do it for himself. He needs to be bounced into it.'

'That's what I thought.'

They looked at each other, smiling in complete accord.

'Jake's gone to sleep,' said Tilda. 'Put him in his chair and he'll sleep for an hour at least, and I'll show you the clothes that Sue has sent for him from the States. I have to say that she's got style. They're really cool.'

The telephone bell startled them: Teresa instinctively cradled the sleeping baby so that he shouldn't be woken whilst Tilda snatched up the receiver.

'Hello? Oh, hello, Piers . . . OK, that's fine . . . Ma's here with me, actually . . . Yes, I'll tell her. Love to Felix. See you.'

'It's OK,' Teresa put Jake gently into his chair. 'It didn't wake him up.'

'Piers sends his love and says, "Are you staying to supper?" He's dropping in on Felix and then meeting a client for a quick half in the pub but he won't be late and he'd love to see you.'

'That's very sweet of him,' said Teresa, gratified. 'Would I be a nuisance?'

'Don't be daft.' Tilda slipped an arm about her mother's shoulders, giving her a quick hug. 'Come on upstairs and see Jake's new gear and then I'll put you to peeling vegetables. There's no such thing as a free supper at Michaelgarth.'

CHAPTER TWENTY-SIX

Felix moved quietly about the flat, carrying the tea-things into the long, narrow kitchen – his galley – putting the biscuit tin away in the cupboard. The half-glazed door opened on to the large square platform of an iron staircase and here bloomed a tiny garden of roses, miniature specimens in pots and tubs. He'd cut a perfect yellow bud for Lizzie.

'Put it in your tooth-glass,' he'd said. 'It'll be in full flower by tomorrow.'

She'd taken it, brushing it across her lips, smiling at him. 'And you'll come and have dinner with me?' His hesitation had been unmistakable. 'You promised.'

He'd nodded and, understanding his anxiety but refusing to let him retract, she'd kissed him and gone away. Now, as he washed the cups and saucers, rinsed out the teapot, his thoughts were full of conflicting emotions. How good it had been, how energizing, to talk openly about the past they'd shared, to fill in some of the gaps. Yet for both of them it was as if Piers were in the room with them, his imminent arrival colouring and reshaping their memories.

'Why?' Lizzie asked, standing beside the birdcage, staring in.

'I'd never really thought about that before, Felix. Not about *why* you and Angel began an affair. It just seemed so right, somehow. You belonged with us, that's how it felt, and yet you had another family.'

He stood beside her, looking at the fluffy chick, perched beside the two little birds; one with its head flung back, beak open in joyous song, whilst the other listened intently, head on one side.

'To explain all that I'd have to tell you how my marriage was,' he answered at last, 'and that's very difficult. Not because I don't want you to know but because it must necessarily be one-sided. I can only tell you how it was for me. Marina isn't here to put her side of the picture. I can only say that I wasn't a serial adulterer. Angel was my only . . . love.'

Lizzie, taking a last look into the birdcage, sat herself down in the other wing-chair.

'Tell me about Marina. Tell me how it all started . . .'

Now, drying the cups carefully, putting them in the cupboard above the working surface, he wondered if he'd managed to be fair. He'd attempted to explain how it had begun: how he had grown to love Marina because she had first loved him and how he'd truly believed that she simply needed to be given the encouragement to allow her confidence to build; that he'd been certain that, with his love to lean against, she could overcome her shyness. He'd tried not to put all the blame on Marina's jealousy, her inability to show physical affection, the silences, but he'd shown how social events had become fraught with dangers because of his friendliness and how innocent conversations were so readily misunderstood.

'Perhaps I should have been more vigilant,' he said. 'I'm sure I caused her pain although it was difficult to know quite how to handle it. But it wasn't simply that I grew tired of being continually judged as a lecherous swine and resented it, the fact is that when I saw Angel I simply fell in love with her. It wasn't just a physical thing. It was as if we recognized each other in some way and there is no doubt in my mind that, if I had been free, I should have asked her to marry me.'

'Were you ever tempted to leave Marina?' Lizzie asked.

'Oh, my dear girl,' he answered sadly, 'each time I left you all I wondered if I were crazy. All that love and laughter and warmth. But there was Piers, you see. Even if I could have brought myself to abandon Marina, I could never have given up my son.' He looked at her quickly, fearful that she might be feeling hurt that he'd been prepared to leave her and Angel, but there was only compassion in her face. 'I loved you,' he told her. 'You were so dear to me, Lizzie, but it was as if you and Angel and Pidge were another world, a different life. Can you understand that? I know that men are able to compart-mentalize their lives in a way that doesn't come easily to most women, and I don't explain or excuse it.' He smiled ruefully, self-mockingly. 'Perhaps I just wanted my cake as well as eating it.'

'And so what happened? Why did you give us up?'

'Marina found out,' he said. 'I think she'd suspected for some time but there was . . . a confrontation between her and Angel. She'd brought you down for a holiday . . .'

She nodded. 'I can remember it, you know. We saw Marina with Piers in a shop – I've no idea which one. I've been looking for it but I can't recognize it although I can remember the smells. Coffee and cheese and stuff like that.'

'Parhams,' he said at once. 'Good God, Lizzie! But how could you have been so certain? You were only seven or eight years old.'

'There was a kind of electric current which seemed to sizzle between them,' she answered, 'and they glared at each other like two cats. Angel squeezed my hand really tightly and I remember staring at the little boy and knowing that he felt that something was wrong too. There was so much tension. But how could Angel have known who they were? Or Marina, for that matter? That's what I've asked myself so many times.'

'They'd met twice, backstage at the theatre and at a party.' He sighed heavily. 'It was a crazy thing to do, to come down on holiday. I knew nothing about it and when Marina confronted me about it I was absolutely thunderstruck. When two worlds collide it has a devastating effect and that's when I saw that I'd have to stop.'

'But it didn't stop then, did it?'

He shook his head. 'I tried to give you up but I failed. In some ways it was easier because Angel was between contracts with the Old Vic and just after that holiday she began working at one of the other classical reps so the whole scene changed anyway. I told myself that it didn't hurt anyone if I continued to visit you and Pidge, and I'm afraid that Angel and I still met up occasionally. Then she came back to Bristol and someone saw us together. Marina gave me an ultimatum.'

'Her and Piers, or Angel, Pidge and me?'

'Oh, darling,' he said wretchedly, 'just don't think it was easy. Telling Angel, trying to explain . . .' and she got up, kneeling beside him so that he put his arm about her whilst staring away the hot, weak tears that burned his eyes.

Felix swiped at them with the tea-towel, cursing himself, glancing at his wrist-watch: nearly a quarter to six. The relief and joy of talking with Lizzie were beginning to fade before the daunting prospect of Piers' arrival. How would he be able to behave naturally with his son after such a meeting? In some ways he felt that he'd betrayed Piers by talking to Lizzie so freely, but he couldn't imagine how it could have been otherwise. Lizzie had the right to a place in his life, to make demands. Yet Piers had rights too: to know that Lizzie had been here and who she was.

'Shall you tell him?' she'd asked almost fearfully.

'Should you mind? It would be wonderful if everything

could be open and above-board but I simply don't know how to begin. He has always been very loyal to Marina and I can't imagine how he might take it.'

'He looks nice, Felix.' She'd sounded rather wistful. 'I wish we could be friends. Does that sound that crazy? Well, I am crazy. Mad as several hatters.'

They'd laughed together, ease slipping between them once more.

'I liked the sitcom,' he'd told her. 'I can't tell you how proud I was.'

She'd grinned at him. 'Aha!' she'd said. 'So *that* was how you recognized me. All this waffle about second sight . . .'

She was so like Angel when she smiled. When he'd tried to talk about her own life, however, the smile had faded.

'Don't ask,' she'd replied sombrely. 'Angel, Pidge, Sam. Oh, Felix, I've lost them all.'

She'd got up then, saying that she must go before Piers arrived, pressing him to have dinner later with her at the hotel.

'Good luck with Piers,' she'd said. 'But the timing still might not be right. Play it by ear.'

Nervous now, praying for guidance, Felix went back to the window to stand beside the birdcage, watching for his son. As he saw him at last, coming up from The Steep with that familiar stride, Felix was filled with fear. The mere sight of him, the sheer reality of that hurrying, purposeful figure, made nonsense of the rehearsed phrases and carefully framed apologies: yet he must make the attempt. He'd betrayed both Piers and Lizzie and now the time had come to repair the damage he'd done.

Felix pressed the button that released the door catch and Piers came in, taking the stairs two at a time, the spectacles case in one hand, his briefcase under his arm.

'Sorry, I'm late,' he said rather breathlessly. 'A bit of a drama at the office and then the traffic was very heavy. Look, I've had to arrange to meet a client so I can't stop more than a minute. Just check them and make certain they're OK.'

Felix took the case and examined the spectacles, trying them on.

'Perfect,' he said. 'I can't tell you how grateful I am. Are you sure you can't stay? I rather hoped I could discuss something with you.'

'I simply can't right now, Father. It's very important that I catch him – it's John Clarke, remember him? – and I thought I'd kill two birds with one stone . . . if you see what I mean?'

He grimaced as if apologizing for his clumsiness and Felix smiled understandingly, laying his hand lightly on Piers' shoulder.

'Don't give it a thought, my dear boy. Thank you so much for these . . . I suppose you couldn't come in afterwards?'

'I'm sorry, Father,' Piers looked harassed, 'but the fact is Tilda's got Teresa with her and I suggested that she might like to stay for supper. It'll look a bit rude if I'm too late and I have no idea how long John might need.'

'I quite understand. Perhaps tomorrow? It's rather important. Will you telephone? It was good of you to come in . . .'

He saw him down the stairs, sending his love to Tilda, and went back to the window, feeling ashamed of his huge relief at being let temporarily off the hook, wondering how to arrange another meeting with Piers as soon as possible. Despite this welcome respite, he knew that he simply couldn't let it slide – if nothing else, Lizzie's presence required speedy action – but it was difficult to see how to achieve his goal.

He saw Piers appear from below him, raised his hand in a salute and remained, transfixed in shocked horror, his hand still upheld as he watched him cross the road and disappear into the porch of the Luttrell Arms.

CHAPTER TWENTY-SEVEN

Refreshed by a shower, Lizzie pottered between bathroom and bedroom, trying to decide what to wear for dinner with Felix. She was buoyed up with a sense of wild elation: she'd found him – and the birdcage – and simply being there in his flat, talking with him, had eased the loneliness that had haunted her for the last few months. His evident delight in her company had given her confidence a boost and – despite her anxiety about Piers – she'd felt an uprush of high spirits.

Crooning to herself 'Can't Help Loving that Man of Mine', hamming it up as she wound the springing tendrils of her thick mass of hair into a low knot at the back of her neck, she sat for a moment staring at herself in the mirror. She made a few faces – it never ceased to amaze her how easily one set of features could be changed into so many different expressions – and wondered how Felix was managing with Piers, trying to imagine what his reaction would be: how he would feel when Felix began to disinter the past. She could picture the scene – Felix in his wing-chair with Piers sitting opposite – but with what words, she wondered, would the scene begin? She tried a few phrases and dismissed them as over-dramatic or pathetically banal. It became clear to her that it would be very difficult for Felix to advance without antagonizing Piers almost at once.

'By the way, you remember that mistress I had when you were a boy . . . ?' or, 'You'll never guess who's in Dunster, Piers . . .'

How would he explain her presence without it sounding impossibly contrived?

'Well, you see Pidge and Angel died quite a while back and when she lost her husband she decided to . . .'

To what? To seek out her mother's lover? After thirty-five years? She could imagine the sceptical look on Piers' face; his 'oh, yeah!' expression. He might think that she and Felix had been in contact since Angel's death and even believe that the affair itself had gone on much longer than Felix had admitted. When she'd asked how he'd explained the presence of the birdcage to his son, Felix had told her that Piers had never asked about it, behaving as if some instinct warned him against seeking an answer that might hurt him.

Slowly her ebullience began to subside beneath a wave of compassion for Piers. It was one thing knowing his father had had an affair, quite another for the mistress's daughter suddenly to appear on the scene. She pulled the towelling robe more closely around her, suddenly chilly, although the evening was still warm. Surely talking about those happenings of so long ago couldn't be too painful? Lizzie shook her head: remembering Felix's face, knowing that this was simply wishful thinking. The trouble with burying emotions very deeply was that, once re-exposed, they were liable to be fresh and raw and every bit as sensitive as when they'd first been hidden beneath thick layers of denial. Even Felix, who was ready to accept the damaging results of his behaviour, had clearly found it difficult to talk to her about certain aspects of the past. How much more daunting it would be to have this dialogue with Piers.

Lizzie began to feel that she needed a drink. She looked at her wrist-watch: not yet half-past six and a good hour and a half until she met with Felix. It had been thoughtless of her to insist on that meeting, knowing that he was to have such an encounter, yet it had been such a joy to see him again that she'd hated leaving him without his promise. Pulling on her jeans, together with a loose linen overshirt, Lizzie tucked her big key into her bag and went downstairs.

The heavily beamed room, with its only window looking into a high-walled court, was dim and it wasn't until she was at the bar, ready to order, that she saw Piers beyond the shoulder of a burly fellow with his back to her, who was leaning with his elbow on the wooden counter. Piers was listening intently, watching his pint, but as Lizzie moved into his line of sight, he raised his eyes and looked at her.

Their glances locked with an impact that shocked each of them equally. His face brightened, as if in recognition – and even pleasure. She instinctively smiled back at him and then, swiftly pulling herself together, she looked away – *slowly, count the beat, don't overdo it* – still smiling, though rather vaguely now, as if embracing the other occupants of the bar with the same casual friendliness. The young barman moved towards her, greeting her cheerfully, but even as he mixed her vodka and tonic, adding the ice and slice of lemon, she was aware of Piers' attention. His companion – noticing that sudden change of expression – had glanced briefly over his shoulder but was now continuing his conversation whilst Piers, though taking his part, still watched her as she took her drink to the small table near the door.

Her heart beating like a clock, Lizzie sat down. Unable to resist, she looked at him again: again that impact! Calmly, she opened her bag and took out the novel she'd put in earlier as a protection against the chatty couple and, opening it, began to read at random. The words jumbled meaninglessly before her eyes whilst her thoughts scrambled about inside her head: it was impossible that he should be so balanced, so ready to be friendly, after such an interview. After all, there was no-one else present with whom he could confuse her and yet he watched her with such ease and, she had no doubt of it, a readiness to speak to her once his drinking companion finished his conversation. Her stomach churned at the prospect and she seized her glass and drank some vodka.

At this moment the friendly couple came into the bar and immediately embarked upon a series of proprietorial enquiries. They hoped that the walk to the church hadn't tired her further? She *was* looking more rested. They were meeting up with friends but would be thrilled if she felt she could join them. She couldn't? A guest to dinner? Oh, they quite understood. Perhaps another time?

Hardly were they seated at a table just behind Piers when their friends arrived; there was a great deal of cheerful greeting, followed by a matey jostling as to which of the males should get the first round in, and at last they all sat down together. Pretending to be absorbed in her book, Lizzie was aware of their little nods in her direction, their voices lowered now as they boasted of their acquaintance with her. The second couple stared across the bar in undisguised interest and Lizzie could feel a faint wash of colour rising in her cheeks. Presently the burly man shook Piers' hand and went out and Piers, picking up his glass, came towards her.

She glanced up at him with the merest lifting of brows, a faint suggestion of surprise, almost enquiry – 'After all,' she told herself grimly, 'I *am* an actress' – but he smiled down at her so openly that she could feel her facial muscles relaxing into a wide answering beam.

It's OK, she told herself, weak with relief. He knows and it's OK.

'You must think I'm a bit of a prat,' he said – oh, how like Felix's voice his was – 'to stare at you like that. You know, I really thought I recognized you—'

'Oh, I know,' she interrupted eagerly, 'I felt exactly the same.'

'And then I heard that couple talking,' he went on, 'and I realized that I *did* recognize you but not the way I imagined. You must be sick to death of people forcing a conversational opening on the strength of it but I have to say I love the advert and that brilliant sitcom.'

'Thank you,' she said after a moment. 'That's . . . so kind. Actually, I'm a very sad person and I love it when people recognize me.' Her voice gathered strength as she recovered from the shock, realizing that he had no idea who she was in relation to Felix and wondering how he'd described her without mentioning her acting career. 'I wish I could be blasé about it but it's a very nice change to be known, actually.'

'How refreshingly honest.' He hesitated, glancing at the empty chair, and she indicated that he should join her. 'I've never met a celebrity before so you mustn't mind if I rather revel in it.'

She chuckled. 'You haven't met one now,' she told him, 'but thanks, anyway.'

'But you were saying that you felt the same thing? Sorry, I just wanted to get my explanation in first so that you knew where I was coming from. Did you think you recognized me too?'

She stared at him: if she said no, then later he must discover that it wasn't true. Confused, with no time to think clearly, she nevertheless felt very strongly that it would be quite wrong to lie to him.

'Yes,' she said. 'Yes. I recognized you. You're very much like your father, Piers.'

He gave a little crack of delighted laughter. 'This is the first time that I can honestly say that I'm very pleased to hear it. But how do you know my name? Look here, this is very mysterious.'

It was at this point she understood that the confrontation

with Felix hadn't taken place: that Piers had made no connections because there were none to be made.

'I knew your father when I was a little girl,' she told him, cursing herself for her stupidity, for not realizing at once that he couldn't have spoken to Felix about her. 'I haven't seen him for thirty-five years but I met him again this afternoon in that little memorial garden behind the church. My name is Lizzie Blake. My mother was Angelica Blake, the actress.'

His warmth had faded visibly as she spoke, and now he watched her warily. She was grateful that his back was turned to the other occupants of the bar and was careful to keep her own expression pleasant so that no-one should guess that anything might be amiss.

'You met this afternoon? By chance?'

'I came to Dunster to find him,' she answered steadily. 'I had no idea whether I would be able to track him down. It was . . . extraordinary to discover that he was so close.'

'Extraordinary,' he agreed drily.

'I took him completely by surprise and we talked about old times but I know that he wanted to tell you about my unexpected arrival,' she'd nearly said 'warn', and bit her lip. 'He said that you were calling in and he would explain it to you.'

As she listened to her voice saying all the wrong things she watched the battle of anger and fairness being played out on his face; noticed the hand resting on the table clench itself into a fist, the thumb caught between the middle fingers.

'I didn't give him the chance,' he said at last. 'I was in a rush and there was no opportunity.'

'I am so sorry, Piers,' she said. 'I know that it's not easy – and you'll probably think it was quite wrong and tasteless of me to come here – but I did rather hope that, after all this time, we might be friends.'

He gave a little smiling frown, as if such a suggestion was preposterous, yet he didn't speak. Instead he picked up his glass and finished his beer in one swallow.

'After all,' he spoke as if he were finishing off some kind of debate with himself, 'none of it was your fault.'

'No,' she agreed, 'but then it wasn't yours, either.'

'That's true.' He looked at her with a hard, bright look. 'But it doesn't really change anything, does it? Will you forgive me if I disappear? I think I should have that talk with my father after all.'

She watched him go – and then turned back to see the other residents gazing at her with interest. Guessing that she was to be invited to join them for a drink, she smiled brightly, indicating the time, ruefully indicating the need to hurry away and change for dinner. She stood up and, taking her glass with her, went upstairs to her room.

CHAPTER TWENTY-EIGHT

Piers crossed the High Street, without glancing up, and took the stairs two at a time. Felix was waiting for him by the window.

He thought: It has come at last. It is now . . .

'I changed my mind,' Piers said, still standing near the door. 'I thought that perhaps we'd better have that talk after all.'

'You met Lizzie.' It was better, Felix thought, to be direct: no stumbling about in a morass of pretended misunderstandings or apologies. 'I hoped to prepare you but it never occurred to me that you were meeting John Clarke in the Luttrell Arms. It must have been rather a shock.'

'Just a bit.' Piers' voice was brittle. 'I made an utter fool of myself, actually.'

Felix frowned, surprised. 'How was that? I guessed that you'd met or else you probably wouldn't be here now but . . . did she introduce herself?'

'Oh, no, don't worry, *she* didn't make the running. I introduced myself to her. I recognized her from that advert, you see, although I couldn't quite place her at first, but when

I realized I went dashing up like a dog with a bone, positively delighted.'

'It was a natural enough thing to do.' Felix kept his voice deliberately flat, aware that Piers was scorching with embarrassment, trying to remove the sting from his humiliation. 'Of course, being Lizzie, she'd have been thrilled that you recognized her professionally. Success is rather new to her, I gather.'

'I can't say that her gratification is of paramount significance to me,' Piers said angrily. 'There are other issues which are rather more important.'

'I quite agree,' said Felix quietly. 'I was simply making an observation about Lizzie's probable reaction. This is the very last thing she wanted to happen, although she was so hoping to meet you at some point. From what she told me I gather that she lost her husband recently and the shock and the loneliness has made her introspective; going back over the past and trying to remember certain things. She decided to look me up, came down on spec and we met quite by chance in the memorial garden. I promised that I would explain her presence here to you when I saw you, so by the time you introduced yourself she would have assumed we'd had this talk.' He gave a frustrated snort. 'She must be feeling pretty confused too. I hope she was . . . intelligent about it.'

Piers was silent for a moment, apparently reflecting on their meeting. 'To be honest,' he said slowly, 'she was. I . . . liked her.'

Felix stood quite still with his hands in his pockets. Aware of a huge liking for his son and great admiration, yet he remained where he was, waiting for Piers to make the next move. Finally Piers raised his head and looked at him.

'Is she my sister?' he asked.

Shocked and dismayed, Felix withdrew his hands from his pocket and held them out in an involuntary gesture of absolute denial.

'Good God, no! Of course she isn't. My dear boy . . .' He remembered the scene with Marina – her question: *I suppose she isn't yours, by any chance?* and the shadow by the door – and closed his eyes in a moment's pain: all these years, Piers had lived with this terrible suspicion. 'My dear boy,' he murmured again, 'I swear to you that there is absolutely no question of that. Lizzie was at least six years old when I first met her.'

Piers took a deep, deep breath and gave a gasping sigh; his shoulders seemed to sag a little and Felix moved forward, taking him by the arm, almost pushing him down into the wing-chair. He began to talk, pouring two shots of whisky, needing to tide them over this dangerous moment.

'They were living in a funny old house in Bristol up near the university. Pidge lived in a flat on the ground floor and Angel and Lizzie rented the first floor and the attic. It was a bit of an odd set-up but it worked very well for all three of them. Pidge could look after Lizzie when Angel was at the theatre.'

As he clattered about with glasses and the decanter, he shot a swift glance at Piers: he sat quite still, staring at nothing in particular, his hands clenched into fists resting on his thighs.

'To make sense of it I shall have to tell you who Lizzie's father was or it might give the wrong impression, but you must give me your word that you don't repeat it to Lizzie.' Piers looked at him, frowning but concentrating now. 'Her father was General Sir Hilary Carmichael.' Felix nodded a confirmation in response to Piers' disbelieving expression. 'Angel never told me his name but I guessed very quickly. He was a war hero with a tragic private life. His wife had been badly hurt in a riding accident. She was not only a cripple, her brain had been damaged in the fall, but he looked after her as well as he could and refused to let her be put away into some institution. I knew of him during the war, of course, he was tremendously popular amongst the troops and everyone called him "Mike", rather like everyone called Montgomery "Monty". Angel simply referred to him as Mike, but once she'd described his background I knew who it was. Pidge had been his driver at the end of the war and he told her when the flat fell empty at the house in Bristol. He owned it, you see. The family owned a great deal of property. Well, after the war he and Angel met and had an affair and, by mismanagement or bad luck, Angel became pregnant. Mike had been very clear that there was no future for her with him and she accepted the situation but decided that she wanted to have the baby. Mike was prepared to support Lizzie financially, up to a point, and saw to it that Pidge and Angel got together in the house in Bristol. Lizzie thinks that the house was Pidge's and that she left it to her when she died but it was simply another of Mike's ways of looking after his daughter.'

Felix pushed the tumbler into Piers' hand and took a much-needed sip from his own glass.

'And Lizzie never asked questions about it?'

Deeply relieved that his ploy to distract appeared to be working, Felix sat down opposite.

'I don't think so. She accepted what Angel told her: that her father was a soldier and he was killed in Korea. Angel and Pidge went so far as to say that he was a King's Messenger, which Mike was at one point and which added a certain lustre to the story, but you have to remember that Lizzie would have grown up amongst war orphans. I think she longed for a father but, as far as I know, she never questioned their version of him.'

'And you fulfilled the role? Up to a point?' His voice was dry.

'If I did then it was inadequately.' Felix wondered how much of the truth should be told and decided to hold nothing back. 'She suggested once that I might like to be her father but I explained that I couldn't, that I was one already. She wanted to know all about you.' He stared down into his glass so that he shouldn't know whether his son was disgusted or angry at this breach of confidence. 'I haven't seen her since she was ten or eleven years old.'

'Four years. You were lovers for *four years*?'

Felix bit his lip. 'Not in the sense you're probably imagining. Angel was lucky to have two or three seasons with the Old Vic in Bristol but after that she went off to one of the other classical repertory companies and I rarely saw her. But although she was away, in Manchester if I remember rightly, I still used to visit Pidge and Lizzie when I was in Bristol. I was fond of all of them, you see, it wasn't just . . . an affair.'

'But why?' At last the question was framed: his voice full of bitterness. 'How could you continue with the affair for so long when you saw how it hurt Mother?'

'Everything hurt her,' answered Felix slowly. 'To begin with it was puzzling when Marina refused to speak to me because I'd been friendly to another woman at a party or while paying a bill, or by simply holding a door open for a pretty girl. When I realized that she was a deeply jealous woman, I tried to help her out of it but nothing worked and, after a while, I was at a complete loss as to how to help her.'

'So you thought that having an affair might do the trick?'

Felix knew that it was Piers' own pain that infused the question with such a heavy note of sarcasm but, nevertheless, he felt a quick deep stab of anger.

'Don't be too quick to judge the frailties of other men,' he said. 'If you have never lived without affection or warmth, never been regularly subjected to icy silences and searing contempt as a punishment for acts of ordinary human kindness or friendliness, then you can't imagine how very lonely and isolated you can feel. Oh, yes, I know that I should have continued to manage without love, content in the knowledge that my wife was loyal, competent and a good mother, but I was weak. Please don't imagine that my affair with Angel was simply a matter of sex. I was offered love and warmth and laughter. There was friendship, human weakness, generosity – oh, so many tempting things in that little house with those three women and I accepted them gratefully.'

He realized that he was staring up at the birdcage and looked away, took another drink.

'The birdcage was theirs?' Piers' voice was unexpectedly gentle.

'Yes.' Felix blinked away a threatening sting of tears. 'Angel got it from somewhere – a prop room, I suspect – and the chick was added later. It was supposed to represent the three of them. Pidge's name triggered it off. She was Charlotte Pidgeon but nobody ever called her Charlotte. When Angel died she asked Pidge to give it to me as a keepsake. I hadn't heard from them for more than twenty years and it was a terrific shock. Angel can't have been much more than sixty when she died and Lizzie was married and living in London. I went to Bristol to collect it.'

'But why did she want you to have it? After all, it must have meant a great deal to Pidge too.' His voice was calm now, interested.

'The end of the affair was a very bitter one. Angel couldn't see why we shouldn't continue in the same way, and we parted badly. I think the birdcage was her way of showing that she'd forgiven me.'

'So why then, after all those years? What happened that broke it up?'

'Marina gave me an ultimatum. I'd tried before then to stop seeing them, after Angel very foolishly brought Lizzie here for a holiday and Marina saw them both. She'd met Angel twice, backstage and at a party, and it took a matter of seconds, I imagine, for her to guess the situation. It was at that time that Angel's contract had finished at the Old Vic in Bristol and she was going to be working in the north for a season. I thought it would do no harm to go on seeing Pidge and Lizzie but then

Angel turned up one weekend and it all started up again, but very spasmodically. Someone saw us together at the cinema in Bristol, mentioned it to Marina and that was that. She told me that she would divorce me and that I wouldn't be able to see you and so, in the end, there was no contest.'

The shrill sound of the telephone bell startled Felix into spilling his drink and he reached for the receiver, striving to keep his voice calm, praying that it wasn't Lizzie.

'Tilda.' He let out a breath of relief. 'Hello . . . Sorry? . . . Oh, yes, he's still with me. Would you like a word?'

He passed the phone to Piers and, wiping his fingers and the base of the tumbler on his handkerchief, went to stand by the window, staring out, wondering where Lizzie was and what she was thinking, imagining what a shock it must have been for her when Piers introduced himself. The touch on his shoulder made him jump.

'I'd quite forgotten about Teresa staying to supper.' Piers smiled a little. 'Not terribly surprising, I suppose, under the circumstances. I think it might be a good idea if I went home now, don't you? There's rather a lot to think about and I feel that we both need a bit of a break.'

Felix nodded, wondering how he should behave, his normal instincts hampered by a lack of confidence. He had no idea what Piers might be thinking and felt that it was his son's right to dictate the next move.

'That sounds very reasonable. I hope . . . I am so sorry, my dear boy . . .'

His voice faltered, suddenly he was exhausted, and Piers assisted him into his chair.

'Thank you for being so open,' he said. 'It can't have been easy. Rest now and I'll phone you in the morning.'

He kissed him lightly on the brow, as he always did, and went quietly away. Felix sat for some moments in silence, too tired to do more than think over all that had just been said, trying to remember Piers' reactions, hoping that he hadn't made a mess of it all. Quite suddenly – with a little stab of guilt – he thought again of Lizzie, remembering their dinner date, and, picking up the telephone, he dialled the number of the Luttrell Arms.

CHAPTER TWENTY-NINE

Back in her bedroom, Lizzie sat down shakily in the armchair by the window, placing her drink on the small nearby table. She couldn't concentrate – couldn't remember exactly what she'd said or how she'd reacted – she only knew that the whole scene had bombed: her timing had been rubbish, her gestures wildly under-rehearsed.

'A perfectly *bloody* performance,' she announced, using her old trick of making something seem less frightening – less important – if spoken aloud. 'In fact, I may have to shoot you. Bounding in there, grinning like some third-rate hooker the minute he looked at you . . .'

Her stomach contracted as she thought about the way she'd responded to his open, friendly look across the bar, recalling that sudden impact which had startled her into such an unguarded smile. And later, when he'd approached her, his unstudied opening remark had bounced her into dropping her careful defences, beaming madly at him like some demented schoolgirl . . .

Lizzie groaned aloud in humiliation, hot with shame, as she leaned forward to rest her head on her up-drawn knees as though to hide herself, but the scene continued to replay itself relentlessly before her inner eye. If only she'd kept her mouth shut, heard him out, but no, but no – she groaned again – she'd had to interrupt him, saying that she'd recognized him too. If only she'd had more sense she might have guessed that his reaction was all bound up in that wretched television advertisement and that he hadn't spoken to Felix after all.

Thinking of Felix had the effect of bringing her upright again, wondering how he was coping with Piers and what he might be saying to him. She picked up her glass and swallowed some of the now-warm vodka, trying to decide at what point she might risk telephoning him. She began to feel nervous and unconfident, fearing that her arrival in Dunster might be as divisive as Angel's was forty years before. She wondered what Angel had hoped to achieve or if it had simply been an impulsive moment of madness. Sipping her drink, Lizzie tried to imagine how Angel had viewed Felix's family; whether her need of him had outweighed any feelings of guilt. It occurred to her that, as a child, she'd assumed that it was perfectly reasonable for Felix to share himself between the two households – although two or three days once a month was hardly a fair distribution of his company – and although she'd longed for him to be her father she'd never resented the boy with the odd name who lived 'in the country' with his mother, rather, she'd been fascinated about him, longed to meet him. How odd that she should have done so, here in the shop in Dunster, without realizing at the time who he and the grim-faced woman were! That meeting had signalled the end of the affair.

It must have been almost as difficult for Pidge to adapt to the separation as it had been for Angel. It was clear that although Pidge had disapproved of that holiday in Dunster – . . . *you'll be relieved to know!* – *not a sign of F* . . . – nevertheless she'd always been pleased to see Felix at the Birdcage, welcoming him, joking with him, preparing a special supper. Certainly there had been no disapproving faces or making herself scarce: they'd been a little family together. It struck Lizzie that Angel must have been possessed of a great generosity in being so ready to share her lover with her friend and child: she'd been so full of warmth and ready laughter. It was so sad to recall that, later, she'd begun to drink heavily, to become unreliable and so get offered fewer and fewer parts. Perhaps, Lizzie thought, her mother had missed Felix more than either she or Pidge had guessed. She pictured her as she'd been in her late thirties.

In the early sixties she is no longer offered the parts of Rosalind or Lydia Languish but she assumes the roles of Mistress Quickly and Lady Sneerwell with enthusiasm – and discovers a talent for the meatier roles in Restoration comedy. Although she's beginning to lose her shapely suppleness, the extra weight suits her, lending her a statuesque beauty, the creamy skin still smooth and eminently touchable. As the decade draws to an end, however, Angel's career has begun to decline. It manifests itself slowly, that lack of self-discipline, the desperate need for another drink. Perhaps it is nothing to do with Felix's defection: perhaps she fails to get an important part she auditions for, or perhaps a play folds but, at some point during the sixties, Angel loses her confidence and becomes unstable, swinging between extravagant high spirits and a kind of bitchy indifference; between affectionate maternalism and maudlin depression.

She makes her way to the café in King Street, which they call Hell's Kitchen, or to the Duke for a drink with her actor friends, sometimes persuading them to come back home with her for a 'jolly', but as the months wear on and still no work is forthcoming she becomes more withdrawn, finding it increasingly difficult to wear a cheerful expression or shrug an indifferent shoulder.

It isn't easy for Angel when she hears that her daughter has been offered the part of Nellie Forbush in a production of *South Pacific*. Angel pretends disdain, which she sees is hurtful but she simply cannot help herself.

'Musical comedy?' Her shocked expression is almost ludicrous.

'It's the *lead* . . .' mutters Lizzie defensively.

'And a first-class touring company.' Pidge's voice is warm and proud. 'Isn't it wonderful? All those singing lessons have paid off. I'm so thrilled, Lizzie.'

'We can't all be Shakespeareans.' It is a hurt response to Angel's reaction but Lizzie smiles gratefully at Pidge.

'Clearly . . .' Angel shrugs; her voice tails away, indicating that such a thing is beyond speech.

Pidge's arm tightens round Lizzies's shoulder as if to ward off Angel's marked lack of enthusiasm.

'You're such a snob, Angel,' she says lightly. 'Or it couldn't be that you're just the least bit jealous, could it?'

'Oh, shut up, Pidge.' The reluctant grin wrinkles her still charming nose. 'It *is* a bit of a shock when your child lands her first major part, especially when no-one is exactly falling over themselves to offer you a job.' She opens her arms to Lizzie. 'Give me a kiss, sweetie, and forgive your old mother for being a bitch.'

It is so typical of Angel during those later years, that switch from sharp-tongued contempt to affectionate gaiety; her smile – self-deprecating but with a twinkle – is a special blend of penitence and joyfulness that demands forgiveness. On this occasion they make it up very quickly, opening a bottle to drink to Lizzie's success; Angel holding up her glass, her eyes sliding carefully away until the glass is brimming, 'Goodness, that's plenty! Here's to you, sweetie . . .' and Lizzie is always ready to accept the olive branch after these outbursts.

Nevertheless, it is almost a relief when the time comes to leave Angel and Pidge in the Birdcage, to spread her wings at last. Yet she always returns; after success or failure it is still home.

The telephone disturbed Lizzie's thoughts, jolting her back to her horror of the meeting with Piers.

'We've had it out.' Felix sounded exhausted. 'It's been very tricky but I think we're still friends. I hope that the worst is over but I have to say that I simply can't face the dining-room at the hotel, Lizzie. Would you like to come over and see me after you've eaten?'

'I'm not hungry, Felix,' she told him, concerned by the ragged timbre of his voice. 'I'd love to see you but I don't want to tire you out any more than you are already.'

'Oh, please come over,' he said at once. 'I'd so like to see you. We can have some cheese and biscuits or a sandwich. I am tired but I feel terribly restless . . .'

'I'll be right there,' she answered. 'I know exactly how you feel. The adrenalin's still racing but there's nowhere for it to go. I can't wait to tell you what a prat I was. But I expect that Piers has done that already.' She heard his chuckle and felt a great uplift of spirits. 'Five minutes,' she told him – and, replacing the receiver, stood for a moment, her hands clasped together in relief and gratitude.

Driving back to Michaelgarth, Piers was surprised at his principal reaction to his father's disclosures: the relief was overwhelming. Now he could fit the missing pieces together and make sense of the puzzle, remembering that moment years ago when he'd stood outside the drawing-room door listening to his mother's accusations.

From that moment forward, he fears that somewhere in the world, waiting to appear, is a half-sister: his father's child. His mother's voice is full of distaste, the words clear, although it isn't until much later that he understands them fully. He doesn't know what a mistress is but the words 'She had a child with her. I suppose she isn't yours, by any chance?' fill him with a nameless anxiety. Hearing his father's exclamation, his footsteps approaching the slightly open door, he flees away but, even as he hides out on the hill with Monty, he thinks about the meeting earlier that day in Parhams: his mother's cold hand gripping his own as she stared at the woman and her child. The mother looked nice – pretty, rather friendly, ready to be faintly amused – and the little girl gazed at him very intently but as if she too might like to be friends.

As he grows up, the awareness of that child's existence hovers at the edge of his consciousness. Once, he attempts to raise the subject with his mother.

'That woman we saw in Parhams,' he begins diffidently, 'do you remember, Mother? Do you know her?'

He sees the all-too-familiar expression – contempt, anger – take possession of her face as she stands at the kitchen table, kneading pastry. She looks neat and sensible in her well-cut tweed skirt with a green, thin wool jersey. She's taken off her rings and he picks one up – the diamond that his father has given her on their engagement – and turns it in his fingers, watching the jewel flash.

'Your father knows her,' she says. 'She's an actress. I met her once or twice in Bristol.'

'But why was she here?' he asks.

His mother hesitates, lips compressed. 'She came here hoping to see your father,' she answers. 'They are very close friends. He spends time with them when he goes to Bristol. In fact he probably thinks more of them than he does of us.'

'But why does he?' he asks anxiously.

She shrugs, pounding the pastry with the rolling pin, her hands white with flour; there is something almost violent in her actions.

'I'm afraid to say that your father is not a particularly loyal person,' she answers at last.

Piers has a feeling that she is *not* afraid to say it; rather, he believes that she has *enjoyed* saying it, that the words have given her some kind of bitter pleasure. He decides after all that he doesn't want to hear any more; he puts down the ring and goes out into the garth, calling to Monty, and as he roams about he wonders if his father truly loves the woman and her child, and why he wants them when he has a family of his own. Perhaps he would rather have a daughter than a son; perhaps that other woman, the actress, smiles more than his mother – from what he can remember of her this might well be the case – and makes him laugh?

For a period of time he lives with two fears: the first that his father might leave them for the actress and her little girl; the second that something should happen to the actress that means that he brings the little girl to live with them. Being away at school helps to keep these fears at bay. However, quite soon after the scene following the cricket match, he is told that the Bristol office had been closed or sold – whatever the reason given it means that there are to be no more visits – and he is able to relax a little. His parents settle into a kind of truce: fewer icy silences on his mother's part but, despite his father's efforts, not much joy either.

One of the things that attracts him to Sue is her cheerfulness, her readiness to laugh, to share. Being in her company has the same effect as coming from a cold, wet night into a bright room with a blazing fire: full of life and warmth. She is irresistible, her energy sweeps him off his feet. His mother doesn't care for her much, but this isn't new. His mother, until then, manages to take the edge off any budding relationship; that curling lip and cool eye – 'Must she wear her skirts quite so short? So common, apart from being quite disastrous with those legs,' or, 'Is she capable of original thought, Piers? I suppose she *can* read?' – destroy his confidence and happiness so readily.

His father always stands up for him, which generally makes

things worse: 'I think she's rather a sweetie,' he says, or, 'When you're eighteen you don't particularly want to take a Nobel prize winner to a party, Marina.'

The cool eyes rake him with contempt. 'We all know in what direction your tastes lie, Felix. I'm hoping for something better for Piers.'

Once, suddenly angry, his father says: 'Should you criticize my taste so freely, Marina? After all, I married *you*, didn't I?'

Humiliated, furious with both of them, Piers leaves them on the verge of a row and, until Sue, simply ceases to take his girlfriends home. After the Royal Agricultural College, he moves into the cottage at Porlock, glad to be on his own despite being away from Michaelgarth.

As the years pass his fears recede but his love for the old house increases and when, finally, he moves in with his young family it is one of the happiest moments of his life. Whenever he sees Michaelgarth standing like a landmark on the hill, as he drives through the archway into the garth or sits in silence in the old chapel, he feels an overwhelming sense of safety and belonging. It is his home. He knows it in all the seasons: washed in gold, its windows fiery as it reflects a blazing midsummer sunset; or with its grey stone walls sombre against the backdrop of a snowy hillside. He loves the peace of the square, elegant drawing-room on an autumn night, its heavy brocade curtains drawn against the roar of a north-easterly gale, logs settling in the grate, a sudden burst of flame casting fantastic shadows in the lamplight. This tranquil atmosphere contrasts satisfactorily with the busy untidiness of his study, with its window into the garth: that small crowded room where Joker likes to curl on an ancient, saggy sofa in a patch of sunshine whilst Piers, distracted from his desk, leafs through some long-forgotten book or listens to a recording of Miles Davis. Sometimes on these occasions he wonders what might happen if this half-sister should appear, demanding her share, forcing him to sell, and he is gripped with an icy dread. He tells himself that he has inherited the house from his mother's family, that Michaelgarth is his now, but he cannot quite quench his fear of losing it. Even so, he has never been able to confront his father, never had the courage to ask that one vital question.

Not until today after he'd met Lizzie Blake. As soon as their glances touched it was as if an empathy had flowed between them: they might have been old friends who'd been separated for years. There was a recognition that went far beyond that of having seen her before on the television. Immediately he'd wanted to speak to her, to be in her company: it was as if he'd fallen instantly in love. It was ludicrous that, after all these years, when his fear at last became living reality he'd been almost less concerned that she'd come back to claim his father's love or Michaelgarth than that he'd be unable to try to form some kind of friendship with her. This unexpected release from all these terrors equally swamped him with relief.

Piers slumped a little at the wheel. At last the waiting was over: the confrontation made, the explanations given. Now he wondered why he'd waited so long. What could have held him back except the fear of hearing an unpalatable truth? His father's story had touched him more deeply than he'd shown: despite his loyalty and love for his mother he knew all about the silence and the sense of isolation.

He could quite see the attraction of the Birdcage for his father, although he still wondered how much the knowledge of the affair had affected his mother. The jealousy and cold-ness had been there from the beginning, this was true, but how much more had his father's betrayal affected her? Piers shrugged the question aside. For the moment there should be no more recriminations. No doubt other questions would arise from time to time, other doubts, but at least, now that the wall of reserve had been broken down between them, he would be able to ask those questions, to fill in the gaps.

This acceptance of the situation allowed his thoughts to drift back to Lizzie: to remember how she'd looked and what she'd said. *I did rather hope that, after all this time, we might be friends.* Of course, he'd made a complete and utter ass of himself, behaved like an oaf and then walked out on her! He groaned a little, wondering what she was thinking, whether his father might explain the situation to her. Deep down he had the feeling that she wouldn't hold his behaviour against him: she'd looked too friendly, too much fun to cling to resentment.

Instinctively he made the connection: no doubt this was how Angel had seemed to his father after the frigid atmosphere of Michaelgarth. Well, he at least had no such constrictions and he fully intended to contact Lizzie as soon as possible. Perhaps she might have lunch with him? Relief continued to flood over him, lifting his spirits, as he drove into the garth, parked the car and went in to supper.

CHAPTER THIRTY

Gemma was the first to waken. Guy lay turned away from her, the sheet thrust down across his legs, and she drew her hand lightly over his brown back. He did not stir and she rolled over, her arms beneath her head, wondering how it was that her adventures with other men never diminished her need for Guy. Perhaps it was because she didn't fall in love with them: she assessed them physically, as one might appraise a partner for a dance or for a game of tennis, and their other qualities or failings were unimportant to her.

She smiled to herself as she reviewed the performance of her most recent partner, remembering how they'd met just before Sophie's marriage to Henry Corbett, whose family had farmed on Exmoor for generations. It had been fun, looking forward to being Sophie's matron of honour, meeting up again with another of their school-friends, Marianne, who was to be a bridesmaid. During school holidays, and even up until the time of Gemma's marriage to Guy, Marianne had regularly spent a few weeks each summer on Dartmoor, sharing her time between Gemma's family and Sophie's. Her boyfriend, Simon, was one of Henry's oldest friends.

'It'll be great to be living near Marianne,' Sophie had said at the small thrash she'd thrown a month or so before the wedding. 'And here's Simon who's going to be the best man. This is Gemma, Simon. You'll have to look after her but watch out for her husband, he's a jealous man.'

Simon, eyebrows raised appreciatively, had taken her outstretched hand. 'And who shall blame him?' he'd asked. 'Hello, Gemma.'

It was odd, she thought as she lay, warm and relaxed beside Guy, how she'd known straightaway that Simon was an adventurer like herself. They'd exchanged mobile numbers on the pretence of his keeping her in touch with the wedding arrangements and she'd seen him when he'd brought Marianne to a fitting in Exeter for their dresses and taken the three of them – for Sophie had been there too – out to a pub afterwards. All through lunch his glance had crossed hers, sliding away again quickly, and he'd touched her once or twice on the shoulder or the arm when passing her a glass: so exciting, those snatched moments, with Marianne sitting beside her, talking to Sophie about the great day and quite unaware of Simon's preoccupation.

How much more difficult on the day itself, with Guy in attendance, to exchange those tiny signals: much more difficult but even more thrilling because of the danger. Knowing that Guy was not at his best in social situations, that he had no ease of manner, no natural gregariousness, Sophie had paired him with Henry's sister, a straightforward young woman who was the junior partner of a lawyer's practice in Taunton, who'd had no difficulty in keeping him entertained. Gemma, seeing them in earnest conversation – arguing a point, forcefully exchanging ideas – had been pleased that he was so well looked after and had given her attention more fully to Simon.

Towards the end of the day he'd extracted her promise that she'd meet him for lunch: a promise she'd been very willing to make. His family owned a company that supplied agricultural machinery and he travelled all over the South-West, visiting farms and markets, so it had been quite easy to meet in out-of-the-way pubs once or twice, but soon Simon was pressing her to agree to a less public meeting. This trip had been a gift from the gods but, even so, it was very risky. Sophie could no longer be relied upon to cover for her as she'd done so often in the past. Once she'd chuckled at Gemma's escapades, admired and envied her attractive, charming friend, but ever since the birth of Gemma's twins, and especially now that she was a married woman herself, Sophie had suddenly become rather strait-laced and Gemma knew that she wouldn't approve of this little fling with Simon.

Frowning as she stared up at the ceiling, Gemma felt the chill touch of fear icing her skin.

'Guy's a tad scary,' Sophie had observed. 'I was crazy about him once, d'you remember, but I'm not sure I'd be able to cope with him when he has sense of humour failure. You have to be on your guard, don't you? I can't imagine how you get away with it, actually. You seem to be on a kind of permanent Tom Tiddler's ground with him.'

'Oh, Guy's OK,' she'd answered lightly. 'I know all the no-go zones.'

'Sounds more like negotiations with a foreign power than a marriage.'

Sophie had laughed it off but Gemma knew exactly what she meant: there was a fastidiousness about Guy, which ruled out certain areas of behaviour. When Guy's puritanical streak was roused his face grew expressionless, his lids drooped almost menacingly over his eyes, and he withdrew behind a barrier of almost unapproachable austerity. As yet she'd always been able to break through that barrier, talk herself out of trouble, and, because her love for him was always in evidence, he'd been prepared to admit that he was over-ready to be judgemental.

During these brief excursions into extra-marital adventures

she never lost her grip on her relationship with Guy and, so far, he'd found no grounds on which he could base his easily roused suspicions. To do him justice he'd worked hard to be more broadminded, to recognize her friendly, affectionate nature for what it was, and occasionally she felt guilty when she was deceiving him. Yet Sophie was right: Guy was not easy to live with and she needed her fix of irresponsible fun just as he needed those long hours alone at sea. And it *was* a fix: an addiction. She was incapable of resisting the opportunity to seize her pleasure and the prospect of a new, exciting partner was as tempting as the chocolate had been – just out of reach in the cupboard – in childhood. She could not concentrate on other things, could not forget its invisible presence: the vision of it was always there, pressing at the edge of her thoughts. Sooner or later she must drag the stool across the floor, climb up and reach into the cupboard for it so that she might feel the smooth stickiness on her fingers and taste the sweetness as it burst upon her tongue.

Simon was fun: he knew of a quiet, private place, a sunny, grassy patch screened by high banks of furze, where he'd spread his rug on the close-nibbled turf before opening a bottle of wine.

'What makes me think you've done this before?' she'd asked idly, leaning on one elbow as she watched him.

'Me?' He'd pretended surprise, indignation even. 'Perish the thought.'

Yesterday, she'd hurried to meet him again, giving Bertie a walk along the way, parking beside his Land Rover Discovery, which blocked any glimpse of their secret place from the road. This time she'd taken her own rug from the car, laying it on top of his so as to make their bed more comfortable. She'd brought a picnic, which they'd shared, and later, much later, she'd lain in his arms, her fingers threading through his hair. It was fair and rather dry, soft to the touch, and a memory fleetingly distracted her.

'You remind me of David,' she'd murmured and he'd answered sleepily, 'David? Who's David? I thought his name was Guy. Oh, and, by the way,' he'd roused himself, 'Marianne knows you're here on holiday. Sophie told her.'

'Did she?' She'd felt languorous and contented in their sheltered corner, so hot that the sun seemed to melt her bones and suck caution from her brain. Bertie lay stretched in the shade of the furze, panting. 'Should I phone her, d'you think?'

He'd frowned. 'What would you say to her? I thought we'd agreed that you wouldn't see her.'

'But then I didn't know that Sophie would be so quick off the mark to spread the glad news. It would be difficult anyway, wouldn't it, to see Marianne? With her being at work in Taunton all day?'

'Mmm. I suppose it would look a bit odd if you didn't get in touch with her, though. Tell you what: if you telephone home between nine and six you'd get the answering machine and you could just leave a message.'

'It's fortunate,' she'd replied, 'that everyone who knows Guy wouldn't expect him to want to spend his evenings socializing, otherwise it might be natural to assume that we'd get together as a foursome.'

He'd grinned, making a comical face. 'That might be tricky. I doubt I could be quite that cool. If Marianne suggests it I might have to invent a few late calls this week. Luckily, in my job I don't have a routine.'

'Don't worry. Marianne will quite understand that Guy wouldn't be easy to persuade. He's having to make a couple of appearances at Michaelgarth, which is stretching his good temper. I think we're quite safe.'

Now, as she turned her head to look at Guy, she felt a pang of remorse at the way she'd described him, although it was true enough.

'Do we have to go to supper again on Friday?' he'd asked. 'We were there on Sunday.'

'Oh, but I want to see my big brother,' she'd protested. 'It would be a pity to miss him and we have to be away on Saturday morning . . . Are you sailing with Matt again tomorrow?'

She'd noticed his guilty frown with amusement but he'd shaken his head.

'I thought it would be a bit much to desert you for three days on the run,' he'd admitted. 'We could have tomorrow together, go for a walk over the cliffs and have a pub lunch somewhere.'

She'd been clever enough to greet the idea with enthusiasm. 'I'd love that,' she'd answered, letting him see her pleasure at his suggestion, 'though I don't want to spoil your fun. Perhaps you could go out again on Thursday or Friday?'

'The tide's making it more difficult to get out early but Matt did suggest a few hours after lunch on Friday.' She'd watched him, seen the moment when he'd realized that a little give and take was in order here. 'Of course I'd be back in plenty of time for supper at Michaelgarth.' He'd added casually, 'It'll be good to see Saul.'

'That's fine then,' she'd said easily – and he'd fetched the map so as to plan their walk.

Simon had been philosophical about it. 'I'll cram my appointments into Wednesday and Thursday,' he'd said, 'and keep Friday free. Usual place, about two-ish?'

She'd been relieved but not surprised to hear his ready acceptance, realizing that their little affair was nearly over and knowing that they would part good friends.

It was important, she told herself, that no-one should be hurt.

Unbidden, an image of Marianne's face as she'd looked on Sophie's wedding day presented itself before her inner eye: she looked so happy, seizing Gemma's arm, smiling at Sophie in her bridal gown and crying, 'Doesn't she look gorgeous?':

happy and trusting. And now Tilda appeared beside her with that direct look, those amazing cornflower eyes, and Gemma heard her saying: 'I miss him so terribly but here at Michael-garth I feel that he's close to us.'

She shut her eyes as if to blot out these images and rolled over quickly, pressing herself against Guy and hiding her face against his back.

'Wake up, darling,' she said, rather desperately, and he stirred, groaning, and turned almost automatically, still half asleep, to take her into his arms.

CHAPTER THIRTY-ONE

For once, Tilda and Jake were downstairs before Piers. She settled the baby in his bouncy chair and stood for a moment in contemplation: it was unlike her father-in-law to be late for breakfast. He'd been on good form the previous evening, making them both laugh, reminding her mother of youthful indiscretions, and Teresa – delighted and protesting in turn – had enjoyed herself enormously. It was later than usual before she'd set off on the half-hour drive back to Taunton but she'd refused to stay overnight, insisting that she had things to do first thing next morning.

Tilda pushed the kettle on to the hot plate, cut some bread for toast, but before she could decide whether she should wake Piers – perhaps take him some coffee – he came in.

'Overslept!' He rolled his eyes at her. 'A quick cup of coffee will have to do this morning. Morning, Jake.'

Despite his evident haste, he looked more peaceful, more rested, than he'd looked for many months. She watched him as he gulped at his coffee, making a face as he burned his tongue, and decided that there was a kind of banked-down excitement about him. He had the air of someone who had dressed with care, as if he might have an important date. Following so closely on his high spirits during last evening his demeanour puzzled her.

'Alison phoned last evening before you got in,' she said, testing him. 'Something to do with your holiday next week? I said you'd give her a buzz.'

His expression changed so oddly that she stared at him curiously. His bright look was transformed as if by shock and he stood quite still, like someone who had just remembered something that might prove an obstacle to a future pleasure. He put his cup down, feeling unseeingly for its saucer, his brow contracted.

'Are you OK, Piers?'

He glanced at her, distracted. 'Mmm? Oh, sure. I'm fine.'

'If you say so.'

The sardonic note in her voice alerted him and he smiled quickly, collecting his briefcase and a cotton jacket, taking another draught of coffee.

'I'm fine,' he said firmly.

Tilda raised her eyebrows disbelievingly. 'Good,' she said. 'That's OK then.'

He paused by the door, head bent a little, biting his lips as he tried to see his way ahead.

'Today is a bit . . . tricky. If I'm going to be late I'll give you a buzz.'

'OK,' she answered. 'Whatever.'

He smiled at her, went out through the scullery and presently she saw the car pass the open window.

Tilda switched on the television, flicking through the channels, and sat down at the table with her breakfast. Eating her toast, talking to Jake, leaning to set his toys dancing on the bar across his chair whilst he smiled gummily at her, she continued to wonder what had happened to Piers. It had been ages – well, before David died – since she'd seen him as light-hearted as he'd been last evening. He'd been so obviously enjoying himself, so carefree; as if he'd been relieved of some weighty load of fear or guilt. Of course it could simply be that something had happened at the office that had solved a long-term problem; eased some financial crisis. He was not in the habit of sharing his problems with her; not, she suspected, because he felt that they were none of her business, but because he didn't want to add to her own troubles. At least he didn't try to make light of them by attempting to move her into another relationship but nor did he encourage her to discuss them. Man-like, she thought, he didn't want to probe about in her inmost psyche but was quite ready to listen if she wanted to talk.

They each suffered from an almost morbid anxiety of upsetting the other by occasional bursts of insensitivity. Sometimes – just now and then – she found that she was able to forget about David completely: she'd be watching a television programme and find herself shrieking with laughter and Piers would wander in and she'd wave at him, still laughing, and then think: oh, God, David's dead and I'm laughing! – and be overwhelmed with shame and horror and misery. It wasn't that Piers had ever looked censorious or wounded – quite the opposite, he liked to see her happy – but nevertheless the guilt was there. It happened in reverse too, and this, she reminded herself, was one of the downsides to living together: in this area they were inclined, between them, to keep opening the wound simply by their awareness of the other's pain.

'But I don't want to forget your daddy; I love him,' she told Jake rather desperately. 'I shall always love him. But how do you learn to live without someone? How does it work?'

She began to unload the dishwasher, putting the things away, longing for David to come in from the scullery.

'What's the matter with you?' he'd ask. 'Got a face like a bottom that's been put in a colander and sat on!'

She thought: He'll never say things like that to Jake. Never see him grow and be proud of him. He'll never play cricket out on the hill with Jake, like Piers did with David, or take him up on Dunkery to watch the sun set, or go sailing out of Porlock Weir.

She wept silently as she'd learned to lest she should upset Jake, her back turned to him, her face buried in the teacloth. As if he sensed her unhappiness, he began to grizzle too, and she wiped her eyes and went to him, lifting him out of his chair and sitting with him at the table. Settling them both comfortably, she unbuttoned her shirt and began to feed him, smiling down at him as he watched her, his tiny hand patting gently at her breast as he sucked.

The car came slowly past the window and into the garth; a door slammed and she heard footsteps crossing the cobbles and coming in through the scullery. A tap on the door and Alison appeared.

'Hello,' she said. 'Not a difficult moment, I hope? Oh.'

Tilda watched her, outwardly calm, as she lifted the remote control to switch off the television. She knew that the 'Oh' – although giving the impression of being taken by surprise – was actually meant to imply that it was rather odd and not quite done to sit at the kitchen table feeding one's baby whilst watching a chat show on the television. Alison wasn't a truthful person, Tilda decided; she existed behind a frame-work of expressions and actions that she would deny should they be challenged. She liked to control without appearing to manipulate: she was self-seeking whilst pretending that her own aims were in the best interest of another person; in this instance, Piers. Almost at once, Alison proved this point.

'I still find it a bit of a shock to see you sitting there when I come in,' she said with a bright little laugh. 'Piers must find it quite a sea change. It was always so quiet when I popped by before.'

'But then you wouldn't have got further than the scullery, would you?' asked Tilda, also brightly. 'Not at this time of day if Piers was at the office, I mean.'

Alison coloured: she disliked the inference that her relationship with Piers wasn't close enough to have merited her being given a key to the house.

'I've brought one of my fatless sponges,' she said, ignoring the remark, placing the cake tin on the table. 'I know how Piers loves them.'

She glanced about her, looking for new evidence of Tilda's habitation, always anxious lest there should be signs of a more permanent occupation.

'Would you like some coffee?' Tilda pulled herself together, remembering that this was Piers' house and Alison was his friend.

Please, she found herself praying to no-one in particular, please don't let it be because of Alison that Piers was like he was last night.

'I'll put the kettle on.' Alison hurried to the Aga. 'Do you drink coffee with . . . you know?'

She nodded towards Jake and Tilda's bared breast as if none of it was quite nice, and Tilda felt a spasm of mirth ripple through her diaphragm. Jake opened his eyes reproachfully and Tilda beamed down at him.

'Occasionally I do. I'd like one, please,' she answered. 'Lots of milk but no sugar, thanks.'

'It's so hot again.' Alison fiddled about, enjoying a sense of being at home in Piers' kitchen. 'Of course, these big old houses are so cool, not like my little bungalow.'

'It's a bit different in the winter with a gale blowing,' said Tilda. 'Rather like being at sea up in my bedroom on that north-west corner.'

Alison looked about for some subject that might put Tilda in her place; that would underline the fact that Piers had had a life before she'd turned up with her baby: a life in which Alison had played a major role.

'I wish Piers would get rid of that old bean bag,' she said. 'Quite insanitary. He said he was going to the last time I saw him.'

'He's probably keeping it for the next one,' said Tilda. 'Anyway, it's clean; I've washed the cover in the machine.'

'Next one?' Alison, putting the coffee mugs on the table, was taken off guard. 'I understood that there were to be no more dogs.'

Tilda's eyebrows shot up. 'You can't be serious! Piers without a dog? He's just taken a bit longer to get over Joker than usual, that's all. There have always been dogs at Michael-garth.'

She moved Jake to the other breast, settling him comfortably whilst Alison watched with undisguised distaste. Glancing up, Tilda caught the expression and Alison looked quickly away, sipping her coffee but unable to allow the subject to drop.

'When we talked about it, Piers agreed that the time had come to try life without a dog,' she said. 'He agreed that a dog is a most frightful tie and that we – he – could have much more freedom without one.'

'Freedom for what?' asked Tilda with great interest. 'After all, dogs never stopped Piers doing what he wanted before. He takes them into the office and in the car with him, and even to the pub. And he has that wonderful Animal Aunt that comes in if he has to go away.' She shook her head, as if dismissing Alison's opinion, as if pretending that she must have misunderstood Piers. 'No, I can't imagine Piers being without a dog for much longer.'

'I think, for once, you might not know quite as much as you imagine you do.' Alison couldn't quite hide her irritation. 'I promise you that Piers and I have talked it through very carefully.'

'Perhaps you were talking and he was listening,' suggested

Tilda, 'which is a bit different.' Stop, she thought. Stop *now*.

'I think that you should remember that though Piers has given you a temporary home it doesn't entitle you to interfere with his private life.' Alison's face was patchily red, her eyes bright and slightly watery with combined anger and embarrassment. 'Just because you are suffering bereavement you mustn't think it gives you some kind of right to batten on to other people's generosity. Piers has been grieving too, and he needs the space and freedom to move on now.'

'Did he say that too?' asked Tilda. 'Along with not wanting a dog, I mean?'

Alison compressed her lips into a thin line, cross with herself for having been betrayed into saying too much. If she said 'yes' then Tilda might confront Piers; if she denied it, Tilda would laugh up her sleeve and see the truth of the situation. She prevaricated.

'Of course not in so many words. Piers is much too unselfish. He wants you and Jake to be happy and to be able to build a new life together . . .'

. . . somewhere else, added Tilda silently. Suddenly she felt a huge depression; a sense of helplessness.

'Jake needs his sleep,' she said, carefully easing the drowsy baby from her breast and covering herself with her shirt. Oddly, she felt a sudden need to hide herself from the unfriendly, prying gaze of the woman across the table. The flash of defiance was quenched and the ache for David had returned. Oh, for the sight of his eyes, always so bright, so keen, smiling into hers; to feel his strength flowing into her numbed body. She laid Jake against her shoulder, gently massaging his small back, feeling the warm wetness of milky dribble as it soaked through her thin shirt. Alison swallowed back her coffee and got up. She felt a little concerned at the look on Tilda's face but had no intention of showing a gentleness that might undermine any of her previous arguments.

'I'll be away,' she said. 'I hope you enjoy the cake.'

After she'd gone, Tilda went out into the sun-filled hall, murmuring to Jake, standing for a moment in the peace and stillness, before climbing the stairs to her bedroom.

CHAPTER THIRTY-TWO

Lizzie was at breakfast when the telephone call came through. She set down her orange juice and followed the girl to the reception desk, wondering if Felix were unwell. He'd been very tired last evening – but quite calm, sure that all would be well, although knowing that there must be a further meeting with Piers.

'The worst is over,' he'd said several times – but not as if he were trying to convince himself, rather as a result of an easing from a huge emotional weight.

Nevertheless she hurried anxiously to the telephone. Felix, after all, had recently undergone major surgery and he might have suffered a setback in the night.

'Hello,' she said urgently into the receiver but speaking as quietly as she could, turning away from the receptionist, who busied herself at a distance. 'Are you OK, Felix? I've been worrying that I shouldn't have come over last night after all the drama but I simply had to know how you were and whether Piers was going to come back with a gun and shoot me.' She waited for his chuckle, which was not forthcoming, and was seized with another stab of foreboding. 'Sorry,' she said. 'I'm rabbiting on, I'm still reeling with all this stuff. Are you OK?'

'Well, I'm certainly not coming to shoot you.' Piers' voice was amused, if a little cool. 'But I *was* wondering whether we might have lunch together.'

Lizzie's hand clutched the receiver in a convulsive grip, her eyes closed in horror. 'Oh, God,' she murmured. 'Oh my *God*! The girl just said Mr Hamilton . . .' She sighed. 'OK. Shall we take it from the top or would you like to hang up now?'

His chuckle was particularly comforting. 'I'm very happy to take it from the top if that means starting again – on both sides. I certainly didn't intend to mislead you. I did actually give my full name but the receptionist probably just caught the surname.'

'It's early in the day and Felix *has* telephoned me here once or twice so it might be confusing,' agreed Lizzie, ready to forgive anything, 'and I should love lunch. That's very . . .' she rejected 'nice', wondered about 'kind' . . . 'that's great,' she finished lamely.

'Good.' He still sounded faintly amused. 'There's a nice pub at Porlock Weir. The Ship. Shall I collect you? Say half-past twelve?'

'Great,' Lizzie repeated faintly.

Can't you think of another word? she asked herself furiously. Aren't you an actress? Don't you work with words?

'Could you be outside the hotel?' he was asking. 'Parking will probably be impossible and I can simply scoop you up as I go past.'

'That sounds . . . fine.'

'Good. I'll see you then.'

The line went dead and Lizzie stood for a second, listening to the buzzing sound, before slowly replacing the receiver. The receptionist smiled questioningly at her as if wondering whether Lizzie might want to make another call.

'Everything OK?' she asked politely, after a moment.

'Abso*lute*ly OK.' Aware that she was grinning unrestrainedly, Lizzie wiped the inane expression from her face. 'Just some rather good news,' she said, hoping that this might account for her odd behaviour. 'Thank you so much.'

She went back into the dining-room and sat down again. The remains of her scrambled egg were congealing gently, unappetizingly, but she managed a triangle of toast, without tasting a crumb of it, and finished her orange juice. She could see that she was destined to make a fool of herself in front of Piers and she groaned in spirit before a rising sense of excitement crowded out this self-condemnation. He wanted to have lunch with her and he'd sounded . . . no, *not* nice, *not* kind, but definitely fun. That chuckle, so like his father's . . . How would Felix react? she wondered. Would he be pleased or anxious at this unexpected move on Piers' part? She hoped that he would approve of her acceptance of the invitation but it would be comforting to talk to him first; check out a few things so as to be prepared. They'd agreed to have coffee together at about eleven and, meanwhile, she'd planned to explore the Dunster Wearhouse. A shopping spree – she must remember to buy some postcards to send to her friends – coffee with Felix and lunch with Piers: Lizzie sighed with pleasurable anticipation, dropped her napkin on the table and rose to leave.

The friendly couple were waiting, leaning out from the chairs, smiling expectantly. They did hope that it was good news? They'd feared at first that it might be some emergency – to be called away from her breakfast like that – but they could see from her face that it couldn't be *too* serious . . . ?

Lizzie beamed at them, bending a little nearer, lowering her voice: 'A call from my agent . . . Hollywood . . . I know . . . quite amazing . . . mind you, not a word . . .'

She passed from the room, still wearing an expression that might cover such an eventuality – exultation blended carefully with just the right amount of dazed disbelief: humility, she decided, was the keynote here – and went upstairs.

It was just after eleven when she climbed the stairs to the flat, having first deposited her spoils at the hotel.

'I've been shopping,' she called up to him. 'I was hoping to find something rather special to wear. Oh, Felix, you'll never guess.' She hugged him as she reached the landing. 'Piers telephoned this morning and has invited me to lunch.'

Too late she saw his warning gesture and, looking beyond him, saw a tall fair girl getting up from the chair by the window.

'This is Tilda,' Felix said, his voice betraying nothing but pleasure that they should meet. 'I'm never quite certain of our technical relationship but she's Piers' daughter-in-law. Tilda, this is an old friend of mine, Lizzie Blake.'

'Hello.' Tilda moved forward, holding out her hand. Her eyes widened with surprise. 'But aren't you . . . ? Gosh, Felix! You never told me that you knew a famous actress.'

'That's because he didn't know he did.' Lizzie smiled warmly at her. 'But then he didn't tell me that he had a positively beautiful granddaughter-in-law either. I think we should take him in hand, don't you?'

'I just loved the sitcom . . . And that advert . . .'

'How sweet of you.' Lizzie could do the 'touched and grateful, tinged with a dash of graciousness' response with barely any effort at all. 'Don't you simply adore the dog? I wanted to keep him but they wouldn't let me.'

'Have some coffee.' Felix drew her further into the room, his eyes amused, not in the least taken in by her act. 'Tilda and I have already started. Would you like a biscuit? And here's Jake, my great-grandson.'

Lizzie stared down at the baby lying in a kind of carrying chair. He gurgled contentedly, chubby fists and bare legs kicking furiously, and Tilda smiled rather shyly.

'He's behaving himself at the moment but I really should be on my way. This was just a quick fix.' She laughed a little. 'I come and see Felix when I feel a bit miz. He always cheers me up but I simply must dash off or the car will be over its time.' She hesitated. 'It's really so good to meet you. Are you staying locally?'

'At the Luttrell Arms.' With difficulty, Lizzie tore her gaze from the baby. 'Until Friday morning.'

'Friday?' Felix couldn't hide his disappointment. 'I didn't realize it was to be so short a stay.'

'I was lucky to get four nights at this time of the year – or so I gather.' Lizzie beamed at them both. 'I would love to stay a little longer, of course . . .'

'Have you tried the other hotels?' asked Tilda. 'Or the second-hand bookshop, perhaps. Cobbles, it's called. The Corleys have a lovely little self-contained flat. They only started self-catering this summer so they might not be fully booked. You can't disappear just yet.'

'Well . . .' Lizzie was a little taken aback by this evident desire for her company. 'To be honest, I hadn't thought much further than Friday. I just came down to see Felix, you see.'

'And you haven't seen Piers yet?' Tilda's friendliness was so genuine that it was impossible to feel resentful at this interest in her affairs. 'Did I hear you say that you were having lunch with him?'

'They haven't had time to catch up yet.' Felix intervened, gently pushing Lizzie down into the wing-chair, putting a cup of coffee on the table beside her. 'We'll have to look into the possibility of other accommodation.'

'You could always come to Michaelgarth.' Tilda grimaced, looking suddenly embarrassed. 'Sorry. I forget that I don't have the right to do things without asking Piers. Not that he minds. You could be in the west wing with me and Jake.' Lizzie looked again at the baby, swinging in his chair, which Tilda was now holding as she might carry a shopping basket.

'He's very good,' she added, lest Lizzie might be put off by this suggestion. 'Oh, *do* mention it to Piers! It would be such fun.'

'Good idea.' Felix stepped in, yet again. 'Although we must let Lizzie decide for herself.'

'Of course.' Tilda looked stricken. 'That's so typical of me. David used to say, "Do try to engage the brain before clutching in the mouth." Sorry, Lizzie.'

'It's very sweet of you to invite me.' Lizzie imagined – just for one mad moment – accepting the invitation and telling Piers about it over lunch. Wild laughter threatened to choke her. 'It sounds terrific fun.' She caught Felix's warning glance and pulled herself together. 'Shall we see how it goes? I'm sure we'll meet again, either way.'

'I hope so.' Tilda clearly meant it. She kissed Felix, grinned at Lizzie and went out, carrying Jake's little chair carefully. They heard the street door close.

'That was . . . tricky,' said Felix.

'I'm getting really good at ad-libbing,' observed Lizzie. 'What a perfectly lovely girl. And just wait until you hear about my latest gaffe with Piers.'

'Are you really having lunch together?' Felix sat down opposite.

'We are. He telephoned the hotel this morning and, naturally, when the receptionist said it was Mr Hamilton I assumed that it was you. I can't remember exactly what I said to him but he must think that I ought to be certified.'

'And he was friendly?' asked Felix anxiously. 'He sounded natural?'

'He was very polite and very charming, and his laugh sounds just like yours.' Lizzie smiled at him reassuringly. 'Is there anything you feel I should know before I humiliate myself any further?'

'I am just so pleased,' said Felix happily. 'It's such a good sign that he wants to meet you again. It means that he's slowly letting go of all his resentment.'

He shook his head, as if words were beyond him, and she reached out to touch his hand.

'I was rather pleased too,' she admitted. 'So come on. Teach me my lines, give me my cues, I want to rehearse this scene before I play it to an audience.'

CHAPTER THIRTY-THREE

Tilda made her way between the dawdling holidaymakers, enjoying the sensation of belonging; happy in this awareness of her own permanency amongst so many visitors. David had often railed at the indecision of strolling couples blocking the path, at being unable to park his car outside his grandfather's flat at the height of the season, but Tilda took it in her stride. The warm sunshine washed the pretty village scene in yellow light, carving sharp black strokes of shade across the sunken cobbled pavement and touching the hanging baskets with their bright splashy colours. She'd had to park in West Street this morning and – as she passed beneath the long, three-tiered, slate-hung walls of the old nunnery, holding Jake's chair carefully away from the traffic – she considered the possibility of starting her own little business here, in Dunster. She hesitated outside the second-hand bookshop, wondering whether she should check with Adrian to see if his holiday let might be free for Lizzie, and decided that she mustn't interfere; paused to look at the display of antique linen-wear in the window of the Linen Basket, which had once been Parhams grocery shop, and resisted an urge to try on one of the gorgeous straw hats that hung in the doorway.

'Can't afford it,' she told Jake, who watched wide-eyed as he was swung along, his own linen hat cocked rakishly to protect him from the sunshine. 'I've got your future to think of, haven't I?'

As she put him into the car, her mobile sang out its silly little tune and she snatched it from the pocket of her satchel-bag.

'Saul!' Her voice was so full of delight that the young man might have been forgiven for imagining that she was more than usually pleased to hear his voice. 'How are you? You're still coming on Friday?'

'Of course I'm coming.' There was nothing to betray the lifting of his heart at that tone in her voice. 'I want to see my godson, don't I?'

'Oh, Saul, you'll never guess who I've just met!'

'No, I probably wouldn't.' He sounded cautious now, trying to disguise a flash of dismay. 'Brad Pitt? Pierce Brosnan? Homer Simpson? I give up. Who have you just met?'

'I was having coffee with Felix and who should stroll in but Lizzie Blake, the actress. Remember that sitcom? *Family Values*? David adored it. And she does that advert with the terrific dog . . .'

'Yes, I know who you mean.' He sighed with silent relief: no gorgeous new man, then. 'How come Felix knows her?'

'He didn't exactly say and I didn't like to ask but she is just *so* nice.'

'And am I going to meet her?'

'I don't know. She's only booked in for a few days at the Luttrell Arms but we're trying to persuade her to stay longer. I hoped she might come to Michaelgarth. Wouldn't it be fab?'

'It would,' he agreed. 'Meanwhile, I shall be down about tea-time, if that's OK?'

'It'll be so good to see you, Saul.' She suddenly realized

how very true this was. 'Oh, listen, I nearly forgot. Did you know that Gemma's down?'

'At Michaelgarth?' He was clearly surprised.

'No, they're at the cottage. Guy had some sailing job postponed and we'd had a cancellation so they're there for the week.'

'That's nice.' He sounded non-committal. 'How are my nephews?'

'Oh, she left the twins with your ma so that they could both have a real break. Guy's getting some sailing with a man he sold a boat to last year.'

'So Gemma's spending time with you and Jake, then.'

'A bit. She's got a few chums over here, you know, but she and Guy will be coming to supper on Friday. Drive carefully, won't you, Saul? Give me a buzz on the way down.'

'Of course.' He heard the rising note of anxiety – ever since David's accident, she'd been abnormally fearful when her friends were making long trips – but kept his voice light. 'Everyone sends their love and tells me that I must bring you back with me.'

A little silence. 'Yes,' she said, rather bitterly. 'I'm sure they do.'

'Tilda, they really miss you.'

'I know.' She controlled that flash of resentment: that a cruel quirk of fate should have suddenly removed her so completely from the company of her friends and the world where she'd been so happy. 'Give them my love, won't you? And we'll see you on Friday.'

She drove carefully away: driving was something she'd had to make herself do immediately after David's death, knowing that, if she lost her nerve, her life – and Jake's – would be impossibly restricted. She was cheered by Saul's call, part of her mind planning the weekend ahead, part still wondering how she might occupy her time and her talents. She'd reached Alcombe before it quite suddenly occurred to her that Piers' high spirits might have been caused by the prospect of his lunch with Lizzie Blake and nothing at all to do with Alison.

'Oh, how I do hope so,' she said aloud. She glanced in the mirror at Jake and then at her watch. If she dashed round the Co-op here in Alcombe, instead of going into Tesco's, there would be plenty of time to see the new golden Labrador puppies over at Huntscott. She'd reserved one charming little fellow several weeks before and the breeder, an old friend of the Hamiltons, had agreed that if Piers really was not ready to have another dog then she'd take him back.

'Don't worry, my dear,' she'd said. 'I'm sure he'll want him. Joker's litter brother is his great-grandfather but I understand how you feel. I shan't have a problem finding a home for him.'

'You won't tell him, will you?' Tilda had asked anxiously. 'I want it to be a surprise for his birthday.'

The breeder had given Tilda's shoulder a friendly squeeze. 'Not a word,' she'd promised.

Tilda put Jake's chair into the trolley, her mind made up. Seeing Bertie had confirmed her conviction that it was time for another puppy at Michaelgarth. Piers should have his present on Saturday at the party whilst Saul was with them to give his support. Saul, like David, was a man of positive action and she could count on him to keep them all going if the moment became too emotional. Tilda made a happy little face at Jake as she pushed him along the aisles, choosing treats for the birthday supper. Her heart gave a tiny jump of excitement: perhaps Lizzie Blake might be one of the party too.

All that morning, Piers was aware of a barely subdued excitement: he worked with one eye on the clock and his thoughts elsewhere. When he arrived outside the hotel there was no room to park and he could only lean across to open the door for Lizzie before driving on again as quickly as he could so as not to cause a traffic jam.

He said: 'Sorry about that, I couldn't quite think where else to meet you,' whilst she was telling him that she'd been nearly run over whilst hopping in and out to look for him. They both fell silent, neither looking at the other, both anxious not to behave as if they were inexperienced teenagers on their first date. It was Lizzie – knowing so much more about the past than Piers – who was able to assume control; to drive the conversation carefully away from banality towards the intimacy that they both needed.

'I love this part of the village,' she observed, as Piers took a short cut up St George's Street. 'It's so incredibly quiet. You can't believe that all that busyness is happening in the High Street when you're sitting in that beautiful little garden.'

He smiled, slowing a little as he passed the school and turned into Priory Green. 'It's rather special,' he agreed.

'It was so odd,' she continued, almost as if he hadn't spoken, 'to see Felix sitting there on that bench. I thought he might be dead, you know, and I needed to see him so much.'

'Why?' asked Piers after a moment. 'Why now?'

'It's one of those trigger points,' she answered. 'I'm sure there are all kinds of clever names for it but I think it's fairly common. Something pretty grim happens, some terrible loss, and you find that you're reassessing your life, trying to understand why certain things happen, but to do that you need to fill in a few gaps and sometimes you don't think of asking questions until it's too late. Well, I didn't. Angel, my mother, died quite young – she was barely sixty – so she hadn't got to that age where you begin to look back and start all that "Do you remember?" stuff. And I wasn't old enough to want to know then.'

'But why should you think that my father would know things about your life?' It sounded abrupt, even aggressive, and he frowned, frustrated by his lack of tact. 'I'm not getting this right.'

'Don't worry about it.' She felt strangely at ease with him. 'I can't tell you how glad I am that you wanted to do this. For us to have lunch together, I mean. I always felt that I knew you, you see. Felix talked about you and I imagined how you might be, as children do. I expect he didn't talk about me.'

'No,' agreed Piers after a moment, moved by the rather wistful note. 'Not as such.'

. . . She had a child with her. I suppose she isn't yours, by any chance?

Lizzie was looking at him curiously. 'Not as such,' she repeated reflectively. 'Do you remember seeing us in Parhams that day, Piers?' She saw his hands tighten on the wheel and bit her lips. 'Sorry,' she said quickly. 'I'm getting this all wrong, aren't I? We come from different standpoints. You saw me as the enemy and I saw you as a friend. We – me and Angel and Pidge – were happy to share Felix but, since we had no choice in the matter, we just accepted the fact that we were lucky to have anything of him at all. You, on the other hand, had all the fear of losing him and we constituted a threat. I can quite understand that, but I just want us to be friends now.' She shook her head, sighing. 'I always go bull-headed at things,' she told him regretfully. 'Putting my foot in it, making assumptions . . . Where did you say we were having lunch?'

The sudden change of subject, the light social tone, didn't deceive him at all.

'I'm having trouble adjusting,' he admitted, refusing the opportunity she was offering him. 'Every time I think, that's all over, it's in the past, another memory or some old tug of loyalty jumps out of the woodwork.'

She turned towards him, relieved and grateful for his honesty. 'Of course it does. Goodness, how else could it be? That's what I meant when I said we're coming at it from totally opposite positions. I'd decided to track down the past so I was prepared for it, as far as I could be, hoping to meet Felix . . . and you. Mind you, I was pretty nervous. After all, you can't just turn up after thirty-odd years without expecting a few surprises. But for you, this is a bolt from the blue. I'm sorry about last evening, Piers. I was unbelievably stupid and tactless. It must have been such a shock for you.'

He began to laugh. 'I felt such a prize idiot. I really thought I recognized you – well, I did, of course – and feeling a real hell of a fellow, chatting up a famous actress . . .'

Lizzie was laughing too. 'You should worry. I behaved like a total prat . . .'

He turned his head, still smiling. 'Shall we take it from the top?' he suggested. 'New readers start here?'

She grinned at him, settled in her seat and stared straight ahead as if at a set. 'Clear,' she said in a sharp high voice. 'OK. Act One. Scene One . . . Take Two. Action . . .' and waited. This time he must call the shots.

'Start at the beginning,' he said after a moment, 'and go on until the end and then stop. Tell me everything you can remember about Angel and Pidge and the Birdcage.'

CHAPTER THIRTY-FOUR

Felix watched them go, his heart beating so unsteadily that he was obliged to reach for the back of the chair to support himself. He longed so much for harmony to exist between these two; hoping that the gentle powers of understanding and friendship might go some way to healing the pain and resentment that still reached forward, long-fingered from the past, to touch and bruise the present. He sensed the current of interest that flowed between them, sparking intermittently into something more than just curiosity roused by times past, and he was seized by anxiety.

He'd laughed aloud as Lizzie hopped from the porch into the road each time a car had come along, startling the driver before leaping back again and waving up to him, miming fright, expectation, and turning the whole scene into street theatre. He knew that it was a means of keeping up her own spirits, refusing to let her nerves take control: behaving just like Angel before a performance. He remembered how she'd greet him with exaggerated relief, clutching one of her cotton wrappers around her, the after-lunch coffee cup rattling in its saucer as her hand shook.

'I can't remember a single word, sweetie, not a word of it. My mind is quite, quite blank. Thank goodness you've turned up, Felix. I do hate the afternoon before a first night. I have this terror that I'm going to say the wrong lines. Once, when we were doing a Rattigan season, I was standing in the wings just before my entrance and I couldn't remember whether it was *French Without Tears* or *The Winslow Boy*. Everything went black. Oh, the horror . . . Felix, I think I need soothing . . .'

That wicked upward look, which spoke volumes of love and need, had never failed to move him; but then Angel had been able to show her vulnerability, gratefully accepting assistance whilst continuing to find her own ways of dealing with it – just as Lizzie did now. Marina had hidden her weaknesses, armouring herself with pride and self-righteousness against his attempts to help her, becoming weighted and clumsy with an iron-clad self-protection, so that each time her jealousy and fear unbalanced her it became more and more difficult to right herself.

Now, watching Lizzie, Felix was pierced with pity and remorse, knowing that, even after he'd finished the affair with Angel, its shadow had lain between him and Marina; an indelible stain that could never be washed away no matter what solvents of affection or penitence he applied to it. He'd betrayed them both: Marina and Angel.

'She began drinking,' Lizzie had said, 'well, she always liked a drink, of course, but more serious stuff. It was a bit of a vicious circle, if you see what I mean. She'd drink a bit, become unreliable, lose her confidence and then drink a bit more. I'd begun to get work myself by then so it was poor old Pidge who took the brunt. It was quite a gradual process; an extra shot of whisky before going down to the theatre, a little sip between acts. She was very naughty and cunning, as you can imagine, and Pidge didn't really have a hope . . .'

He'd tried to imagine that older Angel, unconfident, slowly

losing her professional edge, unwilling to face his own part in her disintegration, his face sombre. Lizzie had carefully stared out of the window.

'It's difficult to know when it really began,' she'd offered. 'I wondered whether she'd been in a play which folded, something like that, or whether she was getting to that age which is so deadly in the theatre: the onset of the big four-o was such a nightmare. These days there's television to take up the slack but there wasn't the scope for Angel . . .'

Even as she'd attempted to ameliorate his guilt he'd been remembering that final meeting with Angel in Bristol. Now those memories came flooding back, driving the thought of Piers and Lizzie from his mind.

As soon as she sees his expression she puts an arm about him, drawing him into that magic circle of emotional security.

'Sweetie, you look terrible,' she says. 'Whatever is it?'

The windows are open, the leaves of the plane tree flickering gold and green in the afternoon sunshine, whilst the drone of the city beats quietly beyond the small green deserted square. He looks about the room: Angel's yellow, silk fringed shawl flung across the broad lap of an armchair, magazines in an untidy pile on the floor beside it; Lizzie's new ballet shoes – the blocked pink satin toes in the process of being darned – standing together on the table with Pidge's work-basket, full of brightly coloured reels of cotton and a fat rosy-pink velvet pincushion; the new, clean, sharp-edged sheet of music – a Beethoven sonata – balanced on the rack of the piano whilst a stack of yellowing, crumpled pages threaten to topple from its shiny lid onto the black and ivory keys; and – presiding over all this dear, familiar scene – the birdcage. He stares up at the two pretty birds, with the small chick beside them on the perch, and his throat constricts with misery.

'Come,' she says, watching his face, 'come, my darling, you look in need of soothing.'

He goes with her for the last time to the warm bed, postponing the brutality of parting, snatching this final offering of comfort and love.

'You've said this before,' she tells him later, wrapped in a long cotton garment, her hair falling over her shoulders, her face pale. 'It's impossible, Felix. We tried it once and it didn't work.'

'It has to work.' He cannot look at her. 'Marina has said she'll divorce me . . .'

She moves swiftly to his side, looking up into his eyes which were turned so resolutely from hers. 'Would that be so bad?' she asks softly. 'Would it, Felix?'

'It's not simply that,' he answers wretchedly. 'She says that I would no longer be able to see Piers.'

'She's bluffing,' she says at once, taking a step back, retying her belt more firmly. 'She couldn't do that.'

'She might be able to. After all, we haven't exactly been over-discreet, have we? If it should come to court . . . '

'No-one would keep a parent from his child.' Rising fear makes her voice tremble. 'It's nonsense.'

'I can't take that chance.' In his attempt to make her understand how serious he is he merely sounds harsh. 'I have to think about Piers.'

'And what about me?'

'Do you imagine that this is easy?'

'I see you for a few days each month, if I'm lucky . . .'

'How often we see each other isn't the point . . .'

They argue in self-defeating circles until finally, hating himself, he raises the weapon of his marriage and prepares to crush her with it. 'You always knew the score, Angel. I've never pretended that I would ever leave Marina. We knew that this might happen sooner or later . . .'

She loses her temper then, battering him with bitter words, accusing him of faithlessness, of cowardice . . . until, suddenly, Pidge appears and Angel turns towards her.

'He's leaving us,' she tells her, almost conversationally. 'He's really going this time, Pidge. What shall we do?'

The sudden outburst of weeping shocks him and he steps forward instinctively, his arms outstretched, but Pidge shakes her head, holding Angel, watching whilst he takes one last look around him before passing through the open doorway and down the stairs.

He'd never seen her again. Even now he couldn't tell if he'd made the right decision. At least he and Marina had come to love each other again at the end, even if it had been a result of her suffering. He had the small comfort of knowing that she'd needed him and he'd been able to give her comfort and affection. Felix took a deep breath: he needed a drink. No point in sitting wondering how Piers and Lizzie were getting on together or brooding over the past; he'd be better off having a jar in the pub with one or two of his old chums, followed by some lunch. He pottered about collecting his keys and his hat and, treading carefully down the stairs, made his way out into the busy street.

Leaving Piers to pay the bill, Lizzie wandered out of the long, low-ceilinged bar, blinking into the bright sunshine. Crossing to the sea-wall she stood for a while, her arms folded on the warm stone, looking down at the small boats which rested, beached and motionless, waiting for the tide to lift them back to life. The long mole reached out into the Channel and, on the spit of land beyond it, three cottages huddled comfortably together, their backs turned against the sea.

Piers appeared beside her, pushing his wallet into his back pocket, looking across to the harbour wall.

'Would you like to walk out to the beach?' he asked.

'I should love to if you've got the time.'

They fell into step together, side-stepping visitors, coming together again, each aware of the other. Lizzie paused on the little bridge to look down into the inner harbour where other boats lay, some rotting into wrecks.

'I wish the tide were in,' she said dreamily. 'It seems impossible to imagine how much water would be needed to fill it up. It must be very beautiful at high tide with a full moon.'

'It is.' He wandered ahead, his hands in his pockets, glancing back at her. 'Perhaps tomorrow evening . . . or Friday? We could have dinner at the Anchor. I can't promise a full moon but I'll check the tides . . .'

He hesitated and she smiled at him, nodded her agreement.

'That sounds nice. But not Friday. I shall be back in Bristol by then.'

He couldn't disguise his disappointment. 'In Bristol? But when are you going?'

'On Friday morning.' She made a regretful face. 'The room was only free for four nights. I suppose I was lucky to get in at all at such short notice but I'm beginning to wish I could stay longer.'

Piers tripped over the extended lead belonging to a small waddling spaniel, apologized to its owner, and reached out to draw Lizzie on to the grassy space in front of the cottages.

'You can't go just yet.' He tried for a light note, which didn't deceive her at all. 'You haven't seen Michaelgarth yet.' He was rather surprised to realize how very much he wanted this. 'Does my father know that you're going on Friday?'

She nodded. 'I mentioned it this morning. I told you about meeting Tilda?' She gave a small chuckle. 'She pressed me to stay, bless her, but it's not quite that simple. I should think that the place is bursting at the seams, although she mentioned a self-contained flat in Dunster. At a bookshop . . . ?'

Piers nodded abstractedly, realized that he was still holding her arm and let it go abruptly. They moved forward again, pacing slowly together, each in a pensive mood.

Lizzie thought: I think he really does want me to stay. Goodness, I've talked myself hoarse but he really seemed to need to know all about Angel and Pidge. He wasn't being polite. Oh, crikey! Should I go or should I stay? How I'd like to stay . . . if he really means it. Felix would like it, I know, and that darling girl. How terrible that her husband, that Piers' son, was killed . . . and the baby . . . Oh God, the baby! Could I deal with that . . . ?

Piers glanced at her from time to time, trying to gauge her reaction. He was astonished at how flat he felt, thinking that she would be gone in less than forty-eight hours. Her story, which she'd told with all the flair of her profession, had given him a great deal to think about, rather as if a missing member of his family had unexpectedly arrived on the scene; someone who could fill in the gaps, who shed new light on old memories: a gentle light that was kind to human failing and softened the hard, black and white edges of preconceived truths. It was impossible that she should disappear almost as suddenly as she'd arrived.

'And anyway,' he said aloud, as if clinching an argument. 'I'm on holiday next week. I can show you round properly.'

Even as he spoke the words he thought of Alison again; since Tilda had mentioned her at breakfast, she'd been there at the back of his mind, a shadow across the expanding light of this strange, new happiness. They'd reached the end of the mole and stood together, staring out across the Bristol Channel to the distant hills of Wales, faint and insubstantial in the hazy heat. Lizzie watched him thoughtfully.

'Perhaps I could check out the bookshop . . . ?' She pursed her lips, looking casual, open to possibilities but not *too* keen – 'If Tilda thinks it's OK . . .'

'Well, it's an idea.' He shifted his weight, thrust his hands into his pockets, made his decision. 'But you might think of staying with us – Tilda and me and Jake – at Michaelgarth . . . just for a few days.' He looked down at her and away again.

'Perhaps it's a bit sudden. After all you don't really know any of us, but it could be rather fun.'

A gull screamed above their heads, wings stretched white against the sky, drifting in the light airs. Lizzie turned, looking back at the high wooded hills above the harbour, shutting her eyes for a moment against the sun's heat and then opening them again to smile at him.

'Thank you, Piers,' she said. 'I should like that very much.'

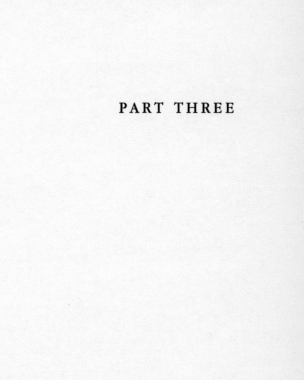

PART THREE

CHAPTER THIRTY-FIVE

Lizzie stirred, drifting between sleep and waking, her eyelids fluttering. Her hands opened and closed, stretched out on the sheet as if reaching for something . . . or someone.

'It couldn't matter less, darling,' Sam is saying. 'You know me. It's part of the job as far as I'm concerned. You know how really good photographers always say that they have to be a little bit in love with their subject to get the best out of them? Well, that's all it is. But you always knew that, didn't you? It wasn't as if it was ever a secret and it's got nothing to do with you and me.'

She struggles to speak, to tell him something important, but she cannot make a sound.

Roused by her efforts into wakefulness, Lizzie dragged the pillows into a soft, supporting pile behind her head and stared out of the window towards the great hill, all green and gold in the early morning sunshine. Loss enveloped her, panic plucking at her diaphragm, and she lay still, looking about her as if by examining and learning the room she might beat down her fears. She'd always found it difficult to remember places accurately although she responded immediately to atmosphere: she knew at once whether she felt comfortable and happy or, instead, uneasy and wanting to be away. Describing a town, a room, was agony for her.

'Tell us all!' Angel commands, as soon as she returns from a visit with a school-friend or, in later years, after a tour abroad, and poor Lizzie screws up her eyes, willing her recalcitrant memory to perform, halting and stumbling through a dull and pedestrian account, whilst Angel rolls her eyes in despair and Pidge grins sympathetically. It is exactly the same with people: she is quickly drawn towards them, or totally indifferent, and very rarely has cause to review that first opinion. So it is with Sam: an instant fascination; an absolute requirement for his company.

'I love you, little Lizzie,' he tells her. 'You've got under my skin. D'you know that?'

She feels herself beaming at him; trying to be cool and sophisticated, failing miserably.

'He's terrifically dishy,' her friends warn her, solo and chorus, 'and he's quite a lot older than you. He's got a bit of a reputation . . .'

Lizzie listens obediently, nodding sensibly, her eyes wide and dreamy with love; she knows these things – and is touched that her friends should care enough about her to wish to protect her – but his age and physical attractions, his predilections for younger actresses, are all part of Sam. He is determined, wily, forceful: even his black hair curls and crisps with vitality: his bright brown eyes either focusing with uncomfortable intensity or flicking to and fro, restless, observant, watchful.

'I love you too,' she answers, not shyly or hesitantly but longingly, needfully. And, later, when the rumours begin – which he never bothers to deny – she takes no notice of them.

'There will always be rumours with a man like Sam.' Angel is comfortingly pragmatic. 'Ignore them if you can and don't play the detective; don't interrogate unless you really can't put up with it. It's part of his job as far as he's concerned and it's got nothing to do with how he feels about you.'

Perhaps it is because she knows that Angel has experienced a similar situation in her own love affair with Felix, and because, like Angel, jealousy and the need to possess have been left out of her character, that she is able to deal with those occasional lapses; and Sam makes it easier simply because he never lies. He treats his infidelities, most no more than drawn-out flirtations, as a kind of necessary occupational hazard: if an actress turns in a better performance because she thinks he is in love with her, well, so be it. He expects Lizzie to be intelligent about it and, because he is never furtive, never shuts her out, but is always careful to make Lizzie feel that she and their marriage are completely separate from these tiresome outbreaks, she is able to accept them. He is discreet and, whenever possible, he makes certain that, in public, Lizzie is always at his side. There are difficult moments, when the current actress believes that he is serious about her, but he is always careful to leave an escape route for the injured party so that she might withdraw with a certain amount of dignity. If, however, any of them refuse to go gracefully, he has no hesitation in being brutal: he never deceives them about his true feelings and he refuses to be blackmailed.

Once or twice the injured party comes to see Lizzie, imploring her to give Sam up, convinced that it is only she, Sam's wife, who stands between their love.

'Sorry, darling, sorry,' he mutters absently, already planning his next production, next seduction, 'the woman has the intelligence of an amoeba. Good grief! She must be raving . . .'

'You're hopeless.' But she stretches out her arms to him. 'Why do I put up with it . . . ?'

*   *   *

The thin, high wailing of a baby roused her and she drew the sheet up to her chin, almost as if it were a kind of protection. The insistent, weak yet demanding cry penetrated her defence and sadness and grief welled inside her: had she been so ready to forgive Sam's lapses because she'd been unable to give him a child? This guilt, growing alongside her own desperate longing for a baby, had made her more vulnerable, fearful of losing him.

A door opened and she heard a light footfall along the corridor. Abruptly the crying ceased, there was movement, the sound of a low murmuring, and then silence. Lizzie got out of bed, humming a little – Blossom Dearie's 'Peel Me a Grape' – peering from the window, concentrating on the room. She bent to inhale the scent of the roses arranged in a pretty silver vase set on the oak chest of drawers, which was placed across one corner of the room. A photograph caught her attention: straddling a bicycle, the small boy frowned in the bright sunlight, staring at the camera almost censoriously.

David, thought Lizzie – and was aware of a tightening of her stomach muscles as panic seized her. Impossible though it might seem, she was here, at Michaelgarth, with Tilda just down the passage and Piers asleep across the garth.

'I can't quite believe it,' she'd said to Felix, after Piers had dropped her back in Dunster after lunch on Wednesday afternoon. She'd gone to the flat early in the evening to find him outside on his big platform, watering some of his pots and tubs. He was in shirt-sleeves, his arms brown; she found that she was looking at his hands. 'It was such a shock – well, you can imagine, can't you? – and I just accepted, "Thank you very much, I'd love to",' she mimicked herself, 'and that was that. And now I'm having a good old panic, Felix, and I'm counting on you to reassure me.' Leaning against the kitchen door-jamb, watching him working amongst the tiny blooms in his miniature garden, she'd grinned suddenly, wickedly. 'Not,' she added with mock-severity, 'that I'm talking *soothing* here, you understand.'

He'd stared at her, his movements arrested, an odd look of mingled surprise and guilt on his face, and then he'd begun to chuckle, the years falling away, so that his face looked almost young again, his eyes gleaming with amusement at old memories.

'Darling Lizzie,' he'd said, with such warmth and love, that she'd instinctively held out her arms to him and they'd met in the middle of the kitchen and hugged each other.

'Am I crazy?' She'd held him away at arm's length, peering fearfully into his face. 'Accepting just like that? After all, I hardly know Piers . . . or Tilda.'

'But you *do* know him, don't you?' he'd asked gently. 'In some inexplicable way you know him because you know me. You've known him since you were a child.'

'Yes,' she'd agreed at last. 'It seems that way. When I saw him in the bar I felt a kind of recognition – and not just because you're both physically alike. And I think he felt the same way.'

'I think so too.' Felix had let her go, turning back to the miniature garden outside the kitchen door, putting his secateurs and a small fork into a painted wooden tool-box. 'I admit that I am amazed that he's invited you so soon, although, to be fair, Piers has never been a procrastinator. He clearly wants to get to know you much better, and, personally, I can't think of a better way of going about it. I'm all for it but then I'm probably as crazy as you are,' a little pause '. . . and we mustn't forget that I have a hidden agenda.'

'And what is that?' She'd watched him, frowning in anxiety as she'd sensed his mood swing towards self-doubt. 'What agenda?'

He'd straightened up, dusting his hands together and then digging them deep into the pockets of his old khaki-drill trousers. Head bent for a moment in thought, he'd stood in the early evening sunshine, brooding, whilst she'd stared at him, almost afraid of what she might hear.

'I'd like to feel that Piers has forgiven me,' he'd said at last. 'Or, at the very least, I wish he could understand and accept my behaviour in the past. It's been between us all these years, that shadow of resentment on his part and guilt on mine, and we've never quite been able to confront it. Now, you've suddenly come among us and we can't ignore it any longer. Once that first huge step was taken it seemed to me that the worst was over and we had a good chance, Piers and I, of restoring our relationship before it was too late. Now you tell me that he's invited you to Michaelgarth – and that place is very special to Piers, remember – so I can't help feeling that he's taken the next three or four steps in one great leap. Good grief! *Naturally*, I'm delighted. By accepting *you*, surely he must have forgiven *me*. You embody all the things that threatened him and yet he's invited you into his home and family, *and* in time for his birthday, so that you'll meet some of his closest friends. Oh, I'm sure that he retains certain reservations but I feel . . . oh, as if I've received some kind of absolution. Of *course* I want you to go to Michaelgarth, but my reasons are not necessarily disinterested ones.'

'But there couldn't be any hidden motive on his part?' She'd sounded troubled and he'd hastened to reassure her.

'Of course not. That's not at all what I was implying.' He'd smiled at her. 'It means so much to me, that's all. To see you and Piers as friends would heal so many old wounds and to imagine you at Michaelgarth with him and Tilda is almost too much to take in all at once. It's beyond everything I ever hoped.'

'Well, then,' she'd grinned back at him, though still nervous, 'let's hope I can put up a good performance. Wish me luck for a truly bizarre first night.'

'You'll be just fine,' he'd said encouragingly. 'It's perfect timing, what with Piers' birthday and Saul down for a few days, and I shall be at Michaelgarth on Saturday. Tilda being there will take all the strain out of it. There's nothing to fear.'

Now, as she prowled about the room, examining the watercolour of an ancient stone bridge spanning a white tumble of water, peering into the built-in cupboards that took up one whole wall, she gave a disbelieving snort.

There's nothing to fear.

She hadn't realized that Piers' birthday was not simply to be a small family affair: apparently she was to be plunged into a full-scale party which, whilst it certainly distracted from her presence at Michaelgarth, filled her with alarm.

'Lots of people will be coming,' Tilda had told her cheerfully soon after she'd arrived late on Friday afternoon. 'Piers has masses of friends and he pays back hospitality by giving big parties every now and then. His birthday was too good an opportunity to miss. And just *wait* until they see *you*.' She'd sighed contentedly, looking at Lizzie with undisguised satisfaction, as if she were a collector and Lizzie a much-prized, highly valuable commodity. 'Oh, how I long to see Alison's face.'

'Who is Alison?' she'd asked anxiously but Tilda, saying lightly, 'Oh, just a rather boring friend', had refused to be drawn any further. Jake had begun to cry, distracting Tilda, and Lizzie had escaped into the garth, wandering about uneasily as she imagined the ordeal ahead, until she'd heard a car approaching. Presently Piers had appeared, walking into the garth with a firm quick step, smiling with pleasure to see her there.

She'd raised her hand casually in return, hastily arranging a relaxed, natural expression – 'Try to remember that you *are* an actress' – as if she were quite used to staying with people she'd known a brief two days and he'd looked at her intently as if trying to gauge her mood.

'Has Tilda been looking after you?' he'd asked – but almost immediately, sensing her tension and guessing that he was sounding rather like an over-efficient host, he'd grimaced self-mockingly. 'It's a bit nerve-racking, isn't it?' he'd asked sympathetically. 'Is it time for a drink? Do we feel we rather need one?'

'Yes,' she'd replied feelingly – and, oddly calmed by his presence, she'd followed him into the house.

This morning, reflecting on the effect he had on her, puzzled by her feelings for him, Lizzie finished her tour of the room, murmured 'Help!' once or twice rather quietly to no-one in particular, and went away to have a shower.

CHAPTER THIRTY-SIX

By the time Tilda arrived in the kitchen Piers had finished his breakfast and disappeared and Saul was standing at the window, staring out towards Dunkery, a mug of coffee in his hand. He turned as she came in, put the mug on the table and with complete naturalness went to take Jake from her, holding him confidently, smiling down at him. Watching him, Tilda's first reaction of pleasure was swamped by an uprush of misery. Just so had she imagined David holding his child, the strong, cradling arms in heart-touching contrast with the weak helplessness; the bobbing, rolling head supported against the broad shoulder. In that brief moment she both resented Saul and, simultaneously, longed to rest against his strength.

'Piers must have been up early. I see he's already had his breakfast.' She poured herself a glass of milk, taking refuge in banalities – 'Ten minutes on the bleeding obvious,' as David, intolerant of any kind of pretence, would have remarked – 'He usually comes down a bit later at the weekends.'

'Too excited to sleep?' offered Saul, making faces at Jake. 'Birthday boy and all that? Can't wait for his pressies?'

'Oh, shut up,' said Tilda crossly; Saul too, always saw

through any kind of subterfuge and once again she experienced mixed emotions: relief at not having to pretend with him and irritation that he refused to co-operate with her evasive tactics.

'Perhaps it's having a famous actress to stay.' Saul decided to steer clear of emotional waters and sat down at the table, holding his godson comfortably whilst finishing his coffee. 'I have to say that I really like her.'

'Oh, so do I.' Tilda's confusion was submerged in a wave of enthusiasm. 'She's so funny, isn't she? And so natural. You'd hardly believe that she's only just met us. I thought she and Piers were old friends but it's Felix she really knows. Apparently she and Piers haven't met for years but you wouldn't really know it, would you?'

'Well, after all,' remarked Saul thoughtfully, 'she *is* an actress – but I know what you mean. Old Piers is the least bit smitten, I thought.'

Tilda looked across at him sharply. 'I thought so too.' A little pause. 'I wonder what Alison will think?'

'Is she that bossy female that gives you a hard time? I haven't met her yet.'

Saul sounded as if he were rather relishing the prospect and Tilda grinned at him challengingly – if affectionately.

'Got your white charger ready, Sir Lancelot?' she asked brightly – and he coloured a little.

'Oh, I know you can look after yourself,' he said, 'but I've been looking forward to a run-in with her. Don't spoil my fun. I'll just slap her about a bit, nothing much . . .'

Tilda laughed. 'You have my permission if she's horrid to Lizzie,' she agreed. 'There's something oddly vulnerable about her, isn't there? She's . . .' Tilda frowned, trying to put her ideas into words, 'well, she's so nicely scatty. Not childish and irritating but . . . sort of genuinely naïve. She can't cope with Jake at all, you know.'

'How do you mean?' Saul looked at her, puzzled.

'She's never had children, you see, and he's so small that she's terrified of him. "Aren't you afraid of breaking him?" she asked. It's quite a nice change, actually. Women of that age usually want to tell me how I should be dealing with him and what I'm doing wrong. All that "Oh, we didn't do that in *my* day" stuff. Well, apart from Alison, of course, who seems to think that a mother and child shouldn't be allowed out in public.'

Saul raised his eyebrows at the bitter note in her voice and she grimaced at him.

'*I* think you're hoping that Lizzie is going to cause trouble between Piers and Alison,' he told her, shifting Jake a little.

They exchanged a conspiratorial glance and as she turned away, beginning to prepare breakfast, he allowed himself the luxury of his natural feelings for her, watching her with longing as she moved about the kitchen. She was so beautiful, so casually elegant, this widow of his closest friend; as unattainable now as she'd been ever since David had introduced them.

'This is Tilda,' he'd said with all that confident ease with which David had been blessed. 'I've told you all about her,' and so he had but nothing had prepared Saul for the reality of her: tall and shapely in the soft clinging stuff of her ball-gown, the thick yellow hair slipping from its artfully casual arrangement and lying in long shining stands upon her neck, those extraordinary eyes . . . The sharp jab of David's elbow had brought him painfully alert.

'This is when you say "hello",' he'd advised kindly – and Tilda had smiled warmly at Saul, taking his hand, ignoring his embarrassment.

'David's such a thug,' she'd said regretfully. 'No finer feelings at all. But I expect you know that?'

'Oh, yes,' he'd agreed, so feelingly that they'd all laughed – and a bond had been instantly formed between them. They'd become a foursome with whichever girl Saul was currently dating and he'd been too deeply and sincerely fond of David to allow his feelings for Tilda to betray him.

'Cereal?' she was asking him now. 'Toast?' and turned in surprise when there was no reply.

'Great.' He looked swiftly down at Jake lest she should see the expression in his eyes. 'Yes, both, please . . . I long to see the puppy.'

'He's arriving later.' Tilda put out bowls and plates, laying a place for Lizzie. 'He'll make his entrance during the party. A kind of canine kiss-o-gram. Oh,' she rolled her eyes in joyful, wicked anticipation, 'I can't wait to see Alison's face.'

Saul shook his head doubtfully. 'I'm beginning to wonder whether I'm going to enjoy this party. Poor old Piers. Does he guess what's in store for him, I wonder.'

Footsteps could be heard crossing the garth, coming in through the scullery, and Tilda put a warning finger to her lips. By the time Piers arrived in the kitchen, Saul was peacefully eating cereal, a sleeping Jake in one arm, whilst Tilda waited patiently by the toaster. Piers raised his eyebrows at the unexpected silence and Tilda, smiling at him, marvelled as she often did at the economic expressiveness of Piers' face: surprise, amusement, a shrewd assessment of the true situation between them were conveyed by the slightest facial movements. Saul turned his head, so as to acknowledge him, and Piers let his hand lie briefly on his shoulder.

'Sleep well?' he asked.

'Like a brick.' Saul set down his spoon and turned in his chair. 'Happy birthday, Piers. Good day for it.'

'It's hot already.' Piers' eyes narrowed affectionately at the sight of his grandson, so contentedly asleep, and – like Tilda earlier – was seized with a spasm of piercing grief at the recollection of all that he had lost. He turned away quickly, as if to examine some letters lying on the dresser, willing down the pain. 'It'll be a splendid evening for a barbecue. I've begun to set it up, but I'm counting on your help, Saul.'

'No problems.' Saul attempted to spread butter on his toast, one-handed, and Tilda took Jake from him, laying him gently in his little chair. 'I'm a real dude when it comes to the barbie.'

Before Piers could respond, a car passed the window and Tilda, catching a glimpse of it, stiffened, making a warning face at Saul. Piers raised his head, listening, and, after a moment, a door slammed and Alison came through the scullery and entered the kitchen. She balanced a covered plate on one hand and held a carrier bag in the other. Saul got to his feet as Piers put down his letters whilst Tilda, with an attempt at a welcoming smile, took another mouthful of toast.

'Goodness!' Alison looked round at them with determined cheerfulness. 'Quite a deputation. I've come to wish you a happy birthday, Piers, since the telephone seems permanently on answerphone these last few days. Oh, and to bring my offering for the party. I felt it was rather a lot for you to manage to feed the five thousand without a bit of help.'

'Not quite that many.' Piers touched his lips to her raised, expectant cheek. 'And thank you for your good wishes . . . and your contribution. This is Saul, David's greatest friend and Jake's godfather. Saul, this is Alison Rowe.'

He didn't qualify the second part of the introduction and she bit her lip as she stood the bag on a chair and took Saul's outstretched hand.

'That looks interesting.' Tilda spoke lightly, indicating the covered plate. 'I hope it isn't a birthday cake or Mrs Coleman will have a fit and Piers will have a serious problem blowing out two lots of candles.'

'It's a trifle.' She set it on the table. 'You can never have too much to eat at these parties, can you? And in the bag there are sausage rolls and a few bits and pieces.'

'It's very kind of you.' Piers was careful not to look at Tilda. 'I'm sure it will be much appreciated.'

He smiled at her but Alison frowned a little, picking up on Tilda's comment. 'What's Mrs Coleman got to do with it?'

'You must have met Mrs C, Alison.' Tilda's voice was brittle; brightly conversational. 'She's Piers' cleaner and she's always done the catering for his parties. Even *I* wouldn't trespass on Mrs C's preserves.'

'I'm not quite a stranger here, Tilda,' answered Alison sharply. 'Of course I know who Mrs Coleman is, although what she has to do with Piers' birthday . . .'

Instinctively the two men intervened: as Saul moved to stand beside Tilda, and Piers began to explain Mrs Coleman's role in the festivities, the door opened and Lizzie came into the kitchen. She'd hesitated for a moment outside the door, hearing Tilda's remarks, catching the name: Alison. In the moment of her entering she took in the scene – Tilda bright-cheeked and defiant, with Saul protectively at her side; Piers caught between family loyalty and friendship; Alison aggressive – and her thespian instincts rushed to the fore. Angel's shade seemed to slip inside her skin, informing her performance – 'I went *right* over the top,' she admitted later to Felix – and carrying her into the centre of the stage.

'So sorry to be late, sweetie,' she cried, bending to kiss Tilda's flushed cheek, beaming at Saul – who grinned instinctively back at her – and moving at once to Piers. 'My dear, a whole orchestra woke me at dawn, plus a cockerel with laryngitis and a sheep with a nasty case of bronchitis.' She shrugged helplessly, palms extended upwards. 'And they say it's quiet in the country. When I went back to sleep I slept for hours and the next thing I heard a car and when I *saw* the time . . .'

Tilda took one look at Alison's incredulous face and burst into uncontrollable laughter.

'Sorry,' she muttered, helplessly. 'Sorry, it's just . . .'

Lizzie turned quickly towards her. 'Was it you who brought the coffee, Tilda?' she demanded. 'Well, it just saved my life when I woke up and saw it there, that's all' – and Tilda, who knew very well that Lizzie had been wide awake and in the shower when she'd taken up the coffee, began to laugh again.

'Alison, this is Lizzie Blake.' Piers, with mixed feelings, took charge. 'I'm sure you recognize her from her appearances on television . . . Lizzie, this is Alison Rowe.'

Once again he failed to qualify the relationship between them, and Alison's smile was glacial.

'I rarely watch the television, I'm afraid. Should I know you?' She touched Lizzie's hand briefly. 'I'm one of those very busy people who don't need to live vicariously by watching ghastly soaps.'

Pleased that she'd rather cleverly managed to imply the area of endeavour in which it would be natural to assume that Lizzie worked, she turned to Piers with a proprietorial smile but Lizzie immediately distracted his attention by kissing him warmly, wishing him many happy returns of the day. He leaned instinctively to receive her salute and Alison's smile faded.

'My husband used to say that television was the last resort of the mentally deficient,' she said, with a light little laugh that deceived no-one, 'and I do so agree with him.'

'Well, lucky old you, sweetie.' Lizzie sat down at the table and took a piece of Tilda's toast, spreading it lavishly with butter. 'I utterly depend on it. Especially the dear old soaps. It's *such* fun seeing all one's chums . . .'

'Coffee?' suggested Saul tactfully. 'I'm going to have some more. Lizzie? Alison?'

Jake woke suddenly, grizzling gently, and Tilda, still swallowing down her laughter, pushed back her chair and went to him.

Alison touched Piers' arm. 'Could I have a quiet word?' She gave a little humorous look that implied that the kitchen was full of lunatics, and led the way out into the garth.

The other three exchanged glances.

'I've heard the term "upstaging" before but I've never seen it done quite so professionally,' said Saul reflectively, making coffee. 'You ought to get an Oscar for that, Lizzie.'

'Coffee will do nicely,' she told him grimly. 'So that's Alison. You might have warned me.'

Tilda stared at her anxiously over Jake's head. 'I can't decide whether it's just me, you see,' she said. 'I wouldn't mind her being antagonistic to me and Jake if I could believe she was right for him. But I'm sure she just isn't and he's sinking further and further in. I can just imagine what David would say!'

Lizzie took another piece of toast. 'Tell me all about her,' she said. 'How it started and all that stuff. Hurry up with that coffee, Saul, and then you can stand near the door and warn us when they come back. I think that Alison is someone I need to know about. From the top, Tilda, and don't leave anything out.'

CHAPTER THIRTY-SEVEN

'My dear Piers,' Alison was saying out in the garth, 'what an extraordinary woman. You didn't tell me anyone was staying at Michaelgarth. Is she here for the party?'

Already it was hot: the warm, still air was fragrant with the scent from the roses, which climbed and tumbled over the high stone walls in clusters of gold and cream and pink; tissue-soft, crumpled faces opening towards the sun. Deep in amongst the woody stems velvety buds, tight packed, showed like candle flames hidden amongst paint-bright leaves whilst higher up, on the entwining, thorny branches, full-blown blooms drooped, their faded petals drifting silently down to settle lightly on the ancient cobbles.

Piers stooped to pluck a just-opening bud, studying it with a deep, grateful pleasure before presenting it to Alison. It stopped her, as nothing else could have done, but even before he saw her face – relaxing from spitefulness into surprised delight – he knew that he'd made a mistake. She would misunderstand the gesture, just as she'd done so often in the past, and even whilst he smiled at her he cursed his own stupidity. Such danger lay hidden in these casual human exchanges: each reading his – or her – own interpretation into words, actions. Some blessed people were naturally, delicately, attuned to the least nuance – others almost wilfully obtuse. Lines of a poem ran in his head:

> Earth's crammed with heaven,
> And every common bush afire with God;
> And only he who sees, takes off his shoes –
> The rest sit round it and pluck blackberries.

He knew that in giving Alison the rose he was allowing her to imagine something that was not true. Nevertheless she was momentarily distracted: the rose, in all its fresh beauty, made it impossible for her to continue to be unpleasant. She turned it in her fingers, breathed its perfume, allowing his offering to quieten her restless, grasping soul.

He thought: In a moment she will put on her shoes again and begin to pluck blackberries – and saw the exact second in which she rejected the gentler powers of generosity and kindness, choosing instead self-importance and conflict.

Turning to him, the rosebud forgotten, she said, 'But who is she, Piers, Lizzie whatever-you-called-her? It was as if you expected me to know her.' She laughed vexedly, as if such an idea were preposterous. 'You didn't tell me you had anyone staying, in fact I wasn't sure what the arrangements for the party were, though I've been trying to get hold of you since Wednesday. I expect Tilda forgot to give you my message. So who is this woman?'

He tried to decide which aspect of her wounded pride he should first address. He knew that he'd upset her by refusing to introduce her as an old friend – or as someone even closer to him – but was still at a loss as how to describe their relationship. He was fond of her but his sympathy for her bereavement, especially coinciding as it did with his own, had misled her, and he knew that he'd allowed it do so without taking steps to prevent it: because of his pity, because her problems and her needs had been a comforting antidote to his own grief for David – whatever the reasons, he'd been a party to the deception. Lizzie's arrival had jolted him out of his apathy but, in truth, he could not say that he believed that he'd been acting fairly towards Alison. He'd known he was not committed, not in love with her, was aware of her expectations, but had gone along with it; it was only now that he was unable to continue to deceive her. He opted for the truth.

'She's my father's friend,' he began. 'I met her once briefly when we were children but my father knew her mother very well. He hasn't seen her for quite a while and then she turned up in Dunster rather unexpectedly. I understand that she lost her husband recently and I think that she's in that rather terrible state of loss and rootlessness. Well, we know that one, don't we?'

Alison, raw with jealousy and shock at seeing an attractive woman so much at ease in the kitchen at Michaelgarth, was unwilling even to allow Lizzie the benison of grief.

'She didn't seem too bereft,' she said, with that same vexed, half-mocking laugh. Even in the grip of this weighted, miserable uncertainty, she would not show herself to be openly, honestly vulnerable. Instead she must attempt to discredit Lizzie in Piers' eyes. 'Personally, I can't stand that type of showing off,' a shrug, 'although I suppose it takes some people in.'

Piers was silent: in her fear and anger Alison rolled the rosebud to and fro between her fingers, shredding and peeling the soft petals into tiny yellow velvet balls.

'Of course I can imagine that Tilda is delighted,' she went on contemptuously. 'Anyone who is remotely well known would appeal to *her*. She's always watching the television, isn't she? I could hardly believe my eyes when I saw that portable TV in the kitchen . . .'

Piers, watching her bitter mouth, the little sneer, the look of fear in her eyes, was reminded of his mother. He wondered if Alison's jealousy were rooted in a need to possess, to control, or whether it sprang from a lack of confidence and low self-esteem. He feared that it might be the former and was gripped with distress: either way, he did not want it to be his problem, yet his compassion for her could not be quite so easily withheld.

'Tilda's good for me.' He spoke lightly, trying to lead her into a calmer frame of mind. 'She and Jake give me so much.'

'Give *you* so much?' Her eyebrows arched in disbelief. 'I should say that the shoe is quite on the other foot.'

'You mustn't forget that you still have your children,' he reminded her gently. 'They might not come home to you quite so often these days but they are *there*, alive somewhere in the world. At any moment one of them might telephone you or text you. There might be a card amongst your letters or a parcel on your birthday, from either your son or your daughter, or they could even appear, wandering in, taking refuge, coming home to recharge their batteries, gather courage or even simply to borrow money. All those privileges are denied me now.'

She was wise enough not to snort as she usually did, to say derisively, 'You call those privileges?' but remained silent, frustrated by his painful simplicity.

'It's not just her company,' Piers was saying. 'I have no problem with being alone. It's simply that she and Jake are part of David and whilst they are around I can feel that he is too. Oh, it hurts like hell, sometimes, but even pain can have its uses. I'm sure you feel like that about Philip from time to time?'

Impossible to answer that she hardly ever thought about Philip, except when a household problem arose: that her desire for Piers blotted out almost every other sensation.

She thought: This is like having some terrible fever. I am in love with him. It was never like this with Philip.

Even without looking at him she was aware of his proximity: the brushing of his shirt-sleeve against her bare arm, the movement of his hands, his quick intent glance. In her mind's eye she saw again the woman in the kitchen, remembering how she'd moved so easily to give that kiss to Piers and how naturally he'd bent his head to receive it. Fear seized her: tall, slender, the thick hair so loosely gathered back, she'd looked quite young as she'd made her entrance, drawing all the attention to herself, making them laugh. Alison had felt clumsy in comparison, heavy and humourless, only too aware that anguish was painting cruel lines upon her face and rooting her flat-footed to the floor whilst the other woman's body was fluid with unconscious elegance and grace.

Perhaps she could be like that; perhaps, even now, she could accept his gesture and let him lead her away from the dark, sterile, boggy land of possessiveness towards the higher, warmer, fruitful ground of generosity. Even as she contemplated it, a burst of laughter from the kitchen assaulted her ears, stiffening her spine; glancing down she saw that the rosebud was destroyed and she dropped its remains upon the cobbles, wiping her finger on her handkerchief.

'I have a present for you in the car,' she said, 'but I was hoping to have a moment alone with you . . .'

Her voice trailed into nothing and she looked away from him, resentment dulling her face. Piers, knowing that he had failed, resisted the usual urge to over-compensate by extravagant words and gestures.

'That's very kind,' he said cheerfully – but making no attempt to suggest a solution that would appeal to her. 'And thank you for the goodies. They look delicious. Mrs Coleman will be here later and Saul's going to help me gather together all the garden furniture. I'm afraid that it's going to be one of those days. Are you sure you wouldn't like to get my present and come back inside to have some coffee while I open it?'

He glanced over his shoulder as Tilda came out into the garth carrying Jake, singing to him.

'No,' Alison said sharply. 'No, not now.' Despair gripped her. 'But I shall see you later?'

'Of course,' he said warmly. 'Don't be silly. Come early and have a drink.' He smiled at her, unable to let her go away unhappy. 'We'll have the present-giving then, shall we? About six thirty?'

Her face lit with hope at this promise and she half wondered whether she should simply get his present and do as he suggested but, even as she heard Lizzie's voice joined with Saul's and Tilda's, the impulse died.

'I'll see you later, then,' she said. 'No, don't bother to see me off. I'll see you at half-past six,' and she hurried out of the garth, climbed into her car and drove away.

CHAPTER THIRTY-EIGHT

Between the cottage door and the gate, ostentatiously placed lest he might somehow be forgotten, Bertie sat watching the packing-up process. All week he'd felt unsettled, unused to his surroundings, puzzled by long, solitary hours in the car. His tail thumped gently each time a suitcase or bag was carried out; ears pricked, he waited patiently for the summons that would mean that, at last, they were going home.

'I'll take him for a walk in a minute,' said Guy, who had tripped over him twice, cursed him elaborately and was now feeling guilty. 'I might as well do it now, before it gets too hot, and then he'll settle down and go to sleep in the car. Do you want to come?'

Gemma shook her head. 'I'll finish the packing,' she said. 'There's not much more to go in and I'd rather get it done. When you get back we'll have some coffee to set us on our way.'

Guy put on his shoes and went outside. 'OK,' she heard him say, 'your moment has come. No, no, not in the car, you daft animal; we're going for a walk.'

She watched them pass the front window on their way up

the hill and then began to make a thorough check of the house. Someone called Mrs Coleman would be over shortly to change the sheets and clean the cottage. Meanwhile Gemma wanted to make certain that nothing was left behind and the place was tidy and clean and in good order. Piers had refused to take any payment for their week's holiday and the least she could do was to keep the changeover work to a minimum.

The wardrobes and chest of drawers were empty; no book had been kicked under the bed, no bathrobe left hanging behind the door. She moved from room to room, possessed with the sense of restlessness that had been with her since early morning, ready to go home: the fun was over and she felt uneasy. The brief sense of belonging was gone, their short tenancy was finished, and she felt a stranger here. She put her head round the door of the sitting-room. They'd never used this room with its open hearth and comfortable armchairs, preferring to live in the big family room across the narrow hall, but she hesitated at the door for a moment, aware of an ambience of continuity: of centuries of day-to-day living. The room, in fact the whole cottage, had an atmosphere of permanence: there was none of the impersonal uniformity of the holiday cottage about it.

Here Piers had lived, first alone and then with his family, before moving back to Michaelgarth and Gemma imagined that she was able to detect his wife's influence at work amongst the bright, pretty hangings and loose covers.

'Sue was brilliant,' Tilda had told her that morning when she'd come for coffee. 'She did everything so well. When the last tenants left, Sue persuaded Piers to let the cottage to holiday-makers. She said it would bring in more money. Piers agreed to try it but he's happier letting it on a long-term basis to a local person, and he's saying that at the end of this summer it will go back to being a shorthold tenancy. I think he's been waiting to see whether I might have preferred to be here rather than at Michaelgarth.'

'And wouldn't you?' Gemma had asked curiously. 'Wouldn't you welcome a bit more privacy?'

She'd longed to ask whether Tilda missed her freedom, longed for some fun, but something in Tilda's clear, tranquil gaze forbade it.

'Not really.' Tilda had considered the question seriously. 'Piers gives me plenty of space, you know. The two wings divide the house quite naturally, and he has his study and we've converted the dining-room to a comfortable place for me and Jake. I find that it's rather nice to have someone around in the evening and we kind of comfort each other without getting too emotional, if you see what I mean. It's Piers I feel sorry for, actually. I'm probably rotting up his private life without realizing it but he gives no sign of feeling trapped. I sometimes wonder what I'd do if he met someone else and it got serious. I doubt another woman would want me and Jake in the west wing. I expect we'd move down here then but, selfishly, I hope it doesn't happen. I feel so much at home at Michaelgarth and I want Jake to grow up there if possible. It's where David was happiest and I want Jake to feel part of that.' She'd looked affectionately at the cottage as they'd sat outside its open door. 'Of course he lived here too, when he was very small.' She'd laughed, shaking her head. 'I just can't get away from him.'

Remembering, Gemma shut the sitting-room door sharply and crossed the hall. Her bag, bulging with various items she might need for the journey, sat on the breakfast bar beside the mugs put ready for coffee. She checked the fridge, taking out a bottle of water along with the last of the cheese and some grapes. There was a drop of milk for the coffee and a few other odds and ends, which she collected and dropped into the waste-bin. Taking Guy's sweater from the back of a chair, picking up the map from the table at the window, Gemma gathered together the last things to be put into the car and made a pile of them on the bar.

She filled the kettle, switched it on and took the cheese and grapes out to the car. The small hamper was crammed between the twins' little chairs and she leaned in, stretching across the nearest seat, so as to lift its wicker lid and put the remains of the food inside. As she closed it she was aware of something being missing; some object that was usually kept here on the back seat. Frowning in puzzlement she went back into the cottage, trying to remember what she'd forgotten. Bertie's bed was already in the back of the estate car, along with his water bowl, and Guy had packed boots and jackets into the well behind the driver's seat.

Gemma took another look around the room, trying to picture the usual contents of the back seat and wondering whether she was thinking of something that hadn't been necessary for this holiday: the padded bag containing the twins' travelling requirements, for instance, had been left at home along with the duffel bag full of soft toys with which she entertained them on long journeys. She shrugged, fishing for her mobile in her crammed bag, checking for messages. It was in the second between thinking about Simon and deciding not to risk a last call to him that she remembered the missing item: her rug. She nearly dropped the mobile, clapping a hand to her mouth in horror, visualizing their last meeting.

'Do we really need two rugs?' he'd asked teasingly. 'Perhaps I should try to get hold of a feather mattress.'

'It's a bit late now, isn't it?' she'd retorted, spreading her rug across his own. 'But perhaps you should consider it for next time.'

'Is there going to be a next time?' he'd asked, pulling her down beside him, and she'd shaken her head as she smiled at him. Afterwards they'd stood talking together, drinking coffee from a flask, collecting the remains of the picnic. He'd bent to pick up the rugs, bundling them together over his arm, talking about Marianne, recounting her reaction when she'd heard Gemma's message on the answerphone. She'd perched on the edge of the passenger seat of her car as she listened to him, combing her hair and peering into the small mirror inside the glove compartment. What had happened after that?

Gemma screwed her eyes shut, desperately trying to recreate the scene. Had he put both rugs in his own vehicle? Putting her mobile on the top of her bag she ran out to the car; hastily she moved the cases that Guy had stacked earlier, lifted Bertie's bed, peered into the wells behind the front seats. The rug was always kept folded on top of the small hamper between the twins' chairs, ready to be wrapped round them if they were chilly or to be spread for them to crawl on during a picnic. It was nowhere to be seen. She tried to steady herself. After all, Guy would probably never notice it was missing and it could be easily replaced. There was nothing particularly special about it: it was the rug she'd taken to school to use on her bed in winter, a cheerful tartan with her nametape sewed to one edge . . . She caught her breath and her heartbeat thudded in her side: she could see that nametape very clearly: 'G WIVENHOE' in blue on a white background.

In a single moment she imagined Marianne putting something into the Discovery – a coat? her walking boots? – noticing the bundled rug and dragging it out to fold it properly.

'What's this?' she'd ask Simon, quite natural to begin with, puzzled by the second rug rolled into their own. 'Where did this come from?'

She'd hold it out to him, not suspecting anything until, alerted by his silence, she'd look at him properly.

Gemma swallowed in a dry throat. How would he react after that first shock? Would he bluff it out – 'Haven't a clue, darling. Can't remember when we last used the rug, can you?' – and try to hurry her into the car? Would Marianne, still puzzled, insist on examining the rug and see that wretched nametape? She glanced at her watch. It was clear that Simon hadn't noticed it yet or he would have phoned her. There was still time to warn him. Supposing she were to text him: leave a message?

'Best not to phone tomorrow,' he'd said. 'Marianne and I will almost certainly be together. We generally shop on a Saturday morning and it would be a bit chancy.'

If she sent a text, would his mobile ring and give him away? She had a sudden horrid vision of Marianne arriving at the cottage, flourishing the rug and demanding an explanation: she saw Guy returning to such a scene, surprise and distaste turning to suspicion and finally to anger. She whirled about and ran into the cottage, seized the mugs and thrust them back into the cupboard, emptied the milk into the sink and threw the carton into the waste-bin. Grabbing their belongings, she raced back outside, looking along the road, willing Guy to appear with Bertie at his heels. There was no sign of them. Back indoors, scrabbling in her bag, she found the cottage keys, which she'd been told to leave on the breakfast bar – 'Mrs Coleman has her own set of keys,' Tilda had said – and dropped them on the pine counter. She felt sick and frightened and, hearing Guy at last, she hurried out, trying to school her face into a smile.

He was closing the gate behind Bertie, who clearly wanted to get into the car, and looked surprised to see her coming out, hitching her bag over her shoulder. Her small, pretty features were sharpened, pinched, and he frowned a little.

'Are you OK? I thought we were going to have some coffee?'

'Oh, darling,' her voice sounded uneven and she cleared her throat, 'I had a sudden longing to get on. Do you mind? I know it sounds silly but I simply can't wait to see the babes, can you? It's been a lovely break but I just want to get home.'

He shrugged. 'That's fine with me but I need a leak before we go. You haven't locked up, have you?'

He disappeared into the cottage whilst she opened the tailgate to let Bertie in and then went to stand by the open door of the car, biting her lips, willing Guy to hurry. Her knees shook and she looked down the road, convinced that she heard an engine. He came at last, slamming the door behind him, and climbed into the car. Waiting in anguish whilst he dug in the pocket of his jeans for his key, took a last glance over his shoulder towards the sea, she realized in those endless moments exactly what she had risked and how much she stood to lose.

Guy switched on the engine, fixed his seat belt, and at last they drove away with Gemma, chin on shoulder, watching the empty toll road reel out behind them.

CHAPTER THIRTY-NINE

Sitting on the seat in the cloistered way outside the hall, Lizzie watched Saul and Piers. She'd left the kitchen to Mrs Coleman and Tilda, whose murmuring voices could be heard through the open window, and was content to sit in the shade, peacefully entertained by the scene before her. Whilst the swallows darted in and out above his head, Saul kept disappearing into the barn, only to return with yet another wooden seat or some dilapidated deckchair. Each would be dusted off, reviewed, and then tested by Saul who lowered himself gingerly on to rotting slats or fraying canvas with such a comic expression of dismayed caution that Lizzie laughed out loud. One ancient deckchair collapsed beneath him with a gentle explosion of dust and powdery wood and he was rescued just in time by Piers' outstretched hand hauling him up as it disintegrated.

As they stood together – Saul dusting himself down disgustedly, Piers chuckling sympathetically – she wondered how difficult it was for Piers to watch Saul and Tilda together, how painful to see Saul undertaking the small tasks that would have naturally fallen to David. Clearly Tilda and Piers were a great comfort to each other and she felt humbled by their bravery: humbled and ashamed.

She was already regretting her earlier behaviour, despite the evident pleasure it had given Tilda and Saul; whatever their feelings about Alison she'd had no right to interfere or to assume that Piers needed her assistance. It was evident, from Tilda's recital, that Alison neither welcomed the presence of Piers' daughter-in-law and grandson at Michaelgarth, nor was she being terribly intelligent about it; nevertheless it was up to Piers to draw his own conclusions. She'd said as much to Tilda who agreed that, in normal circumstances, Piers would have already realized that Alison wasn't right for him; her anxiety, she explained, was that Alison misunderstood his kindness for something quite different and that he was now entrapped by a sense of guilt.

'He's good at guilt,' she'd said. 'My mother says that his mother instilled it in him. Felix had an affair with some woman up-country that lasted quite a long time and Marina took it out on Piers. Made him feel that he had to make it up to her, if you see what I mean.'

It had been rather a shock to hear Tilda refer so casually to a part of her own life – to hear Angel described in such a way – and she'd felt compassion for the young Piers, attempting to comfort his mother whilst trying to understand his father's behaviour. She'd followed Tilda out into the garth, watching Alison go with mixed feelings, unable to detect Piers' reaction and feeling suddenly embarrassed.

She thought: I am like a tourist visiting his life, peering at it and assessing it, without knowing anything about him. What does he truly think and feel? Who am I to think that he needs protecting from his friends?

She'd been quite happy to be alone for a moment when Tilda went away to change Jake and Saul strolled over to the barn to check the barbecue. She'd watched as he'd exchanged a few remarks with Piers who, with a little friendly look towards her as she'd stood in the sunshine finishing her coffee, had gone indoors. She hadn't seen him again until lunchtime: a quick snack of bread and cheese, disturbed by the arrival of Mrs Coleman, laden with bags and boxes. Saul and Tilda had hastened to clear away the remains of the meal, chattering together as they'd filled the dishwasher, whilst Piers introduced Lizzie to Mrs Coleman. Lizzie, who had already imagined her as an elderly apple-cheeked country-woman, devoted to Piers' family over generations, had been obliged to revise her ideas: she was a spare, rather tired-looking woman in her late thirties with a very sweet smile and an air of quiet confidence. It was clear that Piers was very attached to her and she'd given him a quick kiss as she'd handed him his birthday card.

'How very sweet of you, Jenny,' he'd said, opening it at once, reading it and then standing it with the other cards on the dresser. 'Thank you so much.'

'Many happy returns,' she'd said. 'Now, if you'll clear out and give me some room I'll get started, unless Tilda would like to lend a helping hand.'

Piers and Saul had immediately wandered out into the garth, taking Lizzie along with them, and now she sat watching as Saul began to make a pile of the rejected seats, fetching a wheelbarrow and taking them away to be disposed of at some later date. Piers came to sit beside her on the bench.

'I'm disappointed,' she murmured, not looking at him but continuing lazily to watch Saul.

He took in her profile, the half-closed eyes, with an amused glance. 'I'm sorry to hear that.'

'I had it all worked out,' she continued in the same low voice, 'that Mrs Coleman was to be an ancient retainer, jealous of her position here, working her fingers to the bone at Michaelgarth. I'd even pictured her rather like an Irene Handl character. You know the kind of thing? Rather blowsy but clean, very clean, with a spotless overall. Those appley-red withered cheeks and sharp but kind eyes. Oh, and serious shoes.'

'*Serious* shoes?' he repeated, puzzled.

She looked at him. 'You must know what I mean,' she insisted. 'Black lace-ups but distorted by bunions. Heavy and uncomfortable but she always wears them with stockings, even on the hottest day. I'd decided that I might be summed up and found wanting unless I was lucky enough to be approved because of the TV ad but that even then she'd still fear that I was flighty.'

He chuckled, remembering Mrs Penn. 'Yes, I can see how disappointed you must have been. Jenny Coleman doesn't quite fit that identikit.'

Lizzie sighed. 'So much for preconceived ideas.'

'And do you always form mental pictures of people you're about to meet?'

She pursed her lips cautiously. 'Not always. They have to sound interesting, excite the imagination. Some people do it the other way round, of course. They imagine actors to be the characters they portray, especially in anything that has a long run.'

'You mean that you are permanently identified as the delightful if scatty mother of two rebellious teenage sons whose charming but dysfunctional father keeps rotting up your life.'

'Something like that,' she agreed, after a pause.

'Any similarity?' he asked carefully.

'About as accurate as my picture of Mrs Coleman,' she answered. 'I couldn't have children,' she added quickly but with a finality that silenced him.

He gazed up at the swallows, which swooped and wheeled in the hot blue air, vanishing into the dark shadows of the barn to feed their nestlings, arrowing back out into the sunshine: it seemed that anything he might say could only be trivial or inquisitive.

'You, on the other hand, were just as I'd imagined you.' She assisted him over the awkward moment. 'But then I had something to work on. My memories of Felix helped me there. It'll be odd to see him here, both of you together. Is it time for me to go and fetch him yet?'

He glanced at his watch, taking the hint. 'Whenever you like. I hope it won't be too much for him but he can have a rest between tea and supper. It's kind of you to go.'

'And will Alison be here for tea?' she asked lightly. 'Or . . . anyone else?'

'No.' He answered rather too quickly. 'No, it's just family and very close friends for birthday tea. That's how it always is at Michaelgarth.'

'In that case I feel very honoured,' she said, 'especially as we only met four days ago. Of course you could say we've known each other for forty-odd years . . .'

'You're special,' he said unguardedly – and she turned to look at him, surprised and pleased.

'I wish I'd bought you a present now,' she told him. 'Damn.'

His eyes narrowed with amusement. 'You presented me with some wine, if I remember correctly.'

'Yes, but that wasn't a birthday present. That was an early thank-you-for-having-me present.' She shook her head. 'I didn't think that I knew you well enough to choose anything. Now I feel bad.' She hesitated. 'Piers, I want to apologize for this morning. Oh, don't look puzzled: you know very well what I mean. All that showing off in the kitchen in front of Alison. I just felt a bit shy, I suppose . . .'

He gave a shout of laughter. 'Shy?' he said disbelievingly, teasingly – and she laughed with him, comfortable and happy again, her embarrassment suddenly dissipated. They looked at each other, that strange sense of recognition leaping between them until, genuinely shy now, Lizzie made a show of checking the time by her own watch, saying that she must get ready to fetch Felix.

Upstairs in the bathroom she stared at her reflection in the glass, hearing Sam's voice saying: *Love her? How do I know if I love her? Love's such an overused word. I'm not certain I know what it means any longer.*

She turned away from the glass and, going back into the bedroom, sat down on the edge of the bed. Remembering his pile-driver personality crowded out other feelings and she imagined him, as she'd known him best, directing an actor: his hands slicing and shaping the air, his body tensed with the urgent need to convey his precise requirements. She pictured the frustration when those directions were misunderstood, his hands snatching and dragging through his thick wild hair; the excitement when a scene was spot on, one fist punching the air and his face creased with delight. In his company other people faded into insignificance and, in his absence, life was an empty colourless business: one way or another Sam was going to be a difficult act to follow.

Love's such an overused word. I'm not certain I know what it means any longer.

Presently she stood up, found her car-keys and went down-stairs, the words still echoing in her ears.

CHAPTER FORTY

They had tea in the shade of a huge green umbrella, sitting round a big wooden table in the garth. Tilda and Saul sat together on a bench seat with Jake in his bouncy chair beside them whilst the other three sat in the most comfortable of the garden chairs, selected earlier by Piers and Saul. Jenny Coleman had made delicious buttery cucumber sandwiches, thin and light as wafers, and a coffee and walnut cake. They sat in the dappled sunlight idly discussing how Tilda might start up some kind of small business, perhaps working from Michaelgarth, without having to leave Jake.

'So many people work from home these days,' she said. 'There must be something I can do. I certainly can't imagine going back to an office routine although I'm good at organization.'

The conversation continued at a desultory level, with various suggestions bandied to and fro, until it was time to cut the cake.

'My favourite,' declared Piers with great satisfaction whilst Tilda poured more tea. 'How about a slice, Lizzie?'

'Oh, yes please.' She spoke rather dreamily, staring towards the barns. She'd been wondering how Alison might have reacted to this exchange of ideas and noticing that Saul was having very little to say. 'You know this would be a terrific place for people to give workshops.' She accepted her piece of cake. 'I was having a look inside the barns earlier. There's masses of space and you wouldn't have a parking problem. You were talking about running a little tea-room, Tilda, but why not make it into a kind of craft workshop where people come to give classes?'

'What kind of classes?' Felix looked interested, taking his tea from Tilda. 'You don't mean that Tilda should give the classes?'

'No, no.' Lizzie was amused by Tilda's squawk of horror. 'I was thinking of some of the craft workshops I've seen in action. The expert in whatever craft it is – it might be, oh, let me see. Water-colours? Silk-painting? Pottery? Writing? – would hire your barn for a course of lessons, which he or she would advertise. People always need places to hold courses – they call it a venue, such a horrid word – and a place like this, so old and set around this beautiful garth, would attract any creative person like a magnet.'

'So we let the barn,' began Tilda rather diffidently and with a sideways glance at Piers, 'but only on a temporary basis and to lots of different people?'

'I suppose you'd have to see what demand there was,' observed Piers thoughtfully. 'You might have someone who wanted it for the same few weeks each year or regularly once a month.'

'It might be a bit of a headache fitting each class in and keeping a diary of it all,' admitted Lizzie, 'but Tilda did say she likes organizing. I don't think that theatre workshops would work without some kind of stage but you could do mime and dance, I suppose.'

'And would the punters stay overnight?' asked Felix, clearly fascinated by the concept.

'It depends how long the course is and how far they travel,' answered Lizzie, rather pleased by the reception of her idea. 'But the place is stiff with B. & B.s and small hotels. It shouldn't be a problem. The area is such an attraction in itself, isn't it, especially for artists?'

'And I could provide lunch.' Tilda sat up straight, her cake forgotten. 'Home-made soup and rolls, with a rather delicious pudding . . .'

'For which they pay extra,' chipped in Lizzie, grinning at her.

'Would it cost much to put the barn in order?' asked Saul. This was his first contribution.

'We'd need to install a lavatory,' said Piers; he was clearly taking it seriously, 'and fit out a small area so that they could make coffee and so on. And put in some kind of heating.'

'I suppose you could check with the library to see what courses are being given locally,' suggested Felix, 'and then approach the teachers?'

'Brilliant,' said Tilda, 'and the Tourist Board too. It's the best idea we've had yet,' she hesitated a little. 'Isn't it, Piers?'

'It's good,' he answered positively. 'Really good.'

Tilda gave a huge sigh, sat back to finish her cake and smiled at Saul, sensing that he was not as wholeheartedly enthusiastic as the others.

'Come and help me bath Jake,' she said to him. 'I want to try to get him settled a bit earlier this evening.' She glanced at Lizzie, remembering how Teresa always begged to bath Jake, feeling rather awkward. Lizzie – though she smiled upon the baby and showed none of Alison's tiny resentments when he was fed or if he cried – nevertheless made no advances towards him. 'Unless you might like to help me, Lizzie . . . ?' she began cautiously.

'Good grief!' Lizzie looked so terrified that everyone laughed. 'You cannot be serious! I'd drop him or drown him.

No, no.' She shook her head. 'He's so fragile he frightens me to death.'

'Come on, Saul. You're not afraid of him, are you?' Tilda stood up, taking Jake's chair, and the three of them went into the house.

'He's so small.' Lizzie felt her reaction needed further explanation. 'Oh, the responsibility of such a tiny person.'

She frowned suddenly, biting her lip, and Felix, watching her, leaned forward, pushing his plate a little to one side.

'That's a very good idea of yours, Lizzie, about the barn, I mean. What do you say, Piers?'

'It *is* a good idea.' Piers crossed his legs, leaning back in his chair. 'It probably wouldn't cost much to convert the barn but I shall need to look into the planning regulations. Tilda needs something to get her teeth into and this could be a perfect solution.'

Upstairs, Saul leaned against the door-jamb, watching his godson being lowered into his small bath. His legs kicked excitedly as they touched the warm water and he laughed with pleasure at the freedom and his new-felt power. Tilda, kneeling, a towel wrapped about her waist, laughed with him, turning her head from the splashing, the ends of her hair wet. Suddenly she lifted him high up, so that the water streamed down her strong, brown arms whilst Jake gurgled with joy.

Saul was pierced with tenderness: he'd found it difficult to sit silently by, listening to plans that would commit Tilda to Michaelgarth, yet he had no sensible alternatives to offer. From his own point of view he'd have preferred her to be somewhere other than David's family home, where his presence was stamped so strongly, but Michaelgarth was Jake's inheritance and Tilda was safe here. After all, it was almost as much her home as it had been David's, and he knew that, however much she missed her army friends and the social life, this part of Exmoor was where she belonged.

Last evening, with Gemma and Guy joining them for supper, she'd been so much mistress of the occasion, so naturally right as she'd moved about the kitchen and in the drawing-room afterwards. There was a strength and grace about her that had contrasted sharply with his sister's tinsel, doll-like prettiness and, though no-one could be more charming than Gemma when she was in good form, Tilda had some special quality that transcended charm. He'd felt the usual uncomfortable twinge as he watched them together, wishing that he needn't have been burdened with this knowledge, which had made him ashamed of his sister and angry with David. In her innocence, Tilda had been warmly friendly with Gemma, straightforward and low-key with Guy – who disliked anyone fussing over him – and Saul wondered, not for the first time, how she would react if she discovered the truth.

'Forget it, mate,' David would have said. 'It was just one of those things. Life's too short . . .'

Saul experienced a sinking of the stomach as he imagined how those eyes might look at him if Tilda ever found out what had happened between David and Gemma: what might she think of his silence? Would she accuse him of helping to deceive her or understand that he'd merely been trying to protect her? He ached with his love and need for her, wishing that he could take care of them both, and instinctively he went to them, taking the towel from her and holding it so that he could wrap Jake in its soft warm folds. They sat together, the three of them, on the edge of the bath and she leaned against him, her hair dripping on his cotton shirt.

'I love you,' he said angrily. 'That's the trouble. You know it really, don't you, Tilda?'

'Yes,' she said, after a moment. 'Yes, I do know, Saul.'

'I feel so bloody helpless.' He still spoke savagely, yet he continued to hold the child tenderly. 'I feel as if I'm being disloyal to David but I loved you from the first minute and I just have to say it out loud.'

She slid her arm about him, her cheek against his shoulder, remembering Gemma's words: *I can't quite see Saul in David's league.*

How could she describe her great affection for him? 'You're very special, Saul,' she began, 'it's just . . .'

'I know.' He tried to smile, not wanting to distress her by forcing explanations from her so as to ease his suffering. 'Just don't tell me that I'm like a brother to you, that's all.'

She was silent for so long that he turned to look down at her, fear and a faint flickering of hope wrestling together in his breast.

'I can't describe exactly what I feel,' she answered at last. 'David was so . . . all-encompassing. He's such a difficult act to follow – and I can't imagine even thinking about that yet, if ever. But I love you too, only it's cheating to say so when I can't offer anything. I know I'd hate it if you weren't around and I need you to keep me grounded, if you see what I mean.'

'I think so.' He knew he must be content with this much, at least for the time being, but that tiny flame of hope continued to glow within him and his spirits lifted. 'Let's get this fellow sorted and then I must go down and help Piers get the lights up in the garth.' He bent and touched his lips lightly to her hair. 'Don't worry about it, Tilda. I shall be around for as long as you need me.'

She grinned at him gratefully, giving him a hug. 'We both need you,' she told him, and followed him into the nursery.

CHAPTER FORTY-ONE

As she dressed for her rendezvous with Piers at six thirty, Alison cast anxious yet hopeful glances in the dressing-table glass as she passed to and fro before it: as though these short glimpses, taken on the wing, might reveal some unknown side of her, presenting some aspect of which she was rarely aware. The quick, darting figure, wrestling with a zip, dragging a T-shirt over its head, showed a different Alison to the one who sat upon the upholstered stool, staring critically and with dissatisfaction into the triple mirror. Was this how Piers saw her: in motion, flexible? Or was it the other woman, who had tiny lines carved between her brows and a discontented mouth, of whom he thought?

The presence of Lizzie Blake at Michaelgarth had undermined her confidence with far more success than Tilda had ever been able to achieve, and Alison had already tried on and rejected three separate outfits: the first too casual, the second too smart and the third simply boring. The bedroom, which looked into the narrow side garden, was warm and stuffy, the high leylandii hedges preventing any cool current of air. No draughts prevailed in this comfortable little dwelling; it was as sensible and neat as Alison herself, and just as predictable. Labour-saving, economical to run, surrounded by its small well-planned garden, it was exactly the house Philip would have chosen for her present circumstances. A photograph of him smiled condescending approval from the dressing-table.

He would have been surprised, she thought now, if he could have seen her in this present dilemma with discarded garments cast anyhow on the bed rather than hung back tidily in the fitted cupboard. Until Philip's death, clothes had been regarded as necessary items that lent respectability and kept you warm – and the cheaper they were the better he liked them. He could see the sense of paying a little extra for quality that would last for ever – for a tweed skirt, say, or a sensible overcoat – but to buy clothes for the fun of it was beyond him. Fashion was a word that did not enter his vocabulary and if you could find the skirt – or overcoat – at a charity shop, for a quarter of the price when new, then why quibble if the colour didn't quite match the rest of your clothes or the length was three inches shorter than was flattering?

As she tried a shirt with a seventies collar and an unusually vivid magenta stripe, Alison began to have a glimmering of the reason why Philip and his daughter had come to blows so often. Once Alison might have worn the shirt without a thought for it, beyond the need for it to be clean and properly pressed, but now the image of Lizzie in her soft apple-green linen overshirt slithered between her and the glass. She'd looked slender and cool, yet the narrow-cut capris had added a youthful, rather sexy touch to the outfit. Alison, staring at herself in the outdated shirt with the full-skirted frumpy denim skirt, for the first time briefly grasped the agony behind Sara's wails: 'I can't wear that old thing. It's no good letting down the hem. It's the wrong shape, can't you see . . . ?'

Perhaps a Lizzie-figure, blessed with style and grace, had hovered between Sara and her latest crush so that Philip's portentous humour and ill-timed homilies on the dangers of extravagance in the pursuit of vanity must have been hard to bear. Alison, more concerned with exam results than her daughter's social success – and, anyway, much more attuned to Mark's needs – had experienced an almost perverse pleasure in supporting Philip. After all, why should she cut corners to save pennies whilst Sara wasted them on frivolities?

Now, frowning in puzzled frustration at her reflection, she experienced a brush of remorse: she dimly saw that an opportunity had been wasted, a chance for her to draw near to her daughter, to share, had been missed. The fruit of those self-righteous homilies and heavy-handed jokes at Sara's expense had been a bitter resentment on their daughter's part: perhaps a lighter touch, the occasional generosity . . . ? Instinctively Alison rejected what seemed to be a quite un-necessary requirement to review Philip or her own standards. Sara had always been an ungrateful, sullen child, and, as she'd grown older, secretive and critical. Mark was uncomplicated, less touchy, and she'd always found his demands much more acceptable – not that he came home, these days, any more often than Sara . . .

Alison resolutely put her children from her mind and began to unzip the skirt. Surely she must have something that would give her both the confidence to meet Lizzie Blake again and to hold Piers' attention. She was looking forward to the fortnight ahead, to having him to herself. She'd already drawn up a little programme of outings: nothing too demanding but which would give them plenty of time together away from Michaelgarth. She would need to be – she rejected the words 'cunning' and 'resourceful', which smacked unflatteringly of a lack of willingness on Piers' part – tactful, was more the word, in her determination to see that Piers was taken out of himself. At Michaelgarth, especially with Tilda and the baby in residence, the shades of David and Sue prevented him from making a new life. Moving from the house in Minehead had been a very sensible step away from her past: it was time that Piers was encouraged forward.

Alison removed the unfortunate shirt, put it with the denim skirt and began a new assault upon her meagre wardrobe.

Lizzie, sitting with Felix on the seat under the covered way outside the hall, saw her enter the garth and felt an instant surge of unworthy glee. The skirt was fractionally too tight and an unfortunate length, given Alison's short sturdy legs; the blouse was too fussy for a barbecue – in fact it would be difficult, decided Lizzie, to think of an occasion when the shirt could possibly be appropriate – and the sandals, clearly worn for comfort, were heavy and unflattering.

Everything just wrong, poor thing, she thought contentedly, and moved a fraction nearer to Felix as Alison approached. She carried an oblong parcel under one arm and her expression of wariness and aggression was not lightened by the sight of Lizzie and Felix sitting so companionably together.

'Hel*lo*,' cried Lizzie gaily, feeling Angel's influence creeping up on her again. 'You're the very first to arrive. Isn't that nice?'

She felt Felix's silent chuckle reverberate up her arm and suppressed her own desire to burst into fits of laughter. Alison stared at them stonily as she approached but, even as Felix began to rise to his feet, Piers appeared in the doorway of the scullery and called a greeting to her.

'We'll be out in a moment,' he said to the two on the bench and drew Alison into the kitchen.

'Why don't you like her?' enquired Felix, still smiling to himself.

'She makes me want to behave badly,' said Lizzie honestly. 'The minute I set eyes on her this morning I just felt it come all over me. Why is that, d'you suppose?'

'There could be lots of reasons. Alison is, I'm afraid, the sort of person who puts one's back up. It's not simply because there's an absence of that indefinable quality which we call charm; there's a more positive aura of prickliness, combined with a kind of smug sense of her own virtues which is almost offensive.'

Lizzie gave a whistle. 'That's about one of the best put-downs I've ever heard,' she said admiringly. 'Did you have to practise it beforehand or did you just ad-lib your way through it?'

Felix looked shame-faced. 'Sorry,' he said. 'It was just such a relief to be able to say it aloud. I know it's none of my business but the Rowes were never particular favourites of mine and I feel very anxious that Piers is getting quite so involved with Alison.'

'Oh, please don't apologize,' said Lizzie at once. 'I thoroughly enjoy a good character assassination. Piers *does* seem to like her, although I gather Tilda doesn't approve.' A silence. 'I had a very odd feeling this morning, Felix. When I first met her it was rather as if the past had begun to replay itself . . .'

She hesitated again, uncertain how to proceed, and Felix turned his head to look at her.

'With Alison in Marina's role and you in Angel's?' he enquired.

She stared at him anxiously. 'It sounds a bit offensive spoken out loud,' she said. 'I don't mean to be. And anyway, it's not really the same. She's not Piers' wife – and he and I aren't lovers – but there's something sanctimonious about her, as if she owns Piers and I'm some sort of predatory intruder.'

'That is probably precisely how she sees it,' he said. 'You represent a threat and her reaction is fairly natural: hackles up, claws out. As I said, Alison is not the kind of person to whom one naturally feels drawn and, in your case, I imagine she's even less disposed to be pleasant.'

'She was pretty rude when we were introduced,' admitted Lizzie, 'but I have to admit that Piers didn't go out of his way to indicate that she had any special claim on him. On the other hand, I don't want to make waves.'

'Don't you?' asked Felix drily.

She grinned, unoffended by his perspicacity. 'I was pleased that we were sitting here together when she arrived,' she admitted. 'I felt that I was the one who belonged and that she was the visitor . . . What are you laughing at?'

'I thought you made that very clear in your welcome,' he said. 'Very gracious.'

They were still chuckling, leaning together like a pair of naughty children, when Piers and Alison came out into the garth.

'Look at this lovely painting of Dunkery that Alison found for me,' he said with a faintly forced cheerfulness.

He held up a heavily framed oil painting for inspection, whilst Alison stood rather smugly beside him. Lizzie and Felix came to attention, staring at the scene with polite attentiveness.

'Isn't that the hill I can see from my bedroom window?' asked Lizzie brightly, determined to be friendly. 'How amazing that I recognize it! It's very good, isn't it, Felix?'

'Delightful,' he agreed. 'Wonderful effect of light and shade.'

Piers lowered the painting, took another admiring look at it so as to show himself sufficiently grateful and pleased, and suggested that it was time for a drink.

'Good idea,' agreed Lizzie rather too readily. 'Can I do things?'

She could see Alison tense, as if ready to spring into defensive action if she were actually to rise from the bench, and decided instead to surrender any rights she might be assumed to have.

'Not that I've got a clue where anything is.' She turned to Felix. 'Mrs Coleman has made the most wonderful food,' she told him. 'I liked her so much. I wish I knew someone like that who would come to my rescue when I give a party.'

Alison frowned. 'Personally I think she's very over-rated as a cook,' she said.

Her tone was resentful and there was a tiny, awkward silence. Tilda and Saul came out from the scullery, carrying a tray of glasses and a bottle, joking together, and Piers turned to greet them with obvious relief. Felix stood up, asking Alison a question about her garden, and Tilda poured some wine into a glass and passed it to Lizzie. Tilda was looking nervous and she made a little face, taking care to keep her back to the others.

'Don't leave me,' she murmured, taking a gulp of orange juice from her own glass. 'The puppy will be here any time now and I shall need your moral support. I'm beginning to feel that I've made a terrible mistake. Don't disappear, Lizzie. I'm relying on you to carry us through by causing a dramatic diversion.'

A car could be heard approaching; engine cut, doors slammed. Tilda stood quite immobile with expectation but at the sight of the couple who appeared through the archway, shouting greetings and bearing gifts, she let out her breath in a gasp of relief. Piers and Felix went to meet them, Alison following behind, whilst Saul hurried away to check the barbecue. More people could be heard arriving out on the drive and Lizzie straightened her shoulders, breathing deeply so as to control her nerves, whilst Tilda glanced at her, eyes alight with anticipation.

'Here we go,' she said, looking Lizzie over rather critically, as if she were a favourite child about to perform in public for the first time. 'Overture and beginners, please, and all that stuff. Are you ready to meet your public?'

CHAPTER FORTY-TWO

Felix watched Lizzie circulating with a certain amount of amusement and an odd kind of pride. The guests, friends of the whole family not just Piers' particular intimates, were thrilled to have a well-known and popular actress in their midst. They jostled to be introduced, each wanting to tell her their impression of the sitcom or the advertisement – often both – and she received each warm greeting with great charm: a clever mix of humility, gratitude and delight that was irresistible. Almost he could hear Alison gnashing her teeth.

From his position in a comfortably padded chair he observed them all exactly as if they were characters in a play enacted on this midsummer night in this ancient garth, especially for his delectation. Saul was working hard behind the barbecue, wrapped in a long blue butcher's apron, turning sizzling pieces of steak and sausages, whilst exchanging quips with some young people who had been David's friends and were glad to have Tilda back amongst their ranks. She would appear at regular intervals to pat him encouragingly, popping a tasty morsel into his mouth, joking with those friends who, guessing the depth of her pain, were careful to keep the conversation light. Her butter-coloured hair fell about her square, brown shoulders, a skimpy soft cotton vest was held in place by narrow straps, her long legs half covered by a filmy sarong in peacock blue.

Felix felt a pang of pity for Saul, who smiled and smiled, dashing his hair back from his hot face with an impatient swipe of his forearm, accepting Tilda's spasmodic offerings with an over-exaggerated miming of surprised gratitude, which made his friends laugh and which touched Felix's heart. Saul's love was there for all to see – though the boy was certain that he was hiding it beneath his play-acting – and Felix shook his head. He wondered if Saul could fill the space that had been left empty by David's passing. His grandson had been blessed with a quality that drew people like a magnet and held them close: kind, yes, up to a point; aware of the needs of those nearest to him; yet David had added into this mix a ruthlessness that so many women found attractive. The combination had been extraordinary, lending an energizing vitality to anyone who drifted within his orbit, and his early death merely added to the mystique and lent a further unfair advantage: age would not wither David, nor the years condemn.

That deep affection existed between Tilda and Saul was evident, yet was it the kind of love that would capture Tilda's imagination, ignite passion? Once you'd met with the real thing could anything else ever measure up? Felix wondered whether it would be fair on Saul for it even to be tried; yet there might be more to Saul than any of them suspected. At Michaelgarth, until now, he'd always had to play second fiddle to David's brilliant virtuoso performance. Perhaps, now, after David . . .

Felix stretched out his legs, crossing them at the ankle, cradling his glass carefully. Life after Angel – oh! how bleak the future looked after that last meeting with her in the Birdcage; how heavy his heart. His only future salvation lay in making

Marina as happy as he was able, otherwise all was wasted and the finishing of his affair a barren gesture. He was grateful that in the final years there had been that brief late flowering of affection between them: a reconciliation born out of Marina's suffering and nurtured by his compassion for her.

The long June evening was fading, sunset colours – scarlet and flame – dying down in the western sky to be quenched in the purple waters of the Channel. Dusky blue light was filling the garth and the little lamps, which were fixed at intervals along the high walls, cast tiny pools of golden light amongst the stretched, knobby boughs of the apple and mulberry trees, touching tender green leaves to bronze. Lizzie edged into Felix's line of vision, conferring now with Tilda, and his heart moved so suddenly in his breast that he became short of breath and grasped at the arm of his chair. Lizzie's head tilted just so, half in shadow, the bundle of hair, pale in this light, the amused, almost wicked expression reminded him so much of Angel: he could almost hear her voice murmuring some shocking gossip, remembering those funny, bitchy comments breathed into his ear: '. . . so she was droning on, sweetie, about this dreary straying husband of hers, whining about the other woman and saying for the twentieth time, "And she *knows* he's a married man," so I leaned across the table and said, "But, darling, so does he . . ."'

Felix winced with the pain of memory and loss and, at that same moment, Tilda threw back her head, shouting with laughter whilst Lizzie grinned. Alison suddenly appeared between them with an expression of self-righteous disapproval, indicating something or some person neglected so that Tilda made a tiny guilty face and hurried away, leaving Lizzie and Alison locked briefly into a social necessity for communication.

He couldn't hear Lizzie's voice and could only imagine the words that accompanied the expansive gesture and smiling look of pleasure which indicated that the party was going well and the guests were enjoying themselves. Alison's expression was more complicated: common courtesy demanded a civil response but, even at this distance, he could see that she grudged making it. The unwillingness to meet Lizzie's eyes, the slightly curling lip, which was intended to show that Lizzie was an outsider, suggested that Alison was telling her that this annual event was always a success and this year was no different. It was clearly important for Alison to put herself firmly within the family group, to show superior knowledge, thus distancing herself from this unwelcome intruder.

Felix watched, shocked by the power that the past continued to hold. During these later years of his life he'd punished himself, wondering how he could have betrayed his wife and child, condemning his own actions. Now, as he looked between Lizzie and Alison, he knew exactly why; he remembered the icy silences, the bitter comments on one side, and saw the loving generosity on the other. Marina's jealousy had revealed itself in the early years of their marriage and his love for Angel – or, rather, hers for him – had been food and warmth after years of deprivation. Weak? He shook his head: let others try living in a freezer of condemnation and suspicion before judging. Of course, his affair with Angel had merely confirmed Marina's view of him but, by then, what did it matter any more? His only defence was that he'd never before taken comfort from any other woman, never looked aside; only Angel had been able to fuse tenderness, humour, passion into one irresistible whole – and only the threat of being separated from Piers had had the power to persuade him to turn his back on that magic; only his son's security and confidence had made the sacrifice worth the candle.

Watching Lizzie and Alison he prayed fervently that Piers would not find himself in a similar situation. In Alison's proprietorial glances, her attempted, persistent presence by Piers' side as he moved amongst his guests, the apparently casual little touches on his arm, he saw the sticky, binding tendrils of expectation, which, if not torn off, would twine and embrace closer and ever more strongly until there was no escaping their weighty burden. Lizzie had a light touch: she approached with a smile, might even thrust an arm within the other person's with a friendly warmth, before turning away as swiftly and easily as she'd arrived: there was nothing burdensome about Lizzie.

He saw that Piers had joined them, holding a drink, relaxed and at ease. Once or twice he'd seen him wearing a different expression and known that Piers was thinking of David: the first Christmas without him, the first birthday, all these were painful moments to be lived through, learning all the while of the inevitability and terrible, icy finality of death. Felix was glad to see him smiling, saw Lizzie murmur something in his ear and the natural way he leaned a little – only a little, for Lizzie was tall – to hear it, whilst Alison strained, watchful and alert, ready to bring Piers' attention back. It looked like an accident that, in the slight movement towards Lizzie, Piers spilled some of his wine over her hand and wrist so that she gave a little jump, a squeak. He hastened to bring out a handkerchief, mopping at her outstretched hand, laughing with her, and neither saw Alison's angry, vexed face.

It was precisely at this moment that the puppy arrived. He was brought in – amongst cries of apology for the delay – perched in a wicker basket lined with a soft blanket. All floppy ears and huge paws, he watched with no little alarm as he was borne through the delighted group and heard the 'oohs' and 'aahs' of sentimental guests. Piers glanced up from his drying operation, puzzled, whilst Tilda slipped between the watching figures to stand between Lizzie and her mother. The little procession now halted before Piers, the puppy held aloft in his basket, whilst the breeder and her husband burst into the first line of 'Happy birthday to you'. The tune was taken up willingly by the other guests, their shouts ringing round the garth, echoing in the quiet night, and culminating in a chorus of 'For he's a jolly good fellow'.

Felix found that his eyes were full of tears as he watched surprise, gratification and tenderness dawning in his son's face as he stared at the puppy and heard the voices of his friends. They crowded near to pat him on the shoulder, to shake his hand, until finally he was able to reach out to receive the basket that held the golden Labrador puppy: Joker's great-great-nephew. Tilda and Teresa stood together, arms entwined, Tilda's face wet with tears. She turned her head briefly, hiding it in her mother's neck, and Teresa laid her cheek upon the bright hair, holding the girl close in an attempt to comfort and to shield. Then Piers was looking for her, acknowledging that it was she who had planned this surprise, and Tilda was smiling again, albeit shakily, embracing Piers and the puppy together, whilst Lizzie smiled mistily and Alison bit her lips with mortification.

The guests closed round them again and Felix could see no more. He got to his feet with difficulty and, picking up his stick, went quietly into the house.

CHAPTER FORTY-THREE

As soon as Piers turned to search for Tilda, Lizzie moved away. For the first time since the party had begun she felt herself a stranger. All these people shared common memories: a history that locked them into a pattern of school, work, love, in which she had no part. She looked instinctively for Felix, saw that his chair was empty and felt even more alone. A few steps backwards took her into the angle of the west wing and the high garth wall and, lowering herself on to the small bench seat in the shadows, she drew a cloak of silence and immobility about her, hoping she would not be missed.

Everyone wanted to see the puppy, to touch him and exclaim over him: everyone except Alison. Even in this moment of isolation, Lizzie couldn't resist the rueful smile that involuntarily touched her lips. Alison stood to one side, torn between openly showing her fury or pretending that she'd been in on the secret. Studying her, Lizzie felt that 'fury' was not too strong a word for Alison's expression. It was evident that Piers' reaction to – and acceptance of – Tilda's gift showed that not only was Alison's opinion unimportant to him but that he was ready to say so publicly. Lizzie guessed that Alison saw this as a victory for Tilda and Felix as well as any other guests to whom she'd made known her feelings about Piers having another puppy.

What was even more interesting was that Piers was showing no sense of embarrassment or awkwardness. He was too intelligent to imagine that Alison would be indifferent yet he had no hesitation in demonstrating his delight. He held the puppy in his arms, stroking the soft head, examining him eagerly, and Lizzie caught the name 'Joker' several times as the breeder pointed out a resemblance and recounted the shared ancestry. Tilda's face was bright with tenderness as she leaned to kiss the puppy on the nose and touch his floppy ears and, when Teresa joined the little group closest to Piers, she grinned at her mother, who smiled back with an expression of triumphant complicity.

For the moment Lizzie was forgotten: the puppy held the centre stage. She made herself more comfortable, wishing she'd brought her drink with her, glad to be in this quiet corner and out of the limelight. She never had a problem with making a fool of herself if it helped things along, broke the ice or made someone feel better, but she was always content to be an onlooker. She liked to observe body language, gestures, expressions: to the actor the equivalent of the writer's copy. For instance, Tilda was now fluid and supple with relief; she embraced Saul as – his chef's duties abrogated – he came to see the puppy, her arm lightly about his shoulder as she leaned happily against him. Saul admired the puppy with a particular, grateful pleasure, since it had indirectly brought him this warm, loving gesture, and, as Piers stooped to share a joking remark with him, he looked up with a charming, smiling humility that touched Lizzie's heart. She saw that Teresa also watched the younger couple, her rather sharply pretty face softened by a kind of hopeful anxiety. When she looked at Piers, however, Teresa's expression grew more calculating and, seeing through her eyes, Lizzie recognized the attraction that drew women to him: that ease with his own body, the quick, narrow, assessing glance, the humorous twist of his mouth.

It would be easy, Lizzie decided, to be tempted to make the mistake of feeling sorry for Piers. His difficult childhood aside, it was always a natural reaction to feel sympathy for someone who had been deserted. The empowering must always go with the one who leaves: the abandoned one, stranded flat-footed and humiliated amongst the wreck of the relationship, watches the still-beloved one starting a new exciting journey, whilst the unloved one faces into each grey, featureless day and cold, endless night with all the pain of betrayal and despair. Was this how Piers had really reacted to Sue's departure: how much did he suffer? There were none of those tell-tale signs that marked out the lonely ones: nothing subdued or empty-eyed about him: no lack of inner confidence. She suspected that the grief he could not always hide sprang from the death of his son: of course, death was terrible too, but at least you were allowed to cling to the love you'd shared and could relive the tenderness; you could mentally flip through your happy memories, tiny scenes of intimacy neither spoiled by bitterness nor denied by those who need to trash the past so as to justify a new shiny future with someone else.

Lizzie wiped her eyes on the sleeve of her shirt. Crazy, she decided, potty, doolally: sitting on her own in a corner, watching people she'd known at the longest for four days and the shortest for three hours, crying into her drink – except that she'd left it on the table . . . She took several deep breaths, concentrating on that trick of taking stock of her surroundings in an attempt to control herself. Several tables, each with a selection of chairs, were set at intervals about the garth, their wooden legs slightly unsteady on the cobbles, but most of the guests were still standing in groups or choosing some delicacy from the two long trestle tables, which flanked

327

the barbecue. White damask cloths covered these unsightly boards and one table was weighted down with bottles, glasses and plates and silver. On the other, the plates of rolls and tiny sandwiches, vol-au-vents and quiche, had been severely depleted and, before too long, Tilda would carry out the delicious puddings that Jenny Coleman had made earlier.

She saw that Alison stood a little apart with a fair, florid woman: Margaret Hooper. 'Margaret and Geoffrey, Alison's brother, moved down fairly recently,' Tilda had told her. 'Geoffrey has been having an affair and Margaret decided to be drastic. I'm not too sure that Alison is utterly thrilled to have them quite so near . . .' They'd been introduced with a whole flurry of other guests and Lizzie had hardly taken in their names but now, as the two women drew slightly closer together, Lizzie guessed that Alison was sharing her irritation with her sister-in-law. The fair woman pulled in her chin, shrugging her solid shoulders slightly, and Lizzie, hidden in her shadowy corner, saw Alison's face set into sullen lines. A tall man moved just behind them, putting his hand on the fair woman's shoulder, and she glanced back at him with a little jerk of the chin and a grimace that invited him to share in their displeasure at the spectacle.

Lizzie wondered how Margaret Hooper had managed to subsume her husband's infidelity into her daily life; how it had been contained and beaten down so that it could be ignored – or forgiven. 'He did time,' Tilda had said. 'Presents, holidays, crawling . . .' Looking at that fair, high-coloured face, Lizzie could believe that Margaret Hooper had taken her pound of flesh and now, she suspected, her husband was grappled to her with bands of steel: bands forged by complicity, of lying and subservience on his part and a series of demands and whims on hers. Was it possible for a relationship to retain its dignity, its wholeness, once lying and cheating clouded its trust? How had Marina behaved once Felix had broken with Angel? Had she punished him in the same way?

Staring at the Hoopers Lizzie realized that, however illogical it was, she couldn't put Felix in the same category. She closed her eyes, frowning, as if debating with herself: it was almost impossible to judge other people's relationships. Things looked so different when you were on the inside.

'How can you put up with it?' friends would ask when the newspapers or magazines carried photographs of Sam at the latest BAFTA awards with a starlet clinging to his arm.

'It's not important,' she'd answered – and that had been the truth.

'The utter boredom of the young, darling,' he'd say, rolling his eyes with weary impatience. 'They take themselves so seriously. But it's coming . . .' and his face would change, his eyes drifting past her towards the vision he had of each new production. Yet, as the years passed, there seemed to be something missing: the excitement, the passion.

'You shouldn't have left the theatre,' she'd tell him. 'Remember Centre Stage?' and he'd look at her properly, with a kind of painful regret, and reach out to hold her closely. She could smell him now, nicotine and coffee and his own, particular Sam-smell . . .

Tilda sat down beside her and slipped an arm about her.

'Isn't it awful?' she said, almost conversationally. 'This terrible weeping comes with no warning, doesn't it? I've felt it several times this evening; missing David, I mean, and then bursting into tears. I know I can say it to you because you can understand what it's like never to see the person you loved more than the whole world ever again in your life. Come on inside and help me with the puddings. It's quiet in the kitchen and it'll give us a moment to get a grip.'

Wiping her cheeks, trying to smile, Lizzie nodded and followed Tilda across the garth but her heart was heavy and full of guilt.

CHAPTER FORTY-FOUR

Left to himself for a brief moment, Piers saw them go. The arrival of the puppy had brought the party to a climax and now his friends surged and eddied about him, chatting, eating, drinking, and he was able to enjoy a sense of solitude whilst ringed about with conviviality. He looked down upon the soft golden head, felt the weight of the fat, warm body in his arms, and glanced about for a place to sit. A chair beside a small card-table invited him to rest for a moment and he sat down gratefully, the puppy now almost asleep, half-lying up his chest. His friends smiled at him, touched his shoulder, someone brought him a drink but had the sense to leave him alone to catch his breath and take in the scene.

His father was sitting in his padded chair, a glass balanced on its arm, talking to a few old cronies. There was a thin, fine look about him; his white hair sleeked back, his face lively, elegant ankles crossed nonchalantly. Their eye-line crossed and he gave a little approving nod towards the dog, sent a tiny wink, so that Piers, absurdly touched, raised his glass in return. How good it was to sit here in the garth on a midsummer evening, surrounded by family and friends: how good to feel the load of responsibility, of loyalty to the dead, slipping away at last. It was no longer required of him to judge his father or to pronounce upon his actions: he could let it go. If he felt his mother's shade reproaching him, he need not respond to it. His father's explanations, his own experiences, allowed him to understand and to forgive the hurt: his own fear was done away with at last. It was impossible to forgive someone on behalf of another, his mother's pain remained unresolved, but he was not prepared to allow her past suffering to spoil the present. He found himself thinking affectionately of his grandfather, and of Monty, remembering how, when Monty had died at last, it had been Felix who'd bought Piers his first puppy.

With a pang of dismay he realized that Alison was beside him, with Margaret Hooper at her shoulder, and he ruefully indicated his inability to rise. Neither of them was particularly amused at the sight of the puppy, lying peacefully asleep on his back now, his fat tummy exposed, huge paws limp.

'So Tilda got her way,' said Alison with a small mirthless laugh. 'I thought she would. It really is rather too bad of her, isn't it? Poor Piers, she takes advantage of your good nature.'

He smiled politely, reflecting on how much he disliked being referred to as 'poor Piers'.

'You know I was thinking of getting another dog,' he reminded her gently – and saw her colour rise. It would be impossible to pursue this line in front of her sister-in-law without demonstrating her lack of power, and Piers wondered exactly how Alison had represented their relationship to the Hoopers. He'd resented being obliged to ask them to his birthday party – they were acquaintances, not friends – but she'd suggested it, tying up the invitation rather cleverly with the dinner party they'd given and to which he'd escorted her, making him feel, rather guiltily, that a return of hospitality was in order. Left to himself he would have suggested dinner at a pub for the four of them but, with the party happening now, it had been difficult to refuse her.

Stroking the puppy, trying to think of something to say to Alison, he cursed himself for letting their friendship drift so far towards some kind of public commitment. It had become so natural for them to be bracketed together in this small social community and, through a kind of apathy born of grief, he'd allowed it to happen. Lizzie's arrival at Michaelgarth was forcing a slight rift between him and Alison, his ready acceptance of Tilda's present was widening it, and he knew that he must not let this opportunity slip.

'I thought we'd decided that you needed some freedom,' Alison was saying with an unnatural jocularity. 'What with Tilda and Jake so firmly ensconced . . .'

That 'we' jolted him out of his attempted affability, dispensed with his unwillingness to hurt, and a ruthless sense of self-preservation asserted itself.

'But I don't want to be free of my family,' he told her firmly. 'I've told you how much it means to me to have Tilda and Jake at Michaelgarth. As for the puppy, well, he's for all of us. We've always shared our dogs, you know.'

If he'd over-emphasized this other 'we', reminding her that she knew very little about him or his past, he had no regrets. Margaret Hooper was watching him, her lips curling almost into a sneer, and he thought: these are the kind of women to whom men are always the enemy. There can be nothing but conflict here.

Saul appeared beside them, holding two plates, smiling an apology for the interruption but making it impossible for further private conversation with Alison or Margaret.

'Felix says you haven't had anything to eat yet,' he said cheerfully. 'It's always the same at your own thrash, isn't it? Anyway, I haven't had a chance either, so I thought we'd grab an opportunity together. I brought things you can manage with one hand since you're a bit handicapped. What a splendid little chap he is. Have you thought of a name for him yet?'

He rattled on, beaming at the two women but monopolizing Piers, until they moved slightly away and were joined by Geoffrey, who shepherded them towards the drinks. Piers raised an eyebrow at Saul.

'Relief of Mafeking?' he suggested – and Saul laughed.

'Something like that,' he agreed. 'Felix thought that the odds were a bit high. You know, two against one, and, anyway, you needed something to eat. Will you be OK now if I go and clear up a bit ready for the puddings?'

'I think I'm pretty safe at the moment,' Piers assured him. 'Thanks, Saul.'

He looked towards his father, who watched with amusement, and Piers wished suddenly, with all his heart, that this moment of truth had come much earlier in their lives. So much time had been wasted: resentment on his own side and guilt on his father's had marred the instinctive affection that had always existed between them. Now he saw more clearly how bleak his father's life must have been once he'd finished with Angel for ever. Marina had never looked upon forgiveness as an option but her bitterness and disgust had slowly softened into a permanently watchful expectation: whims must be immediately indulged, moods cheerfully endured, needs instantly satisfied. Felix's attention must be centred upon her at all times as proof of his repentance, and never had he been offered the least indication that his sin had been forgiven: rather, there was an almost tangible atmosphere of suspicious vigilance. This had been his punishment: he was never again to be trusted.

His mother's crippling jealousy had shaped his own life until he'd seized the opportunity to get away. After he'd left the Royal Agriculture College he'd been able to move into the cottage at Porlock and, though he missed Michaelgarth, the sense of freedom – of crawling from beneath that crushing weight of watchfulness and criticism of his friends – had been worth it. She'd kept a watching brief, though, subjecting him to sudden visits at odd hours, inquisitions, until Sue had blown into his life like an invigorating, good-natured hurricane, sweeping away his guilt and whirling him beyond his mother's jealous reach. They'd had good times together, no great passion but a good deal of laughter, and then she'd moved on again, rushing away to new horizons and leaving him free again, to be himself.

He bent over the puppy, hiding his expression of horror at the thought of how nearly he'd walked into another ready-made prison of jealous watchfulness and constricting, stifling affection. He saw how cunningly he would be detached, step by step, from those whom he loved and the sense of preservation grew stronger within him. He thought of Lizzie: of her funny ways, ready humour, and the way he felt when that flame of recognition leaped between them. What happened when that flame burned too late: once you were committed to another person? Lizzie or Alison: Marina or Angel? He remembered his father's words: *Marina told me . . . that I wouldn't be able to see you and so, in the end, there was no contest.*

He swallowed the last of his drink and, hefting the puppy up into his arms, got to his feet and crossed the garth to Felix. He went down on one knee beside him so that his father might see the puppy, saw the fine, thin hand laid upon its head with a strange constriction in his throat.

'I was thinking of Grandfather and Monty,' he said. 'How long ago it seems. Remember Spider? How old was I when you brought him home for me? Ten? Eleven? And then Snoopy? David chose that name, of course. *Peanuts* was all the rage and we couldn't talk him out of it. So what shall we call this one?'

Felix smoothed the soft yellow coat and was rewarded with a sleepy lick.

'What about Lionheart?' he suggested – and smiled at Piers' puzzled, questioning look. 'He led the Third Crusade, if I remember aright,' he murmured. 'It seems rather apt, under the circumstances. Third time lucky, perhaps?'

Piers, startled, gave a shout of laughter at Felix's insinuation. It was true that he'd been rescued from his mother's influence by Sue and now from Alison's by the puppy. Perhaps he'd require no liberating from Lizzie: third time lucky?

'Lionheart it is,' he said. 'He's the right colour for it and we'll call him Lion for short. Shall we drink to his health, Father?'

'We'll drink to the three of us,' corrected Felix but, even as he lifted his glass, some friends, overhearing, came crowding round to toast Piers' health again and to exclaim over the newly named puppy.

CHAPTER FORTY-FIVE

After the puddings had been carried out into the garth, Tilda remained on her own in the kitchen. Lizzie went away upstairs on some pretext or other and Tilda made no attempt to stop her, understanding that the occasion must be rather overwhelming to a virtual stranger. It was odd though, reflected Tilda, that Lizzie wasn't in the least like a stranger as far as she was concerned, but seemed more like some relative returned after a long break away from home. Perhaps it was all that moving around – continually adapting to new productions, new casts, new digs – that kept her flexible, reminding Tilda of the women she knew who'd been brought up in military families. They, like Lizzie, tended to be at ease in any company, ready to adjust to unexpected circumstances.

Tilda began to prepare an assortment of cups and mugs for coffee, one ear cocked automatically for Jake-noises, remembering other celebrations here at Michaelgarth: David's twenty-first birthday, their engagement party, Piers' annual midsummer bash. Seeing Piers with the puppy had reminded her of Joker's arrival fifteen years before, when she and David were respectively eleven and twelve years old. She had a photograph of David holding the puppy and laughing, whilst she stood beside him beaming into the camera. Blinking away her tears, imagining David beside her, saying, 'Turn off the taps, love. Life's too short,' she began to spoon coffee into the cups on a second tray.

Those tiny darts of fear that Alison planted with such painful precision had been drawn out and neutralized by Piers himself. Tilda knew that she'd overstepped the line with Alison earlier, but it had been made clear by his public acceptance of the puppy that Alison's feelings were not his paramount consideration. Her insinuations that Piers was hoping that she and Jake might be ready to begin new lives together away from Michaelgarth had undermined Tilda's security, but it was the conversation at tea-time that had truly restored her confidence.

She and Piers had often discussed her plans for the future, but nothing had suggested itself that tied her so completely to Michaelgarth as Lizzie's plans for a small craft centre. She'd been thrilled by the idea and deeply relieved to see that Piers had shown no hesitation in going along with it. Just before the party had really begun he'd paused beside her, touching his glass to hers. 'Here's to our new project,' he'd said – and she'd felt an overwhelming relief and gratitude. Then the puppy had arrived and, watching him holding it, she'd remembered David and the whole way of life that she'd lost along with him and she'd been obliged to shed a few tears on Lizzie's shoulder. It was odd how quickly she'd bonded with Lizzie, and suspected that it was something to do with their both being recently made widows. Just now, for instance, when she'd spotted Lizzie sitting in the dark corner of the garth, wiping away her tears, she'd guessed that Lizzie was experiencing that terrible isolation of someone who'd lost not only their partner but their best friend.

Oh, the pain of it. Tilda bit her lip as she waited for the kettle to boil. 'Get a grip,' David would have advised – he'd never been particularly sympathetic in emotional crises – and she smiled waveringly to herself as she attempted to follow his advice. Footsteps could be heard passing through the scullery and instinctively she straightened her shoulders, her back to the door, practising a brighter smile.

'Well, *what* a success.' Her mother put an arm about her. 'You must be thrilled to bits. Dear old Piers certainly rose to the occasion, didn't he?'

Tilda returned the hug. 'Wasn't it fantastic? And isn't the puppy gorgeous?'

'Perfect.' Teresa perched on the edge of the table. 'Piers is going to call him Lionheart. Lion for short. Isn't that nice? Where's Miss Blake disappeared to? I couldn't believe my eyes when I saw her. You might have warned me, Tilda. I understand she's an old friend of the family?'

'I wanted it to be a surprise.' Tilda lifted the heavy kettle from the hotplate. 'She's so nice, isn't she? I think she's more Felix's friend, actually, or at least her mother was. She was the actress Angelica Blake but she's dead now, and Lizzie's just lost her husband, so she and I have a sort of sympathy for one another.'

'I had no idea.' Teresa was swift to understand. 'Oh, poor woman, and she's been so much fun all evening. And it can't have been easy for you either, darling. Here, let me help you with that kettle. It's much too heavy for you.'

Tilda replaced the heavy kettle and stood aside, watching her mother pour the boiling water onto the instant coffee in the cups and mugs.

'That's round one,' she said, observing the two trays. 'You and I might have to manage with plastic picnic mugs. Let's take these out for starters.'

She followed Teresa through the scullery and out into the garth. Piers was talking to a group of friends, eating a helping of one of Jenny's delicious puddings, whilst Felix sat peacefully, the puppy curled on his knees. The Hoopers and Alison stood a little apart, wearing wary and discontented expressions, but there was no sign of Lizzie.

Alison, flanked by the Hoopers, watched Piers with helpless frustration. Quite early on in the evening she'd begun to realize that the presence of her brother and sister-in-law might not be the advantage she'd first imagined; but now she was frankly resenting them. When she'd finally accepted the fact that Piers was not going to ask her to co-host the party with him she'd nevertheless expected to be given some kind of special role. As the days passed and no such suggestion had been forthcoming she'd been both hurt and angry, and her insistence that the Hoopers should be invited as a return in kind for their hospitality had been, as much as anything, a testing of her own power. However hard she pretended or wished it were otherwise, they were not part of Piers' inner circle and she'd felt a sense of triumph when he'd agreed – although with obvious reluctance – to invite them. She'd silenced an inner murmuring that she'd been over-pushy by reminding herself that it was the least he could do; Margaret, after all, was her sister-in-law, and she and Geoffrey had been very ready to welcome Piers to both family and social events during the last six months. The fact that he'd accepted only one of these invitations was neither here nor there and she was determined that he should be seen to repay their kindness.

Now, feeling irritated by their close attendance, she saw that, without them, she might have had much more opportunity to remain near Piers. She could have insinuated herself into his company, shown herself publicly to be important to him simply by refusing to be detached from his side. As it was, it had been natural for Piers to behave as if she were part of the Hoopers' little family group rather than his special friend, and their watchful ubiquity, which she had at first encouraged, had made it possible for her to be shunted off into their care without it looking odd or rude. In fact it might easily appear to Piers' friends that she had been invited out of a misplaced kindness, with the Hoopers tacked on so as to keep her company.

Alison seethed with impotent fury. Her skirt, finally chosen as the most flattering of her summer garments, was slightly too small, and its polyester content ensured that during the early part of the evening it was unpleasantly sweaty whilst now, in the cool evening breeze, it was clinging clammily at each contact point. She moved restlessly, trying to ease it away from her skin, and Margaret glanced at her with a kind of pitying affection.

'Time to go?' she asked. 'It's getting rather late.'

Alison squirmed with mortification. It seemed impossible that she'd once imagined that Margaret's partisanship might be an advantage in her struggle with Tilda for first place in Piers' affections. She saw now how foolish she'd been to imagine them as a foursome – she and Piers, Geoffrey and Margaret – at the centre of the party. She'd assumed that his invitation to bring her present for him so that it could be opened privately, just the two of them together, meant that she would be at his side when the guests arrived; instead the wretched actress and Piers' senile old father had moved into action and stolen the show, Felix introducing whatever-she-was-called Blake to newcomers as though she were someone truly famous whilst she, Alison, stood by, completely ignored.

To be fair it had been a relief then to see Margaret and Geoffrey; to stand looking on, agreeing with them that it was all rather silly – although it had been necessary for Margaret to be firm with Geoffrey when he'd suddenly recognized Miss Blake from some advertisement and wanted to be introduced to her. She'd made no attempt to monopolize Piers, chatting to his friends as if she'd known them all her life, but it was clear that she'd been told about the puppy.

Alison stared angrily at the offending object, curled up on

Felix's knees. Its unexpected arrival had been a huge shock, a direct challenge as far as she was concerned, as though Tilda had flung down the gauntlet as publicly as was possible. Even worse was Piers' reaction: not one shocked glance in her direction, no embarrassment or awkwardness. Those earlier conversations about whether he should have another dog, her own expressed wishes on the subject, might not have existed and when she'd finally spoken to him, with Margaret firmly by her side, he'd given her a polite put-down. She'd had no opportunity to appeal to his chivalry or his sense of guilt – which she might have done if Margaret hadn't been there, so solid and self-righteous – and then Geoffrey had shepherded them off as if they were a couple of sheep and she'd had no chance to speak to him since. Worse, Margaret had heard that put-down and was now behaving with a nauseous kind of knowing pity.

Alison watched Piers, at ease, chatting with a friend, and felt the now-familiar, desperate need, the longing for him, which made it impossible to back down and slip quietly away.

'You go on home,' she said to Margaret. 'Honestly, I shall be fine.'

'If you're certain. I'll phone you tomorrow.' Margaret turned to look for her husband.

Alison didn't bother to answer: there was no sign of Miss Blake but Tilda and Teresa had just emerged from the house carrying trays of cups and mugs. If she were careful and lucky she might manage to corner Piers while they were busy with the coffee. Watching for her chance she slipped between the little groups of guests, dodging tables, across the garth to Piers.

CHAPTER FORTY-SIX

Lizzie went into her bedroom and sat down on the edge of her bed. She stared out of the open window, watching the moon's glow casting its pale radiance across the high bare slopes of Dunkery Hill: the midnight-blue sky was so thickly sown with stars that it seemed that curtain upon golden curtain opened upon an unfathomable infinity of light whilst far below, down in the valley, steep coombes sliced dark wedges of shadow along the edges of the pale, silvered fields. The sheer immensity of the scene, the deep silence, added to the confusion and sadness that had come upon her earlier as she'd sat on the bench in the garth.

Tilda's warm affection and her sympathy had made it quite impossible to stay with her in the kitchen. Here, at Michael-garth, her ability to hum and dance herself away from reality was beginning to break down and these mood swings between jollity and despair were becoming difficult to handle. Lizzie stirred: this had happened before, this attempt to disguise frustration with optimism, to hide a gradually growing fear behind a wild cheerfulness.

*   *   *

In those early years of marriage with Sam she never imagines that she'll be unable to have children – why should she? – but soon she begins to feel envious of her pregnant girlfriends, to dread the way the hopeful look on Sam's face dies into disappointment when she admits that her period has started after all. It is important to restore his good humour and so she dances and sings him back to high spirits and confidence, waiting until she is alone again before she gives way to her own private despair.

How she longs for a child – Sam's child. She plays the scene in her head so many times; imagining his pride and tenderness, the way he'd hold his baby, believing that it would root him more securely and satisfy that deep restlessness that drives him on to experiment, to reach for higher goals. As for his women, those pretty actresses with whom his name is linked – does she hope that a child might replace them too? At some point her own confidence, her trust in him and their marriage, is undermined by this failure. Her own longing to cuddle her baby, the hungry need to feel that warm weighty little body in her arms, is continually denied in her anxiety to make it up to Sam in some way.

'It's not your fault,' he says, after the results of some tests showed that she is infertile. 'At least not in that way,' and there is a new, terrible, absent-minded kindness about his affection, which fills her with terror.

When he goes to America to direct his first film abroad his absence is almost a relief. She is able to make her generous encouragement – 'Of *course* you must go. It's a fantastic opportunity. I shall be fine and I'll come out as soon as the play finishes' – a kind of present, a reward for his acceptance of her barrenness. When the usual flirtation edges him for the first time into an affair she finds that she is regarding it in the same light: as a kind of consolation prize, which, for those same reasons of disappointment bravely borne, he deserves. She accepts his explanations with the same forbearance and understanding that she uses to deal with his flirtations and is almost grateful for his approval. He begins to work more and more abroad, whilst her own work keeps her between London and Manchester, so that their time together assumes the quality of a holiday: great fun, not quite real, keeping problems on the back burner.

Affairs now become the pattern and she needs to remind herself of Angel's words: *There will always be rumours with a man like Sam. Ignore them if you can and don't play detective; don't interrogate unless you really can't put up with it. It's part of his job as far as he's concerned and it's got nothing to do with how he feels about you.* Good advice, no doubt, but sometimes very difficult to follow. Hard work saves her from her own private despair, from brooding too much on her childlessness, and in time she is able to accept Sam's women as being the same kind of occupational hazard as spending long weeks alone or first-night nerves.

A noise from the kitchen below disturbed her thoughts: the clang of the kettle on the hotplate and the faint murmur of Tilda's voice talking to Teresa. Lizzie frowned, as though she were trying to hear the words, and quite suddenly, as if coming to some decision, reached for her capacious holdall. She riffled through it, coming upon the postcards that she'd bought earlier in the week to send to her friends, and sat for some moments holding them in her hand, staring down at the picture of the Yarn Market.

The Yarn Market is octagonal and dates from the fifteenth century . . .

Lizzie put the postcards beside her on the bed and drew her mobile telephone from the bag; switching it on she began to check for messages. She listened to each of the three messages carefully and then replayed them. Presently she took a pen from the bag and began to write on the back of one of the cards, pausing from time to time to consider her words. When she'd finished writing she took another card from her holdall. She studied it, turning it to read the message, slipped it into an envelope and put both cards into her leather shoulder-bag. She went out on to the long landing, pausing for a moment at the window that looked down into the garth before going downstairs.

Piers saw her come into the garth, observed that inward-turned expression of preoccupation before it was automatically switched to a kind of detached, amused awareness of the scene as if she had stepped suddenly upon the stage. He was seized by a sense of foreboding so strong that, leaving Alison holding her coffee, he crossed the cobbles to Lizzie and took her by the arm.

'What is it?' he asked – and she turned that same bright blank smiling gaze upon him as if he were a stranger. He wanted to shake her, to say, 'Come on, this is me. You don't have to pretend,' and then, just as suddenly, he lost his confidence, remembering that they had known each other for less than five days.

'Come and have some coffee,' he said lightly. 'Although I warn you that you might have to have a plastic mug. Tilda said that you'd gone upstairs for a moment.'

He'd realized that he'd simply left Alison standing alone and now he steered Lizzie back to her, and took a mug of coffee from the tray on the table beside them. Before he released her arm he felt her tense, as though preparing for action, readying herself for a performance.

'It was my wretched contact lenses,' she invented rapidly. 'Quite agonizing sometimes, you know.'

She took the coffee and beamed upon Alison, who stared back at her with unconcealed dislike, furious with Piers for simply walking away in the middle of their conversation.

'I have perfect sight,' she answered coldly. 'I don't need spectacles and if I did I certainly wouldn't feel the need to have all the discomfort of contact lenses. I have excellent long vision.'

'But can you see what's happening right under your nose?' asked Lizzie.

She asked the question so naturally, so intently, as if she were really interested, that Alison actually drew breath to answer it before she saw the true meaning behind Lizzie's words. For one brief second Piers and Lizzie looked at each other with such mutual accord, with such total amused understanding and recognition, that in that moment there might have been no-one else in the garth with them. It was Lizzie who moved first, turning to put her mug back onto the tray and saying, 'The party seems to be breaking up and I'd like to say goodnight to some of these nice people,' before drifting away.

'I must say,' said Alison angrily, staring after her, 'that I wonder if she's quite all there. You read about the artistic temperament and so forth and all I can say is, if that's it then you can keep it.'

Piers gave his distinctive facial shrug: the look that he and Lizzie had exchanged had restored his confidence yet he was still ill-at-ease.

'She's certainly unusual,' he murmured, watching Lizzie crouch beside his father's chair, talking to him while she stroked Lion.

Alison, filled with fresh alarm, sought to distract him.

'She's clearly not normal,' she said acidly. 'I certainly agree with you there, but to go back to what we were saying, Piers, about next week. Knightshayes . . .'

As if on cue, his father raised his head and looked at him, reminding him of that earlier conversation. *He led the Third Crusade, if I remember aright* . . . The way out was clear if he had the courage to grasp it: yet it was difficult to take one's own freedom at the expense of another person. Impossible to explain to Alison that, having met Lizzie, he knew that their own friendship would not develop into anything more; he had no wish to hurt her but how else was it to be done except by plain speaking? He looked down at Alison's anxious, frowning face and glanced again across the garth at Lizzie, who laid her cheek on Lion's head and laughed at something Felix was saying to her. He fetched a deep breath and braced himself.

'I don't think I shall be able to make it,' he said quietly.

There was a finality in his voice and in his expression, and anguish twisted her gut. Some faint instinct warned her that the gentler powers of acceptance and good grace would stand her in better stead at this moment than the arid comfort of bitter words but, consumed by humiliation and defeat, she denied the instinct for those same reasons that, earlier on this same spot, had driven her to destroy the rose he had given her.

'I would never have believed that you were the sort of man who would make a fool of himself over a woman like that.' Her voice trembled with furious misery; her face was plain with disgust. 'It's so undignified for a man of your age to behave like a twenty-year-old . . .'

Tilda was beside them, carrying Lion. She put him into Piers' arms, smiling at them as if she had no idea that she was interrupting.

'Felix is off to bed,' she told him, 'and I think Lion's ready to be introduced to his new quarters.' She gave Alison a friendly glance. 'I think the party's over,' she said gently.

Alison stared at her. There was something symbolic in Tilda's action, as if she were showing that the battle was won and that she, Alison, was on the outside. Before she could respond, Felix joined the group.

'A wonderful evening,' he remarked generally. 'I had no idea it was so late.' He turned his head so as to smile directly at Alison. 'I do hope you've enjoyed it,' he said with affable authority, rather as if he had been the host. 'Goodnight.'

In the face of such implacable courtesy she could do nothing but mutter 'Goodnight' and turn away. Felix laid his hand restrainingly on Piers' arm.

'Don't spoil it,' he murmured. 'Even a friendly remark at this stage will undo all the good you've done. It's kinder in the long run.'

Piers, who, moved by Alison's look of defeat, had been on the point of calling after her – 'Be in touch' or 'See you soon' – looked at his father.

'She'd misunderstand, you see.' Felix smiled at him. 'When you're desperate you can persuade yourself to hear or see what you need.'

'I know you're right,' admitted Piers. 'It's just that I feel rather a heel.'

Felix nodded cheerfully. 'Comes under the heading of "Tough",' he said. 'I expect you'll survive it.'

Piers laughed. 'Fair enough,' he said. 'Have you enjoyed yourself, Father?'

'Very much indeed.' He hesitated. 'I think that Lizzie has done us both a great deal of good.'

He waited anxiously for Piers' reply, his thin hand reaching for the puppy's head, pulling one of the soft ears in a gentle caress.

'A very great deal of good,' agreed Piers – and saw the relief smooth his father's face into a peaceful happiness.

'Goodnight, my dear boy,' he said. 'I'm for my bed.'

People were coming in twos and threes to say goodnight to Piers, to thank him, until finally the garth was empty and he went inside to find Tilda putting Joker's bean bag down on the scullery floor, Teresa and Saul clearing up in the kitchen whilst Lizzie drifted to and fro, generally getting in the way.

'Go to bed,' Tilda said to her, coming in to collect some old newspaper. 'We shall all be off soon. The dishwasher is loaded and we can finish anything else in the morning. You too, Ma.

Piers ought to have a quiet ten minutes with Lion on his own, to let him adjust.'

Teresa continued with her task of scraping odds and ends into the bin, whilst Saul collected empty wine bottles together, but Lizzie did as she was told, said goodnight to Teresa and Saul, gave Tilda a hug and crossed to the doorway where Piers stood with the puppy in his arms. They looked at each other carefully, almost warily, and, shifting Lion's weight, he held her tightly with one arm as she reached to kiss him on the cheek.

'Thanks, Piers,' she murmured. 'It's been really great. I can't tell you . . .'

She leaned against him briefly and then went past him, out into the hall and up the stairs.

CHAPTER FORTY-SEVEN

Piers slept heavily until he was wakened by the closing of a door and the very faint, insistent noise of Lion whining miserably. He rolled onto his back, saw that it was already light and peered at his bedside clock: just after five o'clock. He groaned, knowing that he must go down at about six to let Lion out, feed him and play with him for a while, wondering if Tilda had already been downstairs to see to him. That early period of bonding was a very important one and he didn't grudge it but, just now, he would have preferred another three hours' sleep. At least he could have an hour, he told himself, if only he could get off again. The mournful, piteous noise drifting through the open windows moved him to compassion but he knew that Lion must accustom himself to being without his litter brothers and sisters. He'd soon adjust; Piers hardened his heart and turned onto his side, willing himself to sleep. A car passed along the lane below the house and a blackbird was singing on the hill behind the garth. Piers settled himself more comfortably.

*   *   *

There has been a blackbird singing out on the hill for as long as he can remember. As a small boy he sleeps in the room on the south-east corner facing on to the hill but he always longs for a view of the sea from his bedroom.

He stands at the window in his parents' room, staring across the tawny little fields towards the coast where the autumn gales pile the grey seas onto the rocks below Hurlstone Point.

'Couldn't I sleep in the west wing?' he pleads yearningly. 'In Grandfather's old room. Please.'

He has another reason: he misses his grandfather very much and to be in his room brings him closer, refreshes his memories. He is relieved that his father hardly changes the study where the old man once sat to listen to the wireless and to read his newspaper: it retains his influence, as if he might be found there, dozing in his chair, waking to cry, 'What's up? Where's the fire?' His bedroom still has his books on the shelves, his small personal items lying about, and Piers likes to touch them so as to feel the worn imprint of his grandfather's hand.

'Not yet,' his mother answers inexorably. 'You're too small for such a big room. And anyway, if you were ill or frightened in the night I'd never hear you.'

He is twelve years old when he is assigned the room on the north-west corner of the house, which in due course becomes David's room. Sue suffers far fewer qualms about her son's hardihood and he is allowed to move in at eight years old.

'I have no wish to hear him in the night,' she says. 'The further away the better. I need my sleep.'

David pleads to keep the double bed with the same fervent passion that, later, he has for a motorbike, a sports car – 'She's a real bargain, Dad. I can work on her. She's a beauty' – and the sailing boat that he keeps down at Porlock Weir. 'Just a loan, Dad,' he says. 'After all, it's only money. I've got to phone the owner today or I'll lose it. Don't put that face on, life's too short.'

*   *   *

Piers pressed his face into the pillow. Oh, to see that wheedling grin again, the complicit droop of the eyelid; to lay his hand proudly on his son's broad shoulder and feel the warmth and comfort of those strong, young arms giving him a hug. He stifled the sobs that wrenched his throat and burned his eyes, whilst Lion continued to whine miserably, and presently he flung back the sheet, pulled on his dressing-gown and went quietly downstairs, crossed the hall and passed through the kitchen to the scullery.

Lion ran to meet him, tail waving furiously, and Piers picked him up and held him close whilst Lion dabbed at his cheek with excited licks.

'You'll wake the household if you carry on like that,' he murmured. 'Good boy, then. Good fellow. Out we go.'

He opened the scullery door, set the puppy down on the cobbles and bent to clear up the newspaper. Lion pottered about inquisitively, tail waving cautiously; he sniffed at an empty glass, left standing half-hidden beside the trestle table, and sat down quickly, ears flattened, as the swallows swooped low over the garth. Having disposed of the newspaper, Piers stood at the door watching him, his grief dissipating. After a moment he went away to pour himself a glass of water and when he returned he brought one of Joker's toys: a bright red rubber ball. He rolled it towards Lion, who galloped towards it joyfully, scrabbling with it, trying to pick it up in his mouth, nudging it with his nose. Each time it came to rest, Piers would set it rolling again whilst Lion gambolled to and fro, ears flapping, clearly enjoying the game.

After a while, Piers fetched one of the more comfortable, reclining garden chairs and sat down, suddenly possessed of an enormous weariness. Lion came to look at him, whining a little, standing on his hind legs with his paws on the side of the chair.

'Had enough, old chap?' Piers ran his hand over the soft,

fluffy coat, imagining how much David would have approved of him, able to think of his son now with a little less pain.

Joker's descendant whined again, wagging his tail hopefully, and Piers scooped him up, settled him comfortably, and presently both of them were fast asleep.

Tilda found them there several hours later and took Lion off for his breakfast, suggesting that Piers should go upstairs to shower and dress.

'Coffee?' she offered as he hovered in the kitchen doorway, yawning, but he shook his head.

'I'll have some more water.' He filled a glass and drank thirstily, watching Lion pottering about, exploring his new home. 'Did you come down earlier, Tilda?'

Instead of placing Jake's little chair on one of the kitchen chairs as she usually did, she was setting it on the floor so that he could see the puppy. When Lion encountered the kicking legs, so near to his inquisitive nose, he sat down abruptly, staring in amazement. Tilda laughed, crouching beside them, speaking encouragingly. 'Look, Jake, this is Lion. Isn't he nice? Say hello.' She glanced up at Piers' question.

'No,' she answered, 'I thought you ought to be the one he saw first. You said that you'd like to have that time to yourself with him so I left him to you. I heard him though, last night and this morning. The thing is, with it being so hot, you have to have all the windows open so you can't help but hear him. He settled down quite quickly, actually.'

'Let's hope he didn't keep the others awake.' Piers leaned against the sink, ankles crossed, watching Lion sniffing cautiously at Jake's toes. 'Lizzie's room is right above the scullery.'

'I did warn her that he might be noisy on his first night away from his brothers and sisters.' Tilda stood up and began to assemble her breakfast things. 'She told me that she'd once slept through her host's garden shed burning down, which included the entire family racing round the house and a visit from the fire brigade, and that she'd never found sleep a problem. Waking up, she said, was something else. In fact she made me promise to take her up some coffee if she hadn't surfaced by nine o'clock. I told her that she could sleep until lunchtime if she wanted to but I don't think she feels she knows us quite well enough for that yet. We compromised on ten o'clock.'

'Fine. Well, I'll see if the bathroom's free and be down as soon as I can.' Piers finished his water and refilled the glass. 'I want to find David's old playpen. It came in very useful for Joker and I'm sure we shall need it again now. It's a wonderful way to restrain puppies as well as babies but, meanwhile, if you have a problem just shut Lion in the scullery.'

'Stop fussing and go and have your shower. I can manage a baby and a puppy, you know.' She put two slices of bread into the toaster. 'I hope his arrival in the middle of your party wasn't too . . . embarrassing for you.'

He'd bent to stroke Jake's head gently with one finger. 'If you mean Alison,' he said, after a moment, 'let's just say that I think the timing was perfect. He's a terrific present, Tilda. The best. It'll be fun watching him and Jake growing up together.'

They looked at each other, both thinking about David, each aware of the fact. In a rare gesture he held out an arm to her and she slipped into his embrace, hugging him tightly, her face hidden against his dressing-gown. He stared over her head, his own face momentarily bleak, but when she raised her head he smiled at her, touched his cheek to hers, grimaced and said, 'Oh, hell, I need a shave.'

'That's OK,' she said, courage restored, comforted by the sharing of their unspoken grief. 'See you later. Bang on Saul's door as you go past.'

She put the toast in the rack and poured some orange juice, found the honey and sat down at the table. The door opened and Teresa appeared, pretty and tidy as always, looking refreshed and ready for action.

'Darling,' she began – and paused to give a little cry of delight at the sight of Lion curled beside Jake's chair. 'Oh, isn't that sweet? I heard him whining earlier, poor little soul, but I felt it was best to leave him to Piers.'

'He came down earlier.' Tilda spread the honey on her toast and took a large bite. 'Did he keep you awake with his whining?' she asked somewhat indistinctly.

'No, not really.' Teresa pushed the kettle onto the hot plate. 'Don't get up. I don't want any breakfast yet, I need coffee, that's all. No, I went off to sleep quite quickly last night but I did hear him this morning, poor fellow, and then I heard someone moving about down here and guessed that Piers had come down. Coffee for you?'

Tilda shook her head. 'No, I don't have it very often at the moment. Jake doesn't care for it. The bread's beside the toaster.'

'In a minute. Coffee first.' Teresa sat down opposite her daughter. 'I think it all went off very well, don't you?' Their eyes met. 'I have this feeling that you won't be seeing much more of Alison at Michaelgarth.'

Tilda grinned. 'I have that feeling too,' she admitted. 'I wondered if I'd been too high-handed, bringing Lion in like that, without asking Piers first, but he was saying earlier that it was the best present he could have had.'

'Good for Piers.' Teresa hitched her chair a little, almost conspiratorially, and lowered her voice. 'Do you think he and Lizzie have got something going?'

Tilda frowned thoughtfully, finishing her slice of toast with evident relish. 'They seem terribly well attuned,' she said after a moment. 'Sort of easy together and very happy. They make little jokes and they seem so . . . well, comfortable and then again it seems that they've only just met each other again after years and years. It's odd.'

'Do you know how long it is since she lost her husband?' asked Teresa carefully, aware that she was moving on to sensitive ground. 'I just wondered, you know . . . ?'

'She doesn't talk about it but when I mentioned it to Felix he said he thought that it was fairly recent. As far as I can tell it was because of her bereavement that she decided to look him up again.' She smiled sardonically. 'It's probably too early to start dusting off your wedding hat, Ma.'

'Wedding hat? Who's getting married?' Saul came into the kitchen, heavy-eyed, a towelling robe tied over a T-shirt and shorts. 'Piers just hammered on my door and then disappeared into the bathroom. Bastard.'

'Don't get up, Ma.' Tilda started on her second piece of toast as Teresa, flustered, began to rise to her feet. 'Saul can make his own tea. And no-one's getting married. We were just talking about Alison's frustrated plans.' She winked at her mother. 'We were congratulating ourselves on our tactics. Or our strategies. Or whatever.'

Lion woke up, staggered to his feet and began to pad purposefully round the kitchen.

'Quick,' said Tilda to Saul, 'head him out into the garth before he widdles on the floor. Go on, Saul.'

Saul seized the puppy as if he were a rugby ball, and sprinted away through the scullery whilst the two women laughed and Teresa got up to make some toast. Presently Piers and Felix came in together and the day began in earnest: breakfast was made, plans were discussed. Saul said that he could stay to lunch but needed to be away by tea-time; Felix, on the other hand, wondered if he might go rather earlier if it fitted in with everyone else. He looked content but rather tired, and Teresa offered to drop him at the flat on her way back to Taunton.

'I simply have to get back before lunch,' she said, 'if that's not too early for you, Felix?'

'You're very welcome to stay,' said Piers, wondering if they were being tactful. 'At least help us to finish up the leftovers for lunch.'

'I'll take Lizzie some coffee,' said Tilda, thinking with relief that at least Alison wouldn't come bursting in this morning, 'and then I shall have to go and feed Jake. Don't disappear just yet, Ma.'

She went out, carrying a mug of coffee, and Saul came in with Lion at his heels, chasing the flapping, trodden-down backs of Saul's slippers.

'It's the most fantastic morning,' he said. 'We went a little way out on to the hill and the view is breathtaking. Ouch!' He jerked his heel out of the reach of the puppy's needle-sharp teeth. 'How will you manage to keep Lion inside the garth, Piers? If you could get a gate up it would be perfect for him.'

Before Piers could reply, Tilda reappeared, still carrying the mug of coffee.

'Lizzie's not there,' she said, staring round at them anxiously, putting the mug on the table. 'Where can she be?'

There was a short silence.

'Perhaps it was her that I heard going out earlier,' offered Teresa. 'Lion might have disturbed her and she decided to go for an early morning walk.'

'But her things are gone and the room's quite empty.' Tilda looked puzzled. 'She's completely disappeared.'

CHAPTER FORTY-EIGHT

It took Piers a few moments to control his shock and, more tellingly, the fear of loss that twisted his gut. He heard Saul saying that he'd check to see if Lizzie's car had gone and Tilda telling him that she'd left it out on the drive rather than in the barn; was aware of Teresa putting forward several theories, but it was to his father that he instinctively turned. Felix was watching him with the familiar look of compassion and affection.

'She'll have left a message,' he said firmly, as if in answer to Piers' unspoken question. 'If she's gone there will be a reason for it. There will be a message.'

A message: Piers was seized with new hope but it was Tilda who found the card propped against Piers' breakfast cup and saucer. She passed it to him and, with barely a glance at the picture of the Yarn Market, he turned it over to read what she had written on the back. His eyes swiftly scanned the lines whilst the others watched him eagerly and Saul came back to report that Lizzie's car had gone.

'It says that when she checked her mobile after the party last night she had several urgent messages from her agent.' Piers cleared his throat. 'He was expecting her back at the weekend and she'd completely forgotten to let him know she'd extended her stay. Apparently she has to be in Manchester first thing Monday morning for some filming and she needs to stop off at Bristol on the way to collect clothes.' He paused and then read directly from the card. ' "I imagine you'll all be sleeping late after such a wonderful party so I'll probably sneak away, trying not to disturb anyone. I can't tell you how much I've enjoyed myself. I'm so sorry this has blown up but please give my love to everyone and my thanks." So there it is.' He looked around at them, trying to hide his crushing disappointment.

'I suppose that's how life is,' Teresa was saying, 'when you're famous. She was telling me last night that they're making another advertisement as a kind of follow-on to the first one.'

'But even so,' Tilda sounded nearly as disappointed as Piers was feeling, 'I wish she could have stayed to say good-bye.'

'It's a long drive to Manchester,' Saul said, 'and if she has to stop off in Bristol she hasn't got a lot of time to spare. It would be silly, not to say irritating, hanging about hoping people are going to wake up. After all, we might all have slept until midday.'

'Chance would be a fine thing with Jake around,' said Tilda, almost crossly. 'Not to mention Lion. I expect it was Lizzie going out that disturbed him.'

Piers remembered the noise of the door closing and the sound of the car in the lane. He still held the card in his hand, unwilling to put it down to be read by the others: 'It's meant so much to meet you at last, Piers,' she'd written. He wanted time to study it again in private and suddenly he needed to be quite alone.

Felix got up from the table. 'How would you feel if we went off shortly?' he asked Teresa. 'I don't want to be tiresome but

I feel that a long rest is the order of the day as far as I'm concerned.'

If he'd hoped to deflect the attention from Piers and the card his plan was a success. Tilda looked at him anxiously and her mother rose at once.

'Yes, of course,' she said. 'You must be exhausted, Felix. Not in pain, I hope?'

'No, no.' He smiled at her reassuringly and shook his head ruefully, as if in despair at his own weakness. 'I'm so sorry to break up the party. If Saul doesn't mind collecting it, my bag is ready packed.'

Teresa and Saul went upstairs together, Tilda began to clear the table whilst Piers and his father wandered out into the garth where Lion was sniffing curiously at a bee. Roses turned their papery faces to the sun, two swallows sat gossiping together on the barn roof but, in the middle of this tranquil scene, it seemed to Felix that Piers was the centre of seething mental activity: he could almost hear the thoughts churning in his son's head. His arms were folded across his chest, his hands bunched, whilst the thumbs were clenched between the centre fingers of each fist. Felix waited, watching the puppy, who had now found the discarded ball of newspaper, which he nose-butted gently across the cobbles.

'It seems so odd,' Piers said at last, 'her hurrying away like that.'

He kept his voice low and Felix glanced at him, frowning a little.

'You don't believe her message? It seemed quite reasonable to me.'

'There was something wrong last night,' said Piers. 'Not early on but later, when she came back downstairs right at the end of the party. I've been wondering if that's when she picked up her messages but, if that's the case, why didn't she tell me then that she'd have to be going first thing in the morning? It doesn't make sense. There's another thing . . .' he hesitated as if trying to decide just how significant this thing was that haunted him. 'She hasn't left an address or a telephone number.'

'I see.' Felix looked thoughtful. 'Of course, if she dashed off in a rush she might not have thought about it. She'll probably telephone when she gets to Bristol. One does these crazy things, you know, in moments of stress.'

'I wondered about that.' He paused. 'But you know her address anyway, don't you?'

'Well,' said Felix, taken aback, 'I did once but I'm damned if I can remember it off-hand. I didn't write to . . . any of them very much, you know. Christmas cards, birthday, that kind of thing. I telephoned sometimes, from the office. You see, Angel was generally at the theatre in the evening so the best time to get hold of her was in the afternoon, just after lunch . . .'

He felt a tiny pain in his heart as he remembered. Oh, those conversations. Him in the empty office, receiver held close to his mouth, hunched over the pad on his desk on which he doodled little matchstick figures: Angel in bed, cigarette smoke curling from the ashtray, hair spread on the pillow: 'Oh, sweetie, you can't imagine how much in need of soothing I am . . .'

Felix opened his eyes to see Piers staring at him.

'Are you OK?' he asked. 'Can you remember it?'

Confused, Felix stared back at him. 'Remember it?' he repeated, still thinking of those afternoons, talking, talking, always so much to say. How could he ever forget it?

'The address,' Piers reminded him. 'Can you remember it?'

Felix swallowed, pulling himself together. 'I can't,' he admitted. 'It's gone. They lived in a pretty little square up near the university.'

'Well, anyway, you know where the house is. You could guide me to it, couldn't you, if I found a street map of Bristol?'

Felix raised his eyebrows, taken aback at Piers' insistence.

'My dear fellow,' he said. 'Yes, I suppose I could. But, goodness, it's more than thirty-five years ago . . .'

'But you went to collect the birdcage.' Piers jolted his father's memory. 'How long ago was that?

'Fifteen years?' Felix hazarded a guess. 'The trouble is that places change. One-way systems, that kind of thing.'

'Cities don't change that much,' said Piers firmly. 'Not in the residential areas. I'm sure that between us we'll find her.'

Felix smiled at him, secretly delighted by his total acceptance of Lizzie and all that she represented.

'I'm sure we will,' he agreed. 'Of course, we could check with the Luttrell Arms. She'd have given them her address, wouldn't she?'

Piers looked at his father with admiration. 'Brilliant,' he said, 'but would they give it to us?'

'I'll ask,' said Felix. 'After all, they know me well enough. I'll give it a try when I get into Dunster and I'll ring you.'

'Thanks.' Piers looked suddenly self-conscious. 'I'm probably over-reacting,' he admitted, 'but I've just got this feeling that something is wrong. Why did she come now, Father? Did she actually tell you?'

Felix frowned, trying to remember the meeting in the garden. *I came to Dunster to find you*, she'd said. Because it was as if he'd been waiting for her – because it seemed so right that she should be there – he hadn't questioned her. Not then. Later, when he'd tried to talk about her own life, she'd looked sombre. *Don't ask*, she'd said. *Angel, Pidge, Sam. Oh, Felix, I've lost them all*.

'She said something about losing her husband,' he said. 'And, of course, Angel and Pidge are gone. I assumed that after her husband's death – being all alone, clearing things out in the house in Bristol, she'd started down that road to the past that we sometimes go along after a trauma in our lives. We try to reconnect to things or people we've lost along the way; we look for our youth in old photographs and letters.'

He remembered Pidge's last words to him: *Remember the way we were*.

'I think,' he said carefully, 'that for a short period in Lizzie's life I was important to her and, in her grief, that particular time came back to her. I know it sounds odd but I never went deeply into the question of why. You didn't ask her?'

'Yes, I did,' he answered. 'She talked about trigger points; that when something grim happens you re-evaluate your life. She didn't actually talk about her husband, if I remember correctly, she simply said that with Angel and Pidge dead she decided to find you in the hope that you'd fill in some of the gaps for her.' He shook his head frustratedly. 'At times like that you're not really thinking straight enough to cross the t's and dot the i's, are you?' He gave a short laugh. 'Well, *I* wasn't.'

'You'd had a shock,' began Felix cautiously – but Piers smiled at him.

'Don't worry,' he said. 'No more recriminations. I just don't want to lose her now, that's all.'

At that moment, Tilda and Teresa came out into the garth, followed by Saul carrying Felix's overnight case, and Felix could do no more than grip Piers' hand in gratitude and relief.

'Give me a buzz later,' Piers murmured, 'when you've had a rest.'

They went out in a group to Teresa's car; there was a flurry of kissing and farewell and then the car moved off, everyone waving.

'I'm going upstairs to find the playpen.' Piers scooped up the now-recumbent puppy from the cobbles and settled him on the bean bag in the scullery. 'Bed,' he said firmly.

Lion opened a sleepy eye and stretched comfortably.

'He and Jake will be able to go into the playpen together,' observed Tilda. 'That should be fun.'

Piers went away upstairs but, as Tilda and Saul reached the kitchen, a car passed the window; the engine was switched off and a door slammed. Tilda hurried to the scullery door, with Saul close behind her, both wondering if Lizzie might possibly have returned. To their surprise they saw Marianne crossing the garth. Her face was grim and over her arm she was carrying what appeared to be a rug.

'Hello, Tilda,' she said, ignoring Saul. 'Is Gemma here, by any chance?'

CHAPTER FORTY-NINE

They gave way before Marianne, backing into the kitchen, where she stood looking about her as if she suspected that they'd hidden Gemma in a cupboard.

'What's the problem?' asked Tilda, mystified by Marianne's expression. 'I've just told you that she's not here. She and Guy went yesterday morning before the new people arrived in the afternoon. Saturday's changeover day.' She stared at the rug that Marianne held. 'Did she leave that behind? Did you manage to get together after all?'

'Yes and no,' said Marianne. She flung the rug on the table as if it were a gauge of war. 'I mean yes, she left her rug behind, but no we didn't manage to get together. *We* didn't, she and I, but she managed to get together with Simon. She got together very intimately with him, if you see what I mean.'

'No,' said Tilda after a moment. 'I don't think I do.'

Saul said nothing: he stared at the rug.

'I see that Saul has no contribution to make.' Marianne folded her arms but Tilda could see that her hands were shaking. 'Well, it's a wise man who knows his own sister, isn't it, Saul?'

Saul thought: It's all going to come out now. All of it – but still he did not speak.

'Gemma left her rug by mistake, you see.' Marianne was talking to Tilda again. 'After one of their intimate little moments behind the gorse bushes, or wherever, Simon very stupidly wrapped both the rugs together by mistake and put them in his car. I found them just now when we were putting our walking gear into the Discovery. "What's this?" I ask him, all innocent.' She began to re-enact the scene in an almost violent self-parody as if to demonstrate her disgust with her own obtuseness. 'I said, "Oh, *look*, it seems we've got two rugs. Wherever can this have come from?" and there's a silence, as if he hasn't heard me, so I turn to look at him, holding up the rug.' She seized the rug so as to demonstrate, and Tilda flinched. '"No idea," he says, all indifferent. "Haven't a clue. That picnic with the Corbetts? Does it matter? Let's get on, shall we?" But by this time, you see, I've shaken it out and had a good look at it. "What's *this*?" I cry. "There's a *name*tape! Oh, good, we'll be able to give it back. Now what does it say?" And there it was, large as life in blue and white, "G Wivenhoe".' She showed them the nametape almost triumphantly, thrusting the rug under their noses, but when she spoke again the furious self-mockery was gone. 'This time, when I look at Simon, he's got the kind of expression you never want to see on the face of someone you love.' She dropped the rug again, leaning across the table, her weight on her fists, and now her voice was low; savage with rage and misery. 'Guilt, Tilda. That's what I saw. And fear. And shame. I felt frightened too, and sick in my stomach. So I asked him, "Want to try again?" and when he tried to bluster his way out of it I said that I was going straight down to the cottage to ask Gemma. So then he told me the truth and I went straight to the cottage but there's no-one around and so I came up here.'

Tilda was almost afraid to move. With her sharp white face

and taut body, Marianne looked as if she might shatter: every piece of her was bone and sinew and stretched muscle. Any response would sound futile after such an outburst, and Tilda looked at Saul for assistance.

'Gemma's not here, Marianne,' he said quite calmly. His face was expressionless. 'We didn't know anything about this.'

'But you're not surprised, are you?' She gave a little mirthless snort. 'Of course you aren't. Why should you be? Knowing Gemma, I don't know why I should be surprised either. I just thought she might draw the line at her friends.' Marianne glanced almost speculatively at Tilda, who'd stretched her hand towards her, and Saul instinctively clenched his stomach muscles as if preparing for a blow. 'Although I don't know why I should think that,' she added, shrugging. 'After all, she didn't draw the line at David, did she?'

Tilda dropped her hand and grew still: she watched Marianne warily as if she were dangerous; as if she were weighing up what she might do or say next.

'Is there any point to this?' asked Saul desperately. 'For God's sake, Marianne . . .'

'What's the matter, Saul?' Marianne was beyond sense or compassion. 'We all know your sister's a tart—'

'Wait,' said Tilda. 'Please wait. What did you mean about drawing the line at David, Marianne?'

'Did he never tell you about the steamy fortnight's leave he spent with his dear friend Saul on Dartmoor? I was there too, wasn't I, Saul, staying with Gemma? We made up a very happy little foursome. I think you were beavering away in London, Tilda.'

At the look on Tilda's face, Saul stepped round the table as if to catch her should she fall. She held out her arm as if warding him off, staring at him as if she were having difficulty in placing him, studying his expression, remembering her conversation with Gemma.

*Someone like David would be impossible to forget . . . God,
he used to make me laugh . . . The unknown quality, that's
what we want and that's what David had . . .*

'So it's true?' she questioned him, dazed – and turned away
abruptly when he could not deny it.

'You weren't married then,' he said urgently, ignoring
Marianne. 'You weren't even engaged—'

'Shut up,' said Tilda abruptly. 'Go away, Marianne. You've
done what you came to do. Saul can give the rug to Gemma
next time he sees her. Please just go away.'

'Oh, no.' Marianne caught up the rug again. 'No, I shall do
that myself. I want to see her face when I give it to her. I want
to spoil things for her just as she has for me.'

'Stop it!' cried Tilda. 'Just think about what you're saying.
Think of Guy and the twins and all the hurt. It won't do you
any good, Marianne, and there are the children. If it makes
you happy to spoil someone's life then you can congratulate
yourself on spoiling mine. Now go away.'

Above their heads, Jake began to cry, a high thin wail. The
rage passed from Marianne's face and her shoulders sagged a
little. She looked away from Tilda, confused.

'Sorry,' she muttered. 'Sorry, Tilda. I thought you knew.
Look, it wasn't like that . . .'

'I'm going upstairs to fetch Jake,' Tilda said. 'I should like
you to go before I get back, Marianne.'

She went out of the kitchen and Marianne hesitated for a
moment before dropping the rug on to the table. She and
Saul looked at one another, neither could think of anything to
say, and finally Marianne turned away. He stood quite still
until the sound of the engine had died in the distance, then
he folded the rug very small and put it out of sight, on the seat
of one of the chairs, just as Tilda came in carrying Jake. Sitting
down at the table, holding Jake on her lap as if he were a
shield, she stared at Saul accusingly.

'You knew,' she said, 'and you never told me.'

Anger began to stir inside him, tightening his muscles. 'No,' he agreed, 'I never told you.'

'I still can't quite take it in,' she said. 'David and Gemma . . . and all this time I never knew. Even then, down at the cottage when she was saying those things about him, I never guessed. You all knew and I was like some silly kid . . .' A spasm of humiliation passed over her face. 'I suppose David asked you not to tell me?'

'Oh, please,' Saul said wearily. 'Let's not do this. Think about it, Tilda. Would you really have wanted me to tell you that David and Gemma got a bit carried away one summer? At what point do you think I should have broken the news? And how? Remember that I didn't know you then and, even if *you* felt that you were committed to David since play-school, *he* might not have felt quite the same until you were engaged. Perhaps I should have announced it at the engagement party.'

'But I don't know that, do I?' she asked angrily. 'I mean how do I know that he didn't play around *after* we were engaged? I can't ask him, can I? I can't see his face or look into his eyes and he can't reassure me. Can't you see how awful this is for me? He can't explain so that we can laugh it off together and then go and make love. He can't tell me that she was nothing to him, that he only loved me. That's what I always believed, you see. We were always so . . . together.'

'Of course you were,' agreed Saul impatiently. 'No-one's denying that but, for heaven's sake, Tilda, David wasn't a plaster saint. You know he wasn't. He lived by his own rules, as if there was never going to be enough time for all the things he had to do, and he was likely to simply take off at any moment on some crazy stunt. There was always that unknown quality about David. It's one of the reasons you loved him.'

Tilda hugged Jake more tightly. It was as if Gemma was there beside her, smiling that sideways smile, smoking her cigarette: *The unknown quality . . . that's what David had* . . . Jealousy and hurt gripped her and she closed her eyes against the picture of Gemma and David together. *God, he used to make me laugh* . . . It seemed intolerable that it should have happened and that Saul had known about it all this time. She wondered what had David said to him about it? 'For Christ's sake don't tell Tilda. After all, it was just a bit of fun but she might not see it in the same light and life's too short for misunderstandings . . .' She could almost hear his voice.

'I think you ought to go, Saul,' she said with difficulty. 'I can't . . .' She shook her head. 'Please just go.'

'OK,' he said grimly. 'I'll go. But just listen for a moment, Tilda. It wasn't I who was unfaithful, and I refuse to be David's scapegoat because he isn't here to answer your questions. I can see that I was a fool to remain in David's shadow all this time, waiting while you got over your grief and being around in case you needed a shoulder to cry on or to listen while you talk about David, and I'm coming out of that shadow right now. Either we've got a real relationship ahead of us, which will stand and fall on its own merits, or there's nothing but a card at Christmas and my role as Jake's godfather. You have to look at me, Tilda, and see *me*, Saul, not David's friend who might make a tolerable second best.'

She stared at him, shocked, whilst Jake kicked and gurgled in her arms, and he picked up the rug from the chair and turned away. Even if she'd been able to make any conciliatory offering, the sight of the rug closed up her throat with a rush of conflicting emotions. The shock was too raw for her to be able to deal with the pain and humiliation as well as taking in the things that Saul had said. She had no idea how long she sat in that state of numbed confusion but suddenly she heard voices in the hall – Saul and Piers talking together – and in a moment of panic she stood up, hoisting Jake firmly into her arms, and hurried past the still sleeping puppy and out into the garth. The covered way outside the hall offered a certain protection and she sat on the bench in the shadows watching for Saul to emerge.

She was certain that he would look round for her and see her sitting there, at the back of the garth in the little cloister, and then he would come over to say goodbye. It was a kind of test: if he saw her then she would speak properly to him, try to explain. He and Piers were in the kitchen now, she could hear their voices through the open window and could see Piers moving about. Presently Saul came out through the scullery, carrying his bag, and she tensed expectantly, seized with a sudden longing to call out to him. She remembered how, earlier, she'd longed to rest against his strength whilst resenting him because he wasn't David, but now, as he walked with long strides across the cobbles, she saw him for the first time as his own person, without the shadowy figure of David beside him, and she felt a clutch of terror at the thought of losing him. He'd already slung his bag into the car and had climbed in by the time she called out to him. The sound of the engine drowned out her voice and by the time she'd risen to her feet, the small hatchback had reversed at high speed out of the barn and shot away down the drive.

CHAPTER FIFTY

As they travelled together into Dunster, Teresa's conversation was mostly about Tilda. Felix listened patiently, perfectly content with contributing very little to what was threatening to become a monologue, thinking about Lizzie. Deep down he feared that there was something more than a pre-arranged rehearsal behind her flight and he felt a very real sense of dread at the thought that he might not see her again. Surely, after this meeting, which had brought so much joy, he simply couldn't lose her again as once, so many years ago, he'd lost Angel? She'd hugged him tightly at the end of the party.

'Oh, Felix,' she'd said, 'don't you find all this utterly bizarre?'

He'd known exactly what she'd meant: that she should be here at Michaelgarth as a guest at Piers' birthday party, befriending his family, bringing with her those echoes from the past.

'Bizarre,' he'd agreed, smiling down at her, 'and wonderful,' and he'd seen the tears brimming in her brown eyes. 'And thank God,' he'd added, 'that Angel bequeathed me the birdcage, otherwise I might never have found you again.'

'It was so many things all coming together that began it,' she'd sighed, 'but the birdcage set me searching and then I found the card. Oh, Felix,' she'd looked suddenly distressed, her voice grew urgent, 'I've been such a fool . . .'

Someone had interrupted at that point, wanting to say goodbye to Felix; Lizzie had drifted away and he hadn't seen her again. He swallowed in a dry throat, his hands clenching on his knees, remembering how he'd walked away from the Birdcage, nearly thirty-five years before, and never seen Angel again . . . To his surprise he realized that Teresa was still talking.

'The trouble is, Felix, that mourning can become a *habit*, a kind of means to its own end, if you see what I mean. I've noticed that if it goes on too long, some mourners are able to delude themselves that grief lends a nobility to the extent that anything else is almost indecent . . . Well, nearly. Of *course* Tilda misses David – good grief, we all do – but I can't bear the thought of her wasting herself at Michaelgarth . . . Not that I don't think that it's wonderful of Piers to have offered her and Jake a home – it absolutely saved her life, I'm sure of it – but it would be so easy for her to sink back and not *bother*. After all it's nearly a year since David died and she's only twenty-six . . . Oh dear, Felix, I can hear myself sounding utterly heartless and it's not a bit like that, really. I adored David, and I can see that he'll be a difficult act to follow, but she needs to be able to move on . . .'

Concentrating on listening to her, interjecting encouraging noises here and there, he thought about his grandson with the usual pang of sadness and loss mixed with a sense of waste at his early death. From babyhood David had lived at top speed, as if he'd known that a great deal of living must be packed into a very short time. Felix hadn't seen much of him as a child – Sue had been too busy to accompany him on visits to his grandfather and Felix had always been morbidly conscious that he mustn't wear out his welcome at Michaelgarth – and, as a young man, it seemed that he'd never stopped still in the same place for more than five minutes together. He'd drop in at the flat from time to time, staying long enough to drink a cup of coffee or a glass of whisky before he'd be up and away again, calling farewells as he raced back down the stairs, waving up at his grandfather from the street below. Felix was always grateful for these visits, delighted to see the boy and to feel that energy revitalizing his own old bones, but he was careful not to make demands and, given the time David had spent at boarding school and then in the army, they'd never had the chance to become really close.

'I have to say that I'm very fond of Saul,' Teresa was saying now, as they drove up The Steep, 'and I think Tilda is too – fonder than she realizes – but one has to be so careful with the young. They tend to snap one's head off at the least thing . . . Now I shall come up with you, Felix. No, I insist. You're looking very tired and I shall feel more comfortable if I see you settled in your chair and resting before I leave you. I can just squeeze in here if you get out first.'

Felix, who had intended to pay a visit to the receptionist at the Luttrell Arms, decided to go along with her plan. He knew that she would question him and he had no intention of telling her that Lizzie had left neither address nor telephone number. Her kindness was rather a nuisance because now he would have to climb the stairs twice – and he felt alarmingly weary and his hip was hurting – but he eased himself out of the car and went to open his front door, waiting for her to lock up and join him.

The envelope was lying on the mat and she picked it up for him before preceding up the stairs. She looked round the sunny room approvingly, put down his case, which he'd forgotten, and suggested that she should make him a cup of coffee before she went on her way.

'That's very kind of you,' he said firmly, 'but I shall be fine now' – and then wondered guiltily if he should have offered her some kind of refreshment.

'I must get on,' she was saying, 'if you're absolutely certain there's nothing I can do. Get some rest, Felix; you look as if you could do with it. It was a good party, wasn't it? No, don't come out.'

She went down the stairs and, once he'd heard the front door close behind her, he sank back into his chair, grateful to be alone at last, closing his eyes for a moment. He dozed for a few moments and woke suddenly, realizing that he still held the card in his lap. His name was scrawled on the envelope and he opened it without curiosity, guessing it to be from someone in the town: an invitation or news of some forthcoming event.

He drew out the card with its black-and-white picture of the Yarn Market and stared at it for a moment before turning it over to read its message.

Darling Pidge,

So here we are and the cottage is sweet.

Lovely weather but it's rather a trek to the beach for poor little Lizzie's legs. Dunster is the most gorgeous village but – you'll be relieved to know! – not a sign of F. I haven't given up hope, though!

Love from us both. Angel xx

Shocked, he reread the words, his dazed brain fumbling towards an explanation. The only reasonable one was that Lizzie had put it through his door earlier that morning. Was this the card Lizzie had spoken of: the starting point for her journey to Dunster? Had she found it in a drawer, or between the pages of a book, and so begun to examine the past more closely? He remembered Piers' question – Why now? – and suspected that the card had been the real catalyst. But why had she left it for him, pushing it through his letterbox on her flight back to Bristol? Examining the black-and-white picture he saw that barrels were stacked inside the Yarn Market whilst a horse with a cart waited patiently beside it, but otherwise the village was remarkably unchanged. *No sign of F.*

Smiling now, touched by the poignancy of the card and its power to re-create the past, he imagined Angel writing it: dashing it off with that blend of wickedness and vulnerable hope that so characterized her. No, no sign of F, and her spirited attempt at adventure had brought the whole flimsy structure that supported their love crashing about their heads. The smile died from his face as, turning the card restlessly between his fingers, staring up at the birdcage, he relived the painful scene that followed.

'I saw that woman today in Dunster,' says Marina. 'That actress. She's your mistress, isn't she? She had a child with her. I suppose she isn't yours, by any chance?'

His heart thumps in his side as he stares at her disbelievingly. Angel and Lizzie in Dunster? It can't be true – yet, deep down he knows that it is: that Angel has made some daring, crazy move that threatens them all. Even as he prepares to answer her he sees the shadow beyond the half-open door and, with a vexed exclamation, he puts down his tumbler and moves swiftly across the room. He hears the footsteps running across the hall, out through the kitchen but by the time he reaches the scullery both Piers and Monty have disappeared.

He turns back into the kitchen, knowing it is no use to look for them, and finds Marina waiting for him. She is wearing a full-skirted summer frock with a square-cut neckline and big patch pockets, its waist clipped in with a wide, white belt; the light blue cotton is splashed with a pattern of cornflowers and it is pretty and fresh and cool-looking. Her hooded stare and crossed arms, however, are at variance with such a garment, and he is suddenly washed through with despair.

'Piers was outside the door,' he explains. 'I hope he didn't hear.'

Marina raises her eyebrows. 'Isn't it a bit late to worry about that?'

'I don't want to upset him,' he says – and she laughs.

'I'm afraid that you should have thought of that before moving your mistress and her child into the village.'

'I haven't done anything of the sort. If Angel and Lizzie are in Dunster then it's because they are on holiday somewhere nearby. It's not against the law to take a holiday on Exmoor, you know, but I promise you that I had nothing to do with it. I had no idea that they were anywhere near here.'

She watches him disdainfully, chin high. 'But you don't deny that she is your mistress?'

'No,' he admits, after a moment, 'I don't deny it. I see her when I go to Bristol.'

He doesn't include Pidge or Lizzie in this statement: Marina would never understand how closely knit the lives of all four of them have become. Let her believe what she imagines to be the truth: that this is about lust and personal gratification. We are as big or small as the objects of our love – the phrase slips into his mind, though he can't remember its source, and all he can think at this moment is how small Marina's requirement to possess seems beside Angel's generosity.

'And the child isn't yours?'

'Of course not,' he cries impatiently. 'For God's sake, she's nearly the same age as Piers.'

She is prepared to accept this but her eyes narrow thoughtfully.

'So you don't know where she's staying?' He shakes his head. 'A pity,' she muses. 'It would have been an excellent opportunity for you to go and see her.' She lifts her eyebrows at his surprise. 'In order to tell her that it's all over.' Felix remains silent. 'Because if it isn't, Felix, I shall take steps to divorce you,' she explains. 'And since this is my house, I should have to ask you to leave it at once. I should also make quite certain that you wouldn't be able to see Piers. I think you'd find it difficult to prove yourself a good example to a small boy once all the facts come to light.' She straightens her shoulders and uncrosses her arms, plunging her hands into the deep pockets of her frock. 'So which is it to be?'

He feels diminished and humiliated: he wants to shout at her – or walk out – but there is Piers.

'I can't leave Piers,' he says.

Her contemptuous smile indicates that she believes that he is a coward – that he is using his son as a front so as to maintain his position at Michaelgarth and his status locally – but she nods, satisfied.

'You'll let me know once you've told her, won't you?' she asks.

'I have no intention of scouring Dunster in the hope of finding her, if that's what you mean,' he retorts angrily. 'She might be staying anywhere. I shall wait until after the weekend and then I'll telephone to see if she's back in Bristol.'

She shrugs. 'Just let me know,' she reminds him, and goes out of the kitchen and upstairs, leaving him alone.

He stands quite still, thinking about Angel and Lizzie, wondering where they are, consumed with a longing to see them. He is furious with Angel, yet frustrated by the knowledge that she is near at hand but utterly out of his reach. For a brief moment he contemplates giving it all up – leaving Michaelgarth and his family and going to Bristol – but, even as he considers it, he is distracted by a noise: the frantic beating of a butterfly's wings against the window-pane as it struggles to gain the freedom of the open air. As he goes to its aid, opening the kitchen window wide and watching the butterfly soar out into the sunshine, he thinks for some reason of his father-in-law. He remembers the old man's goodness, his wisdom and generosity, and the love he had for Piers, and it seems as if David Frayn is standing beside him, his arm laid along his shoulder, instilling courage.

Felix sighs a deep, deep breath and goes out, crossing the garth, up on to the hill, to look for his son.

CHAPTER FIFTY-ONE

He stirred as if waking from a dream, stretching his legs and his shoulders, and finally got to his feet with an effort. Yet his memories accompanied him into the kitchen so that, as he spooned coffee into the mug and waited for the kettle to boil, his thoughts ran on, unreeling steadily from scene to scene. He carried his coffee back to his seat beside the window, sipping slowly, holding the card again and rereading the message; remembering his meeting with Angel at the Birdcage.

'Why?' he asks, holding her by the shoulders, giving her a little shake. 'Didn't it occur to you that it might ruin everything?'

She abandons her instinctive approach – the penitent but mischievous look that has got her out of so many scrapes – and stares up at him.

'I just needed to *do* something,' she says soberly. 'When you wrote saying that you couldn't come I simply had this feeling that it was over anyway.'

'But why should you think that? I haven't changed.' His hands drop away. 'Have you?'

'Of course not,' she answers impatiently. 'Would I have come down to Dunster if I'd changed? It's simply that time is running out, Felix. My contract here is finished although I hope to come back for another season in a year or so. I suppose I thought it might force us into some kind of action.'

'It certainly did that,' he says drily. 'Marina has given me an ultimatum. No, Angel,' he shakes his head at her hopeful expression, 'I can't leave Piers. That's the ultimatum. You or Piers. He's only a year older than Lizzie, and Marina knows very well that once our relationship comes out in the open I wouldn't have a hope in hell of getting custody. They might not even let me see him. I simply can't risk it, Angel.'

'But what shall we do?' It's as if, even now, she hasn't really thought it through or envisaged the destruction her action has brought about. 'We can't not see each other, sweetie.'

He stares at her despairingly. 'It would be almost impossible anyway,' he says at last, 'with you in Manchester.'

'But I shall get home,' she says quickly. 'Lizzie is staying here with Pidge and I shall get back as often as I can.' She watches him, suddenly afraid. 'You'll still come to see them, won't you? You can't abandon Lizzie, Felix. She needs you.'

'I've given my word to Marina—' he begins, clenching his fists in frustration – but she cuts in quickly.

'But not about Lizzie or Pidge. She wouldn't have thought about them, would she? Or did you tell her about the way we are?'

'No, of course I didn't tell her. Christ, Angel . . . !'

'So you could come to see them on Sunday evenings just as you always have,' she pleads. 'I shan't be here so what difference does it make? Please, Felix. It means so much to Lizzie. And to Pidge. You belong to all of us, not just me.'

It is clear that she is beginning to understand the extent of the damage and her distress is so genuine that Felix holds out his arms to her.

'Oh God,' she mutters, holding him tightly, 'I think we both need some soothing, sweetie,' and even at this moment, with the months ahead without her stretching empty and bleak, he can't help but smile. He promises that he will continue to visit Lizzie and Pidge at the Birdcage and deep down, though unacknowledged, is the hope that sometimes Angel will be there too, for holidays, between contracts: he knows, guiltily, that it is not quite over.

Now, finishing his coffee, glancing out of his window across to the Luttrell Arms, Felix suddenly remembered his errand. He looked at his watch, wondering how long he had been daydreaming, imagining Piers waiting impatiently for his telephone call, and got up quickly. He threaded the postcard between the bars of the birdcage, so that he could glance at it from time to time, feeling that it belonged there, and picked up his stick. Feeling unsteady, rather dizzy, he went downstairs carefully, let himself out into the sunshine and crossed the street.

The receptionist was friendly and prepared to be helpful but explained that the hotel's policy forbade any such information being given. It wasn't until he was unlocking his door again that Felix was seized by the obvious solution to the problem: the answer that had been under his nose since he'd arrived home earlier that morning but he'd been too caught up with the past to see it.

'Fool,' he muttered. 'Damned fool.'

As he closed the door behind him the telephone began to ring and he hurried up the stairs, trying to ignore the aching, which was beginning to numb his left leg, making him awkward and slow. At the top of the stairs he was obliged to pause, breathing heavily, his leg almost useless now, and he just managed to grasp the receiver, knocking it from its rest, before he collapsed face downwards on the carpet.

* * *

Hearing Piers shouting her name, Tilda came running to the top of the stairs, staring anxiously down at him.

'What's wrong?' she cried.

'It's Father,' he said, his face drawn and frowning with concern. 'I telephoned him just now but although the receiver was lifted there was a crash, as if he'd knocked something over or fallen, and then nothing. I'm going straight into Dunster.'

'Oh, my God!' She put her hand to her mouth. 'Shall I come with you?'

He shook his head. 'No point. Stay here with Jake and Lion. I'll keep in touch.'

'Have you got your mobile?' she shouted after him and heard his faint response as he hurried out.

She paused, listening, wondering if Jake had been disturbed and whether she should go back to her ironing, which she did in the nursery, or check that Lion was still safe inside the playpen. There was no sound from the nursery so she went downstairs, checking her mobile for messages for the third time since Saul had left Michaelgarth. Earlier she'd imagined she'd heard an engine and, convinced that he'd returned, had hurried out into the garth to meet him. She'd been surprised by the depth of her disappointment, conscious of Piers' raised eyebrows when she came back looking irritable and rather foolish.

'Thought I heard a car,' she muttered – and Piers, who had remained diplomatically silent on the subject of Saul's sudden departure, had given that facial shrug she knew so well.

Now, as she watched Lion playing with Joker's ball in the safety of the playpen, she tried to analyse her sense of loss. Of course, she told herself, she'd known Saul for years: he'd been around, part of her army life, like one of the family, and she'd come to rely on him heavily since David's death . . .

With a little shock she realized that she was now much more concerned with Saul's leaving than she was with David's dalliance with Gemma. Standing in the sunshine, gazing down at Lion, it was difficult to re-create that feeling of betrayal, of something being ruined, in the face of this more recent loss. The past, at this moment, had moved to some distant point, no longer of immediate concern and therefore less painful. Putting things right with Saul had become much more important.

She wondered now how she'd been able to tell him to go: why his living presence had seemed of no importance in the light of this new evidence of David's behaviour. When she'd said that Marianne had spoiled her life she'd meant it – it had seemed, at that moment, as if remembering David would never be the same again – but Saul's unexpected reaction had jolted it into proportion. What he'd said had been reasonable enough and, although she still felt a sick misery at the thought of David with Gemma, the knowledge of it refused to be invested with quite the same sense of drama she'd experienced earlier.

She could imagine David's retort: 'Past history, love. Done and dusted. Don't lose your sense of proportion, life's too short.'

Her mobile beeped and she wrenched it from the pocket of her jeans. It was Piers.

'I think he's had a stroke,' he said rapidly. 'He's breathing but unconscious and there's a nasty gash on his head where he caught it on the corner of the chair when he went down. The ambulance is on its way. Look, I'll phone you from the hospital.'

'Oh, Piers,' she gasped. 'Oh God, will he be OK?'

'I hope so,' he said grimly.

Tilda put her mobile back into her pocket, thinking about Felix, feeling frightened for him and suddenly lonely: if only she hadn't reacted so dramatically earlier Saul would still be with her now. Supposing Felix were to die . . . ? She lifted the puppy from the playpen, holding him against her cheek whilst he licked her face enthusiastically, taking comfort from his warm, wriggling body and trying not to think of the fragility of human life. Supposing Saul were to have an accident on his way back . . . ? She forced back her fears, feeling confused and miserable, taking refuge in immediate action.

'Lunch-time,' she told Lion. 'You first, then Jake. Come on,' and she carried him into the scullery.

CHAPTER FIFTY-TWO

On her way back to Bristol Lizzie spent most of the journey castigating herself for her behaviour during the previous week.

'A week!' she exclaimed, reverting to the habit of talking aloud: her old trick of feeling less alone and holding anxieties at bay. 'Can you believe it? A week ago you hadn't met any of them. Well, except for Felix, of course. It's crazy to have become so involved with them in so short a time. But then you *are* crazy. Potty. Nuts. Doolally. I mean, why did you have to behave like that?'

She groaned in dismay at the memories: practically picking Piers up in the bar; confusing him with Felix on the telephone; doing an 'Angel' when she'd met Alison. It seemed that she was never able to act normally. As soon as another person came within her orbit it was as if the curtain swished up, the spotlight flashed on and she was thrust out into its glare and straight into her routine.

'Shuffle *hop* step tap ball change. Shuffle *hop* step tap ball change. Shuffle *hop* step shuf*fle* step shuffle *step* shuf*fle* ball *change*.'

She hummed the rhythm aloud, hearing the tap mistress's voice shouting the steps above the clatter of tap shoes on the painted cement floor. From that tender age she'd been taught that once the curtain went up you had to smile; even in the backest of back rows with no-one looking at you, still you must continue to dance and mime. Animation was essential and you learned to continue to sing for your supper even after the show was over.

'The trouble was,' she told herself, 'that you'd begun to practise the part of the brave but abandoned woman and then, suddenly, everything spiralled out of control and you were stuck with it. Not that you ever actually said that Sam had died; not in so many words.'

It was an attempt to justify herself – but even as she spoke the words aloud she knew that she was being specious.

'I lost my husband three months ago,' she'd said to the travel agent and now she could remember the shock of the words; how they'd seemed to jump from her mouth, to lie there on the counter in front of her. The woman had accepted them at face value and behaved accordingly, with deference and pity for the newly bereaved, and she, Lizzie, had made no attempt to explain but instead had been seized with a fit of hysterical laughter: teetering on that fine line between bitter tears and mad laughter, which she'd walked so precariously since the telephone call from the States.

Lizzie shook her head, replaying the scene, hearing the words clearly in her head: 'No, no,' she should have said to the woman. 'Not lost him as in "dead". No, I've lost him to another *woman*; to an actress who is much younger than I am and who is expecting his *child*. I couldn't do that, you see,' she might have said to the woman across the counter. 'I couldn't *give* him a child and, now that someone else has, he's in this terrible *state*. He wants her and the child but he doesn't quite want to let me *go*. Oh, he feels very *badly* about it,' she would have been almost shouting at the travel agent now, 'because I've tried not to make a fuss about his little flings, and after all *I* wanted a child just as much as *he* did and I've felt so terribly guilty, but this was one bloody fling *too far.*'

Lizzie pulled the car abruptly over to the side of the road into a lay-by, switched off the engine and rummaged for a tissue. Tears streamed from her eyes as she seemed to hear Sam's voice in her head, explaining it all during the phone call.

Immediately she answers the telephone she knows that it's happened again – that there's another woman who has fallen for him – but this time it's different.

'She's pregnant,' he says, and his voice is an unbearable mixture of embarrassment and pride; shame and excitement. 'She's says it's mine.' A long pause: she is too clenched with shock and fear to speak. 'I think it probably is,' he mumbles. 'Look, it's terrible to bounce this on you but I wanted you to hear it from me. You know how these rumours get about . . .'

'Do you love her?'

Her voice, cool and almost impersonal – rather as though they are discussing someone else's problem – cuts through these unbearable apologies and explanations. He is silenced for a moment.

'Love her?' he repeats slowly, at last. 'How the hell do I know if I love her? Love's such an overused word, I'm not certain what it means any more. Look, I'll grab a flight out—'

'No,' she cries sharply. 'Don't do that. I want time to think.'

He talks on, quickly, persuasively, and she knows at once that he is hoping to exercise the same control, the same excuses, he's used throughout their marriage.

'No,' she says desperately. 'No, Sam, I'm not prepared to be a kind of ageing head wife, relegated to the background like some old dowager so that you can spend nearly all your time with your new family whilst I get the occasional weekend thrown to me like a bone to a dog,' but when he talks about the expected baby and she hears the longing in his voice, she begins to lose hope. He will choose the younger woman who can give him a child: the one thing he has never had.

As the weeks pass it becomes clear that his new mistress is using the unborn baby to make demands.

'You can't blame her,' he says with a kind of pleading desperateness, 'for wanting the child to have its father around.'

'And you can't blame *me* for wanting to have my husband around,' shouts Lizzie. 'But I suppose that doesn't matter. I don't get any say in this, do I? Because she can make a baby I can be chucked away as if our marriage means nothing. And don't tell me that you love me. Like you said last time we spoke, you just don't know what it means any more. You probably never did.'

She slams down the receiver and sits trembling: I've lost him, she thinks. I've lost him this time.

He doesn't ring back and after a few days she writes to him saying that, as far as she is concerned, it's over between them. It is a shock to find how quickly the rumours get around and it is a relief to be able to leave London, closing up the flat for a month, and returning to the Birdcage. Still no word comes from him and she imagines him with this new woman, pictures him holding the new-born child.

The message from him on her mobile comes as a shock: 'I shall be in the UK at the weekend. Looking forward to seeing you.' Then the two messages from Jim: 'Don't forget that you're supposed to be in Manchester on Monday.' And the second: 'Sam is trying to find you. He's on his way to the Birdcage but I haven't told him where you are. Give me a buzz.'

Sitting by the roadside, drying her eyes, Lizzie took a very deep breath and pulled herself together. It was only to be expected that Sam would come back from the States to discuss their separation. Despite the forward leaps of her vivid imagination, picturing him as a proud father, it was only a few months since he'd broken the news of the pregnancy to her. The legalities regarding divorce must now be set in motion. She sat on for a few moments, thinking about Piers and Felix. She'd allowed them to believe that she was a widow; she'd accepted Tilda's compassion and friendship under false pretences. How precious their welcome to Michaelgarth had been; how right it had seemed to be part of their family just as, years ago, Felix had been a necessary part of the little group at the Birdcage. How could she have explained to them that she'd been misleading them; trading on their sympathy and goodwill?

Last night, sitting in the garth, watching them with their friends, she'd known that it would be impossible to explain. Being bereaved was such an excellent reason for the journey back to the past: it lent a glow of respectability – even necessity – to what might otherwise be regarded as a tasteless adventure. To appear amongst them, the daughter of the woman who had threatened that very family she now so much admired and envied, might be seen in a very different light without the dignity of bereavement to support it. She had put Felix at risk, threatened his relationship with Piers and, effectively, lied to Tilda.

She thought of Felix, old and frail but with that same ability to give love and compassion; of Piers, to whom she'd felt such an odd attraction, familiar, easy, yet exciting.

At least, she told herself, she'd done no harm. In fact, according to Felix, she'd actually restored their relationship, helping them to break down the barriers of guilt and resentment at last. So let it rest at that.

Lizzie blew her nose, straightened her shoulders and started the engine. The roads were quite quiet and she drove the remainder of the journey uneventfully. The little square near the university was empty and she was lucky to find a parking space not far from the front door. She took her bag and one case, the rest could wait, let herself in and climbed the stairs. Once inside she dropped the case outside her bedroom door and stood listening: someone slammed a cupboard door and opened a drawer. She crossed the hall and went into the big room just as he came round the end of the piano, tall, wide-shouldered, dressed as always in black, carrying his coffee.

'Hello, Sam,' she said.

CHAPTER FIFTY-THREE

She'd forgotten the effect of his pile-driver presence, the physical force of his personality. In her present vulnerable state she wanted to put an arm across her face as if to ward off that black-hole magnetism that even now pulled and tugged at her.

'I wondered if you might be here.' She kept her eyes away from him in an attempt to resist any temptation. 'I'm afraid this is just a quick turn around for me. I've got to be in Manchester this evening.'

'So Jim said. He's such an old watch-dog where you're concerned, bless him. He was as non-committal as ever and I couldn't think where you might be. I'll make you some coffee.'

'Thanks,' she muttered. 'I've got some washing to do and I'll need to pack.'

'Been away?' His voice was friendly, interested; when she didn't answer, he added, 'It's good to be back in the old Birdcage again.'

There might have been no cataclysmic telephone call, no new mistress, no baby: he was the same old Sam who was about to attempt the ultimate compartmentalization of his life. Surely there must be some change in him? She looked at him cautiously, curiously, and he smiled back at her, that treacherous smile that usually melted any defence she'd erected against his wily persuasiveness.

'I felt that too. I was very glad to be home again.' Lizzie was proud of the calmness of her voice; she decided not to dissemble. 'But then it always was a place of refuge for me.'

She had a feeling that she'd said something like this to him once before and she saw a tiny irritated frown crease his brow, rather as if there was something rather tasteless in referring to other similar occasions where he might have been at fault. He gave the coffee a swirl with a spoon and brought it out to her.

'Look,' he began – and she gave an involuntary little smile at this familiar opening to past confessions. *Look, it couldn't matter less . . . Look, she doesn't mean a thing to me . . . Look, this has got nothing to do with what's between you and me . . .*

'Look, I've been thinking,' he went on, 'that it needn't make too much difference. We spend so much time apart as it is, don't we? I shall still be coming back to the UK. It hasn't changed how I feel about you, Lizzie. I don't think anything could . . .'

She heard him out, watching him with a terrible sadness, yet something was missing from his delivery: there seemed to be a faulty connection and his magnetism no longer produced such a strong, powerful beam. It flared intermittently, now blazing, now dying, and during each short power cut she was able to boost her own courage.

'No.' She shook her head at last. 'No, Sam. I understand your plan for keeping me on the back burner as a kind of insurance in case this new affair is a terrible mistake, but I've told you before I have no interest in the position as head wife of a seraglio. Oh, I know,' she held up her hand as he protested against this job description, 'I know that you're still fond of me and all that stuff but the answer is still no.'

He stared into his mug, his massive shoulders drooping a little, and she felt a spasm of tenderness for him. His thick black hair was still wild and unruly, though streaked through with silver, and he looked as strong and tough as ever. There was something so achingly familiar, so extremely desirable about him, as he sat hunched above his coffee.

Two voices jostled in Lizzie's head. 'I suppose if I really loved him,' said one miserably, 'I'd give him anything he wanted.' The other said brightly: 'Shall I ask him if he's realized that he'll be a septuagenarian when his child starts university? Or how he might feel if this baby doesn't go full term? If there *is* a baby. Stranger things have been known to happen and he's a good catch for a young, aspiring actress.'

With an effort of will she banished both voices, swallowed some coffee and went to fill the washing machine. She heard his chair creak back as he stood up and she braced herself for the next round.

'We haven't said any of the really important things,' he said, leaning against the sink, watching as she hauled things from her case and pushed them into the machine.

'Oh, I think we have.' She straightened up, pushed the necessary buttons. 'There is only one really important thing, isn't there? Your new mistress is expecting your child. Nothing else really matters.'

'Look . . .' There was a kind of grieved impatience in his voice now, as if she were being wilfully uncooperative. His hands, fingers stretched and stiff, began to slice and square the air as if he could push and shape it into his own design. 'I've already told you that you *do* matter. This need not necessarily be an either/or situation.'

She managed to chuckle quite naturally – after all, she told herself grimly, I *am* an actress – and picked up the empty case.

'Not only but also?' she suggested. 'Not only a faithful, accommodating old wife but also an exciting, desirable, new mistress with the must-have accessory baby? Don't tell me she's happy for you to remain married to me?'

She watched embarrassment, frustration and a certain cunning follow in quick succession across his face and waited, still staring at him, eyebrows raised.

'Well, no,' he admitted. 'Because of the baby, you see, but—'

'No,' she said firmly, trying not to show the pain. 'I don't do "buts" any more, Sam. And I don't want to talk about it any further. Just go and get on with it and stop trying to have it all. You've got away with it for far too long.'

She crossed the hall and went into her bedroom, shutting the door behind her, but stopped just inside, alert and unmoving. Presently she heard his footsteps running down the stairs and the front door close with a sharp click. She relaxed suddenly, her whole body sagging as tension flowed out of her only to be replaced with an overwhelming misery. After a moment, still angrily swiping the tears from her cheeks, she flung the suitcase onto the bed and began to pack.

Piers took the stairs two at a time, glanced into the sitting-room but went straight on through to his father's bedroom. He'd brought a small overnight case with him and now he began to pack it with pyjamas, a dressing-gown, some slippers. Pausing to look round the tidy room he wondered if there were some small item he could take back to the hospital; some personal possession to stand on the locker beside his father's bed. There were several photographs standing on the chest of drawers along with his silver-backed hair brushes, a square leather box containing tiny trays for his cufflinks, a small transistor radio.

Piers bent to look at the photographs more closely. The largest one was of Tilda and David at their wedding: Felix stood between the laughing couple, his top hat at a jaunty angle as he stared smilingly out at the camera. Tilda was holding Felix's hand, laughing at some long-forgotten remark, but David was looking with tremendous affection at his grandfather, one arm along his shoulder. How handsome he looked in his uniform: how confident and proud and utterly indestructible: how impossible to believe that he wouldn't come strolling in, his jacket slung over his shoulder, jingling the car keys in his pocket.

Behold, I shew you a mystery; We shall not all sleep, but we shall all be changed, In a moment, in the twinkling of an eye . . .

Piers had a brief momentary vision of a butterfly soaring upwards into the sunny spaces of the hall, yellow wings shimmering in the dazzling light, and he experienced again that transient sensation of delight and peace. Oddly comforted, he picked up the photograph, tucked it into the bag, and paused to examine a small black-and-white snapshot in a worn leather frame. His younger self beamed back at him, straddling his brand-new, shiny bicycle, his own grandfather standing beside him with his pipe in his mouth and Monty at his feet. He remembered the proud moment; his mother on one knee so as to steady the old Brownie camera, squinting down, whilst his grandfather growled at Monty to sit still.

He slanted it towards the light, running the ball of his thumb lightly across the faded print, remembering his mother and that sense of something dark inside her: some kind of banked-down anger that had eaten away at her peace and happiness just as relentlessly as the cancer which had destroyed her later. Even now, he was not quite certain what it was that she had required of him but he *was* sure that he had failed her.

The trouble is that Daddy doesn't care. If he really cared about you . . .

He thought of his father lying in the hospital bed, the bruise livid on his pale brow; his hands thin and frail and motionless on the neatly turned-down sheet. Looking back, he realized that out of confusion and hurt he'd held him at a distance, influenced by those invidious words dropped like poison into his ear. By the time he was old enough and confident enough to make his own judgements the habit of a kind, polite formality had already been established between them and, even after his mother had died, the barrier remained.

'You can't die now,' he'd wanted to say, holding one of those hands gently lest he should crush it in his anxiety. 'Not *now*, just when we were getting it together.'

He looked about the bedroom, wondering if there were anything else which his father might like to see when he opened his eyes, and then went through to the sitting-room.

He thought: It's a pity I can't take the birdcage.

Even as he rejected the idea, knowing that it was far too large and unwieldy for a hospital ward, his eye was caught by the odd shape of the card stuck between the bars. He crossed the room and took it down, seeing at once that it was an early version of the photograph of the postcard Lizzie had left for him that morning. Turning it over he read the message, frowning a little: why should his father have a postcard sent from Angel to Pidge nearly forty years before? Before his mind could furnish a satisfactory answer his attention was drawn to the address and he gave a cry of triumph. This was the message he'd been hoping for, whether from Lizzie herself or from Felix was unimportant; to Piers it seemed to have been sent direct from the gods.

Tucking the postcard into his wallet, he collected his father's shaving things from the bathroom, packed them into the case and hurried away.

CHAPTER FIFTY-FOUR

By the time he arrived back at Michaelgarth the sun was setting and Tilda was sitting in the garth, waiting for him. She went to fetch him a drink whilst Lion gambolled to and fro, ears flapping, tail wagging madly.

'He's going to be OK.' Piers took a big mouthful of whisky and looked up at the swallows swooping above him, relaxing for the first time that day. 'Apparently there is no reason why he shouldn't make a good recovery, it was quite a minor stroke, but the blow on his head was rather a sharp one. He'll be home before too long, all being well.'

'He'll come here, of course.' Tilda rolled the ball for Lion and sat down beside Piers. 'He won't be able to manage in the flat, will he?'

She looked away from the trestle tables and the barbecue, still standing witness to last night's party. So much had happened since Saul had stood there, cooking sausages, laughing with their friends, and she was still shocked and oddly disorientated. She'd received a text message from him earlier which read: 'Back safely, thanks for the weekend' – and she was wondering how she should respond to it.

'No, he won't be going back to the flat.' Piers set down the glass. 'That will be a difficult one for him, I'm afraid, but I hope he'll see how impossible it would be. He'll need looking after for a while.'

'I was thinking about it,' said Tilda. 'I've had plenty of time today for thinking. I know that we've made the dining-room a place for me and Jake but we don't use it all that often. It would make a good bedroom for Felix, until he can cope with the stairs again, and the cloakroom is just across the passage. And if you took those cupboards out of the scullery there would be room for a shower unit.'

He smiled at her, grateful that she was not seeing Felix's impending arrival as a nuisance.

'That's a very good idea. I'd been trying to work it through, trying to decide where he'd be happiest. Of course, if he recovers quickly, he'll be able to use the stairs and I know that he'd prefer that. I don't want him to feel that he's a burden. I hope he'll think that he can make his home here but we must wait and see.' He gave a little chuckle. 'Four generations of Hamiltons at Michaelgarth; it's rather a nice thought. At the same time I don't want you becoming a kind of nurse – after all, you've got Jake to look after – so I've decided to ask Jenny Coleman to come in on a regular basis, if you're happy with that idea?'

'I think that's sensible. I'm very happy to muck in, you know I'll do whatever I can, but I was thinking . . .' She hesitated. 'I'm wondering if the time's come for me to get about a bit more.'

He glanced at her, took another sip of whisky, and wrenched his mind away from his father's needs.

'Well, that sounds pretty good to me. How do you define "getting about" exactly?'

She sat back in her chair, winding her hair up with her hands, twisting it into a rope and letting it fall again, seeking some kind of explanation that would not necessarily involve

David. He saw her almost begin to speak, and then reject the words, and was seized with compassion for her.

'Am I right in thinking,' he began carefully, 'that there was some problem this morning? I understand that Marianne turned up and then Saul left in a bit of a rush. I don't want to interfere but I can see that something happened to upset you.'

Tilda drew her heels up onto the chair seat, wrapped her arms round her knees and decided that she should tell him the truth.

'It's really about David,' she began anxiously, rather as if she were warning him.

'Yes,' answered David's father drily. 'I had a feeling it might be.'

'It's probably silly of me,' she began rapidly, 'and I know I got a bit OTT about it but Marianne came over with a story about Gemma and then let slip that she'd had a bit of a fling with David. Gemma, that is, not Marianne.' She was rushing on, almost gabbling, needing him to have the facts quickly. 'It was before we were engaged but, even so, I felt really horrid about it. It was when he was staying with Saul on leave and I felt that Saul should have told me about it. I can see now that it was unreasonable but I was shocked and hurt, and Saul and I had a row about it. I asked him to go and he said that he wasn't going to be David's scapegoat and that it was time that I saw him, Saul, as a person in his own right.'

'That sounds perfectly reasonable,' said Piers, when it seemed that Tilda had finished. 'Saul's a young man with his own life ahead and he's getting tired of waiting to know how you feel about him. After all, it's very clear how he feels about *you*.'

Tilda stared at him. 'But I don't *know* how I feel about him,' she said rather tremulously. 'I missed him terribly after he'd stormed off and I suddenly saw how much I'd miss him if he weren't around. But I don't know if that's just because I've sort of got used to him being there.' She swallowed, pressing her lips together. 'It's not that I don't love David . . .'

'My dear girl.' Piers stretched a hand across the table and gripped her arm. 'There's no question in anyone's mind about how much you love David, let's get that straight, but no-one expects you to make a career out of widowhood. *I* certainly don't. Sudden death numbs us, the shock cripples us, and it takes time for the life to flow back. I've never imagined that you and Jake would stay here for the rest of your lives. Michaelgarth is your home for whenever you need it, and it's Jake's inheritance, but you must look upon it as a base not as a commitment.'

'I miss my friends and army life,' she admitted, staring straight ahead, her chin on her knees. 'But each time I've been back, I've felt like a kind of intruder. They all feel badly about David and it's like I told you before, being a young widow is bad news. It's like they feel it's a contagion they might catch and, let's face it, their lives are chancy enough without that kind of superstitious fear each time they see me.'

'Then break the Gordian knot. Next time you go up for some party or a ladies' night or whatever, I suggest that, instead of staying with one of these married friends, you let Saul put you up in a hotel. Go and see *him* and stay with *him* and see how you feel then. As soon as Jake is old enough, leave him here with me and Jenny Coleman and give yourself the chance to be with Saul – not as David's widow or Jake's mum but as you, Tilda.'

'It's not that I don't love it here too,' she said quickly. 'You know I adore it here with you at Michaelgarth. I feel that we belong here too, me and Jake. Oh God, I feel so confused!'

'My poor Tilda.' Piers shook his head. 'This doesn't have to be some kind of contest for your affection: Saul or David.

Michaelgarth or Aldershot. Love is not a finite commodity, there's enough for everyone. Stop fretting and move on. I know what David would say. "Go for it, love," he'd say. "Life's too short." '

She turned to look at him, then, her eyes shining. 'I've been telling myself that,' she admitted. 'Oh, Piers, it's just that it's difficult to know my own feelings. Lizzie's idea about the little craft centre in the barn was such a good one.'

'It will still be a good one in five years' time, or ten. Give yourself some space, Tilda. Michaelgarth's not going anywhere and neither am I.'

She uncurled herself and stood up. 'Thanks, Piers. You've been great.' She grinned at him. 'We'll have some supper soon, say, half an hour, but first I need to make a phone call.'

He watched her go, smiling to himself, and then took the postcard from his back pocket and studied it.

Darling Pidge,

So here we are and the cottage is sweet.

Lovely weather but it's rather a trek to the beach for poor little Lizzie's legs. Dunster is the most gorgeous village but – you'll be relieved to know! – not a sign of F. I haven't given up hope, though!

Love from us both. Angel xx

He turned it in his hand, remembering the scene in Parhams, hearing other voices.

I saw that woman today in Dunster. That actress. She's your mistress, isn't she? She had a child with her. I suppose she isn't yours, by any chance?

He realized that, like Tilda, he no longer needed to feel that there was a contest for his affections: he did not have to choose between his mother's possessive love or his father's generosity of spirit but could accept them both. He was free at last. He scooped up Lion, who was lying at his feet on the cobbles busily chewing at the laces on his dekkies, and submitted to having his face licked.

'You'd better come with me,' he murmured. 'You can explore the study and get acquainted with the shades of your ancestors. I have a letter to write.'

CHAPTER FIFTY-FIVE

After several false starts and screwed-up sheets of writing paper, Piers managed to compose a letter with which he was fairly satisfied. Because he didn't want Lizzie to feel embarrassed he began by offering all kinds of reasons for her sudden departure, excuses for her hurrying away without leaving any means of communication, but this began to be so complicated that it finished up by reading as a veiled condemnation. In the end he decided to play it straight.

Dear Lizzie,

We were all so sorry that you had to dash away early on Sunday morning. It was such fun having you here and I'm sure you must have realized exactly how much you've done for my father and me. When he and I talked at the party I knew for certain that your coming to Dunster had made it possible for us to break down the barriers of misunderstanding built up over the years and start a whole new relationship. How can we thank you for all that?

The sad thing is that later that morning, once he'd gone

back to the flat, my father had a slight stroke and a nasty fall and is now in hospital. I'm assured that he'll make a good recovery in time but you can imagine that the shock of it put an end to the party mood. He looks very frail, poor old boy, and I'm hoping that when he's ready to leave hospital he'll agree to come back to Michaelgarth until he's strong again. As far as I'm concerned I should be very happy for him to make his home here, and now – as a result of your visit – it might just be possible that he'll consider it.

I hate to break this news to you out of the blue like this but I feel that you'd probably like to see him, and anyway I think you have the right to know. In your rush you forgot to leave us an address or a telephone number but I found an old postcard with your address on it in Father's flat, stuck between the bars of the birdcage, and it seemed to be a kind of message as if you'd left us a means of contacting you, so I hope I haven't breached any etiquette in writing to you.

I hope the filming goes well and I'm also hoping that you'll be back in Bristol soon so as to pick this up. It would mean such a lot to me to visit you at the Birdcage and fit in the last pieces of the jigsaw puzzle. I couldn't be away long at the moment, for obvious reasons, but if you feel that you could put up with me for an hour or two I would be very grateful. You could drop me a line to the address above or ring on my mobile or on the house telephone, both numbers at the head of the letter.

Yours ever,

Piers

He read it through critically but, before any more misgivings could persuade him to destroy it and begin yet again, Tilda put her head round the door.

'Supper's ready,' she said. 'Or is it a bad moment?'

He smiled at her, folding the sheet of paper in half and pushing it into the envelope.

'A very good moment,' he answered and looked at her again, more closely. She blushed rosily, failing utterly in her attempt to look casual, and his eyebrows rose in that familiar facial shrug. 'Looks like you've had rather a good moment yourself.'

She grinned. 'I've just been talking to Saul,' she said airily, shrugging a little. 'Making a few plans. You know?'

'Oh, yes,' he said feelingly. 'I know.'

'Look at Lion,' she said, still feeling shy, trying to distract him. 'He's recycling your waste paper.'

Lion lay on the hearthrug, surrounded by tiny shreds of the rejected letters and thoroughly enjoying himself, whilst Piers watched him, thinking of other dogs, hearing his grandfather's voice: *What's up? Where's the fire?*

Tilda slipped an arm through his, touched by the expression on his face, feeling a huge affection for him.

'Supper,' she reminded him – and he nodded and they went out together, with Lion trailing them, across the hall and into the kitchen.

Lizzie picked up her letters from the small table in the lower hall and climbed the stairs wearily, sorting through the envelopes as she went. Nothing from Sam, but she was hardly expecting a letter from him. He'd left a text message earlier in the week: 'I'm sure you're right. I shall miss you like hell.' Now it was all down to the lawyers. She puzzled over the envelope with the unfamiliar handwriting and peered at the postmark – Dunster!

Slamming the front door behind her, dropping her case, she went into the big room, ripping open the envelope. Her eyes raced across the written lines, her hand clenched unconsciously against her heart; relief and gratitude showed themselves on her face – and then it reflected the sudden shock.

'Oh, no!' she murmured. 'Oh God! Poor Felix.'

Lizzie sat down at the table, staring at nothing, small scenes playing before her inner eye. Even now she wasn't quite certain what impulse had driven her to leave the postcard with Felix, thrusting it through his letterbox on her flight to Bristol. She'd taken it with her to Dunster as a kind of talisman and now it seemed, after all, that there had been a further part for it to play in this odd drama. Lizzie read the letter again, hearing Piers' voice through the words, wishing that she could be there with them at Michaelgarth.

She knew that before she could see any of them again, however, they needed to know the truth. Although she stared at the carefully printed telephone numbers for several moments she simply couldn't bring herself to ring him: how would she begin? What would she say? Much easier – if more cowardly – to write to him, explaining her own situation. Once he knew the truth he could decide if she would still be welcome. Thinking anxiously about Felix, frightened lest she should lose her nerve, she went to Pidge's bureau and found some writing paper. Back at the table she sat down, thinking furiously. Presently she began to scribble.

My dear Piers,

Thank you so much for writing to me. I can't tell you what a shock it was to read about Felix! I am *so* sorry. I hope that he is getting better. I wanted to telephone but then I lost my nerve. The trouble is, Piers, I ran out on Sunday morning because I was feeling guilty. I *did* have to go to Manchester, that was true, but the thing is that I'd let you all imagine that I was a widow and things got out of hand.

The truth is that my husband is having an affair, one of a long series over the whole of my marriage, and the girl is pregnant and he wants her to have the child. You might remember that I told you that I couldn't have children and somehow this was just so unbearable, so terribly painful. I felt that I'd really lost him this time, and those were the words I used to Felix. He assumed I meant that Sam was dead and I let him go on thinking it.

That evening when I sat watching you at the party I suddenly felt that I was a fraud; that I'd come among you all under false impressions and I felt very ashamed. You'd all been recently bereaved and here was I playing a part and deceiving you all. It was especially awful since Tilda had been so sweet to me, thinking that we were both in the same boat. When I went upstairs I saw the message from my agent reminding me about the filming on Monday but also saying that Sam was on his way to Bristol, and I panicked.

It has meant so much, Piers, to see Felix after all these years and to meet you too. I used to think about you so much when I was little. Felix was there when I really needed the comfort of a father and I shall never forget his kindness and the love he showed me. But it was obvious from the way he talked about you that you were so special to him and I always longed to meet you. It's been a little miracle, this Dunster week, much more successful than poor Angel's was back in the fifties! I can't get over you finding the postcard like that. It was coming across that card in a book that set the whole thing in motion for me and I'm so glad that I decided to leave it for Felix.

Of course I should love to see him, of *course* I would, but only after you've told him and Tilda the truth about me. Sam was here at the Birdcage when I got back on Sunday morning and I somehow had the strength to say that it was all over between us. He's gone back to the States now. If you feel that you can all still trust me I should very much like to see you, Piers, any time over the weekend, although I shall be dashing back to Manchester again on Monday.

I've put both telephone numbers; the mobile should get me almost anywhere.

Love to you all,

Lizzie

She copied his address on to the envelope, went back to the bureau to find a stamp and, seizing her bag, she went hurrying downstairs, out of the front door and round the corner to the postbox.

She had a telephone call from him early next evening: short and to the point but his voice was warm and she knew at once that she'd been forgiven.

'He's regained consciousness and we've been able to talk, though not for long,' he reassured her at once. 'I'm just going to see him. If it's OK I could be with you late on Sunday morning, just for an hour or so.'

'For lunch?' she asked quickly. 'You'll stay for lunch?'

She could hear the smile in his voice. 'Lunch sounds good,' he answered. 'Everybody sends their love and we're all looking forward to seeing you again.'

'I'm looking forward to that too,' she said, truly meaning it, and then didn't quite know what to say next.

'I must dash away to the hospital,' he said, as if understanding her dilemma. 'I'll give Felix your love, shall I?'

'Yes, please,' she said. 'Thanks, Piers. See you on Sunday.'

CHAPTER FIFTY-SIX

When Lizzie went down to open the door to him on Sunday morning she saw that he was carrying the birdcage. Seeing her face change and grow pale Piers hastened to reassure her, guessing her sudden fear.

'Don't worry, he's much better,' he told her. 'It's simply that he's going to be with us at Michaelgarth for some time and he decided that this should be back where it belonged. He said that I should tell you that he thought that it had done all the good Angel intended and it was time that it went home.'

She smiled but her lips trembled. 'Darling Felix,' she muttered. 'How odd it's all been. Oh, Piers, it's good to see you. Come upstairs. Pidge's flat is let now, so I can't show it to you, but I want you to feel at home here.'

He saw that she'd left the doors open, as if there were an invitation to go where he pleased, but he followed her into the big room, setting the birdcage down at the end of the long table and looking about him. So this is where his father had been so happy with Angel and Pidge; this is where Lizzie had grown up. On the piano stood a publicity photograph of

Angel and he went to look at it, remembering the woman he'd seen in Parhams: this was the woman his father had loved.

Lizzie was watching him and he smiled at her. 'She looks nice,' he said. 'Where's Pidge?'

She indicated a smaller photograph: a smart, attractive dark woman with an intelligent face in army uniform standing beside a big staff car. He examined it, rather as if he were fitting together the pieces of a jigsaw, and then looked about the room again, trying to imagine how it had been all those years before.

'I know you can't be away too long,' she said, 'so lunch is more or less ready. Have a potter while I put it on the table.'

He wandered out and she saw him glancing into the bedroom, staring up the small staircase which led to the attic, and presently heard him go up the stairs to the little room. She'd felt it important that he grew familiar with this house where Felix had spent such short but vital periods of his life; meanwhile she'd prepared exactly the same lunch which she'd made as a puja for Angel and Pidge before her journey to Dunster: smoked salmon with chunks of lemon, rings of tomato in a vinaigrette with herbs, thin slices of cucumber in mayonnaise, and new brown bread. She'd chosen the same dishes: round, white bone-china for the salmon; oval, blue earthenware for the tomatoes; a yellow bowl for the cucumber. Lizzie knew that Pidge and Angel would have approved: they would have liked to see Piers here in the Birdcage, having lunch at this table where they'd sat so often with his father.

'It's lovely here.' He was back again. 'All bright and airy but friendly too. I like your Birdcage, Lizzie.'

'Come and sit down,' she said, pleased. 'Tell me everything. How Felix is, first, and then all about Tilda and Jake and Lion.'

They talked together about Felix, about Sam, learning each other; Lizzie put cheese on the table and made coffee but still they continued to talk. At last the afternoon shadows edged silently across the sunny room and Piers sighed, knowing that he must leave.

'So you'll come?' he asked, pushing back his chair and standing up. 'I can tell Father that all is well and you'll be down to see him soon? It will mean so much to him.'

'I promise,' she said. 'If you're certain . . . ?'

'Oh, I'm certain,' he assured her. 'You can't imagine what you've done for us, Lizzie. I promise you it far outweighs your small sins of omission. What my father said is absolutely true: if you hadn't come to Dunster there's no way he'd have been able to accept my invitation to convalesce at Michaelgarth so wholeheartedly as he has done. We're both looking forward to it.' He watched her for a moment. 'The trouble is,' he said at last, 'that I have my own agenda here and I can't pretend otherwise. Nevertheless I would hate you to feel pressured into coming to Michaelgarth simply out of compassion for my father now that he isn't well. There's an element of blackmail in it, isn't there? Your friendship with my father rather includes all of us as a package.'

She smiled at him, remembering Felix's words when he heard that Piers had invited her to Michaelgarth: *. . . that place is very special to Piers, remember . . . By accepting you, surely he must have forgiven me. You embody all the things that threatened him and yet he's invited you into his home . . . I feel . . . as if I've received some kind of absolution . . . It's beyond everything I've ever hoped.*

'You can't possibly guess how relieved I am to know that I'm still welcome,' she told him. 'I behaved very badly. You are all suffering the effects of real bereavement and I took advantage of a misunderstanding and then ran away. You have the right to be angry, and Tilda probably most of all.'

'We're all hoping you'll come back to Michaelgarth,' he said. 'I know that you'll be good for all of us, including Tilda. She's been jolted out of her mourning in a rather horrid way, which she might tell you about, but she's decided that she can move forward now although it's going to take some courage. When I explained your situation she was totally sympathetic and said she thought you were very brave. We know that you have your own life and your work but it would be very nice if you could find time to visit us now and again.'

'I'd like that,' she said. 'I'd like it very much. And I certainly want to see Felix very soon. The trouble is I can't quite say which day next week, it depends how the filming goes . . .' She clapped her hands together in frustration. 'Tell him it will be as early as I can make it.'

An idea struck her and she went to the birdcage and opened the little door. Very carefully she unwound the fine wire that bound the yellow chick's feet and released her from the bar. She looked at her for a moment, gently stroking the faded fluffy coat with her finger, and then held her out to Piers.

'Give this to Felix with my love,' she said. 'It's a token. A symbol. He'll know what I'm trying to say.'

She put the chick into Piers' hand and he held her on his outstretched palm, touched by this gesture and not knowing how to react. Lizzie helped him through the difficult moment.

'Be careful with her,' she advised as, not quite certain how to transport it, he finally wrapped the chick carefully in his clean handkerchief. 'She might look like she's just out of the egg but she's a bit of an old boiler, actually.'

He chuckled, holding out his arms to her, and she hugged him. 'I must get back,' he said, knowing that it was right to leave now, however much he might long to stay with her. 'We'll keep in touch.'

'We'll keep in touch,' she agreed, 'and I'll be down next week. Give Felix my love. Tell him he's got to get better because I need him. Tell him . . .'

'Tell him what?' prompted Piers gently when she seemed lost for words.

'Tell him to remember how we were,' she said at last.

She stood at the top of the stairs so as to see him off and

then went back to watch from the window. She saw him cross the road and get into the car without looking back but, as he pulled out, he glanced up and blew her a kiss. She waved to him, her eyes suddenly full of tears, and then turned back into the room.

The familiar scene comforted her but there seemed to have been some kind of change: the atmosphere was still peaceful, yet there was a new air of hope and expectation. She sat down on the sofa, drawing Angel's yellow silk shawl about her, staring at the birdcage: it looked odd without the little fluffy chick, who had spread her wings at last and was already embarked on a new stage of her life. Sitting there in the quiet room, listening to the voices of the children drifting from the square and watching the dappled shadows cast by the plane tree, Lizzie thought of Angel and Pidge, feeling them near at hand, content and approving.

She wiped away the last of her tears with Angel's shawl and rose to her feet. Picking up the birdcage, she crossed the room and reached to hang it on the hook above the piano. It swung gently for a moment and then settled, back where it belonged again, and she paused to look more closely at the two little wooden birds. So delicately painted were the tiny feathers, blue and green and yellow, that it seemed that they must stir: that at any moment the folded wings might be stretched for flight. One had her head thrown back, beak parted in joyous song: the other had her head on one side, as if listening.

Lizzie smiled at them, her heart full of gratitude and love. 'Welcome home,' she said.